the
Headshrinker's Brigade

Leslie Tourish

TREATY OAK PUBLISHERS

PUBLISHER'S NOTE

Cover Illustration by Desarae Lee
Cover design by Kimberly Greyer
All rights reserved.

**Printed and published
in the United States of America**

Available on Amazon

TREATY OAK PUBLISHERS

ISBN: 978-1-943658-34-3

Dedication

For John and Lauren

^{the}
Headshrinker's Brigade

Chapter 1

On most days, Julia Longley felt like a passable fraud. But on Friday night, as she sat in the newspaper editing room next to her friend Graham while he ran through his day's photos, this belief slid under her skin like electricity.

Static and garbled voices screeched from the police scanner and sent shards of pain through her head. A seed of a migraine flowered into exquisite pain and heralded the promise of more to follow.

She shot her hand up to the dusty shelf above her and lowered the volume. The mechanical voices dropped to a murmur in the cramped editing room. She sighed and settled herself back onto the stool, nudging a 300mm telephoto lens next to her elbow out of the way. *God, why did there have to be so much news in a newspaper?*

Graham turned from the computer monitor, his sky-blue eyes wide in mock surprise. "Why, Miss Julia, does it bother you that, as we speak, there's a two-eleven happening behind the Payless shoe store?"

"Absolutely not. Break-ins never disturb me," Julia said. "I was having a hard time hearing you, that's all. Now go on. You were saying?"

"Okay, weirdo, if that's your story, go ahead and stick with it. But if one of us comes into the lab and the scanner is set to where only dogs can hear it, then you're on our short list of suspects."

Prickly warmth spread over Julia's face. Considering how often she muted the scanner, she made a mental note to be more vigilant about cranking it back up when she left the room.

"Fine." She reached up with an exaggerated groan and increased the volume. "But how can you stand the thing? It's all code this and code that."

"It won't kill you to learn the police codes. You might actually get some great shots that way—in case no one's told you this factoid." Graham gave Julia a wry look.

"I know the codes." Julia paused. "Sort of."

Graham shook his head and a curl of blond hair fell from under his frayed baseball cap.

"You need a haircut."

"Don't distract." He smiled before turning back to the computer screen.

"Anyway, here's an amazing photo of a kid hanging onto this pig for dear life. See how he has his leg wrapped around the porker's belly?"

Bathed in the silver glow of the computer screen, Julia leaned forward and drank in the image, remembering why she had become a photojournalist. A photograph of a determined five-year-old boy, dressed in cowboy hat, stiff new jeans, and scuffed cowboy boots filled the monitor.

She smiled. "Yeah, that's cute."

"Well, we don't stop at cute. Check out this next shot." Graham clicked the mouse to the following frame, in which the kid's expression had turned grim. His straw hat floated three inches behind his head, and he clung sideways to the galloping pig.

"Oh, I like that one better! Did I ever tell you it's not fair you're so good?"

"Every day for the past two years. That's what makes coming to work at this rag so rewarding," he deadpanned, his eyes never leaving the computer screen.

"Now for the final shot." He tapped the mouse and Julia

laughed. The little boy had hit the rodeo arena dirt with a look of surprise and shock that made O's of his eyes and mouth. Only the back half of the pig was in the frame, its cloven hoof and corkscrew tail a blur. Graham swiveled toward her, his nose and cheekbones sunburned from covering the rodeo assignment earlier that afternoon. "So what's the verdict?"

"No-brainer." Julia nodded to the computer. "Tuckus in the dirt needs to run on a front section. Is it for metro? Please don't say it's for sports. They'll bury it below the fold, next to a basketball story."

"Hmm, you may be onto something, Longley." He ran through his images from the day's shoot again. "Let's see what bull-riding pics I have that should satisfy sport's need for speed."

In the hallway, approaching footsteps grew louder by the second. Julia turned around as the evening city editor, Sean, a wiry, compact man with a severely receding hairline, appeared in the doorway, his mouth a tight line. He stared at them for a heartbeat as his face went from pink to red.

"You're just sitting there? Can't you hear what's going on?" Sean pointed to the police scanner.

"Nope." Graham bumped up the volume. "But now we can."

The room filled with the urgent voices of dispatchers, EMS, and police. The words "motorcyclist" and "massive head wounds" echoed in the editing room. Dread sluiced through Julia's veins.

It's my fault we missed that.

"Who's on tonight?" Sean said, his hands balled at his hips.

"That would be me." Julia winced then grabbed her camera bag and turned to the editor. Even though her heart hammered in her chest, she kept her voice level. "What size hole am I shooting for?"

"If it's good, give me a vertical. If it's average, I'll need a horizontal for the lower right corner," he growled over his shoulder as he left.

Julia rubbed the back of her neck and turned to Graham. "Thanks for not busting me."

Graham shrugged. "No one likes the scanner, but it's where the news is. Take my raincoat, cause this storm isn't supposed to pass for another hour or so. Now be a pal and shoot something crappy so you can save Tuckus in the dirt here." He nodded at his picture. "I want it to run above the fold, big and bold."

"I'll do my best to be mediocre." Julia grinned and slipped on the raincoat, which swallowed her. Graham, at well over six feet, was twelve inches taller than her.

She squinted as she walked from the dimmed lights of the photo lab into the fluorescent glare of the main newsroom. Nearing deadline, editors and reporters sat hunched and focused over their keyboards. To her left was a desk littered with discarded reporter's notepads and newspapers, and across the back of the empty chair hung Nick's suit jacket. Her boyfriend was the only reporter who wore a suit to the office, which stood in stark contrast to the rest of the staffers, who sported variations of rumpled khakis and button-down shirts. The sandwich she had made for him this morning sat half-eaten by his keyboard.

"Nick covering the accident?" Julia said to Sean, her voice casual.

His face had returned to its normal, pasty color and he didn't bother to look up from the story on the screen. "Yep. Your man should be there by now."

Of course. Nick was always five minutes ahead of her. Fueled by this image, she rushed out of the building into a steady rainfall, toward her seven-year-old Honda Civic. Fat raindrops drummed the roof as she glanced into the rear-view mirror. Her pale, triangular face stared back, framed by chestnut-brown hair plastered against her forehead. Julia rubbed between her eyebrows and felt a t-shaped worry line. She was sure she didn't have this particular wrinkle when she started as an intern with the paper her senior year of college.

After pulling out on the street away from the squat, two-story, beige-brick newspaper office, Julia drove the route she assumed Nick had traveled minutes before. The windshield wipers slashed the bulleting rain in front of her and left momentary clear swaths on the glass. She pressed down harder on the accelerator.

"Damn motorcyclists," she muttered. "What fool rides in a storm?"

A lanyard and identification badge, with her name and headshot printed above *The Elston Daily News* logo, swayed back and forth from the rearview mirror in large, drunken circles. She snapped it off and looped it over her head to reduce at least one distraction.

Elston, a mid-sized city between Austin and San Antonio, had managed to keep its small-town feel, despite the ever-encroaching growth all around it. It was her home-town, but since working at the newspaper it was as though a veil had been lifted, and, like now, she was discovering the hum of the grid where the town really lived.

A signal light ahead turned yellow. Did she dare run it? Glancing left and right, she determined the cross streets looked clear, inhaled, and gunned it. The light turned red as she sped through the intersection. Her heart drummed in her chest and she barked a laugh. It would be ironic if she got into a bigger accident than the one she was chasing

Why didn't Nick tell me about the accident?

"Stop being such a girl!" she muttered.

As a journalist, he owed her no special favors. But as her boyfriend, would a heads-up be that out of line? She swallowed a lump in her throat and tried to push away the sly voice in her head that whispered, while she was a competent photographer, she wasn't an exceptional reporter like Nick. His drive for the story was breathtaking and intoxicating, which drew her to him. At the same time, she hoped his passion would rub off on her and bless her with the same glow.

Julia shook her head to dislodge the sticky thought—like melted gum on the bottom of a shoe—cranked up the mobile police scanner on her dash, and sped to catch up to the news story happening without her.

* * *

A MOTORCYCLE FORK AND WHEEL pointed up into the cloudy sky as the mangled wreckage flickered red and blue from the police and EMS light bars slicing the darkness. Gas fumes spiked the air, and Julia's eyes watered as she scanned the scene. The bike lay defeated and crumpled in the gutter on a curve of Mill's Crossing Road. Julia shuddered at the thought of the force that had twisted the metal like tin foil.

Lord, I wonder what shape is the rider in?

Stepping with care over a severed headlight ten feet from the motorcycle, Julia circled to find her best angle. She pulled out her Nikon with a 28mm wide-angle lens and framed her shots with the spokes of the wheels as a focal point. A police officer walked in front of the accident with a flashlight and swept the beam left and right. Julia dropped to her knee, turned the camera vertically, and snapped off a dozen pictures as the officer examined the crushed side of the gas tank.

This could be the shot.

Julia aimed and fired off a dozen more, relieved she might have something for city desk this time. She gazed over the whole sorry mess and sent out a prayer for the motorcyclist who lay in the ambulance attended by EMS.

Some of the photographers at the paper bragged about how quickly they could be first on the scene, but to Julia it felt more like aiding and abetting mass rubbernecking. As she walked amongst the wreckage, she was reminded of her aversion to the scanner, the town crier of mayhem.

While one of these photographs would probably get her out of the doghouse with the editor, it would almost certainly bump Graham's rodeo shot off the front page. The image of the little boy riding the pig needled Julia, fated now to be reduced to the size of a postage stamp and crammed into a corner of the sports page for tomorrow's paper. The odd mix of companionship and competition in the newsroom filled Julia with uncertainty—she lacked the hunger for hard news that fueled the other photographers and reporters. She bristled when the editors called her "Kid Photographer Jules" because she brought in picture after picture of children, snapped at the parks, the mall, and neighborhoods.

For a moment, she toyed with the idea of deleting the motorcycle and cop shot from her camera and instead give the city desk a mundane overview. Wasn't Graham's picture worth it? She caught a glimpse of Nick's car parked at a crooked slant up the street, the hazard lights flashing. She shoved the camera back into the bag, the pictures safely embedded on the memory card.

An engine roared to life behind her and Julia jumped out of the street as the ambulance pulled away from the curb with a heavy sway. She glimpsed through the window the paramedics leaning over their patient as they worked, intent, but not especially hurried. Not a good sign.

With the ambulance gone, the powerful headlights of a police squad car silhouetted two figures. One man talked and gestured toward the bottom of the hill, while the other took notes and nodded. Even from a distance, Julia recognized Nick's broad shoulders and military-straight posture, his feet planted firmly apart. His natural confidence elicited trust, as evidenced by animated gestures from the cop, who appeared to have fallen under Nick's charm and was now a fount of information.

Julia considered walking up and joining their conversation, but doubt nibbled. What would she say? Any question she posed now would only point out her lateness. Besides, she felt sodden and unkempt under Graham's bulky raincoat, which was so long it dragged the ground in spots.

As though pulled by a magnetic force, she pivoted around and headed back to her car. A dark glisten on the pavement to her left caught her eye. Despite the rainwater coursing down the gutter, a thicker liquid trickled down the center. Julia stepped wide to avoid walking through the excess gas and oil.

Back in the car, she started the engine and the lights from the dashboard bathed her in a warm glow. She turned on the radio, letting Bach's lush "Concerto in A Minor" fill the interior of the car, closed her eyes, and exhaled a deep breath. After a moment, her stomach unclenched. Punching the radio off with one hand, she grabbed her cell phone and dialed the news desk. It rang once before the editor answered. "City desk," Sean barked over the tapping of his keyboard.

"It's Julia, I think I have your vertical. I'm going to send it now. Hang on."

She cradled the phone against her ear and plugged her USB cord into her camera and uploaded the images to her laptop. Scanning through the pictures she found her photo, even better than she remembered, and hit send. "Okay, you got it."

"Good. Nick should be sending me his copy in the next ten minutes. Hurry back here, I want to go over some of the pictures with you, see if we have anything decent for the jump page." A click and the line went dead.

Of course Nick would have his write-up ready before she even skidded to a stop in the paper's parking lot. Julia imagined him seated in his car as the flashers rhythmically blinked off-and-on, while his fingers flew over the laptop at ninety-words-per-minute. Tight copy would unfurl in a perfect who, what, when, where, why, and how of the accident.

A few months ago, she and Nick had argued about the black humor of journalism expressions, found in phrases such as, "If it bleeds, it leads." Conceptually, Julia hated the idea of a person's suffering being used to sell papers. Nick had only shrugged, reminding her that a free press means you don't cherry-pick the news, you cover *all* the news. While she supported First Amendment rights as much as the next person, she felt her point had been brushed aside. Besides, who was she to argue with Nick, especially when his byline dominated the front pages and his investigative stories filled the paper's lobby wall with reporting awards?

Julia gritted her teeth, started the car, made a sharp U-turn, and floored the accelerator until the engine whined like trapped bees as she raced through the evening city streets, chasing down another deadline.

Chapter 2

The recessed lighting cast a murky glow in the vestibule at the condo's entrance, as Julia strained to find the lock in the brass doorknob with her key. Cool air fanned her face and neck when she pushed open the door, the rooms a constant seventy-two degrees, a temperature Nick believed to be perfect for beating back the woolen blanket of Texas summer heat.

With her shoulder cocked, the camera bag slid down her arm and she stashed the gear behind the modular couch with a heavy thud. The 200mm lens stuck out a few inches, interrupting the smooth lines of the low-slung couch. By habit, Julia nudged the lens back a few inches until only the chocolate leather showed.

She nabbed an apple from a cobalt-blue bowl on the kitchen granite countertop and took a hungry bite, sinking into the plush cushions of the couch and allowing her muscles to relax. The editors had indeed bumped Graham's rodeo picture over to sports, and then ran her shot even bigger than originally planned. Her image depicted the officer training his flashlight beam onto the mangled motorcycle's chrome muffler, creating a starburst effect. If it wasn't so gruesome, it could almost be seen as art. When the photograph was mocked up on the page, Sean had whistled approvingly and said, "Another great shot, Longley."

She contemplated sending Graham an apology text with the offer of lunch at El Gallo, her treat, as a Tex-Mex salve to reduce the sting. Instead, she laid her head back onto the couch and chewed, her jaw slowing with each bite.

Weariness like wet cement filled her bones.

Before she left the newsroom half an hour ago, she'd stopped by Nick's desk and asked him about the rider's condition. With his dress shirt sleeves pushed up, revealing the embroidered N.M. on the cuffs, Nick flipped through a reporter pad thick with notes.

"He didn't make it, Jules," Nick said, glancing up. His blue eyes, tented under dark eyebrows, were bloodshot. "Even if he had been wearing a helmet, at the rate he was hauling ass, his head still would have cracked like an egg. He'd been partying at the Foxy Box, so there you go. I won't need toxicology to know alcohol was involved."

Julia felt ill from the image of the rider, a twenty-something kid, sailing through the air before colliding with the concrete curb on Mill's Crossing.

Nick shrugged. "I've got to roll on this, babe. See you at the house in about an hour," he said, then went back to typing more dense text that scrolled along down the computer screen.

And with that, Julia had been dismissed.

One more bite and the apple was done. In her hand, the core turned yellowy brown at the edges as Julia imagined the guy, probably close to her age, out on a Friday night at that dive bar. His bank account may have been pumped into four figures after the deposit of his paycheck. Life might have felt fine while he joked with his buddies around a pool table haloed in blue cigarette smoke.

But did anyone try to stop him from driving drunk? And those friends who had watched their pal saunter out of the bar two hours earlier, would they spend the rest of their days wishing they had confronted him at the door? When he fished his keys out from his front jean's pocket, would they imagine themselves over and over, plucking the keys away and telling him the ride to his house was on them?

Julia twisted until she could see the kitchen trashcan across the room and wondered about the likelihood of her tossing the apple core and actually sinking the shot, rather than having it ricochet off the rim and sliding in a wet streak across the hardwood floor. To stand and walk meant moving from her comfortable nest. She took aim at the center of the trashcan and cocked her right hand to launch the core when her gaze snagged on a rusty brown blotch at the bottom edge of her Nike running shoe.

Lowering her hand, she leaned forward to study the smear along the shoe's white and aqua piping. Not mud, too thin. With her index finger, wet from the apple, she brushed over its surface and a crimson ribbon unfurled behind. Julia's stomach clinched and she dropped the core and brought her foot in closer for inspection.

She examined the dried, sticky dab on the end of her finger before realization bloomed and adrenalin spiked through her veins.

"Oh my God," she gasped. "It's his blood!"

With trembling hands, she yanked off both shoes, not bothering to untie them, and turned them upside down, which revealed a dark blotch embedded in the tread of her right shoe. She padded in her socks to the kitchen where she dumped both shoes into the deep, stainless steel sink. Holding her hands in front of her face, a streak of rusty brown ran down the tip of her left index finger. Saliva filled her mouth as her stomach lurched again.

She twisted the faucet and thrust her hands into the rush of warm water and watched the blood turn to pink and sluice down the drain. After squeezing liquid soap into her palm, she scrubbed her hands until they were covered in pale soap bubbles.

I've been walking around for two hours with a dead man's blood on my shoes.

A trickle of sweat beaded down her temple. The sneakers, which lay on their sides covered in pink soap scum, seemed alien. Julia grabbed a plastic bag from under the sink and took each shoe by its dripping laces and plopped them inside until the bag strained with the sodden weight. She dropped them in the trash with a heavy thud.

A moment before, the room was expansive and airy, but now the walls loomed closer. Julia escaped the living room and pulled back the heavy sliding glass door. It rumbled open and she stepped outside onto the small, concrete patio overlooking the busy street below.

Inhaling deeply, she filled her lungs with the humid air that carried a musty scent of sycamore tree pollen. On the street a car honked, and the rush of traffic noise invaded her ears as she leaned against the railing and took in the downtown landscape, a glittering grid of orange sodium streetlights and brick office buildings. The image of the twisted motorcycle in a pool of gasoline came to her, and now she suspected when she stepped over the gutter to avoid the rainwater, she may have walked through the man's blood.

She gulped deep breaths until her inhalations slowed and her heart didn't hammer against her ribs. Her hands trembled as she slid the door open and returned to the living room.

In the foyer, keys jingled, and then Nick breezed through the front door, loosening his tie. At the sight of his lanky frame, relief swept through her. With easy grace, he crossed over to Julia, cupped her face in his hand, and gave her a warm kiss that tasted of clove gum and burnt coffee.

"Hey, hot shot," he said. "How's my number one photog?"

"Fine," she lied and reached out for his hand, but he had already slid past her toward the kitchen, pulled his reporter's notepad out of his hip pocket, and tossed it onto the kitchen table. The refrigerator door creaked, followed by the hiss of a beer bottle as Nick opened it. Julia sank back onto the couch, but avoided the opposite side where she had sat earlier. "I'd like one," she said, but Nick had already crossed the room, sat in the armchair, swung a leg over the cushioned side, and tipped his beer bottle toward Julia like a king dubbing a knight.

"Awesome photo. City desk ran it six columns wide."

"Yeah, I saw. What kind of guy was the rider?"

Nick cocked his head as though trying to recall a distant fact. "Joe Hernandez. Twenty-four-year-old guy, worked as a mechanic at the Ford dealership. He had his bike pretty souped up, probably why he was able to pop it so fast on that short road. Too bad he forgot the laws of physics don't give a damn how cherry your ride is." Nick shrugged, then took a long draw from his beer.

Julia narrowed her eyes. A thickness rose up into her chest and she struggled to keep her voice modulated. "He died, Nick. I was there. I stepped in his blood."

Nick's lip curled up and he sat up straighter. "I hate that. God, what a mess. You didn't track anything in the house, did you?"

Heat flushed through her body and her voice rose. "What the hell! He died. You care more about your birch wood floors than the fact that I walked through a dead man's blood?"

A shadow of anger flickered across his face and he gave Julia a lingering glare. He blinked and relaxed back into his chair, his snarl reshaped into a smile.

"Of course a man's life is more important than my floors. But—," he said in a lowered voice, smooth as warmed honey. He paused to drain the rest of his beer. "People die all the time. I forget this is still new for you. You're just hitting a learning curve."

There it was: Nick's ability to sugarcoat the sting of an insult.

Choosing her words with care, she said, "I'm no longer a cub shooter. I've covered my share of accidents and half of them with you. This was a human being, a guy named Joe, not just space-filler for the front page."

The thickness in her chest broke and she swallowed a sob at the thought of the motorcyclist who may have woken up this morning and drank his cup of coffee while gazing out his kitchen window. Did he kiss a girl at the bar earlier while she ran her fingers through his hair? Such simple acts were his last and he had no way of knowing there would be no more coffee or kisses. That an everyday life could blow up was a reality Julia had known since her parents' divorce when she was a child, yet Nick seemed blind to that.

And while working at the newspaper, she had been summoned to witness emergency after emergency and cover such events with excruciating detail. The hot air balloonist tangled into electrical high wires, the house fire with children trapped inside, and the countless auto accidents were all stories that popped up like a thunderhead on a Pacific-blue summer day. She showed up and captured images that told as true a story as she could, but afterwards she felt hollow inside for hours, sometimes days.

A cloak of sadness drew itself over her as she tucked her legs up to her chest and put her head down on top of her knees. Nick walked over, took her by the hand, and pulled her up to him. Relief flowed through Julia as he held her and rubbed her back until her sobs slowed.

She pushed up from his embrace and studied Nick's eyes, framed under starling-wing black eyebrows. *God, he's too handsome for me.*

"You must think I'm such a girl."

"No," he said as he folded Julia back into his embrace, his voice rumbling into her ear. "You're my sensitive artist. Your photographs are special, and when people see them, they get pulled into my stories. We're a team that way."

Nick shifted and Julia sat up straighter to face him. "But being the raw nerve will pull you down in this business. It's never easy to see a life gone too soon." He brushed back a strand of her tangled hair behind her ear. "When I started reporting, lots of stories took me to some pretty low places, too." Nick's face took on a faraway look, but then he snapped his gaze back to her. "Sure, I've got feelings, but I also have editors and readers who count on me. Emotions have to take a back seat to facts."

"But I can't just shove my sadness away." Her tone was flat.

"If you cry every time you cover a story then you need to grow some professional-grade thick skin. Especially if we're ever going to get out of this bush-league paper. There are worse news stories than a Friday night crack-up."

Heat rose to her cheeks and she pulled back. "And just how do I do that? How do you do that?"

Nick stared at her unblinking for a full twenty seconds. "I didn't kill the guy, Julia," he said, each word as distinct as ice cubes dropping into a glass. "I'm just the reporter who was at the scene and fortunate enough to get my facts straight so the readers will know what happened. Including his friends and family. Don't they also have a right to the truth? It's not personal—it's our job. It seems your job needs to be to figure out how to get tougher."

She gasped, all argument flown away like scattered birds.

Nick stood up, stretched, and then went to the kitchen, tossing his empty beer bottle on top of Julia's wet sneakers. "I'm going to bed. We're both tired, so let's just chalk it up to that and get some sleep." He avoided her gaze and walked toward their bedroom.

Julia closed her eyes until the door shut with a small click.

What just happened here? She tucked her knees up to her chest again and tried to shake the image of Nick's stony face out of her mind. *He's right, we're both tired. Everything will snap back to normal tomorrow.*

Coldness seeped into her heart and she shook as she pressed her knees deeper into her chest. She stared out their floor-to-ceiling windows to a twinkling town where people and laughter seemed far away. But her eyes remained resolutely dry.

Chapter 3

A noise scattered Julia's disturbed dreams and she woke under the lemon glare from the vellum window shades above her. The brightness promised a blistering summer day even though the clock read 6:43 a.m.

She turned to an expanse of rumpled white sheets where the sight of Nick's pillow, concave from the weight of his head, greeted her. The coolness of the cotton slipped through her fingers as she ran her hand across his empty side of the bed. Had he left the condo already? Sleep had evaded her until nearly two a.m. because she felt too raw to relax. At long last, she crept into their bedroom and folded herself next to Nick, careful not to jog the bed. His breathing was calm and measured, so she hadn't been sure if he was asleep or pretending to be.

A cabinet door closed in the kitchen and Julia let her head fall back—at least he was still here. Her robe was slung over a chair. She grabbed it, put it on, and padded down the hallway to the kitchen, following the scent of freshly brewed coffee.

Nick leaned against the counter reading the paper, his dark hair wet and combed back, slick as a seal's. Looking up, he gave her a smile and nodded to the coffee pot. "Just in time for a cup of joe, that Hawaiian stuff you spend too much money on."

"Kona. And it's worth every penny," Julia said.

Rather than going to the coffee pot, she went to Nick,

and he wrapped his arms around her. Neither one spoke for a minute as Julia felt his steady heartbeat through his t-shirt. Nick kissed the top of her head and Julia stepped back to smile up at him. Last night's exchange lurked on the edges, but rather than bring it up, she let him pour her cup of coffee and accepted his offering. The thick, ceramic cup warmed her fingers.

"You're up early," Julia said, after her first sip.

"Golf with Zach. We tee off at eight, sharp, but it'll be a quick round since we're only going nine holes."

Zach was the publisher's son, a sallow guy in his early thirties who usually kept to himself, pouring over spreadsheets in the upstairs administrative offices. On occasion, he would trudge downstairs and mill around the newsroom to bother the staff with his brief, stilted conversations. It was awkward all the way around, and generally understood by the staffers as a task he did at his father's urging as a show of involvement in the newspaper he would someday inherit.

Yet somehow Nick had forged a friendship with Zach, and their Saturday morning golf games had become routine these past six months. If Zach worked across the street as an insurance agent, Julia had wondered more than once, would Nick be dragging out his golf clubs to tee off at eight in the morning with the guy?

"That sounds like fun," Julia said without much enthusiasm.

"It'll be okay. Zach's dad might join us to talk to me about writing some editorials," Nick said as he picked up his golfing gloves off the counter. His nonchalance seemed studied. "But it looks like you're going to have the real fun today." He tapped a paragraph on the sports page spread open on the kitchen table.

Craning her neck, Julia read the blurb about a college

basketball tournament thirty miles away, with the first game starting at one p.m. This week she was on the weekend and late shift, no one's favorites, and scheduled to start work at noon.

She groaned. "Maybe it's Graham's assignment?"

"Doubt it. He covered the rodeo yesterday. Odds are you get this one, babe. As they say, forewarned is forearmed."

Julia drew in a sharp breath, and then released it. High school basketball tourneys were an all-day affair spent crouched on the floor sidelines in an attempt to shoot pictures of seven-foot giants in a blur of constant motion. Her attention had to be split between focusing on the action in her viewfinder and being cognizant of a basketball whizzing at her from her blind side, or worse, gettng mowed over by a player and their sinewy, sweaty arms and legs. And the noise from the crowds and the clock buzzer! Her ears rang for an hour after she'd left the gymnasium last year.

Nick's cell phone trilled on the counter and he snagged it. "Nick here." Right away, his jaw muscles knotted. "Oh, good morning, Mom."

Julia considered if she had time to crawl back in bed and pull the covers over her head. Mrs. Meyer's staccato voice bounced across the kitchen, tinny and insistent.

Nick's face took on a hard expression. "Uh-huh. Let me check the calendar for that weekend. See if it works for Julia's schedule, too."

Her voice on the other end of the line grew louder and Nick pulled the phone from his ear. After grabbing his cup of coffee, he scuttled down the hallway. "Mom, it will not make the weekend more complicated—"

He disappeared into his office and closed the door behind him.

Julia could not decide if Nick's mom disliked her or

just the idea of her. She suspected Mrs. Meyer's chilliness toward her stemmed from the past year that Julia and Nick had lived together with neither engagement ring nor wedding plans in sight. Nick had made the regrettable decision to inform Julia of his mom's opinion of her moving in with him in two words: shacking up. Shame had filled Julia and she told Nick that, in the future, he didn't have to report back to her all the facts.

From behind the door came the muffled rise and fall of Nick's voice, but his impatience was unmistakable. Curiosity won over Julia's discretion as she edged down the hallway. She stopped when Nick said, "Don't scatter bibles at me, Mom. You might knock over one of your vodka bottles. Julia's got a right to live here if I want her to."

Julia sucked in her breath. Nick kept his silence as he listened for a full minute to Mrs. Meyer's response.

"Who said what to whom at the officers club last night is none of my business. Dad keeps his opinions to himself and do you notice how much better that works out for everyone?"

The few times Julia had spent time with Nick's father, her impression had been of an impeccably dressed, graying Air Force colonel, his lips pressed together as his wife rattled out her list of complaints about whatever was offensive or outrageous that week. And before every visit, Julia vowed she would shed her quiet-as-a-mouse reputation and wade in there with opinions of her own, only to wilt under the force of Mrs. Meyer's convictions.

Every time Nick's parents visited, Mrs. Meyer maintained a pinched quality around her nose as if Julia wasn't quite the potential daughter-in-law she had imagined.

"Okay, so now that we've got what you like and don't like out of the way, pick a weekend," Nick said.

A bead of sweat slid between Julia's breasts as she

edged down the hallway and back to the kitchen. A visit from Nick's mom? Great.

The office door opened and Nick walked out, his face flushed as he slipped the cell phone into his pocket. He raked his hand through his short-cropped hair. "Dad might be able to command his troops, but he has zero control over Mom."

He leaned against the counter and stared at the opposite wall, their fragile bubble of peace burst. A sunbeam shifted between the slates of the wooden blinds and blazed against the toaster's chrome, scattering harsh shards of light through the room.

"Your mom is welcome anytime," Julia said, "but does she have to make it so obvious that she doesn't like me? I mean, we've been together for two years!"

"She never liked any of my girlfriends. Blow her off, Jules. Don't let her get to you. If she does her thing, nitpicking and complaining, and then you try to please her, she'll only find something new to nag about." He reached for his car keys.

"Well, thank you for defending me. Again," Julia said as she shoved her hands deeper into her robe's pockets.

"Always, darling." Nick picked up the golf clubs parked by the kitchen table and hefted them onto his shoulder. "See you tonight. Don't forget to dodge those basketballs." His lips brushed hers, and then he whistled down the hallway.

From the first time she'd met Nick, he'd riveted her attention—nothing about him felt safe. The photo chief had been taking her on a tour of the paper during the interview. As they walked in the newsroom, Nick was in a hallway, athletic yet graceful, talking to a reporter. His broad shoulders tapered to a trim waist, no doubt achieved by a routine of crunches at the gym. As she passed, she dared to glance up at him and he gave her a curving smile, his indigo eyes, ringed with thick eyelashes, fixed on hers. She stumbled slightly, forgetting how to place one foot in front of the other, and Nick reached out to steady her elbow, never dropping his gaze. His touch radiated an electrical current from her arm throughout her body, and with that, Julia was hooked. To date Nick had been unimaginable, so when he asked her out a month later and they kissed after a candlelit dinner, to live without him soon became unthinkable.

And he'd stood up for her, to his mom even! Still, something distracted Julia's attention like a moth batting against a porch light, and she kept going back to Nick's clipped tone on the phone. If he could be this abrupt with his mother, would Nick to be as dismissive to Julia if she were to become his wife?

* * *

EVERYONE KNEW THE EVENING and weekend shifts at the paper were the most unpredictable due to people's wonkier behaviors coming out more once the sun set. The photographer who was on that rotation was usually glad when it was done and passed on to someone else. However, the land of sports dominated the evening schedule: basketball, football, soccer, baseball, golf—events spliced into quarters, innings, and rounds while chasing after one ball or another.

Raised by her working mother who had neither time, interest, nor money for such luxuries as sports, growing up, Julia had made her second home the public library, where books were free and the adventures between the pages took her into faraway worlds. Julia had learned about sports on the fly while covering the events and prayed no one had caught on to her cluelessness when she was on assignment.

She strolled into the photography department, a rectangular room with a large table in the center, piled with equipment and large monitors. Julia's photo vest sagged under the weight of the short-telephotos and wide-angle lenses stuffed into the zippered pockets. Her battered Nikon dragged on her neck, anchored by the 300mm lens snapped into the camera body. With her every step, metal clicked against metal. A small headache gave signs of blooming behind her right eye and she took deep breaths to visualize exhaling away the pain. Such headaches came more often lately, a glaring fact she tried to shove away with increasing futility.

The photo chief, Michael, a graying man who'd been at the paper for decades, and a new-hire shooter named Larry, stood at the counter hunched over a camera with its back cover removed. The gold and green of the circuit panel was flayed open like a dissected animal.

"Camera casualty?" Julia set her own camera down next to them with a thud.

Neither one looked up as they intoned in unison, "Mirror box locked up."

Julia logged onto the computer and clicked open her assignment file, praying her name wasn't attached to the basketball tournament. "I hate when that happens," she said over her shoulder. The day's photography assignments popped up on the computer screen.

From behind her, an out-of-breath voice said, "You wouldn't know a mirror box if it bit you in the ass."

"Well, hello to you, too," she said, and turned around as Graham walked sideways through the door. He lugged his lighting equipment case, which was big enough to bury a body in. "Still pissed, I see?"

He held up his right hand with the finger and thumb about half-an-inch apart. "Tuckus got reduced to the size of a postage stamp, just like I told you would happen. But I got my revenge."

"How?"

Graham dropped the case and camera bag down then straightened up his reed-thin body. "I posted it on the wire last night. Got a call half an hour ago from a buddy on the San Antonio Express-News that they picked it up. Ran the mother huge."

He paused a beat and cocked his head. "Hey, I know ... Let's share the good news with sports."

Sticking his head out the door, Graham yelled toward the sports desk, "Hey, you princesses! San Antonio ran my rodeo picture so massive you could salute it!"

Someone yelled, "Salute this!" Laughter floated back. Graham chuckled and shook his head. "Philistines." He flipped open the case and rooted through lighting umbrellas and skeins of thick electrical cords.

With a rueful wince, Julia smiled, and then turned back to the computer and scrolled through the assignments until she stopped, her smile fading, the headache spiking deeper behind her eye. Photographer: Julia Longley. Carter Auditorium. Three to nine p.m.

She groaned at the prospect of the entire afternoon and evening spent at Carter Auditorium with a roster of high school basketball teams and their noisy fans blasting air horns. Wait, who's the reporter? She prayed and scrolled down the assignment document. Reporter: Toby Schmidt.

"Hell." Julia slumped into her chair.

"What's up, buttercup?" Graham said as he plugged in two battery packs.

"I'm going to the basketball tourney. With Toby."

"Ouch," Graham said, and snapped the case shut.

"Here's what you do if Toby drives. Take trash bags. Lots of them. You know, the commercial grades. One to sit on and the rest to start bagging up all the crap around you."

Michael chimed in. "Maybe we could do a story on car hoarders. Are there such people?"

"Sure there are," Graham said. "How else do you explain Toby?"

Larry, who struggled at reattaching the camera, said, "The last time I rode with him, I couldn't even see my feet for all the fast food bags on the floor. I'm no Martha Stewart, but ..." He shrugged.

"Aw, we need to lay off Toby. He's okay. Maybe a little talkative, is all," said Michael, as if going for the higher road.

"Talkative." Graham snorted and rolled his eyes. He leaned toward Julia. "Trash bags and ear plugs."

* * *

GLANCING AT HER WATCH, JULIA realized she had already spent twenty minutes searching for Toby throughout the newspaper building. She knew he was still on the premises—his car remained parked haphazardly half on half off the curb. With each passing minute, their window evaporated for making it courtside by the tournament's starting buzzer.

Last year, she'd arrived ten minutes late to a game because Toby had gotten them lost. By the time she trotted up to the gymnasium floor, print and television photojournalists and their gear already lined the perimeter. Immovable, they'd staked out their spots and squatted, like Easter Island statues, while she edged, crouched, or knelt around the court to shoot the tournament over their heads. Her thighs and knees had ached for days after the game.

Julia's feet hurt from the weight of the camera gear as she searched the accounting department, the breakroom, upstairs conference room, and the front administration offices. Twice she circled the outside of the building, knowing how fond Toby was of his frequent smoke breaks.

At last, fuming next to the sport writer's car, Julia closed her eyes and visualized the newspaper's layout. The sun, high in the sky, baked everything in sight. Julia wiped sweat off her forehead with her sleeve. Short of crawling through the attic, where had she missed? "Oh dammit," she said as she pivoted and looked at the back of the building, windowless and stretching past the parking lot. "Not the press room."

As Julia marched into the cavernous room, the blue off-set web presses, rising two-stories above her, sat ink-stained and silent. A few men in the back wiped down the conveyor belts of the soy newsprint, but otherwise the press room was empty.

Wait. Julia heard something. She turned back to the press room and walked in a few more paces.

There it was again. A muffled guffaw. But only one person was laughing. Toby!

Julia bee-lined for the break room at the shadowy end of the building. Her cameras clinked against each other like castanets, keeping the rhythm to her increasing pace. As she approached, Toby's words grew louder. "What were they thinking with that line-up? I told the coach just the day before what I knew would win against McKinney High. Place Johnson first, for sure Gomez next because he seems healed enough from his injuries to me, then—"

Toby lolled at a scuffed-up table with his back to Julia, his neck-fat rolled over his plaid collar, empty energy drink cans lined up in front of him. Three press guys sat in uncomfortable silence as though they'd been trapped in their orange plastic chairs for a long time. Three pairs of glazed-over eyes lit up when they saw Julia.

Toby swiveled around in his chair and his face jack-o-lanterned into a huge grin. "Hey, there you are! I went looking for you, but needed to grab some papers for the coaches first. Then the guys and I got into a debate ..." He waved his hand at the three men who were already on their feet and pushing their chairs back like shanghaied escapees.

Julia willed restraint and said in a low voice, "Toby, we're late. Do you have everything you need, because we've got to move. Now."

"Yep, got it all here. Wait, let me grab those papers." Toby reached for a stack of newspapers on the floor next to the now vacant room. "Well, let's go, Miss Rev-Em-Up."

She narrowed her eyes at him. As they exited out a side door toward the parking lot, she reached into her camera bag pocket for her keys. Toby put up one meaty paw. "Stash the keys, J. I'm driving. You're too poky and I know the back roads to the arena. Time is apparently of the essence here."

"Oh no, Toby, really. You drove last time."

"We were late then, too, as I recall, and we still got there with minutes to spare."

They reached his car, a look-at-me canary-yellow Ford Mustang with dealer plates. He swung open the passenger door for Julia, in what appeared to be a gesture of chivalry. An empty soda can rolled from the seat out onto the parking lot with a plink. Magazines, newspapers, and Taco Bell bags covered the car's interior so that it was anyone's guess as to what was splattered on the upholstery or sticking to the floorboards.

"Oh, shoot—let me clear you a space." He thrust the

stack of newspapers into Julia's hands. Grabbing armfuls of trash, he heaved layers into the backseat. Papers and food wrappers escaped the car and settled around the tires while others caught a breeze and drifted down the parking lot.

Julia glanced around to see if anyone watched this spectacle. She gripped the armful of newspapers. "Really, we can take my car. It's just on the other side of the parking lot."

Toby stopped as he held a tattered *Sports Illustrated* magazine in one hand and a Burger King super-size cup in the other and looked at her as though she'd sprouted broccoli for ears. "First, everyone knows I only drive American."

Julia considered letting him know she'd missed that edict from on high, but held her tongue as he continued to heave the magazines to the backseat floorboard with a thud.

"And I for sure don't ride in four-cylinder rice burners such as yours. But with this baby's V8 chewing up the miles, watch our little lateness problem fade away in my dust." With the seat and floor somewhat cleared, Toby grabbed the papers from Julia, and chucked them into the half-filled backseat. "We're good. Let's go!"

Julia lowered herself into the seat, which was patterned with concentric stain circles, and nestled her camera gear at her feet, careful to not allow the cameras to come in contact with the sticky mats. A musty funk wafted from the upholstery, assaulting her nostrils, and behind her left eye, pain bloomed as her headache stretched a tentacle toward the center of her brain. She wondered if this was what a migraine felt like.

Toby turned the key in the muscle car's ignition and the engine rumbled to life. He floored the accelerator and the car screeched from the parking lot into the street.

"Man, it's hot in here." Toby cranked up the air conditioning and unleashed a blast of cool air.

"Oh, good, air," Julia said, as she leaned back into the seat.

Toby patted the dashboard. "Oh yeah, Mellow Yellow here can pump out the AC like an arctic blast."

Cheered by a fresh audience, Toby continued. "Yep, in fact, I got the Shelby for a steal from my dad's car lot just a month ago."

Her headache pounded as she puzzled out his words—Shelby and car lot. "Oh, you mean the model of the car," Julia said. It was as though her mind was floating above her body and she was observing their conversation. A tremor quaked through her body and her heart thudded against her ribcage.

Toby shot her a puzzled glance. "Yeah, right—the car you're traveling in, *remember*? Earth to Julia. Oh, here's the exit. It snuck up on me."

He took a hard left onto the highway entrance ramp, gunned the engine, and then zipped in behind a semi-truck rumbling down the interstate. The motion rocked Julia against the door and she glanced down at her fingers, pink and curled in her lap. But why were they numb and far away, as though on the ends of long stalks? Is this what it feels like to untether from reality, as though her mind were a balloon and the anchoring string was snipped? The sun beetled in from the window and sweat popped up on her forehead and neck. The interior of the car seemed too close as she stretched out her legs and watched her feet disappear into a drift of trash on the floorboard.

"Did I ever tell you I used to be the sales director of previously owned cars at my last job?" Toby said.

I'll bet, Julia thought, but out of duty said, "Director, huh?"

"Well, I was the only one working the lot. It was more of a one-man lot, at least that was how my dad put it when he assigned me there. But whenever I had a new customer, we'd almost always end up talking sports. See, you've got to find that common spot where you and the customer can connect." With a jerking motion, Toby turned left and swung around a truck, its chrome bumper hovering a few feet past the windshield.

Julia grasped the car armrests. "What the hell, Toby!"

"Granny driver," he said, pulling out a cigarette from the pack nestled in his front pocket. From the same pocket, he produced a lighter and lit the cigarette, exhaling a thin stream of smoke into the windshield, which billowed back into Julia's face. Coughing, she fanned her face and rolled down her window. Hot air buffeted around her as she glared at Toby.

He raised both eyebrows. "Oh jeez, sorry." He held up his lit cigarette. "But the drive will be my only time to grab a smoke before the game. I'll crack my side, too." Before Julia could stop him, he rolled down his window halfway and the car's interior roared like a wind tunnel.

Toby now yelled over the noise. "So my dad said, 'Since you like jawing so much about sports with the customers, why don't you write about the games?' I'd written for the school paper in high school, and he remembered all that. Soon as he said it, *boom!*"

Julia jumped as Toby hit both sides of the steering wheel with his fists. "I knew he was right. I actually forgot how much I used to love covering the games."

A piece of waxed paper with a grease stain in the center floated past Julia. The silver spike of pain etched deeper and waves of agony radiated behind both eyes. A new fear bubbled up. *What if I'm going to be sick?* The idea of throwing up in Toby's car filled Julia with panic. When she turned to stare out the window in a desperate attempt to change the view, her hair whipped into her eyes. In her side mirror, the dark shape of a motorcyclist approached, and a moment later the rider slid into view beside her. He rode parallel to Julia, dressed in black leather that shone dark under the brilliant sun. Even the helmet was jet black, with the ebony-smoked visor clamped down and obscuring his face.

As if feeling her gaze, he bent his head toward her and appeared to look at her. The moment was intimate, as though something private passed between them.

Then, like thunder clapping on a cloudless day, the man snapped his head forward, gunned the engine until the front wheel rose off the pavement blurring beneath him, and pulled away. Julia smothered an urge to call him back so she could ride on the back of his bike, her arms wrapped around the warm leather of his jacket, and let escape fill her lungs with fresh air.

As he shot in front of the car, the sight of his feet gave her a jolt. The biker wore the same brand of shoes as the ones she'd dumped into the trash can last night. A thin dam broke, and the memories of last night's accident flooded Julia. For a wild moment, she wondered if the biker fading into a vanishing point three car-lengths ahead of them was the same man who had died the night before. His piercing stare still reverberated through the center of her heart.

Cold sweat broke out on her temples, and again she experienced that upward tug of floating near the car's dome light. She struggled to form the words, *I'm going to be sick*, while Toby flicked his cigarette butt out the window before reaching into his pocket for his next one.

He clicked the wheel of the lighter and brought the end of his cigarette into the blue flame until it glowed orange. "Now the first game I covered as a freelancer was the Wildcats during their playoffs game against the Hutto Hippos. Even though I didn't know shit about reporting, I must say it was a mighty fine piece."

Toby paused to take a drag on his cigarette and exhaled a stream of smoke, most of which drifted toward Julia. "Do you remember that story? You were on the sidelines and looking off in a whole other direction, and this corn-fed wide receiver, big bruiser of guy, came flying off the field and almost clipped you. I'm pretty sure my yelling your way saved you from getting run over. Remember that?"

"Toby, I don't—"

A hand appeared outside on the upper left corner of the windshield. In horror and wonder, Julia watched the hand reach up, grab a corner of the windshield as though it were a sheet, and then rip it from left to right, taking away her view of the approaching highway in front of them. A dark, caramel-colored darkness descended, and her breath rushed out of her lungs as if a straitjacket had cinched her ribs. Whipping her head around, all she could make out were dark shapes and shadows.

"I can't see the road ahead, Toby!" she cried, finding her voice. She clutched her throat as she turned to Toby, searching as though she peered at him through layers of smoked glass.

He stared at her, the cigarette dangling from his lower lip. "What?" he struggled, for once at a loss for words.

Heart hammering in her chest, Julia sobbed, "I'm not sure if I'm having a heart attack or a stroke, but I can't see! Everything is so dark!"

Maybe it was the words "heart attack" and "stroke," but this seemed to break Toby's paralysis. "Let me pull over." Toby jerked the car roughly to the right. The Mustang swayed across two lanes and kicked up gravel from the shoulder of the road.

He's going to kill me before I die! "No! Just take me to

the hospital!"

"Oh, yeah, right," he said, relief evident in his voice. "Wait, we're coming up on the exit we need in two miles. Hang on, Julia, I'll get you there."

She closed her eyes and found a bit of reprieve in the total darkness behind her eyelids. Julia prayed, *Please don't let me die, God. There's so much I want to do.* A quieter, more analytical voice answered from within. *What are you doing now that's so special?*

Julia screwed her eyes shut tighter, clung to the armrest like a shipwrecked sailor hanging onto a broken piece of mast. Her body rocked as the car angled off the highway and Toby shot down the exit, miles away from the basketball tourney.

Chapter 4

Julia perched on the edge of the sofa in the cramped psychologist's lobby, holding the folder with the test results that the hospital had run two days earlier. The spine of the folder was damp from her sweaty hands. Nick slouched beside her, sunk into the couch as he flipped the pages of a sports magazine with restless energy.

She pushed a pair of oversized sunglasses up the bridge of her nose before realizing they already were up as far as they could go. Her vision was coming back bit by bit, but had taken a strange turn, as though a filter in her brain had been stripped away and everything she saw had begun flooding in at an alarming rate. Yesterday, while camped out at home waiting for today's doctor appointment, Julia grabbed a pair of Nick's Ray-Ban aviator sunglasses to block out all the crowding detail. Behind this smoky curtain she found a measure of relief and hadn't taken them off until bedtime.

Nick reached over and gave her shoulder a quick squeeze. "Take it easy, sweetie. The doctor will be here any minute, and then you can work on getting this stuff squared away." He tossed the magazine onto the coffee table.

They were the only ones in the windowless lobby ringed with chairs, arms chipped and worn, as if from nervous hands picking and gripping the ends. So was that what her vision problem was to Nick? Stuff needing to be squared away, like a rickety end table that could use a good dose of wood glue and a vise clamp?

Julia forced a smile and nestled up against his shoulder. "From your lips to God's ears."

Nick snorted. "If God listened to me, the Cowboys would have made it into the playoffs."

A door swung open opened and a pudgy man stood in the doorway wearing a plaid shirt so crisply ironed that the creases on the sleeves jutted out. "Ms. Longley?" he said, which seemed obvious since no one else was there.

"Weebles" popped into Julia's mind, followed by mortification. *Did I actually say the word out loud?* Julia jumped up and said in a too-chipper voice, "That's me!"

"I'm Dr. Bruce Donovan. I see you brought in some paperwork, so let's go to my office and dive in, shall we?" He made no comment about her sunglasses, but stepped aside as she walked toward his office.

Nick gave her a quick wave. "Be here when you get out." He reached again for the magazine.

Transfer complete, she thought, followed by a sting of resentment. Again she struggled to clamp down her chattering mind. Julia prayed, *Please don't let this be Tourette's Syndrome. I can't be blurting crazy stuff.*

The doctor's office was large and spacious, as though it had sucked up all the square-footage and windows from the lobby. Crimson and emerald woven Panamanian prints jockeyed for wall space with the more somber framed degrees and licenses. With smooth efficiency, Dr. Donovan settled into his chair, balanced his tortoiseshell reading glasses on the end of his short nose, and spread out the report on his rounded Buddha belly. He gestured for Julia to sit across from him, in a chair next to a massive teakwood desk.

She watched him scan the tests results, knowing they all said the same thing: there was nothing physically wrong with her. He scooped up the papers and slid them back into the folder. "These are the kind of tests you want to pay for, Ms. Longley. All negative. And yet you land at a psychologist's office. Not exactly how you wanted to spend your morning, I'm sure."

The room became blurry, and Julia wondered why Dr. Donovan offered her a tissue box. A tear dripped off her nose before she realized she was crying. She pulled a couple of tissues and his small kindness loosened a hot bubble inside her chest. With an assured move, as though this routine had been done many times in his office, Dr. Donovan scooted a metal trash can near Julia's knee.

Wiping her face and blowing her nose, she said, "I'm terrified to be here and grateful to be here." A pause, and then she shrugged. "No offense."

"Oh, none taken, Ms. Longley. People don't seek me out just to plumb the depths for the fun of it."

Julia threw a sodden clump of tissue into the trash can. It made a dull thump. "I didn't used to cry like this. Rarely, in fact," she said, rubbing her nose on her sleeve. The heavy sunglasses, now slick with tears, tumbled to her lap. Without thinking, she picked them up and placed them on Dr. Donovan's desk next to her. "Oh, and call me Julia. When you say Ms. Longley, I look over my shoulder for my mom."

When did he start scribbling notes onto that legal pad perched atop his belly? Tilting his head a few degrees, Dr. Donovan said, "And if your mother *were* in this room, what would she say to you?"

"How's tricks?" Julia said in an attempt to sound jokey.

"Really? Last week you had what appeared to be a massive panic attack out on Highway 95, were rushed to the hospital, subjected to a whole series of tests, and were finally deemed by the ER doc to have ..." He glanced at his notes. "'Hysterical blindness'?" Dr. Donovan leaned forward. "And she'd still be that flippant?"

"Mom's not exactly the Rock of Gibraltar. Whatever problems I had, she found a way to trump them. She didn't used to be that way, but after the divorce, she just sort of, I don't know … deflated. I learned to handle problems on my own."

Dr. Donovan's pen swept across the notepad. "How old were you when they divorced?"

"Oh, I was nine, but really their problems started a lot earlier, when Mom found out Dad was having an affair. He's an attorney, and the other woman was his client, who was going through a divorce. Wendy didn't waste too much time being single," Julia said with a bitter laugh.

A memory floated up of her mother confronting her father with a hotel receipt she had found. Her mother's face contorted with rage as he stood stony and refused to meet his wife's eyes. Julia tucked herself behind a door in the hallway, peeking into her parents' bedroom, not understanding what was so awful about that small piece of paper. She held the new Siamese kitten her father had brought home an hour earlier. The kitten's heart beat through his soft fur, and Julia understood the gift was a token of guilt, not love. Helpless to stop it, she had watched with horror as her world had crumbled.

The doctor's office pulsed with light and the tapestries took on aggressive details. Hard edges were everywhere. Hands shaking, Julia reached for the sunglasses on the desk and slid them back on. The room retreated to gloomy shadows.

Dr. Donovan scribbled in his notepad. "What do you mean, she didn't waste too much time being single?"

Taking a deep breath, Julia plowed on. "Dad divorced Mom, then weeks later married his mistress. Can you believe it?"

"Yes," he said in a mild tone. A silence stretched between them as he waited for Julia to continue.

Julia wiped her eyes with her sleeve. "So, fast forward. Mom loses the fifteen-room house to Dad, because as he told her, she couldn't afford to keep it on her secretary's salary. He moves Wendy into our old home practically the day after we move out."

"Wendy being the evil stepmother?"

"Evil, anorexic stepmother. Mom and I land in a crappy duplex near my school, so I can keep my friends and teachers. At least there was that."

Dr. Donovan peered at her over the top of his notepad, but said nothing.

Julia sighed. "Actually, keeping my old school helped. It's amazing how big the small things can become when everything you thought was solid turns out to be just sand."

"Your mom tried."

"She did. But after a while, trying got too heavy for her," Julia said, remembering her mother's closed bedroom door and the hours of silence from the other side. "Dad tried in his way, too, but Wendy didn't exactly welcome me into my new old home when I showed up for my two-weekends-a-month ritual."

Dr. Donovan cocked his head to one side. "What was that like? Going to your former home and seeing your father married to the woman with whom he had an affair?"

"Weird. Across-the-board weird. I had to act as if their arrangement was as natural as the sun rising in the west, and above all, I could never bring up any uncomfortable facts."

"Such as?"

"That I was miserable. And I couldn't tell anyone that Mom was a ball of resentments, always rolling over the same ground of how she had worked to put him through law school, soothed him when he lost cases, and put up with his neglect for years. Except when he wanted something. Then he'd turn on the charm and she'd get suckered in, and fall for it all over again."

"So Dad can be charming?"

Julia barked a harsh laugh. "Dad could charm the horns off of Beelzebub while trying to figure out how to steal his pointy tail."

"Well, you know what you call someone like that, don't you?"

"A lawyer?" Julia chortled.

Dr. Donovan's eyes twinkled. "Actually, I believe most lawyers are ethical. However, a person as charming, manipulative, and self-serving as you say your father is, might fall more on the sociopathic scale. Successful people can move up the ladder, so to speak, because they aren't burdened with whether something is right or wrong. Or how their actions might affect others."

Julia shook her head and smiled. "I guess Mom was onto something when she called him 'The Shark'. Said he was always on the move, could never sit still."

"Yes, running from oneself can be time-consuming." He turned a fresh page on his notepad. "So, parents divorced. Neither one was emotionally available to you. How did you cope?"

Julia blinked. "Cope?"

"What did you do with your thoughts and feelings?"

She sighed. "Kept out of the way, mostly. Read a ton of books in my room, or stayed at friends' houses until their parents kicked me out around dinner time."

"Sounds lonely."

Julia remembered long afternoons of sitting on her unmade bed, back against the headboard with skinny legs propping up a library book, as she willed herself into the stories of *The Hobbit* or *Watership Down*. Their worlds were richer and more tangible than her own.

"Lonely can be like air. You don't think about air, it's just something your lungs breathe in and out," Julia said. "It never occurred to me to think of it as a problem I could do anything about."

Dr. Donovan leaned in. "So stuffing your feelings and wants, that was a way you got through the day?"

A lump formed in her throat and Julia nodded.

"And today. How do you ask for what you want?"

"What I want? Well, usually I'm okay ..."

Do I ask for what I want?

An image came to her of a pinball machine with the silver ball swatting from one flapper to another. She was good at following directions from parents, teachers, editors ... and now Nick.

"You're shaking your head, Julia," he said. "So I take it that putting yourself first is not a natural response?"

"My first response is how I can get the job done."

"And that was what happened the day you had the panic attack?"

Her heart thudded. "Yes, I wanted the assignment to be over. Sports isn't exactly my thing, and the reporter was really getting on my nerves."

Dr. Donovan sharpened his gaze. "What exactly do you like about work at the newspaper?"

"Well, I like ..."

Her mind flipped through her recent assignments. A bakery opening, a semi-truck rollover, a city council meeting, several high school basketball games, a shot of kids messing around on the park jungle gym, and a trial of a woman who poisoned her husband over several weeks with dollops of antifreeze in his coffee until, near death, his symptoms were medically diagnosed and she was arrested.

"Last week, I took some pictures in the park. Just kids hanging upside down on some playground bars. I hung upside down with them, and the best shot was of them grinning like loons with their hair all dangling down in spikes."

Lifting his head from his notes, Dr. Donovan said, "You hung upside down with them? Why?"

"I wanted to see what they were experiencing," she said, then grew silent. Why had she done that? She could have shot them straight on and gotten the same picture. The warm glow from the fun of that moment had lasted almost an hour.

"You like to relate to people. Closely."

"I guess so."

"But in your job, you might not always be able to do that, what with accidents, sporting games, and murder trials. Is that right?"

"Like my boyfriend says, in journalism you need to stay on top of the stories. Always on the move," Julia said, a protective edge in her voice.

Dr. Donovan nodded toward the lobby. "While your boyfriend might say that, what do you say?"

"What else can I do? And why are you questioning me this way? Do you think I can't be a photographer?" Her chin jutted up a notch.

His eyes softened as he leaned forward. "I don't have an opinion. But some part of your mind may have a different idea. Your vision has been altered. And I think we both know, it's hard to be a photographer if you can't see."

Julia sputtered. "Wait, what? Are you saying my brain shut down so I can't see? So I can't do my work?"

"If your brain hated your work so much, and you weren't listening to other distress signals, then, yes," Dr. Donovan said, leaning back into his chair. "Some deeper part of you may have done this to slow you down and get your attention."

The obviousness of what she'd endured since the horrible afternoon in the car with Toby shot through Julia. All the previous minor panic attacks in the past six months, which she had ignored and chalked up as being too busy and too tired. She'd been revving herself up to get through difficult shoots, aware of the habit of competition that fueled the newsroom and pushed her. She wasn't driving the show, the show was driving her.

To her surprise, relief unlocked a hard knot inside her chest, followed by a sharp sense of danger. "What will I do if I can't take pictures?" she said, hating the plaintive tone in her voice.

"I don't know, but let's talk about it more next time. I'll have you take some personality and career tests, just to see what you're naturally drawn to, what might be a better fit." He reached for his appointment book.

Better fit meant letting go, accepting defeat that she couldn't cut it in the newsroom. Heat prickled up her neck and into her face. *What am I going to do? What else can I do?* She groaned, dreading the conversation when Nick would tell her to toughen up and get over it.

On autopilot, Julia made the appointment and let Dr. Donovan escort her to the door. As she walked into the lobby, Nick was chatting with a petite young woman who leaned toward him from her chair. Her radiant expression was familiar to Julia—women seemed to be dazzled by his white teeth against smooth, tanned skin and those deep, ocean blue eyes. Nick laughed and ran a hand through his mahogany hair, scattered with gold strands bleached through from hours playing golf with Zach.

The woman glanced up at Julia and a guarded look flickered across her face as she straightened. Nick followed her gaze and said in a bright voice, "Hey, that went quick. Ready to go?"

As they left the lobby, the woman slipped a business card into her purse with a furtive motion. Julia gave Nick a sharp look. What had Nick and Dr. Donovan's next patient been chatting about while she had been in the next room talking about her frayed mental health? With his hand firmly on her back, he guided Julia out the door into the street's noise and glare. She arched her spine to avoid his touch, but once she got into the passenger's side of the car she collapsed into the seat and into herself, too spent to give a damn about anything

Chapter 5

Booklets and papers were scattered over the kitchen table like unruly fish scales as Julia hunched over her computer and answered questions from the *Strong Interest Inventory*, one of the tests Dr. Donovan had assigned. She finished one page, hit the next button, and another page loaded up with the question, "Do you like preparing dinner for guests?" She selected "Like."

"Do you like dangerous activities?" "Strongly dislike," she chose.

"Do you like leading soldiers in drills?" She glanced up at the clock, groaned, and selected "Indifferent," wondering how many more questions she could endure. At least she was already on number 277. Dr. Donovan had instructed her to reply with whatever answer first popped into her head. At least in the condo she felt as close to normal as possible, no vision distortions as long as she hunkered down inside these known walls.

Scooting her chair closer to the computer screen, she read, "Do you like taping a sprained ankle?" Her mouse hovered between "dislike" and "strongly dislike" when three knocks on the front door interrupted her. She stood up, stretched her stiff back, and wondered if Nick had forgotten his keys.

When she opened the door, Graham appeared, doffing a red cap with a white Texas Rangers "T" stitched across the crown. "Hey, slacker. You still holed up here?"

"You're talking to me, aren't you?" she said with gratitude in her voice. She stepped aside as Graham breezed in through the door. "Yeah, I've always had a firm grasp of the obvious. And speaking of which," he said as he pulled out a bent envelope from his back jeans pocket, "this is from the photo crew. Don't expect Shelley or Keats. Especially from guys who've never heard of Shelley or Keats."

Grinning, Julia ripped open the envelope and on the cover of the card stood a black-and-white dairy cow in a field, staring out placidly, with the words arched above its head, "A Little Get-Well Poem from Us." Below it read:

"Work on Getting Well.
Don't You Ever Quit,
Or We'll Be There in Person
To Give You Lots of ..."

Inside, the card read, "Encouragement." Three signatures from the photographers were scrawled below, but only Graham's had a note: "Get off your ass and get back to work."

"Sweet," she said with an eye-roll. "Especially yours."

"What can I say?" He plopped down in an armchair. "And to think I chose to swing a camera rather than sweat it over a keyboard. Pity, really. A wasted life."

Julia laughed, but felt a stab of envy at Graham's casualness. A few weeks ago, she had joked right along with him. Their banter had flowed as they'd told each other their stories about what happened when they covered their assignments. Now a wall separated them, with Julia on the other side.

He sharpened his gaze. "So how are you doing, J? You've been keeping it on the low-down, hunkered down here this week. And Nick, well, you know how he is. Holds things close to the vest."

No love lost between Graham and Nick, Julia had noticed. Whenever Nick came into the photo department,

Graham tended to give him a quick "hi" before busying himself with editing or checking equipment. Before, she had chalked it up to Nick seeing friends as friends and work as work, with little mixing between the two. Another reality she was rethinking.

She waved at the table covered with papers. "I'm only goofing off, trying to figure out my life and what I'm going to do next."

"Next, huh?" Graham blew a low whistle. "Is there a Ouija Board hidden under there?" He stood up, ambled over to the table, and picked up a test pamphlet entitled, "Myers-Briggs Type Indicator."

Julia stood next to him. "I wish. That might be less work. Dr. Donovan is having me take all these career and personality tests. He thinks part of my problem is—"

The words caught in her throat. Inhaling, she tried again, her voice low and tremulous, "He thinks part of my problem is job burnout and anxiety. I may have something called a conversion disorder. That's why, when I go outside, my vision gets all distorted. I'm okay here in the condo and can make it into the hallway. But when I step outside, everything crowds in and I feel like, I don't know …" She shrugged, a heaviness pressing into the center of her chest. "Like there's not enough air and all the buildings are crushing down on me. I'm afraid I'll never have my life back."

She hadn't vocalized her thoughts before, but with the words out there, she knew this was the engine driving her fears. That, and Dr. Donovan's belief her problems stemmed from past traumas. It was as though a bruise, long protected and hidden, had been clobbered.

Silence stretched between Graham and Julia. His face filled with compassion and he gave her a long hug. "I'm sorry you're going through this, Julia. But you're going to be all right. You and the doctor will figure out what you need to do next." His words, careful and parsed, caught Julia's attention. "I still want to get back to work. I'm good at it, remember? That's what I've trained to do these past two years. Plus all my work in college." Gazing out the window, she realized what she hadn't said. Photojournalism was all she knew and the idea of reinventing herself was terrifying.

Graham jerked his chin toward the far living room wall, lined with her framed photographs. "We all know you're good. Even I couldn't have come away with some of those shots," he said with a smirk as he elbowed her.

Her photographs gleamed behind glass panes: A mother and her eight-year-old son wrapping their arms around each other while their home burned in the background, an elderly Hispanic woman praying as she grasped her rosary beads between knuckles gnarled with arthritis, and a sheriff, with a pot-belly and buzz-cut so close his scalp shined through, leaning back in an office chair with his feet up on a desk. He stared unsmiling into the lens while a fluffball Pomeranian sat perched in his lap, yawning.

Julia shrugged. "I look at them and it's as though they were taken by a different person. It all seems so far away. I miss photography. It's all I know. I can't imagine anything else." She pulled out a kitchen chair and plopped down. "You met me when I was an intern, like three years ago, so you know how hard I worked to become a staffer. How can I walk away? I'm still paying the student loans. I've invested a small fortune in camera gear!"

Graham grabbed another kitchen chair, turned it around, and sat opposite her, straddling his long legs on either side.

Ichabod Crane popped up into Julia's head. *Don't say it,* she ordered her mind, praying for that much control.

"Yeah, you've been in the newsroom a while, that's for sure. But we both know you're not going to set the world on fire with hard news," Graham said quietly.

Julia raised her voice. "Hey, wasn't your mission here to cheer me up?"

"Let me finish," he said, with his palm held up. "I can recognize one of your pictures without seeing the byline. You capture some spark, like you see with your heart rather than with your eyes."

A smile tugged at the corner of her lips.

"But that doesn't mean sparks happen only behind a Nikon."

"What do you mean?" Julia's smile dissolved.

"I mean, you can put your energy into other things, something better for you than running up and down the sidelines of a football game. In the rain. On a Friday night. Personally, I think that's kind of fun, but maybe not your kind of fun." He shrugged.

War twisted inside her. She did want to shoot again, but she also would like nothing more than to kick her camera bag into a closet and latch the door. But then what? All this talk made her bones ache.

"You're lucky," Julia said with a sigh. "You love what you do here at the paper. All of it."

"You're lucky, too, J. Sometimes, you stumble across luck, and sometimes you've got to chase the bastard down," Graham said. "Give the doc a chance. At least he's got you looking at options."

But all options led her away from these past years of security, a security she hadn't felt since she was a kid when both her parents lived under the same roof before the fights began. *The Elston Daily News* had given her a direction and led her to Nick. And it seemed as if Nick would lead her to a home and maybe even a family of her own. It was as if her foot was poised over a cliff while she prayed the clouds below were built of sturdier stuff than mist.

Chapter 6

As Julia stirred a pot of miso soup, its steam curling up in thin ribbons, evening shadows stretched across the ceiling. She breathed in the salty scent, watching honey-colored bubbles break the surface around her spoon.

This is normal. I'm doing something normal, this is better.

Liar, the quiet voice retorted, as she thought about the trip to the grocery store a few hours earlier. She had promised Nick this morning that she would force herself to get outside and not hide out. *Hide out* being Nick's words, not hers.

After latching the door behind her, Julia had taken a deep breath and walked down the breezeway, placing one foot in front of the other, determined to leave the safety of the condo. Once out on the sidewalk, however, her knees had buckled as if she were trudging through shifting sand. Office and apartment buildings loomed, and Julia sensed their weight leaning in, ready to crush her under tons of bricks. As though some mental filter were stripped, the excruciating details of window awnings, streetlamps, signs, and speeding cars all clamored for her attention. It was as though a firehose of data was streaming into her brain. She whirled around, intent to crawl back, not just to the condo, but under the covers of her bed.

In an effort to quiet her chattering mind, she'd closed her eyes and counted ten deep breaths as Dr. Donovan instructed, until the pulse in her ears slowed.

"Oh dear God, just let me get to the Wag-A-Bag,"

she whispered as she inched the two blocks toward the convenience store, her eyes narrowed to slits against the kaleidoscope.

Once inside, she opened her eyes and found that details didn't crowd as much, but she still felt like a deep-sea diver tethered to a sputtering oxygen air hose. Up one aisle, and then down another, she crammed groceries into her hand basket, shopping more from impulse rather than anything as organized as a list.

On the way to the check-out, a kiosk of green pinot grigio bottles caught her eye and she added one to her stuffed basket. This trip deserved a bottle of liquid courage, she thought, as she unloaded her basket onto the conveyor belt. Her odds and ends trundled along to a junkie-thin clerk whose right arm crawled with a tattoo sleeve of manga warriors riding twisting Chinese dragons. He grunted a greeting and methodically scanned the groceries.

Did a dragon's tail unfurl from around his wrist to curl around his ring finger? Julia had willed herself to hand him a credit card despite her impulse to abandon her bagged groceries on the counter and flee the store. Which was worse, for that sight to have been real, or to have been just another perverse trick her mind was trotting out? Never before had she prayed so much. She'd hoped Somebody was listening.

Now safely back at the condo, she gave the soup one more stir and turned down the burner on the stove. The front door opened and Nick strolled in, golf bag over his shoulder and several file folders cradled in one arm. He stashed his bag in the corner of the foyer and frowned at the sight of the kitchen table covered in papers. She had been taking more career assessment tests. Without comment, he tossed his folders on the table's edge, away from her strewn booklets.

"Hi, babe," Julia said, wiping her hands on a kitchen towel.

His frown melted into a casual grin. "Hey back at you. Sure smells good. This your miso?" He wrapped his arms around her, and Julia leaned into his chest, wishing she could bottle this moment.

"Yeah. I went down to the store and picked up a few things," she said in an offhanded way.

"Good," he said. "See, no big deal, right?" He kissed her on the forehead and moved to pour himself a glass of wine from the open bottle on the counter.

"No big deal," she repeated, and then reached up to a top shelf for soup bowls.

"Here, let me help." In one sweeping motion, Nick scooped up her paperwork and his folders from the table then piled them in a corner chair. Julia's career test and her interest inventory peeked out from under the stack.

She stifled a protest at the sight of them buried and creased. Which surprised her. After all, why should she care? Only an hour ago she had been grumbling as she penciled in answers as to whether she liked, or disliked, job types such as accountant, dance teacher, rancher, or television announcer. She was only finishing these tests to humor Dr. Donovan anyway.

She turned back to Nick. "How was the newsroom today?"

"Well, I wrote an editorial on the new waterline expansion proposal," he said, leaning against the counter. "Spent the morning on it and put together a tight, eight-hundred-word piece. Zach really loved it."

"Wow, that's great," Julia said, making her eyes look wide and thereby attentive. "When did he tell you that?"

"While playing golf this afternoon. He and I went out to lunch at the club then met his father on the course so we could go over some editorial ideas."

"Your weekly golf outings with Zach seem to be paying off." Julia pushed her wine glass away and crossed her arms. "Isn't this your third editorial this month?"

"Fourth, actually. And there's talk of me having my own editorial column, and you know what that means," Nick said, his face flushed from either the wine or excitement.

"Managing editor?" she said in a flat tone, knowing the answer. She thought of their current ME, an older man who had been teetering on retirement for the past year and who insisted upon being called Bud. Only Nick called him Mr. Whittlesey.

"Say it with gusto, darling!" He laughed. "This is good news, for both of us."

Julia stared at him, surprised by the word *us*.

"Well, yes, of course that's good news. There's not much *us* to a column you're writing. But I am proud of you," she said as she poured soup into their bowls. Nick brought them to the table, and they ate in silence.

After a few minutes, Nick reached across the table and covered her hand with his. "Your fingers are freezing." He scooted his chair closer to Julia before taking both of her hands into his and rubbing warmth into them.

His muscled hands encased hers, and an unpleasant thought flashed through her mind. These hands had slipped his business card to the woman in Dr. Donovan's lobby.

For the past week, some silky, insidious voice in her head had whispered about that event, refusing to let her be. Every time the memory popped up, Julia batted it away with the argument that maybe she'd misunderstood what she had seen. Surely Nick would never be that brazen. He'd even been more attentive to her since the appointment. Yet the doubt slid under the surface, even now as she willed her hands to be still while enveloped in his.

"It's been tough lately, I know," Nick said. "But you're doing better every day and you'll be back in the newsroom by next week, right?"

She struggled to form a careful answer. "I want to go back, but not next week. Besides, I'm seeing Dr. Donovan tomorrow to go over the career stuff. Maybe newspaper work really isn't for me."

Nick snorted and let go of her hands. "Get back on the horse that threw you, darling. You're great at what you do! Besides, we're a team, right? I miss seeing you flitting around the newsroom."

Julia frowned at the flitting image. "A two-for-the-price-of-one package, you're saying?" Julia asked, a frost of sarcasm in her voice.

"Sure, you and I could be a power team," Nick said, not catching her tone. "Look, maybe I haven't been supportive enough for you. You know how I get caught up in a story and let everything else fade." He shrugged, as if that was an unpleasant fact beyond his control.

Julia cocked her head. "Not supportive enough?"

"Maybe if I had given you more security, you wouldn't have had this episode."

Heat flared up inside Julia's chest. "An episode? You make what's happening to me sound like a TV program. Like *The Young and Crazy!*" She pulled her hands away from his and made air quotes in front of his startled face. Had he not understood the hell she'd gone through these past weeks?

After a pause, Nick threw his head back and laughed. "See, that's what I love about you, Jules. Your sense of humor. That's going to pull you back." The smile slipped from his face as his gaze softened. "Bring you back to us. I want to take even better care of you."

"I'm feeling a little freaked out here. What are you talking about, Nick?"

With the front door behind her, Julia was overcome with a desire to escape. Yet the image of her walking down the darkened street filled her with dread. She couldn't trust her brain to send the proper signals to order her legs to stand. If she tried now, she would crumple to the floor like a puppet with cut strings.

He rested his hand on her thigh and she resisted the urge to flick it off. "Julia, what if we set a date?"

"Date?" she said, her mind clamping down, refusing to comprehend.

"Not the Saturday night variety. The forever kind."

He slid his hand up her waist and pulled her close.

Oh dear God. He's proposing.

She had imagined so many scenarios where Nick would ask her to marry him. In her imaginings, the answer was always the same thrilled "Yes!"

Now that the moment had arrived, she could only gape. Her mind whirled and sudden heat flushed up her neck into her face as the answer she'd rehearsed in her mind so many times caught in her throat. Her eyes cut back to tests buried under Nick's folders on the chair. Marriage offered a shot at a merry-go-round's brass ring of happiness, but would it also choke off paths she had just begun to consider? And what if she didn't get better? Or worse, collapsed again?

"Nick, you know I love you. I can't believe you're asking me to marry you while I'm in this state."

His arms wrapped around her tighter.

Julia paused and took a wavering breath. "But since I am in this state, I don't know if now is the best time to be considering a marriage proposal."

His arms retracted and he stepped back with a furrowed

brow. "How much time do you need?"

Her mind struggled to come up with a number. Days? Weeks? Months might be pushing it.

"Give me a few more sessions with Dr. Donovan, okay? I want to get back to my regular life again, but I want him to help me figure out better tools."

Nick, who loved all things mechanical, nuzzled her gently on her lips as his hand lingered on her breast. "Sure, honey," he said, fixing those impossibly blue eyes on her. "But it's not as though we have all the time in the world."

Julia hugged Nick while her mind offered up an image of her pinned down into the center of a clock, the minute and hour hands circling round and round. And binding her tighter and tighter.

Chapter 7

Nick steered through the morning traffic and hummed along to the radio as he took a sip of coffee from his stainless-steel travel mug. Julia sat in the passenger's seat and stared out the window, biting her lower lip. Deep in her thoughts, she jumped when he said, "How 'bout if I pick you up after your appointment with the doc? I've got to run over to city hall for an interview with the mayor."

Julia swiveled toward him and frowned. "I thought you were going to come in with me to hear the test results. We talked about it … last night."

Nick honked at the car in front of him, who as far as Julia could tell, had the audacity to go the speed limit. "Hurry up, dude," he muttered, then whizzed by the driver, who shot Nick a withering glare.

"Well, now I know we're not rushing because of me," Julia said, swallowing her disappointment.

"I'm sorry, but the call came in from the mayor's secretary while you were in the shower. She said he'd be in today for a few hours and she scored a meeting for me." He reached over as though to put a comforting hand on her knee but, instead, he punched on the radio and Dwight Yoakam's "Guitars Cadillacs" pulsed through the car.

Julia raised her voice over the fiddles and soaring steel guitar riffs. "Why would she tip you off to her boss's schedule? Don't they usually keep journalists out, not in?"

Nick snorted. "Believe me, news flows both ways. I help the mayor and city council members get their agendas out there, and sometimes the favor is returned. If you know how to get on the right side of a secretary, then they can return the favor and be a solid source."

"Administrative assistant."

Nick gave her a quizzical look.

Julia leaned her head back in weariness. "They're called administrative assistants. Not secretaries." She noticed him thin his lips and they drove the rest of the way to the clinic in silence, until he glided the car to a stop in front of the clinic.

He rolled down his window and appeared to address the lamppost. "Do I pick her up in an hour?"

She followed Nick's gaze to Dr. Donovan, who stood in the recessed doorway of his office with his satchel briefcase slung over a shoulder.

"Make it an hour and a half," Dr. Donovan said as he strolled toward the car. He stooped down and peered in at Julia. "Hi there. Ready to start?"

Julia fumbled with her purse, struggling to unlock her seat belt, and said to Nick in a low voice, "Why is he standing out here?"

Nick shrugged. "If I'm a few minutes late, don't start blowing up my cell phone, all right? This interview might go over. And don't fret over what he says about your tests. It's probably just the standard stuff he has everyone complete."

She scrambled out, shut the door, and turned to the open passenger window. "Okay, but how long—"

Nick's profile slid by as he maneuvered into the traffic and Julia realized he hadn't even put the car in park.

Dr. Donovan gave her a nod from the sidewalk. "At least he's prompt."

She cast a glance back to Nick's car as it disappeared into traffic, and then she took stock of where she was—

outside. The road felt rubbery, as though she had sunk into the pavement up to the tops of her shoes. As though she had split into two parts, her mind seemed to float, and she could almost see herself from above, shock-still on the side of the road. In rushing out of the car, she had forgotten that her brain would promptly be entering this funhouse of anxiety, what Dr. Donovan called *dissociation*.

Morning sun ricocheted off the plate-glass window behind Dr. Donovan and bright spots danced before her eyes. The psychologist hurried to her and touched her elbow. "I thought we'd take advantage of this beautiful weather and review your results at the sidewalk café next door."

She blinked and gave her head a quick shake. How could she manage anything as complex as making it to the restaurant three doors down, its red-checkered table-cloths lifting and falling in the breeze like flags at a finish line? She looked over and could see them from here, their cheerful colors vibrant and aggressive.

Keeping a slow pace beside Dr. Donovan, she pleaded, "You don't have to do anything special for me, really. We can go back to your office."

"Oh, it's no problem at all," he said, steering her toward a small sidewalk table and pulling a chair out for her.

Julia lowered herself into the wrought-iron seat and gripped the edge of the table. Waves of nausea flowed over her. "I don't know if I can handle over an hour of this, Dr. Donovan. It's too intense. Really, let's go inside your office. Besides, aren't there like some sort of privacy issues here? What if others can hear us?"

He had been rifling through his briefcase, but stopped, blinked, and glanced around. "Others?"

Julia dared a peek around and saw the empty, half-dozen patio tables. "Well, yeah, now. But what if others come and sit by us?"

Dr. Donovan waved a dismissive hand. "We're not discussing your inner workings via ink-blot here. Just your personality inventories and preferences. Besides, at this early hour the café is usually empty. I think I'm their best customer."

As if on cue, a waitress approached them with two menus and a coffee pot. Her nails, an inch-long and painted lapis-blue, were curved around the coffee pot's handle. "Hey, Dr. D. Need these?"

"Not for me, Phoebe. But for my friend here, yes."

For a second, Julia wondered if this had something to do with Phoebe's manicure. The answer came in the form of a menu the waitress placed in Julia's hand.

"Would you two care for a cup of joe?" Phoebe asked as she produced a pad and pen from the front of her apron.

"Hell, yes," Julia said, grateful for something she actually did want. Followed by a quick, "I mean, just coffee, please." She cast her eyes down as heat rose into her cheeks.

The waitress arched an eyebrow at her, but said nothing as she filled their cups until they brimmed and steamed then walked away. Julia glanced at her wristwatch and groaned. Only five minutes had passed since Nick had dropped her off.

Dr. Donovan said, "Shall we begin with your Myers Briggs Personality Inventory?"

Julia nodded and took a sip of coffee. She winced at its acid bite, but kept her eyes straight on the psychologist. I'll just focus on his mouth. Listen to his results, drink this bad coffee, and go home.

"Your test results show you to be an INFJ, which stands for introverted, intuitive, feeling, and judging. This personality type tends to be sensitive, introspective, has a strong moral base, and a desire to do work that is meaningful. An individual wired like this needs to connect deeply with people, otherwise they can become depressed and anxious. They also tend to be leaders, not followers."

The word *leader* made Julia cock her head. Had she ever led anything?

"What?" said Dr. Donovan. "You're frowning."

"That last thing, about being a leader, it just doesn't fit me. It sounds kind of, bossy, you know? Maybe the test got it wrong."

He gave her a piercing stare that made her squirm. She wasn't used to people looking at her as if her thoughts were typed across her forehead. Julia rocked back and forth, until Dr. Donovan seemed to be noting this behavior. Silently she commanded herself to stop, and her body stilled.

"Yes. I could see why you would think that, although it's been my experience that some of the best leaders don't always start off as such. Sometimes life's circumstances nudged them in a direction where they had to show up and do something."

Julia's furrowed her brow deeper. Either you're a leader or not. Could a person learn such a thing?

Dr. Donovan picked up the document and continued. "INFJs tend to cluster in the helping fields, such as teachers, clergy, doctors, dentists, counselors, and psychologists. They are also heavily represented as musicians, artists, and photographers." He looked up and grinned at her. "So you see, you found a job that falls into your personality type."

Hope candled in Julia's chest. "So my career does fit."

"Yes, of course. As long as the work you're doing is meaningful to you and you have creative power over your day." He paused, putting down the document. "Does that sound like your current mode of employment?"

Her hope wavered. "Well, no," she said. "Not every day. My friend Graham gets all charged up with the assignments. And sure, I have those days, too." But when was the last time she had come back from a shoot all excited? Graham's sense of purpose filled the photo lab as he whistled and joked. An image came to Julia of her soaking up Graham's happy energy while she hung back along the edges. Not in the inner circle. She flinched.

"Perhaps Graham's job is a better fit. Whatever effort he puts into his work, he gets even more fulfillment back," said Dr. Donovan, handing Julia a one-inch packet, which weighed only ounces but sagged in her hand like a brick. Weakness seeped into her muscles, along with the realization of what he was telling her—covering daily news had not caught hold of Julia and filled her up.

"Let's go over these together, shall we?" he said, as he scooted his chair closer to the table, as though cozying up to a fire before diving into a fat novel.

Julia glanced at her watch. Nine minutes past the hour. She took a deep breath and turned to the first page.

* * *

TWO HOURS AND THREE CUPS of coffee later, Julia was on a first-name basis with Phoebe, the lapis-nailed waitress who discretely slipped the check to Dr. Donovan.

Phoebe turned to Julia. "Whew. I'd look as glazed as a Krispy Kreme doughnut, too, if I'd had to go through all that stuff. Give the girl a break, Dr. D."

Julia smiled, even though her head swam from all the characteristic traits, statistical leanings, and probability of outcomes Dr. Donovan had slogged through with her.

He snapped his briefcase shut. "Oh, I think the torture

for today is finished." He handed the waitress a twenty for the five-dollar check. "No change, Phoebe."

She rewarded him with a brilliant smile and a wink for Julia before leaving.

Rubbing her temples, Julia scanned the test booklets in front of her. She picked up the Strong Interest Inventory, and read aloud a phrase. "Connection and empathy. What does that mean? I'm connecting all day with people."

"In covering stories, sure. But to really know people and find out what makes them tick, you have to dive deeper. A photographer is always on the move and that deprives you of connection. Your personality type is sometimes known as the Joan of Arc because of the desire to save others." Leaning forward, he thumped the tests with his index finger. "But you can't save anyone unless you save yourself first. Your personality type can also be prone to neurotic behaviors if you're not in a nurturing, supportive environment."

"What if I were to try and become a ..." She picked up the career list and pointed to the top line. "A therapist? Isn't that a problem if I'm already crazy?"

Dr. Donovan's face broke into a mischievous grin. "Why, my friend, it might actually be an asset. I'm joking, of course, but it does take someone left of center to be a therapist. And you are not crazy. Maybe stressed to the point where the brain's visual cortex has shut down."

He added, "Temporarily."

"I know. That whole conversion reaction thing you told me I have."

He stared at Julia straight into her eyes. "Yes, but that whole conversion reaction thing is also your salvation. Neuropathways shut down and forced you to seek out answers. Possible answers are before you, and ..." He pointed back to one page of a report. "You scored high on the empathic scales, so being a therapist falls into your skill sets. You may have hidden gifts in helping others, and by so doing, maybe help yourself along the way."

Julia's fear twisted into anger. "But I don't want to change! I can barely handle this paper job. What if I'm a train wreck at something new? I'm a mess inside, so how am I supposed to reinvent myself?"

The coffee cups jumped and clattered in their saucers. Julia stared at the table in surprise before she noticed her hand was curled into a tight fist next to her place setting. Had she just pounded the table?

As though the outburst hadn't occurred, Dr. Donovan said, "To change nothing is still a choice. You may decide to find a way to adjust to your career, given more time. People reinvent themselves all the time. At least if we're growing, we do. Change doesn't happen all at once. Sometimes it's not one day at a time, but one moment at a time. Make one right decision then choose the next."

She stared at him and frowned. Nothing was that simple. Was it? And what if she made a change, and then life turned more on its ear?

A high-pitched squeal sliced the air and Julia turned to see a woman pushing a baby stroller in front of the florist's shop across the street. A pink-cheeked toddler arched in her stroller and waved pudgy fingers at the flowers, chortling with excitement. The mom crisply angled the stroller a few inches away from large, white plastic buckets stuffed with roses, tulips, sunflowers, and daises. The child stretched a determined, tiny hand out from under the stroller's hood and nabbed a lemony-yellow chrysanthemum then dug her fingers deep into the bloom's center. Mom and child turned a corner leaving sunshine petals to drift in their wake.

That would be my kind of photograph.

She imagined the cool touch of her camera and Zeiss

telephoto lens in her hands as she captured the pair with the chrysanthemum petals floating behind in midair. Her breath caught in her throat as she sat erect and glanced up the road crammed with parked cars hugging the curb and pedestrians ambling up and down the sidewalk. Whipping around behind her was more of the same. Everywhere were people, shops, telephone poles, parking meters, and store-front signs coming to her at a normal pace rather than in an aggressive rush of visual overload. The filter in her mind had snapped back into place and she was part of the world again. Deep waves of gratitude washed over Julia.

"Dr. Donovan—"

But he had stood up and was snapping his briefcase shut. "You don't have to search, he's right there. Dr. Donovan nodded toward the street in front of the café. Nick's car and his impatient face in the open driver's window blocked the view of the florist shop.

"Hey, Jules! You ready? I've circled the block twice and couldn't find a parking space." The car behind Nick honked his horn as if to punctuate the statement.

Grabbing her purse, she stood and turned to Dr. Donovan as he handed her a manila folder. "Here are your test results," he said. "And call my service for your next appointment."

Before he could walk away, she placed her hand on his arm and her words came out in a rush. "I can see. Just now, everything is looking normal again!"

The car horn blared louder and longer this time, and Nick waved to the driver behind him to go around.

Dr. Donovan raised his eyebrows. "And just in time, no?" He tapped her folder and gave her a nod.

She trotted out to the car and when she closed the door, she noticed Nick's florid cheeks and clenched jaw. Before she could apologize, Nick pulled into the stream of traffic while Julia clutched the folder against her chest like a shield.

"There must have been six cars behind us," he said. "I've got to get back to the newsroom, so I'll drop you off in front of the house, all right?"

"Okay."

Julia pressed her hot forehead against the cool glass of the passenger window and marveled at the unremarkable world that was sliding by without assaulting her senses. She considered telling Nick her vision was better, but couldn't muster the energy.

Underneath her weariness, an electric current coursed. Regaining her sight solved a huge problem, but opened up more, as if dominoes were stood in snaking spirals that fanned into different directions. A tap into one domino would set the rest into a clattering motion.

What direction would they take? Could she make the one good choice? Then continue to the next good one, then the next? As the town slipped by outside the glass, Julia closed her eyes and her head dropped back as she let darkness envelop her.

Chapter 8

Shouldn't the second week back at work be better than the first? So far, it wasn't.

Julia rubbed her neck, then straightened and returned to scrolling through the day's assignments on the computer. Her morning would be spent covering a geriatric exercise class at the YMCA—the lifestyle editor had requested enough pictures for a full-page spread—a review of a new restaurant, and a pet-of-the-week portrait at the animal shelter. She checked the other photographers' assignments—the governor's press conference and a veteran's rehab story—and her suspicions were confirmed. They definitely got the meatier stories and left her with a heaping plate of fluff.

The photo editor, Michael, breezed by and gave her a quick hello. There was a definite chill in the air from him and the other photographers since her return, as if they didn't quite know what to make of her. Perhaps they worried that what she went through might be catching. Graham, thank God, was her one unchanged friend. When she had first walked back into the photo lab, he'd said, "Hey, look who's back from the funny farm! You know, Jules, I'd pull that one myself if I could, except they'd probably never let me out."

"They'd never let you in because you might teach the crazies your old tricks," she shot back with a grin.

Graham barked a laugh and gave her a quick hug. He whispered, "Welcome back, sister green-eyes."

Her smile didn't fade when she'd walked past the other

photographers who'd mumbled their hellos. Maybe it wasn't going to be all that hard to slide back into work after all, she'd told herself as she picked up a thick stack of letters and magazines that had collected in her mail basket.

But that bright spot had dimmed with each day as she'd shot one lackluster assignment after another. Was this how factory workers felt while they counted down the clock until their shift was over? The chill waves coming from Nick hadn't helped either, as he continued to smart from her dodge to his marriage proposal. When she'd shown him the list of potential new careers after her meeting with Dr. Donovan, his argument was that school takes time and money, and wasn't she tired of wasting time and money with all these doctor visits? Plus, he had added, wasn't she back to normal? What needed to be changed? Defeated, she had tucked the career list away into the top drawer of her desk, feeling as though she were shoving pieces of herself in amongst receipts and bills.

She shrugged her camera bag onto her shoulder then walked into the newsroom, buzzing with reporters on the phone and editors focused on the monitors in front of them, scrolling through copy. Nick lingered by the far elevator doors, typing into his phone. Wasn't he supposed to be attending the morning staffing now? The managing editor, probably wondering the same thing, walked up and spoke to him.

Nick pointed to the ceiling where the second story comprised the publisher's realm of Zach and his father's offices. Bud's face clouded but he said nothing as the elevator doors opened and Nick strode inside. When the doors slid shut, the managing editor trudged to the staff meeting with his shoulders hunched and brows furrowed. He passed Julia without comment and his eyes down.

Julia frowned. Her boyfriend's callous disregard of

Bud, only to partner up with Zack, had increased during her weeks away from the newsroom. As she made her way through the newsroom, the seed of a panic attack sprouted. She pushed the side door open of the building that led to the employee parking lot, put her hands on her knees, and then leaned forward, taking deep breaths, just as Dr. Donovan had taught her.

Oh Jesus, not this again.

Her pulse quickened even as she forced herself to inhale and exhale at a slower rate. Then it finally dawned on her: Nick was switching camps from the newsroom to the business office and she had known all along—seen it all along—but had refused to understand it. Could this be why she felt a chill from others in the newsroom?

"What game is he playing?" she muttered to herself. Was she willing to sign up for life of sleuthing out his agendas?

Julia picked up her camera bag that had slid to the ground. It now felt like it was stuffed with stones. She slogged to her car, grateful for the simple comfort of her first shoot being older ladies, with hair tinted blue and pink, pumping three-pound weights with bird-thin hands and wrists. Julia envied these women, their choices of whom to marry, how to raise kids, and how to balance work achieved years ago. On autopilot, she slung the camera bag onto the floor of her car, started the engine, and headed to the community recreation center.

* * *

THE MORNING ASSIGNMENTS TUGGED Julia through an hour at the YMCA water exercise class, interrupted when she had to rush to an apartment fire set ablaze by an untended candle left too near curtains, and then a quick jog to a new Thai restaurant for a food shot for a restaurant review piece. It took Julia forty-five minutes to set up the commercial soft-box lighting rig, which left her only five minutes to shoot the picture. Plates of steaming curried dishes were brought out under the direction of the chef, who was impatient to get back into his kitchen and prep for the lunch crowd.

She arranged and shot the dishes as artfully as she could, inhaling the savory sauces that spilled over gleaming mounds of white rice until her stomach growled. At the end of the session, the chef gathered the dishes, walked into the kitchen, and dumped all the contents from the bowls into a trashcan.

Julia groaned. By the time she entered the animal shelter for the weekly adoption feature, her plan was to get the shot in less than ten minutes, and then go grab some lunch.

A burly man hunkered at the front desk behind a computer, stabbing at the keyboard with his meaty index fingers. Julia struggled to remember his name. Phil or Bill?

Glancing up from his computer screen, he peered at Julia from under a mop of unruly hair. "Hey, it must be Monday if the paper people are here. Let me see which lucky critter got picked to be your rag's POW." A few hunts and pecks on the keyboard, and he said, "Here it is, Pet of the Week will be Trixie, cat cage 127."

"Is the shelter full?" Julia said, trailing behind him as he unlocked a back door to the animal kennels.

He shrugged. "We're always full."

The dogs' yelps and barks echoed against the concrete walls and hallways as the animals paced behind their wire enclosures. Julia averted her eyes from their pleading faces, each animal desperate to escape such a noisy, cramped place. The acidic smell of bleach wafted in the air, barely masking the undertones of urine and poop. If misery had an odor, this would be it. Whenever she snapped a dog or cat's picture, she escaped the shelter's cacophony with the hope her picture might help that animal win the publicity lottery. She liked to imagine some tenderhearted newspaper reader, who, over their morning bowl of corn flakes, turned the page, saw the animal's headshot staring back, and became instantly hooked.

The shelter worker stopped before a cage, wiggled his hands into brown leather gloves, and reached in to pull out a scrawny, brown-and-tan striped cat who hung limply. All the fight had been wrung out of her. Phil—or Bill—held up the cat, who couldn't have been more than four months old, and peered into its face. "Nah," he said, shaking his head, "this one ain't no calendar cat. She's too puny and she's got a weird notch in that ear. Let's see if we can find you someone prettier."

He plopped her back into the cage where she collapsed, as though her bones were thick molasses. Julia bent down and peered into the shadowed enclosure. Lamp-lit yellow eyes stared back unblinking, their corners crusted with green mucus.

"Here's your GQ cover dude." He heaved out a pumpkin-orange tabby who regarded Julia with a baleful stare.

With a twist of her wrist, she popped on a short telephoto lens to the camera, framed the shot, and fired off three quick pictures of the slouching tom. She dropped down to one knee and was lowering her camera bag to the ground to stuff her Nikon into the main compartment, when something patted her right shoulder.

With a quick gasp, she looked up. A burnished paw stretched from cage 127, patted one more time then withdrew. A pink index card with the name "Trixie" was printed out in thick, black strokes at the top of the cage. Those yellow eyes ringed in crust stared as Julia moved forward an inch. Now the notch in the ear was more visible, and Julia noticed it was dime-sized and poorly healed. The cat's gaze flickered away from Julia's as though her reserve of energy had burnt off. She tucked her paw back under her thin body and closed her eyes, like a toy winding down.

Julia rubbed the half-grown kitten's head with her index finger. Trixie's eyes remained shut, but she offered up a thread of a purr, which sent faint vibrations up Julia's fingertips. A chink loosened in Julia's chest. If she left this cat in the shelter, it would be dead by the end of the week from either infection or desperation. And just like her imaginary reader eating corn flakes while scanning the paper and coming across a pet-of-the-week picture, in a blink, she knew that this cat was her cat.

Without a doubt, Nick would despise not just this cat, but any cat and all the guarantees of scratched furniture and feline hair balled along the edges of his grandfather's 1930's Persian rug. But as furious as he might become, would he actually stop her from adopting the cat if she stood her ground? She inhaled deeply, no longer minding the smells, and her lungs expanded as though they hadn't taken a full breath in a long time. Let him bitch, came Julia's answer. She straightened her back.

The shelter guy shifted from foot to foot, ready to leave. "It's Bill, right?" Julia said. "I think I might take this one here home with me."

He raised his eyebrows then shrugged. "Jerry, actually, but it's all cool. If that's the one you want, okay, but you may be racking up the vet bills. This puny gal's going to have them."

Twenty minutes later, Julia strapped a borrowed travel pet carrier into the front seat of her car as she muttered, "He'll just have to deal with it." She had an image of Nick's stony face, but shook her head and peeked into the crate's mesh front. "Right, Trixie?" The cat stared back with rounded, frightened eyes.

She tossed in the bag of antibiotics that Jerry had given her to treat Trixie's conjunctivitis, along with the name of the vet who had spayed her the week before. "You need to follow up with the vet, since he's the one who addressed her intact ovary problem," Jerry said when he handed the carrier over to Julia. "Bring the carrier back next time and have fun with your little dude."

As she pulled into traffic, the reality of what she had done hit home. First, she needed to go to the pet store and buy food and bedding, and from the smell of her new pet, a stout cat shampoo. Once she got Trixie settled in at the condo, she'd have to dash back to the paper. If no one was hogging the editing stations in the lab, she would just make her five-p.m. deadline for the news and lifestyle desks. Just. Her heart thudded in her chest. Taking deep breaths and exhaling slowly while she counted to ten, her hands slowed their shaking.

She braked at a traffic light and closed her eyes. Nick was going to insist she take the cat back. Worse, she could see herself caving.

Weight settled on her shoulders until they sagged. Should she turn around now and head back to the shelter? Tell Jerry she'd been impulsive and had come to her senses after she'd traveled three miles? And how many times had she taken one tentative step forward, only to scuttle back when things got tough? Her fear kept her safe yet also equally stuck. She pushed the heels of her hands into her eyes until she saw stars, but still a tear seeped through and traveled down her cheek.

A questioning meow made Julia jump. Trixie had a voice after all, and she pushed her front paws against the metal mesh of the crate. She meowed, louder.

Julia placed her finger against the mesh and felt the warm softness of Trixie's pad. Anger roiled in her chest and her breathing shallowed out. A taste of copper crept under her tongue. How could she fight for what she wanted if she was the first one in line to deny herself?

Blue flashed across the Honda's dusty windshield and Julia glanced up as a woman ran across the intersection. Slung over her shoulder was a backpack with "Elston State College" stitched in red silk. Watching the woman stride up the hill, Julia knew the sidewalk led to the school's main administration building, a place she'd been to several times covering stories.

As the light turned green, the student took a right and disappeared up the hill. Julia imagined herself walking up that hill and entering a classroom. An ache of yearning flooded her. *Has the time passed to reinvent myself?*

"Now," she whispered, gripping the steering wheel until her knuckles showed white. "Now is my time."

Not bothering with a blinker, she turned left in front of two rows of cars. They blasted her with their horns as she sped up the hill. From the scratching, clawing noise, she knew Trixie had slid into a corner of the crate.

"Sorry, girl!" Julia said, as she sped into the main building's parking lot and whipped into a parking space. Before her were the pink stucco walls, punctuated with brass window frames of the admissions office.

Like the Trixie decision, Julia pushed away her yapping logical mind for the second time in one hour and grabbed her purse, which had tumbled to the floorboard underneath a heap of reporter's notepads and cat medications. Before she could slam the car door shut, Trixie let out a mournful meow.

Midday sun poured down and Julia knew the interior

would soon be stifling, making Trixie wonder what new shade of hell she had landed in. The goal of hitting her deadlines was shrinking, so Julia wrenched open the car door, pulled out the cat carrier, and lunged up the walk. Julia swayed from the bulk and prayed she didn't look like a crazy, drunk cat lady.

A low-slung desk of cherry mahogany was at the back of the lobby and behind it sat a woman with long brown-and-blond-streaked hair. Nestled on her tiny ski-slope nose were a pair turquoise, cat-eyed glasses, and her mouth pursed as Julia approached.

Shoving the carrier up against the desk and hoping the woman wouldn't be too investigative, Julia asked, "How do I start the graduate school process?"

Surprise flickered across the woman's face and she hesitated. For a wild moment, Julia feared she would be told, *no, desperate people need not apply.* Instead the woman leaned forward. "All right, I can help you with that, but what is that box? If it's an animal carrier, you know, we—"

Tilting forward to block her vision, Julia raised her voice to mask the noise of Trixie, who had begun to shuffle around in the crate. "I just need to pick up any forms or packets. You know, graduate school materials."

Frost edging each syllable, the woman inclined her head. "Yes, I know graduate school materials," she said in a way that Julia could imagine her making finger air quotes. "For which area of study?"

Oh shit. Her thinking hadn't extended that far.

"Isn't there some general application I can fill out now then figure out the details of the actual degree later?" Even as the words came out, she knew how dumb they sounded.

A rattle came from below near Julia's knee. Was Trixie biting the wire mesh? Julia nudged the carrier and the cat stilled.

Miss Eye Glasses was having none of it. "No," she said with a flat stare. "You have to apply for a particular department. You *do* know the department you're interested in, don't you?"

Heat rose up in Julia's cheeks, as she tried to remember the career list she and Dr. Donovan had gone over, what he called her short list. Teacher? Preacher? Beekeeper? It was as though a door had closed and cordoned her off from her memory.

The carrier rattled and no one could mistake Trixie gnawing the mesh. Then the cat gave a low growl.

"Okay, that's a cat." The woman leaned across the desk and her two-toned hair swept the surface. "Pets are not allowed in campus buildings, so I'm going to have to ask you to remove your animal."

The carrier swayed from the cat's frantic attempts to flee as she slammed her body from one side to the other.

Was Julia going to miss her deadline, walk out of here without the admissions packet, and possibly return Trixie to the shelter, all for nothing?

Decide!

An image flashed of Dr. Donovan sitting across the cafe table, as he went line by line over her strengths and traits. He was emphatically telling her something.

"Counseling program," Julia said. "I'd like the information packet for your counseling program."

The woman stopped giving the carrier the evil eye and stepped back as though she had forgotten Julia was there. "Oh, well, okay, I can get you that." She took her time walking to a side room and returned with a sheath of paperwork, which she handed over with a reproachful expression. "Send in your application to the education department, the deadline is next month. Our animal policy you now know."

Julia accepted the packet in one hand, grabbed the carrier in the other, and spoke above Trixie's escalated caterwauling cries. "Thank you and so sorry about this," she said as she backed toward the door.

The woman only thinned her lips. Julia burst out the door and into the fresh air. All around her were emerald lawns and towering oak trees that spread their limbs almost to the red-tiled roofs of the Spanish-style buildings.

Can I really make this happen? Get into graduate school?

She walked to her car, careful not to bump the now blessedly silent carrier. The hard afternoon sun deepened Julia's shadow to an inky black as the mica chips embedded in the sidewalk shimmered like diamonds. Her hands trembled as she slid the cat carrier into the front seat. Whether it was from fear or excitement, she couldn't tell.

Behind the wire-mesh door, Trixie turned up her sad, totally done-in face. Julia put her finger between the mesh and scratched the cat under her chin. "Let's strap you in, girl, and take you home. How about a can of tuna and an old beach towel for a bed? From here on, it looks like we're improvising."

The phone rang and a picture of Nick lit up the screen. She dropped the ringing phone into her purse, backed up, and drove home with the packet in her lap.

Chapter 9

The college library doors closed behind her with a soft swoosh as Julia walked a well-worn path to her favorite corner with the two over-stuffed armchairs. She trailed a finger along the book spines as she passed between the shelves. She hoped Fiona had staked out their spot, and smiled when she found her friend nestled in one of the chairs, absorbed in a thick textbook. Two paper cups of coffee sat steaming on the windowsill, one of which had the word "soy" written on the side.

"There you are," Julia said, dropping her new leather purse next to the chair and kicking off her high heels.

"Here I am," Fiona echoed, peering through dark brown frames that matched her almond eyes and sleek, bobbed hair. After putting her book down, she picked up the two coffees and handed Julia the non-soy cup.

Julia took a sip, closed her eyes, and sank back with a sigh. "Better."

"Hard day pounding the pavement?"

She reached down and rubbed a foot. "Actually, the interview went okay. The psychiatric hospital was nice enough and they said they were looking for an extra intern to work their adolescent unit. I guess teens could be interesting. I just hope they don't expect me to wear these shoes. My feet have only known sneakers."

Fiona snorted. "Try being me. I'll be expected to wear business suits every day. Maybe on casual Fridays I can wear one-inch heels." She tossed her book, *Marketing Strategies for Non-Profit Organizations*, and it landed on the small table in front of them with a heavy thud.

"You can always change your degree plan back to therapy track, you know," Julia said.

Fiona arched a manicured eyebrow. "You be the voyeur. I actually enjoy budget analysis. Who knew, right?" She sipped her coffee.

Julia shook her head and smiled. They had clicked as friends when they met two semesters ago in their first class, maybe because they were as opposite as yellow from blue. Fiona squirmed during lectures when the professor provided techniques designed to open up emotional channels for clients—most of these techniques involved asking probing questions. However, the true torture for Fiona came the day members of the class had paired up to conduct mock therapy sessions, with one student being the "therapist" and the other, the "client."

Julia had glanced a few times at Fiona as her face grew more pinched while she struggled through the exercise with a fidgety male classmate. By the hour's end, Fiona's cool surface had cracked, with the color high in her cheeks and her skirt rumpled from where she had wiped her sweating hands. The class had barely wrapped up before she beelined it to the graduate department office and switched tracks from counseling to public administration.

When Julia had asked her why, Fiona answered with her chin tilted up a few degrees. "I'd rather make sure a clinic has enough grant money to keep the electricity turned on so people like you can save the world."

Julia had thrown her hands up in mock surrender, because she knew her friend was right. However, Julia had loved the exercise. She'd been paired with a mousey girl, who at first barely made eye contact, but by the end of their session was chatting away and expressed disappointment when their time was up. Julia had found it fascinating to study the myriad ways people maneuvered the thorny twists of being human.

"Any leads on an internship yet?" Fiona said.

Stretching out her legs, which felt weird in stockings, Julia crossed them at the ankles and said, "One more interview left. That place on the south side of town, you know, Elston Mental Health Clinic."

"Seriously?" Fiona cocked her head and frowned.

"Serious as a heart attack."

Fiona whistled a long, low note. "Didn't that place almost get gas-bombed by one of their clients a few months ago?"

"How can a place almost get gas bombed? Either it did or it didn't." Julia bristled, surprised at the heat in her voice.

With a slight eye-roll, Fiona said, "I stand corrected. But still, a client! One of their own, who, let's not forget, cruised up to the clinic on a skateboard while packing a gas can ... at least that's what I read in the paper. Bad luck for him, and good luck for the clinic, when he went inside and asked for a book of matches." Fiona shook her head and took another small sip of her coffee. "I wonder what tipped off them at the front desk? The smell of gas fumes?"

Julia laughed, despite herself. But she didn't meet her friend's eyes as she picked a fleck of lint from her jacket. "The only thing that got blown up was the story in the press. Even Nick said it was a bunch of nothing."

Fiona raised an eyebrow. "Speaking of Clark Kent, what does he think about you applying at Elston MHC?"

"Not much." She found another tiny piece of lint to pick on her skirt.

The silence between them stretched.

"Okay, okay ... because he doesn't know yet." Julia sat back in her chair as if pinned and met her friend's troubled gaze.

"Now, I agree that keeping Nick in the dark might be a good plan in case you're not offered a position. No need to poke the bear just as an exercise. But what if they take you on? Elston is the last stop for this population before they skid all the way off the grid. Expect an opinion from Nick when you tell him his fiancée will be working at the Clinic of Perpetual Prozac. And don't hold your breath for an 'atta girl'."

Julia's sat up straighter. "Look, you're being a snob. They're people like you and me, just with lower incomes. And we're not exactly rolling in dough ourselves, so let's have a little compassion here."

Fiona's expression softened. "Sweetie, you are so right. As we speak, Mother Teresa is smiling down on you and aiming one of her sandals at me. But this isn't about you doing good deeds among the poor. This is about you working with people who could be seriously mentally ill. Do you feel the couple of classes we've had are going to cut it if things get rough there? 'How do you feel about that?' may not be your best tactic against Mr. Gas Can."

During Julia's interview that morning at the psych hospital's adolescent unit, the floors had shone under their layers of wax, and the staff, dressed in crisp scrubs, had nodded at her stiffly as they breezed past in the halls with clipboards cradled in their arms. The group session she'd observed was a circle of either deflated or defensive teenagers, book-ended by two therapists reading out loud from a handout on cognitive thinking errors. Was Muzak piped in, too? Even Julia had to keep pinching her forearms to stay alert. That psych hospital would certainly earn the stamp of approval from Fiona and Nick.

Sighing, Julia reached over and touched her friend's knee. "Hey, I know you're right. I have a feeling I'm going to get a call back this week from the hospital telling me I got the job." She added in a lighter tone, "Besides, tomorrow at the Elston Clinic is just good interview practice, right?"

"Right." Fiona fixed one of her sharp, appraising, bird-like glances on Julia that always made her squirm.

Julia switched her gaze to the window and watched the wind sway the tops of the cottonwood trees. In even as something as simple as finding a summer internship, was she going to have to get the stamp of approval from Nick? She didn't want to start over only to fall back into pleasing others. She drained her coffee cup and tasted a bitterness lurking under the sweet as the lukewarm liquid slid down her throat

Chapter 10

Just get out of the car, Julia scolded herself for the second time. Or was it the third?

But in their ten and two positions, her hands still gripped the steering wheel, slicked with sweat, her knuckles popcorn-white. Beyond the windshield, dusted with grit and smashed bugs, squatted a brick, single-story building built circa late sixties as a store, which had now descended into its current reincarnation as a mental health clinic.

To the right of the door hung a chipped wooden sign with the name Elston Mental Health Clinic. The windows were shuttered against the morning light by venetian blinds, bent from people spreading open the thin metal slats with thumb and forefinger to peer out from the dark interior.

Julia squinted. Something was written inside the letter o in Elston. By reflex, her hand went to her Nikon with the 200mm lens, which she still kept beside her on the passenger seat. As she peered through the viewfinder and turned the barrel on the lens, the letter popped into focus. Someone had scrawled a sad face within the faded circle.

"Lovely," she muttered then frowned. Why hadn't anyone bothered to wash away the graffiti? Was it apathy or tacit agreement?

Sweat trailed down her left temple and her bangs flattened against her forehead. Not wanting her armpits to be next on the sweat parade, she pushed open the door into the June heat. At nine forty-five in the morning, the air around her had already reached ninety degrees. An extra résumé jutted from the corner of her purse, which she pushed back down as she picked her way toward the clinic, not trusting her balance on high heels. A growing blister complained from her left pinkie toe, but Julia kept her gait steady and refused to baby her foot. While this interview would probably end up going nowhere, she wasn't about to walk in limping and wincing.

She pulled open the glass door and the metal frame gave a high-pitched squeak. Needs oil, thought Julia, as she exited the glare and entered a gloomy hallway. After a few blinks her eyes adjusted and a pumpkin-orange couch swam into view, its surface scattered with torn *People* and *Popular Mechanics* magazines. Fraying duct tape held one corner of a cushion together.

"May I help you?" a disembodied voice said.

Julia jumped and looked up as a young, petite Hispanic woman behind a counter slid the glass partition open with an arm ringed in an impossible number of bracelets. Her short-bobbed hair framed a heart-shaped face, which she tilted at Julia and gave a large smile.

"Hi, I'm Julia Longley and I have a ten o'clock interview with Mr. Bridgeman."

"Oh, sure, he's in. Just follow me." As the receptionist led her down the hall, Julia caught a light waft of her jasmine perfume. The woman cocked her head back. "I'm Mona, by the way. You here for a clinician internship?"

"Yes, I am."

"Well, good luck. We haven't had an intern for a while. Not that we don't get students who come in to interview, we get quite a few of those."

"If they interview, how come they're not hired?" They stopped before a semi-closed door at the end of the hallway. Mona ignored Julia's question, but said in a low, conspiratorial voice, "Listen, you want to make a good impression?

Say you like fishing."

"Wait, what—?"

Mona opened the door with a flourish. "Hey, Walter, your ten o'clock is here. She finally decided to get out of the car." Heat rose up into Julia's face. Great, now they think I'm a weirdo. Those bent venetian blinds flashed into her mind, perfect for spying, as she walked into the clinical director's office.

Hunched over some sort of a contraption at his desk, Walter Bridgeman was a tall, lean man with short-cropped blond hair and a sprinkling of gray at his temples. Faint purple hues under his deep-set green eyes gave him an older, more worn look, even though he appeared to be in his mid-thirties, younger than Julia had expected. More handsome, too. He stood up and extended his hand, for the moment abandoning his view through the circular lens of a large desktop magnifier. Under it, a small vise clamped a tiny starburst of canary-yellow and periwinkle feathers.

Walter shook Julia's hand, his warm fingers encircling her tiny hand in his strong grip. She hoped he didn't notice how cold her fingers were.

"Good to make your acquaintance, Ms. Longley. Please, have a seat." He gestured toward a chair, the seat hidden by a stack of manila charts.

Julia hesitated. Was she supposed to move the charts, or should she sit somewhere else?

Walter glanced around his office, which was utilitarian, with no artwork or creature comforts, as though seeing it for the first time. "Oh, shoot," he said, his tone apologetic. "Let's make you some room here."

He grabbed an armful of charts, which revealed a battered Naugahyde chair, and searched for an open space to dump them. Not finding one, he shrugged his muscular shoulders and let them drop to the floor behind his chair. A puff of dust rose and fell.

Walter turned to Mona, who leaned against the door frame with an amused grin as though she were seeing this scene from Julia's eyes and said, "How long did she stay in the car?"

Mona's Cheshire-cat smile widened. "I timed her at fifteen minutes."

"That's better than the last one," Walter said. "Twenty minutes, as I recall." He gave Julia a wink.

What was the etiquette here, exactly? Was she supposed to wink back and congratulate herself that her trepidation was five minutes shorter than the last poor soul's?

"Yeah, except that woman drove off. Never even got out of the car," Mona said as she closed the door with a jingle of jewelry.

Walter chuckled, sat down in his chair, and swiveled toward Julia. "So there you are. You already have a leg up on the competition, as you didn't leave tread marks in the parking lot. Now you're applying for a clinician's internship, right? Where did I put your résumé?" He rifled through a pile of paper to the right of his magnifying glass stand.

Julia laced her fingers together and laid them in her lap. Should she reach into her purse and hand him her résumé? Would that give the impression she had expected the director not to have his act together?

"Here it is!" He pulled out a crinkled sheet of paper from a pile that bore little resemblance to the crisp résumé she had mailed two weeks ago. Walter smoothed the accordion folds out of the linen paper then squinted at the page. "It looks like you're starting a second career after working as a photojournalist. Why the switch?"

The memory of the smeared blood on the sneaker floated up to Julia and she pushed it back. Sweat popped up on her forehead. "I loved photography, but I was ready for a change. You know, to do deeper work by connecting and helping others." Her lips stretched into her pluckiest smile. She was grateful she had anticipated this question and had memorized a handy answer.

"Huh," Walter said, as he paused to give Julia a penetrating stare before reading on. "So this would be your first internship before you graduate next year."

"Yes, sir, although I've been volunteering at the graduate school counseling office this past semester," Julia, said in a casual tone.

Please don't ask me how many people actually showed up at the student office, she prayed.

The student office was an infamous low-traffic corner of the campus. The four Saturdays she worked last month had fetched her a total of three students: two homesick freshmen and one hung-over guy seeking to score some Xanax.

"So I see." He dropped the résumé back into the pile behind him. Rubbing his eyes with the heels of his palms, he gave a sigh. "Look, in case you haven't noticed, this place isn't exactly a four-star rehab spa. We are understaffed, way underfunded, and a magnet for all the local crazies. If you see someone walking around town wearing a tin foil hat, they're probably one of ours."

Walter held up his hand, as though Julia were about to protest. He needn't have worried as she only gaped—her capacity for words had flown like panicked birds.

"I know, I know. As clinicians we're not supposed to use the word crazy. We say someone is 'psychotic' or they have a 'personality disorder.' But," he continued, pointing his finger up to the stained ceiling tiles, "sometimes that word fits, especially for our frequent fliers."

"Frequent fliers?"

Walter warmed to the topic. "If you had experience working in a prison, that would give you a better feel for our clients here at Elston."

"Are you saying your clients are criminal?" Julia asked, her pulse quickening in her throat. Before she could stop herself, she took a quick peek behind her shoulder, where the only thing that lurked were several fishing rods propped up in a corner.

"Oh no. Nothing like that," Walter said in a reassuring tone. "Well ..." His gaze turned to a middle distance, as though scanning through a catalog of names. He shook his head. "Most aren't criminal per se, as in dangerous. Their behaviors fall more on the mischief scale, if you get my point. Usually they find themselves to be the victims of crimes."

Julia shifted in her chair, crossing her legs, and then her ankles. Did he tell her these things to scare her off or simply trot out the clinic's facts? Fiona's stern face flashed before Julia, her fierce, swallow-wing eyebrows scrunching up as her friend hissed, "Run!"

Julia swallowed hard. Hear him out, she told herself, politely shake his hand, thank him for his time, and then go.

She had received a phone message from the hospital administrator's assistant yesterday evening that they were offering her the adolescent unit's internship. All Julia had to do when she got to her car was call the woman back to accept the job, and then have an entertaining Elston Clinic story to tell Fiona when she saw her next. Her exit plan helped to slow the pulse in her throat.

"Trouble often finds our clients because they don't have the best coping tools." He reached across his desk and picked up a manila folder three inches thick and soft from the wear of many hands. "Here is a good example of our everyday client," he said, pulling on some reading glasses that had been buried underneath fanned spreadsheets.

Walter opened the chart and scanned pages covered in dense, hand-written notes and said, "This is a twenty-seven-year-old woman who has been our patient for eight years. She's improved this year, now that she's decided antipsychotic medicine really does keep the voices in her head to a low murmur."

"Eight years? Just to get someone medically compliant? Does she work with a therapist?"

"For talk therapy? Yeah, she's on therapist number five. I worked with her for two years. Her current therapist is Paul Krebs, but we call him Paulie. He's more of a marriage counselor, but since we're short-handed, this lady is now on his caseload." He tossed the file on his desk where it landed with a dull whump. "And eight years is nothing. Many of our clients have been with us for fifteen or more."

Walter pulled the next file off the stack. It had "Volume Three" scrawled on a corner. "This gentleman has chronic depression and an avoidance disorder not helped by the fact he lives out by the lake in a trailer that's barely standing on its blocks. He says he won't move out until he finds the right girl, which will be quite the trick since he's forty-two years old and odds-on gay."

"Wow," Julia said in a small voice.

The file in Walter's tanned hands was also dense with session notes about the lake client.

"Look," Walter said as he settled back into his chair. "What we strive for on our clients' behalf is improvement, and on the best of days we're lucky to get them stabilized. We don't want them hearing voices coming from electrical outlets or having cops call us because one of our people has been stealing their mail. It's never a fun day when a client is brought to the clinic in the backseat of a cruiser accompanied by a mental health deputy."

He sat up straighter and spread out his hands with the palms up. "Success for our people is when they get a minimum-wage job. Major celebration is when they keep that job for six months. To work here, your view has to be long in order to see improvement through the years."

He tapped the folder in front of him with his index finger. "Years," he repeated. "You might want to think about who we are, especially since you're so new to this field."

Silence fell between them as Julia cleared her throat and searched for something to say. While he hadn't come out and said she was too inexperienced for the job, his unvarnished truth made his point clear. Still her gaze traveled to the charts, thick with people's stories of how they were trying to make sense of their lives. Didn't she know that feeling?

Behind Walter a flash of blue and gold winked. To break the mood, and maybe find a quick exit, she said, "All of that gear on your desk, is that part of someone's treatment plan?"

Walter plucked a tiny hook from the vice's grip and twirled it between his thumb and forefinger until the blue and gold feathers blurred into an optical illusion of emerald. "No," he said with a laugh. "Not for them. This is for me. I have a thing about making fishing flies. Given the chance, I spend as much time as I can casting my line out on the rivers to see what's biting."

After tossing the lure back onto his desk, Walter passed his hand over his eyes. "I'm honest because anything else takes too much time. We're swamped. You seem nice, but nice doesn't cut it here. It's been my experience that the nice ones come in with their hopes high, but leave after a few weeks with their tails tucked, apologizing all the way."

"Who does make it here?"

"Realists. People who have worked in a small-town community mental health clinic before and can tolerate the red tape. And stubborn people who are driven and don't give up. And I'm not saying you aren't all those things, but we might be too tough a steak for someone just cutting her teeth."

He stood up, signaling that the interview was done. Julia scrambled to collect her purse, feeling both relieved and dismissed, as she followed the director down the hallway. At the lobby, Walter extended his hand. "Wish I could give more encouraging news. But from our side, there's nothing we hate more than the sound of a box of newly printed employee business cards hitting the trash can."

She took his hand, and this time noticed the calluses on his fingertips. A working person's hand. She might have been hurt to be brushed off so quickly, but the kindness in Walter's eyes made such a petty emotion shrivel.

Still, an oily and heavy doubt twisted in her gut. What if she stayed? Could she handle it? Could she be strong enough? Stubborn enough?

From down the hall came a muffled woman's yelp, which caused Julia to pause and glance in that direction. She let go of Walter's hand. "Thank you for your time, Mr. Bridgeman."

A veil fell across Walter's face. Had disappointment flickered in his eyes? He stepped back and said, "Sure, and after a couple of years in the field if you wish to apply again—"

From an interior office came the crash of shattering glass that made them both jump.

A woman's high-pitched scream was followed by a

man's deeper bellow. "You bitch! You crazy bitch!"

Another man's voice, high and reedy, spoke in a rapid, placating tone.

"Oh, Jesus," Walter said as he spun from Julia and raced toward the escalating voices. Mona rushed out from her receptionist's area and almost collided with Walter in the lobby. They looked at each other and said in unison, "The Petersons!"

Chapter 11

Silence slid around them as Mona stood perfectly still and Walter tiptoed down the hallway with his head cocked toward the closed door on the left. With a bang, the door flew open. Mona flattened herself against the lobby wall while Julia gave a small cry.

A fireplug of a woman, dressed in a baggy camo T-shirt, her thin legs sticking out from frayed denim shorts, backed out into the hallway. Pointing a trembling finger, she shouted into the room she'd come from, "Take her! You can have her! She's only a cousin. I have tons more of those, or do you want to group email all of them your smutty love letters?" Not bothering for a reply, she turned and bolted through the front door into the sunbaked parking lot, which bathed the dark lobby in a flash of paparazzi light.

A deeply tanned man strode out. "Don't walk away from me, Nadine Peterson!" he shouted. His faded red tank top stretched across his belly while his denim shorts were a tad bit less frayed.

The couple might have been around forty, but due to their coffee-bean-colored skin, bronzed from years of sun exposure, Julia guessed they could have been younger. Walter's words, "lake people," popped into her mind.

"We have fifteen more minutes left in our session!" the tank-top man called out as he pointed back to the office.

Julia, Walter, and Mona watched from the lobby as Nadine skidded to a stop, pivoted around with her middle finger extended, and yelled, "Here's something you can talk about in your fifteen minutes! Go back in there and jaw with

Paulie about how you're walking your sorry ass home! You two can process your feelings." She waggled her fingers into air quotes. "About how sad you're going to be to find your crap throwed out in the front yard. How's about I call up my snake of a cousin to come fetch your belongings? Shouldn't take long, considering she's only three trailers away. But I guess you know all about that, now, don't you?" She trotted to a bird-poop-splattered red Ford truck that listed to the left, and yanked open a mismatched, aqua-green door.

Snapping to the fact that therapy hour was indeed over, the man shouted, "Oh no you don't!" He barreled after her with his flip flops slapping the pavement.

Thin and curved as a question mark, a second man popped out from the office and glanced at Walter, Mona, and Julia through smudged glasses set askew. A painfully short haircut might have given him a military look, but nothing else about him fit that bill. Sweat streamed down the sides of his flushed face as he followed the couple, his notepad still clenched in his right hand. He called after them, "Justin! Nadine! Stop! You're both flooded right now! Come back inside and let's find a way to close the *exits!*" His voice cracked a few notes higher on the word exits.

Walter and Mona followed Paulie out to the parking lot. Julia, flummoxed as to what do to next, found herself trailing behind them as Justin reached the side of the truck.

Justin yanked at the locked car door as Nadine revved the engine into an angry growl and Paulie danced from side-to-side, pleading with them to "deescalate." Justin, in mid-yank, turned and snapped, "Shut it, Paulie. This here is all your fault! See what all your honesty bullshit got us! If you love your woman, you protect your woman. Jesus, you don't get all honest on them."

Having rolled down the car window an inch, Nadine

yelled through the crack, "Don't you blame him. The blame rests with you and Mr. Happy there in your trousers. Back yourself up from my truck, lessen you want your toes flattened."

Walter turned to Mona. "Get Angel and Glen on the phone. Tell them we need containment. Now!"

Mona shot back into the clinic, her bracelets clinking like castanets. In a few long-legged strides, Walter joined Paulie and spoke in a low tone to the counselor, who was staring at the couple as though in a trance.

Julia shuddered and woke from her own trance-like state. *What am I doing?* Her Honda sat at the far end of the parking lot and her fingers inched toward the keys in her purse. If she slinked away now, would it be considered from Walter and Mona's point of view as discretion or cowardice?

Nadine gunned the engine and began backing the truck up with Justin hanging onto the door handle. Through the space in the window, the couple continued to spar.

Julia grabbed her car keys. *Screw it*—she was so out of here.

Walter and Paulie leaped to either side of Justin and attempted to pull him from the truck door. The three men crab-walked beside the truck as Justin pleaded, "Please, baby, you don't want to do this! You know those emails don't mean nothing."

Nadine ignored him and came within inches of running over his foot.

Justin jumped back and almost lost a flip flop, then slammed his fist on the truck roof, and yelled, "Dammit, Nadine, don't leave me here! I need to get to work!"

She gave him a serene smile before putting the car into drive.

"Nadine, stop!" Walter called. "We don't have the staff

today to bring Justin out to your house."

Stabbing his finger to a spot on his notepad where something was written, Paulie added, "Justin opening up about the affair is a step toward moral integrity. This is how you build back trust!"

Nadine's Mona Lisa smile melted into a dark scowl. She hit the accelerator and Paulie and Walter jumped out of the way. Justin's round belly jiggled as he lunged for the truck bed and grabbed something in the back. He stepped back, a long, black rope unspooling from his right hand.

Julia's hand flew to her mouth and a gasp escaped as she tried to make sense of what she was seeing. Was that a jump rope?

Justin cocked his arm back and ran after the truck. Realization hit and Julia yelled, "Watch out! He's got a bullwhip!"

The whip arched high into the air above him in a slow-motion, upside-down u-shape, before Justin thrust his arm down. A loud crack rang through the air as the whip thwacked across the cab's roof, its tasseled end dangling in the middle of the windshield before what Julia could only imagine was Nadine's shocked face. The truck's brake lights lit up as it came to a jarring stop.

Crack! Justin rounded to the driver's side and landed his whip again across the top of the cab.

Nadine yelled, "Now you've done it, asshole! When I get home, I'm torching your crap! When you see smoke, you'll know it's adios to your new Wranglers!"

Justin edged toward the front of the cab, the whip handle raised high, poised to slice down. The rest of the whip hung behind him and trailed like a dark lion's tail. "Get out of the truck and talk to me! You're not running away again. I want to work this out and I'm tired of chasing after you!"

"With a bullwhip? You moron!" She slowly cranked down her window a few more inches, revealing her face splotched with red. She yelled to Walter and Paulie as they approached, "Do you see the crap I put up with?"

Paulie's tone took on an air of gentle entreaty. "Come on, you two. This isn't going to solve anything. Justin, drop the whip before the sheriff deputy comes. No real harm done yet, right guys?"

Next to Julia came a voice, "Too late for that." She jumped and found Mona next to her, shading her eyes and looking across the street at the growing crowd. A sheriff's patrol car was pulling up the curb with its siren off but lights flashing. The crowd took its time stepping back a few paces, but their eyes stayed trained on the drama surrounding Nadine's truck.

Mona sighed. "Cue the cops."

Julia's sliver of an escape window had snapped shut, and she groaned. *Oh, Lord. What if I have to stick around and give a witness report to the deputy?*

Nadine, either unaware or uncaring of the uptick in drama, reached down for something on the floorboard.

"Drop it, Justin!" hollered a baritone voice from the far side of the parking lot. A beefy man, who may have played football in high school a decade ago but was now soft in the middle, strode towards the truck. Bright red splotches stood out on his cheeks, which matched the crimson in his plaid shirt. By his side trotted a shorter, wiry man, dressed in black whose forearms were covered in sleeves of blue, red, and green tattoos.

"Are those guys with the clinic?" Julia whispered to Mona.

Mona nodded. "Yeah, that's Glen and Angel, our caseworkers. God help us if they have to do a take-down with the Petersons in front of all these looky-loos. We'll be writing up incident reports till closing time because of this." Mona folded her arms across her chest as her jaw jutted forward. "Paulie has got to learn to control his clients better than this."

"A takedown? Here?" Julia said.

The smaller caseworker yelled to the deputy, "We've got this—just give us a second."

The officer appeared relieved as the crowd shuffled behind him. In the knot of people, Julia caught a glimpse of the long tube of a telephoto lens.

"You ain't got shit, Glen," Justin shot back, "because there's nothing going on that Nadine and I can't settle on our own!" Even though Justin struck an aggressive, wide stance, he had lowered the bullwhip so it lay coiled and docile at his feet with the handle dangling from his fingers.

"Drop the whip completely or we're dropping you alongside it," said the caseworker Julia now knew to be Glen. His arms were cocked by his side, displaying powerful biceps.

"Call off your dogs, Paulie!" Justin yelled, fixing his gaze on the counselor who cradled his notepad in front of his chest like a shield.

Paulie stood behind Walter and peeked around his shoulder. "Now you know they're called case managers, not—"

Justin screamed. Nadine, who must have found what she had been rooting for, depressed what appeared to be a nozzle of bug spray from the car window and doused Justin from head to chest. Bellowing, he dropped the whip and thudded to his knees, wiping his eyes furiously. "Help! I've been gassed!"

Nadine scrambled out of the truck, snatched the whip triumphantly, and crowed, "I got him! He's disarmed! Arrest him!"

In tandem, Glen and Angel jumped forward, grabbed

Nadine, and pulled her arms behind her back. She kicked and screamed, lost her balance, and toppled sideways. Glen took her into a bear hug and twisted his body, making it so that he absorbed the jolt of their fall after she landed with an *oomph!* on top of him.

Angel stepped into the middle of their tangled arms and legs, grabbed Nadine's thumbs, and crisscrossed her wrists. He called to the deputy, "A little help here, okay?"

The deputy broke from the crowd and hurried over while pulling a pair of handcuffs from his belt.

"Don't cuff me! I was protecting myself! It was self-defense!" Nadine yelled. "Put the cuffs on Zorro with the whip over there! He's the one who needs arresting."

The deputy snapped the chrome handcuffs around her wrists and hauled her up.

"This man needs medical treatment first, ma'am, then we'll sort out who is facing what charges," the officer said, before speaking into the Walkie Clip strapped to his shoulder and requesting an ambulance.

Tears streamed down Justin's flushed face as he squinted up from where he sat on the ground. "I'm not just some man, I'm her husband!"

"You've got no one to blame for that but yourself, buddy," the officer said with a shrug.

Unburdened from Nadine, Glen stood up and brushed gravel and dirt out of his hair. He turned to Angel. "Okay, you ready? One, two, three." They took Justin by his elbows and hoisted him up from his kneeling position before relinquishing the gasping man to the officer. In unison, the caseworkers escorted Nadine to the squad car.

A few people from the crowd of about two dozen jeered but stopped when the deputy gave them a warning look. Nadine's head snapped up and she stared at the people across the street.

The scene had expanded with the arrival of the news crew from Channel 7. Their van sported a small satellite dish on the roof, and their logo was splashed on the side with the words, "All Information, All the Time." A leggy woman, who seemed to be poured into a tight chartreuse Chanel knock-off suit, gripped her microphone and tugged at her cameraman's sleeve as if to move him faster to the front of the crowd. The cascade of blonde hair that fell past her shoulders was blinding in the mid-morning light.

Julia's lip curled and her eyes narrowed. Calliope Smythe. Julia had worked at news events around Calliope, with her ridiculous British-sounding name and nose-bleed stiletto heels, long enough not to be fooled by the television reporter's camera-ready gloss. If Ms. Smythe wanted something, she'd run over anyone standing in her tiny, size-two path.

The cameraman, now in the approved position, zoomed his video camera onto Nadine, who swayed and stumbled between the caseworkers as they walked her to the patrol car. She glanced around like a trapped rabbit. Exposed to the media and on-lookers, her anger burned away and left an abashed nakedness in its place. Nadine's knees buckled and one of her sandals fell off. Glen and Angel strained under her dead weight to keep her from falling and moved her along.

A fierce need to protect Nadine welled inside Julia, and instinctively she sprang forward and ran to pick up the sandal. Julia reached the trio in the middle of the street and said, "Ma'am, you dropped your shoe. Let me walk with you until you get into the police car." She nodded her head toward the crowd. "Just until you're out of view."

For a flash, Julia was aware she was probably ruining Channel 7's shot, and a mean spike of gladness went through her. The small thrill was tempered by the uncertainty that filled Nadine's face at the sight of stranger in front of her.

Angel gave an exasperated sigh and said in a low voice, "Thanks for the shoe, lady, but this is clinic business. Step away."

"I just interviewed here at the clinic," Julia blurted out. She pointed to Walter who stood off the side watching them, his head set at a quizzical slant.

As they reached the squad car, the officer opened the door and deposited a weeping Nadine inside. Glen squatted next to her. "Nadine, sweetie, give me your foot."

Like an obedient child, she stuck out a foot, displaying toenails painted bubble-gum pink. With a gentle swoop, he slipped it on then stood up, wincing as he massaged his lower back. "Well, get a move on, girl, and sign up," he said to Julia. "We could sure as hell use the help."

Angel and Glen trotted back to the clinic as the squad car drove off and an ambulance lumbered in and parked next to the red-faced Justin. Something caught Julia's eye and she scanned the crowd only to stare straight into the smug contempt of Calliope, who swiveled her pretty head to say something to a person behind her.

Julia lifted her gaze and jumped at the sight of Nick. His hands were on his hips, and his gaze bore into hers. His lips were pressed into a tight, thin line.

Chapter 12

In a measured motion, Nick placed his beer down on the scarred table at their favorite booth at The Cedar Door, his eyes still not meeting Julia's. He traced his finger over the layers of initials and dates carved into the grain of the weathered oak planks.

Julia inched forward to reduce the distance between them. The bar maintained a swirl of blue haze, even though smoking had been banned for years. Someone had punched Johnny Mathis's "Chances Are" into the Wurlitzer jukebox and the rich notes spiraled around them, making their distance that more painful.

After another moment, Nick raised his gaze to hers and, as if they'd been in mid-conversation, said, "You know, I'm really trying to be supportive here, Jules. I can't tell you I've been on board with this whole change of career thing, but I'm trying, all right?"

Julia reached across and wrapped her fingers around his wrist, bumping and sloshing her glass of Chardonnay. "You have, Nick. I'll admit I didn't think you'd be all about it at first, but this last semester you've been very helpful." While he had groused when she first told him she'd decided to go back to school, saying she was giving up on newspapers too soon, he fell into a sullen sulk after she signed up for classes and filled out student loans applications. A few weeks before classes started, however, he surprised her by paying for the books and first semester tuition. When she threw her arms around him after he handed her the check, he said in a gruff tone, "It's just a little seed money to get you going on your project."

Still, a half-smile had played on the corner of his lips when she had kissed and held him tight.

Now his grim face told her what she had suspected all along—he wanted her to return to the newsroom. He also wanted her back with him at home rather than gone to classes or the library, and their lives back to how they used to be. Maybe it was the late midnight hour, but fatigue flowed through her. Tomorrow's edition contained the story about the clinic brawl that Nick himself had written. Julia swallowed, afraid to ask, but more afraid not to know.

"How big is the story going to run?" she said. Might as well acknowledge the elephant sitting between them.

"I was able to get city desk to bury it on page seven of metro with only two paragraphs and no art."

Slumping back into the booth, Julia sighed. "Good. It could have been a lot worse. Thank you."

Graham shot the brawl, so Nick must have killed the photograph, too. Her cheeks prickled with heat, knowing she was on the other end of a news event that had been downplayed by her fiancé.

"I suppose that's one way of looking at it. But when we heard the chatter come across the scanner letting us know there was an altercation with a weapon at the Elston nut farm and I knew you were there ..." He took a long draw from his beer mug. "Let's just say it was adrenalin-pumping."

"I'm sorry. I can imagine it looked a lot worse than it actually was."

Nick stared at Julia as if too stunned to speak. "It looked worse than it was? My imagination couldn't have conjured what I saw when I drove up! There you were, front row and center, with a guy brandishing a bullwhip while some crazy lady is hosing him down with bug spray. A domestic! Every cop I know hates domestics because they're powder kegs."

He wagged his finger and barked a laugh. "Luckily, Channel 7 couldn't use the video with the woman getting arrested since you blocked their shot. And don't think everyone there didn't realize what you were doing."

Calliope Smythe's smug expression lurking behind her microphone popped into Julia's mind. She ground her teeth. "What do you care about Channel 7?" Anger rose in Julia's voice. "And how did you know I ruined their shot?"

Waving his hand to dismiss her, he shot back, "That's beside the point. You were in a tussle between two hillbilly drunks."

"Justin wasn't drunk. He was upset because Nadine found out he was having an affair with her cousin at the trailer park—"

Nick shook his head and spat out, "Who. Cares!"

Julia stared at him, breathless.

"Who cares who he is, what psycho sad sack he's married to, or why he brings a bullwhip to a knife fight? I don't care and neither should you! You were where you didn't belong. You didn't have the authority to jump into their little drama, nor the training." He sat back, cheeks flushed, his eyes blue glittery diamonds.

Julia gasped. "But that was why I was interviewing, to get the experience!"

A couple at a table next to them glanced their way, and she lowered her voice. "I've got to start working somewhere and this is only for a summer internship."

"I understand. I also know a neon sign when I see one. And that message is for you to work the rehab hospital gig, with puny teenagers and burly guards."

"That job is still up in the air," she said then pressed her lips together. While technically true, the ball had been in her court to send the administrator her references and it somehow kept slipping her mind. She shifted more than once, took a deep breath, and unloaded the bomb she had carried for the past twelve hours. "Elston Clinic offered me the job before I left, and ... I took it." She rushed the last bit and cringed.

Nick laughed. When she only stared back at him, the silence between them stretched out, long and twisting. Julia almost wished he'd yell a little bit, just to break the tension. Finally he grimaced, and then took a deep, slow drink of his beer.

"Yeah?" he said in a flat voice devoid of curiosity, as he thudded down his empty beer mug.

Julia's words tumbled over each other. "When the clinical director saw I was able to help deescalate the situation, he asked me to submit my application and references ..." All of the other rehearsed parts of her speech flew away like dandelion seeds. She shrugged. "So I did."

After the squad car had rumbled away with Nadine sequestered in the back, Julia had watched Glen walk up to Walter and speak to him. Both men glanced at her before Walter shook his head twice. Glen leaned in closer to the director and gestured toward the clinic before shrugging his former linebacker shoulders and walking away.

Walter had heaved a sigh, glanced at the retreating caseworker, then walked up to her. "Well, it looks like there might be an opening here after all. If your references check out." She had glanced at the shabby, sunbaked clinic and imagined the handful of characters she had just met, rambling around inside it, and she felt a tug. The word "yes" had leapt out of Julia's mouth before the warning bells in her mind could stop her.

Nick rubbed his temples while Julia held her breath, willing herself to stay silent. Finally he looked up. "For the record, this is a terrible idea. And I want this to be only a summer gig, all right? Once you have your hours, then you move onto something different. Something not involving yahoos brawling in the streets."

Julia's breath came out in a whoosh of relief. How long had she been holding it? "Of course," she said, reaching for his hand, feeling the warmth of his fingers wrapping around hers. "Only the summer. It'll fly by like that."

"You get them to assign you only the easy nut jobs, Jules. I mean it. Eventually, when you get your degree and license, then you can open up your own office. Have your own private practice."

She angled her head up at him, a flicker of hope candled. This was the first time Nick seemed on board with her new direction. Smiling, she said, "Someday I'm going to have my own office, my own practice. I love that idea. It will get better—you'll see."

He studied her face in a calculating way. "That might work out. After you graduate next year and we get married, you can open up your own shop wherever I find another job. You being mobile and flexible could come in handy. After all, I can't stay at this rinky-dink paper forever, now can I?" He gave her hand a firm squeeze, then drew it to him to kiss the top of her knuckles.

Silent alarms went off in her gut and she shivered when his lips brushed her flesh. *He loves me*, Julia reminded herself, not for the first time. She frowned at the thought of how often she had been telling herself this lately.

Chapter 13

Julia wiped a wad of paper towels soaked with bleach cleaner across the surface of her desk, and then inspected the wet folds. The towels came back grayish with grime, which was better. At least they weren't charcoal black like her first two passes. She straightened, stretched her back, and fought wooziness from inhaling the strong bleach fumes trapped in the windowless office she had been assigned, a former junk room.

She was glad she'd kept her expectations low. Julia tore off more paper towels, soaked them in cleaner, and went after the desk surface a third time. A knock made her jump and she turned to find Walter filling up the door frame. He was taller than she remembered, and his nose had a fresh sunburn on the tip. Under his eyes, however, a bluish tinge belied weariness.

"Settling in?" He glanced around the room with the dull green carpet crushed flat and dust outlines from where boxes had been stacked. The long drape of a spider web swung from a buzzing fluorescent lighting fixture in the center of the ceiling.

"Shining it up a bit," Julia said, striving for a chipper tone.

Walter scanned the room. "I told the janitor to clear out some stuff we had stashed in here, but I guess that's all he did. This room hasn't been used in a couple of years. Since our last intern. If I'm remembering that student correctly, he probably didn't bother to clean it when he left. Well, drop your scouring pad and come meet the rest of the crew.

We're having our Monday morning meeting in the conference room."

Trailing behind Walter, Julia smoothed her hair and tugged down her shirt, which had hiked up on one side. The conference room, another hopeful term for a somewhat larger, windowless room next to the kitchenette, held a rectangular table crammed into its small space, around which five people were seated.

The caseworker, Glen, who sported wraparound sunglasses, glanced up at Julia and gave her a quick nod, before sinking deeper into his chair to face a spot on the wall. His eyes could have been closed, for all Julia knew, the lenses were so dark.

Next to him sat Angel and Mona with a chart spread open before them, both in a conversation so animated that they didn't notice her. Across the table and sitting by himself, Paulie doodled in a corner of his yellow legal notepad. His head snapped up like a startled rabbit when Julia entered the room. He then tucked his head down and focused on his notepad, scribbling in a tight scrawl, as his ears took on the glow of a sunrise pink.

One woman, who looked to be on the far side of fifty and had a cropped, butter-gold helmet of hair, stared straight at Julia. She served up a thin smile made vivid by her cranberry-colored lipstick, the warmth of which didn't quite reach her appraising eyes. While the chair next to her was open, Julia slid onto the one next to Glen.

Walter sat at the head of the table, glanced over at Glen, and said in a dry tone, "Nice shades, Mr. Parnell. Is the room a bit too bright for you this morning?"

Glen jerked his head and looked around, as though surprised to find himself in the middle of a meeting. Pulling off his glasses, he tucked them into the front pocket of his plaid shirt with mother-of-pearl snap buttons. "Dang.

Totally forgot I had those bad boys on. Okay, boss. Proceed with the meeting. I'm ready to be illuminated."

Angel craned his neck and peered at Glen. "Let me illuminate you, bro. Step a little closer to the Visine bottle next time. Your eyes are total road maps."

"Totally worth it, my hair-challenged friend. I killed last night." Glen chuckled.

"Wait," Walter said, as he passed around copies of a handout with "Weekly Agenda" typed on the top. "The Foxy Box is now having karaoke on Sunday nights, too?"

"You got to come off the river, man. The Box has been karaoking the house on Sunday for months. A table of ladies requested I sing "Blue Eyes Crying in the Rain." Twice! Earned me a phone number." He dragged out a crinkled napkin from his front jean's pocket with a lipstick kiss in the center and a number scrawled underneath.

Angel barked a laugh and gave Glen a high-five, while Mona rolled her eyes.

"I'll take my version of wildlife over yours, Glen," Walter said in a monotone. "Now our first topic is an obvious one. We have a new intern, Ms. Longley, who will be with us over the summer. So welcome." He nodded toward Julia, who felt the heat rise into her cheeks.

Everyone murmured their welcomes and gave Julia a smile, except for the blonde woman, who tilted her chin down a degree and sat up straighter, reminding Julia of a cobra alerted to movement. Julia struggled to keep her smile from slipping.

"You've seen our two caseworkers in action, Angel and Glen. And you met our family therapist, Paulie," Walter added.

Paulie's ears pinked even brighter, but he managed to give her a tight nod.

"Lastly, this is our senior clinician, Ms. Marlene Foster.

She'll be assigning you your clients and supervising you this summer."

"So glad you could join our team for a bit, dear. Always nice to have extra assigned help," Marlene said, drawing a hard sibilant s sound on "assigned."

Julia nodded and wished for a glass of water. Her mouth couldn't have been drier if she had packed it with cotton balls. This woman was her supervisor? Great. Clearly, Walter had tasked her upon Marlene and now Marlene saw Julia as one more thing with which to contend.

For the next hour, the staff discussed the clients' status reports, which caseworker was going out to what service call, what concern a therapist had about a particular person, and who needed coordination with outside agencies. Julia tried to keep up, but after twenty minutes, she just let the conversation flow over her, the details like rushing water. How could the staff keep all these people's lives in their heads?

Finally Walter stood and stretched, signaling the end of the meeting. "Oh, and Mr. Jenkins said he's retiring as our evening janitor, so I'm researching a new cleaning service. It'll be hard to replace him, but if you know of anyone, let me know."

With a glance at the grubby corners in the conference room, Julia didn't think it would be all that hard to replace Mr. Jenkins.

"And Julia?"

She snapped her head up.

Walter stood with Marlene next to him. "Why don't you two visit in Marlene's office and she'll go over your new client list?"

Julia followed behind the straight back of the trim woman and tried not to clomp and drown out the precise clicks of Marlene's heels as they made their way down the hall. Tucked into the back of the clinic, Marlene's office stuck out like a well-manicured thumb. One wall contained a built-in bookcase artfully arranged with books, carvings, and pottery that came across as arresting rather than cluttered.

Gesturing to an armchair upholstered in a red-and-gold tapestry, Marlene took the chair opposite, a petite Quaker-style rocker. Julia sank into the buttery softness of the cushions and sighed.

"Comfy?" Marlene crossed her legs at the ankles in a practiced manner.

"Totally. What an amazing space you've created. I can imagine your clients must love being here."

She arched an eyebrow. "Some more than others. But if you've been practicing as long as I have at the clinic, then you tend to make your office your home away from home."

From a small table next to her, Julia picked up what appeared to be a Murano hand-blown glass paperweight with concentric circles of pink and blue nestled into the center. "How many years have you been here, exactly?"

"Approximately twenty-five. But when I calculate exactly, then that would make it twenty-six years and some months." Marlene's smile cut deeper into the corners of her cheeks.

The paperweight grew heavy in Julia's hands and she gripped it so it wouldn't slip and clunk to the ground. With deliberate care, she placed it back on the table. "Twenty-six years! Then that must mean you've been here since …" Julia realized she was about to wander into a social tar pit.

Marlene finished the sentence. "Since the beginning of my career? Yes, I realize that's a long time, especially to stay in a clinic that others may view as, shall we say, a stepping stone? However, as you get involved in people's lives, they have a way of becoming intertwined into your own, and the years do spin by. And at this point, I've seen some of my client's children as clients."

Unsure whether to congratulate or sympathize with such a statement, Julia nodded as her mind scrambled to find a neutral hook. She was relieved when Marlene went to her desk and came back with a stack of a dozen folders and handed them to Julia.

"I've picked some people from my client list who might benefit from a fresh perspective. At least for the summer."

"Do I contact them?"

"Mona will alert them and put them onto your calendar. Most of them may welcome this temporary change. Of course, they know they're coming back to me at the end of August."

Marlene opened the door and Julia awkwardly stood up while grasping the charts in her arms. But the phrase "most of them" snagged Julia's attention. What about the others?

"Call out if you need any help with these people. Although my notes are thorough and you should find everything you need."

"Um, okay. I'll get on these right away," Julia said as she stepped out into the hallway.

Marlene's smile tightened beneath cool, humorless eyes as she closed the door, leaving Julia in the hallway, wondering if it was too late to call the hospital and beg for the adolescent counselor job back.

Chapter 14

Mona's voice drifted up from under Julia's desk. "Lower the monitor cable down now." Picking through a tangle of cables on the desktop, Julia extracted a thick, gray, insulated cord attached to the back of the smudged monitor and threaded it behind the scarred furniture. She held her breath and hoped she wasn't going to hit Mona on the head. "Is this the one?" Julia asked, uncomfortable with the office manager lying on the grimy carpet and scrabbling around in all the dust just to get her computer hooked up. A jingle of her bracelets was the only response. The computer whirled and the monitor blinked on, washing the top of the desk in cool light.

"You got it, Mona. Here, let me help you get up." Julia backed away from the desk.

Mona crawled out backwards then turned around. A dust bunny dangled from a lock of hair by her jaw. Julia reached over and plucked off the gray clump. "Really, I could have set up the computer myself. You didn't need to get all grubby for me. It's a dust mite farm down there."

Mona pulled up a chair and sat down in front of the computer. "No worse than most of our offices." Glancing around, she added, "Well, maybe this is a bit worse. But you'll get it shaped up in no time, I'm sure. You've got that look to you."

Julia raised her eyebrows and wondered exactly what look that was. In fact, she felt useless standing next to Mona, who was a hum of efficiency as she typed into the keyboard, her red nails clicking and purposeful. "Damn." Mona frowned into the monitor. "The keyboard's frozen." She clicked the mouse a few more times. "The mouse works, but the keyboard is definitely stuck." She gave a humph and said, "Okay, I don't have all day for this." She picked up the phone and punched in an extension number.

After a few rings, someone answered and Mona said, "Paulie, I picked your old keyboard out of the zombie pile and I'm trying to set it up for the intern. But it froze up like it used to with you. How do you unstick it?"

Anxious, rapid murmuring flowed from the phone until Mona cut him off with an impatient, "No one said you broke it. I just want you to come over here and show me the thing you did to make it work."

Faster murmuring from the receiver.

Pivoting her body away from Julia, Mona hunched down over the phone and said in a tight, low voice, "Really, Paulie? A client coming in the door any minute? If you think all I do here is take your breakfast taco orders, then let me set you straight. I also make your appointments."

There was a short murmur from the phone to which she said, "That's the spirit."

Mona hung up and made a tsk-tsk sound. "You know, sometimes the only difference between the staff and the clients is that we have the keys to this joint."

Unsure how to respond, Julia said, "You know, I'll bet if I fool around with this thing, I might get it to work."

There was a light tap at the door and Julia turned to find Paulie standing there, round-shouldered with hands in his pockets, his gaze fixed a bit to the left of her.

"Hey, Mr. Fix-It. Come on in and rescue us damsels in distress," Mona chirped as she got out of the chair and motioned for him to sit.

Ignoring her, Paulie slouched over to the desk, picked up the keyboard, flipped it over, and gave it two hard raps with his knuckles. He placed it down and typed in keystrokes. Words began to crawl across the monitor.

Mona laughed and clapped him on the back. "You did it! What's the trick?"

A ghost of a smile flickered across Paulie's face. "No big deal. Just give the J key a couple of knocks. That unfreezes whatever gets frozen."

Mona pulled up a chair and began opening up folders on the computer, leaving Julia and Paulie to stare at each other over her head. Julia stuck out her hand and said, "I don't believe we've formally met. I'm Julia, otherwise known as 'the intern'."

He shook her hand in his moist grip. "I guess when you dropped in the day you interviewed, I didn't exactly cover myself in glory."

Julia squelched a desire to give him a hug. "I don't know what I would have done with that couple if it had been me. Maybe grab a net?" She giggled.

A smile flitted across his face. "With tranquilizer darts."

Julia snorted. "So are they divorcing?"

"No, the easy way out is not the Petersons' way. They're all patched up now and will see me later this week. But with them, who knows what the next session will bring?"

Glancing up, Mona said, "Girl, don't joke too much about nets and darts. You may need your own supply, once you see the client list Marlene has sent you."

An opened document on the monitor displayed a single column of names. Julia and Paulie leaned in over Mona and squinted at the screen.

Paulie whistled a low note. "Golly."

"Damn straight, golly," Mona said. She glanced up at Paulie. "Can she do this?"

He straightened and said in a matter-of-fact tone, "Appears it's already been done."

Alarmed, Julia skimmed the list of names as if she could suss out who they considered to be such bad news. "What are you talking about? What's the problem with these people?"

Mona and Paulie exchanged silent expressions, both with the same scrunched-up eyebrows.

Paulie said, "Uh, it seems Marlene has given you a group of people whose level of functioning may not be a good match for someone with, well, your current level of training. I guess some have stabilized in the past year and—"

"Stabilized?" Mona squealed. "What do you mean? Cut the bull crap, Paulie." She turned to Julia. "Sweetie, let me be the first to explain. She's dumped her problem clients on you. Must be Marlene's version of taking a summer break."

"Now I wouldn't go that far," Paulie said with little conviction in his voice.

Stabbing her finger at the monitor, Mona's lacquered nail clicked on the plastic surface under one name. "Morris Pennington?"

"Who's that?" Julia asked, trying to keep her voice from quaking.

They replied in unison, "Gas can bomber."

Oh boy.

"But to be fair, he's doing much better, especially since Dr. Sharma increased his antipsychotics. I saw him in the lobby last week and we had a pretty intact conversation."

Rolling her eyes, Mona said, "Yay for Thorazine."

Panic bloomed into Julia's chest and she inhaled deeply. "They're generally safe, right? Otherwise, Walter wouldn't have agreed to it."

Mona shrugged and scanned the list again. "Walter

may not know yet. A lot of these people are long-timers, but maybe Marlene's thinking they need a break from her, too."

"That could be it, a fresh point of view," Paulie said in a pseudo-confident voice without looking Julia in the eye.

"Hold up," Mona said as she squinted at a name on the screen. "Rowena Horn? You think Rowena will be all charged up about a fresh point of view?"

This was maddening for Julia. It was as though she was walking into the middle of stage play. "Now who's that?"

"Rowena is well …" He raked his fingers through his hair, leaving disheveled rows.

"A P-I-T-A," Mona finished. "A pain in the ass."

"I believe the technical term is a Borderline Personality Disorder," Paulie replied mildly.

He addressed Julia. "She has a weak ego structure and her moods are highly reactive to her negative thinking. Rowena's fear of abandonment triggers her to push people's buttons, which, ironically, increases the likelihood of rejection by others."

"My word's better," Mona said as she turned to Julia. "You tell Marlene to take that one off your list. Rowena will eat your lunch."

Julia became aware of the walls closing in and a buzzing noise drilled inside her head. Her legs shook and she struggled to keep from pulling Mona out of her seat so she could sit down, as there were no other chairs. How can a simple list of names turn into such a messy tug-of-war?

She wanted to be quiet and think. No way could she ask to cull a person out of this list of strangers without raising Marlene's suspicions. And if she admitted to Marlene that Mona and Paulie had warned her away from specific clients then they would get into hot water for interfering. She imagined Marlene's imperial face. Conspiring might be her new supervisor's word for their impromptu meeting here. With a shudder, she knew that to ask for anyone's removal would be the beginning of the end for her at the clinic. And with the summer already started, no other internships were available.

"I don't have a choice," Julia said, as she perched on the edge of the desk, her only option without lowering her shaking body to the floor. "I've got to accept this list as is. If I tinker with it, she'll know I know something that only an insider would. And that insider is you two."

Silence enveloped the room. Mona bit her lower lip and Paulie gave her his unblinking owl stare. Mona then cocked her head at Paulie, and again a silent agreement passed between them.

She turned to Julia and clapped her hands together. "All righty, then! Let me pull you some client charts." She headed toward the door. "Let's just say you've got some interesting reading to do."

Paulie trailed behind Mona, but hesitated at the threshold. "You know, for all it's worth, I'm down the hall if you ever get stuck. I know how it is when you first start here. How can you work with clients if you've never worked with clients, right? But there it is. We just stumble around and somehow we figure it out."

A lump rose in Julia's throat. "I'll take you up on that, Paulie. Probably sooner than later."

He ducked his head as his face flushed, and then slipped out the door.

Julia sat in the chair and scooted closer to the monitor, running her finger down each name on the list. She said each person's name out loud as if to chase away their newness, but in the back of her mind, she could almost hear Nick's voice, paternal and smug. *Didn't I warn you about this?*

Chapter 15

They lay wrapped around each other in their bed, tight as coiled ivy. A summer breeze blew from the half-opened window and rolled off their bodies, moist with sweat. The window above them framed a purpling heaven as Julia rested her head on Nick's chest and listened to his heart slow to a normal beat.

"This is my favorite part, holding each other and letting everything just be," she said as she arched her back with contentment.

Nick slid his fingers up and down the small of her back. "Definitely the top five for me."

Julia swatted his shoulder and laughed. "Scoundrel. And for that comment, you have to do as I say and open the window all the way. I want to feel all the breeze."

"Aye aye, Captain." He stood, pulled at the lower edges of the window, and pushed the frame up. A cool gust of wind puffed the gauzy curtains back so they floated around Nick's naked torso. The distant sound of downtown traffic settled around them and the streetlights gilded his straight nose and high cheekbones with amber.

Not for the first time, Julia felt a jolt at his physical presence, as though he were a Michelangelo's sculpture come to life. *He's so beautiful.* But needling doubt followed: *So why is he with me?*

Pushing the thought aside, she said, "If we have children, I hope they look like you."

He cocked his head and gave her a slow smile. "And rob them of your Irish green eyes?" He crawled back into bed and smoothed his hand down the dip of her waist before letting it rest on the top of her hip. Julia drifted into a drowse until Nick broke through. "Speaking of kids, we need to get the horse back in front of the cart. With the wedding plans, I mean." Swimming back awake, Julia said, "What? It's on track."

"Not according to Mom. She called today and went on about how she hasn't heard from you about floral centerpieces."

Julia groaned and rolled onto her back, all the delicious feelings draining away. She and Nick had joked about eloping, but as time wore on, she'd wished they had just hopped a plane to Las Vegas and done the deed. Could the fallout from the families have been any worse?

The wedding plans had started as a family-and-friends garden ceremony in her mother's backyard. When Julia told her mother about the engagement, her mom had hesitated for a moment before offering her home as the wedding site.

While the house itself was modest, the backyard was spectacular. In the years following the divorce, her mother had thrown herself into transforming the weed-choked yard into a jeweled plat that overflowed with tea roses, hibiscus, and blue salvia under her careful planting and pruning. Clouds of butterflies floated among the beds of lavender, a living testament to her desire to create beauty after such a disappointing and draining marriage. Julia quickly agreed to the surprising offer, before her reclusive mother could think better of it and change her mind.

For a week, they pored over bridal planning magazines and possible menus before settling on a wedding cake recipe found in her grandmother's well-worn cookbook, an orange-infused concoction drizzled with a pearly shell of icing. Her grandmother had written in her tiny palmer script, *Yum!* next to the picture of the cake.

Julia's delight in how the plans were taking shape deflated after Nick's mother had caught wind of their ideas. She'd insisted on meeting with her and her mother over lunch to, in her words, "See if I can aid in the tiniest way to the kids' big day."

In Mrs. Meyer's precise and polite manner, she scanned their notes jotted down in a battered spiral pad and suggested alternative thoughts, until their homey plans were swept away like crumbs off a table.

By month's end, the garden wedding of fifty had ballooned into a Scottish Christmas wedding of two hundred for the following year at the First Presbyterian Church, to be officiated by Nick's mom's close spiritual adviser (her words), the Bishop Winston. This last bit of information Mrs. Meyer delivered over a downtown bistro lunch as Julia and her mom sat in silence across from her, stabbing their forks into spinach salads and avoiding eye contact with each other.

Julia's appeals to Nick for backup were met with only a shrug. "Well, she does know everyone, and if anyone can pull strings, it's my mom, the puppet master. Let her work her minions and take a load off us, right?"

Julia's dad wasn't much better when she called him at his office for advice. She'd long ago stopped calling him at his home, as his wife tended to swoop in on the phone calls with a nosy cheerfulness that made their conversations grind to a quick stop.

"Sweetie, I'm a trial lawyer, not a wedding planner," he'd said. "Now should you ever need a divorce, then I'll fix you right up. And let me tell you, if you think weddings are expensive, you haven't seen anything until you go through a divorce."

Thanks a lot. Julia replaced the receiver as gently as she could with shaking hands, fighting the urge to slam the phone down on the table.

Last week, Julia had almost tripped over a FedEx package propped in the doorway with three floral arrangement books crammed inside. Several dozen pages were tagged with yellow sticky notes and covered in Mrs. Meyer's bold, all-caps script: GOES WELL WITH OUR COLORS! LOVE THIS ONE! COULD BE NICE NEXT TO THE GROOM'S CAKE!

Julia had tossed the books on the couch unopened. She'd thought about it for a minute, threw a blanket over them, and went into the kitchen for a glass of wine.

Now, looking into Nick's expectant face, she realized she hadn't so much forgotten about the centerpieces, as scrubbed them from her mind.

"How about red roses and holly?" Julia said, naming the first red-and-green plants she could think of. "That could go with the whole Christmas theme."

"Seems all right, I guess. You don't sound too enthused." He raised himself up on an elbow and fixed her with a penetrating stare that made her squirm.

"Enthusiasm takes time and time's been in short supply lately, what with finals and getting ready for this internship," Julia said, smoothing out a fold on the sheet and avoiding his gaze.

Nick slid his hand from her hip. "Yeah, but that's all handled, right? Finals are done and you're set up in that place."

Not for the first time, Julia noticed Nick's reluctance to say the name of the clinic. "My last final was two days ago and I spent all of yesterday turning a grubby storage room into a space marginally fit to see clients in."

"Okay, but it is only a summer job and our marriage is for the rest of our lives. Getting this wedding launched needs to be our main goal."

"Launched, huh? Why is it I'm getting a picture of you and me strapped to a rocket with your mom pushing the go button?" Julia said as heat rushed into her face.

"Seriously? C'mon, Jules. Lead, follow, or get the hell out of the way. If you like roses and holly, then fine. I don't care if its milkweed and prickly pear, just let my mom know so I can get her off my back."

Julia gritted her teeth and willed herself to take deep breaths. "Let's make a pact. You never tell me to lead, follow, or get the hell out of the way again, and in exchange, I'll call your mom tomorrow and tell her we decided on the roses and holly theme. As in *we* decided, you and me."

The edge in her voice made her shiver, and she wasn't sure if she liked it or not. But it felt true.

He grew quiet and appraised her. "What's with all the heartburn? You don't strike me as the bridezilla type."

A membrane broke and words tumbled out. "This new job is hard, harder than I imagined. Some of my clients probably shouldn't be assigned to me at all. And the therapist, Marlene, who gave them to me? She may have done it out of spite because she didn't like being saddled with supervising me." She searched his face for support.

The frown lines deepened between Nick's brows. "You decided you wanted to work with crazy people, and now you're surprised you've got a few tough ones? Then snap your fingers and come back to the paper. Graham and the guys would be glad to have you, especially with how low-wattage their new shooter is turning out to be."

Julia sat up in bed and stared at Nick.

He shrugged. "What now?"

"I'm not asking for a solution!" she said in a loud voice.

"What are you asking for?" he shot back.

Julia's thoughts darted like rabbits dashing through a labyrinth of tunnels. She took a deep breath and softened her tone. "I want you to listen to me. I'm not asking you to fix this, but I'd like to be able to talk to you about this problem without you going straight into an action plan."

"This problem? It seems like lately it's been a conveyor belt of problems." Nick sat up in bed and faced her, the sheets pooling around his waist. "You don't like newspapers because hard news is too stressful? Bang, you quit the paper and dump our old life. Now you're halfway through graduate school and complaining about being in the same room with real crazies. And mind you, not safe textbook crazies, either. How can you now be surprised that your stress-o-meter has buried the needle into the red?"

Julia grabbed the blanket and wrapped it around her shoulders, tightening it until it had no more give. "All right, pact number two. Don't call my clients crazy. That's insulting and wrong. They may be neurotic, but if someone listened to us right now, they would say we're the ones talking crazy."

A surge of protectiveness for her clients roiled up within Julia, many of whom she'd barely begun to work with, and her reaction was as instinctive as surprising. It was as though her loyalties had thrust root systems deep into new soils without her knowledge.

"Why can't I give advice? You've got a problem and I see a clear answer. When your neurotic client shows up, just listen to their sad tale of woe, ask them how they feel about it, and then let them go on their merry way. That should hold them until they see you next time."

Julia made a strangled noise in her throat, but Nick held up his hand. "Jules, we've got to look at the bigger picture here. This job will be done in August and we're getting married in eighteen months. We're creating our own special thing here, so don't get rattled by some office drama."

His words stacked around her like bricks, and she struggled against feeling flattened. "It's not that simple," she said in a low tone.

Still, her emotions betrayed her, and her voice cracked. "You're lucky because you love what you do. But I'm still searching, and I want to be charged up about what I'm doing, too. I love you, but my world can't just be about us. Just like your world isn't all about us."

Nick opened his mouth, then paused. He slid his arm around her shoulder. "I want you to love your job, but we also know what happens if you get overstressed."

Julia winced at the reminder of her breakdown. Doubt and weariness crept in like damp fog, and she shivered. "This is all new to me, Nick. I'm scared about how to handle the clients, but I believe some staffers at the clinic will support me. And I need for you to be supportive also, okay?"

The ice in his blue eyes melted and he lowered his arm until it wrapped around her waist and he drew her close. "I guess this is a learning curve for both of us. It's only until the end of August."

Julia nodded, not so much in agreement, but because her words had dried up. Suddenly she was bone tired and only wanted to cuddle with Nick, feel his warm breath against her, and shove this conversation away.

But long after he had drifted to sleep, a worry wiggled and wormed its way through her thoughts. *Does Nick lump me into his crazy category?* And would this always be a doubt festering between them that he's the strong one and she's the weak one?

Julia closed her eyes tight against the buzzing thought, but it persisted. What if he was right?

Chapter 16

By the third morning at the clinic, Julia felt a little less jittery. So far, her clients had been polite and chatty, like Mr. Pfeiffer, who now sat in her office wearing a green plaid flat cap. Tufts of snowy hair sprouted from his ears.

"So I told her, 'Look, I don't care how many dancing cats are on some e-card. It don't make no difference to me. But the only real way to go is with an actual card with a stamp on it. That shows you spent some time, shelled out a couple of bucks, and, Lord help us, actually wrote in legible cursive a note saying 'Happy Birthday.'"

"Well, sure, I see your point, but for younger people like your granddaughter—"

"Respect! They just don't get plain manners. Although with my son being her daddy and all, what do you expect? Apple didn't roll far from that tree."

Several rapid knocks on the door made Julia jump. Mr. Pfeiffer said, "My Timex says I've got thirty more minutes." He tapped the face on his watch.

The door swooshed open and Angel leaned into the doorway, the fluorescent lights shining off his bald head. "Sorry, Mr. Pfeiffer, but I've got to end your session early today. Mona will help you to reschedule. Need to steal your therapist here for an emergency."

Julia's client heaved himself up and squinted at Julia. "This just proves my point. The whole world is in one damn hurry."

Angel's pinched face evaporated Julia's relaxed mood.

He stepped aside to let Mr. Pfeiffer pass through the door. "What gives?"

"Sorry to bust up your session like that, but we've got a problem with one of your clients."

"Really? Who?" Julia cast through her mind the handful of clients she had met with thus far. No one seemed to have been in an immediate crisis.

Angel ran his hand over his head. A cartoon band aid clung to the side of his scalp as though he had shaved in a hurry. "I don't think you've met her. A woman named Rowena Horn. She's one of the transfers that you'll be working with this summer. Mona said she came in last week to see Marlene. It ended up with those two having some kind of dust up."

"Dust up?" The name nagged at Julia, and then she remembered this was the person Mona and Paulie had warned her about.

"I'll explain in the car, but we've got to head to out now."

"Wait, why am I going? Is this common for therapists to go to their clients?"

Angel raised his eyebrows and paused, as though he had never considered the question. "Elston Clinic helps poor people. Poor people have more needs. So they call us to help them get their needs met," Angel said as they walked down the hall.

"Well, sure." Julia felt naïve in needing the obvious spelled out.

When they reached the front lobby door, he opened it for Julia. "Rowena's claiming she's being held captive by the clerk at the Gas-N-Go. And I don't have time this morning to deal with her police charges or being committed in-patient for being a threat to other people."

"But what if she is a threat to other people?" Julia's voice trembled.

"She wouldn't hurt a fly. However, the hurt Rowena puts on herself, now that's some bad mojo."

* * *

THEY DROVE IN ANGEL'S CAR, a meticulously clean compact with a sun-faded dream catcher swinging from the rearview mirror. Mid-morning light reflected off his tattooed forearms and Julia tried to puzzle out one of the tattoos inside his left arm, of a young woman's face with a name inked in looping letters. Was it Maria or Marta? He spoke and she snapped her attention back to his face.

"Rowena's ticked, but nothing new there. The wind blowing wrong gets her angry. Dollars to donuts, this has something to do about her talking with Marlene. Mona told me she left their meeting with a wild look in her eye. I was scheduled this week to go by her house for a well-check visit, but now I guess I get to conduct my session at a gas station." He swept his hand forward, as though the scene with Rowena was happening on top of the hood of the car. "This had better not throw my day off because I'm already behind on my case calls."

"So what's happened between Rowena and the clerk?"

"Mona tried to get more details out of Rowena during the phone call, but she just started shouting she needed help because the clerk was oppressing her. Then, click! Line went dead." He pulled off the highway loop onto an exit and took a sharp right. "With Rowena, it's like, 'Here we go again.'"

"Again? How do you mean?"

"Rowena and other people don't mix. She's always getting her knickers in a twist about somebody doing her wrong. Well," he said, staring ahead as he turned down a street pitted with potholes. "It looks peaceful from the outside. Thank God, no cops."

They drove past two gas pumps and parked the car in front of a convenience store that slouched toward one corner, with the right side a good foot lower than the left. Julia trailed behind Angel as he opened the glass-and-metal front door. A sign taped at eye level read: "Cold Beer and Live Bait Special." A clerk glowered behind the register, her folded arms appearing to cage in her ample chest. "You them people," she said, not bothering with a question mark.

Angel seemed unfazed by the clerk's bluntness. "Yeah, where is she?"

The clerk chin-pointed toward the magazine and newspaper aisle where the top of a dark head peaked. Angel and Julia rounded the aisle to find a squat, avocado-shaped woman leafing through a thick fashion magazine at a leisurely pace. Her eyes, however, were anything but relaxed as they snapped and sparked under her thick unibrow. Her hair was cut as though someone had plopped a bowl on top of her squarish head and snipped all around, leaving a mess of uneven strands. Her bulldog jaw, which she clinched so tightly the muscles knotted on either side, dwarfed her tiny pug nose.

Rowena brightened at the sight of Angel, but then saw Julia. Her frown bunched her unibrow more tightly together. In her pudgy arms, she clutched what looked to be a half-dozen magazines, which she mashed deeper into her bosom, as though fearful Julia would walk up and snatch them from her.

Without warning, Angel stopped and Julia almost bumped into him. Keeping his voice neutral, he said, "Hey, Rowena. Got a call you needed some help. What's going on?"

"If I step a toe outta here, that woman up there says

she'll call her manager and have me banned from the store," she said, in the deep alto voice of a chronic smoker without the rasp. She leaned forward and whispered, "Can she do that?"

"The manager has that right, especially if she suspects she's seeing, let's say ... a trend," Angel said in a careful, even manner.

Rowena's throat flushed and her cheeks pinked as she sputtered, "If I own them, then I ain't stealing them! No way, no how, am I paying for my own magazines twice."

Angel held out his hand. "Let me see these for a second, okay?"

Rowena handed them over without a fuss. He thumbed through them, their spines making a thwacking sound. "So you brought into the store *Hot Rod Essentials, Vogue, Men's Health, People, Highlights, Knitting Today*, and *Texas Monthly?*"

She rocked back and forth from her heels to her toes, and stared up at the ceiling as though deep in concentration. "Maybe not the *Hot Rod Essentials* and *Highlights*. But the rest are sure as shit mine."

He raised his eyebrows and held up a magazine with the cover of a woman tugging on a sheer T-shirt over voluminous breasts that threatened to spill out from the top. He read the headline aloud, "How to Increase Your Testosterone with Sex Exercises."

"Why can't a woman read *Men's Health?*" she snapped.

"Because women just don't," said a voice behind them.

They all turned to find the clerk standing with her hands on her hips. She hooked her thumb to the front counter. "Look, this ain't no detective movie. We know who did what. What's I need is this here problem resolved and you people out of my store before paying customers come in."

A low, grumbling growl rose up from Rowena. Angel darted in front of Rowena and handed the magazines to the clerk. "Here they are and we're sorry for the disturbance."

The clerk shook her head. "They're all smashed and crinkled up. I can't sell 'em like that."

"All right, I'll buy them. Or rather the clinic will. I guess we need new magazines for the lobby anyhow," he said with a sigh as he followed the clerk as she marched back to the counter by the door.

Over his shoulder Angel called, "Oh, Rowena, this is Julia. She's going to be working with you this summer."

In dismay, Julia watched Angel's retreating back before she turned to Rowena's disapproving face. Silence spread between them.

Julia took a deep breath and attempted a chipper tone. "Well, yes, that's right. I'll be your therapist this summer, with Marlene supervising, of course! So it won't be like we're starting from scratch or anything." Her voice squeaked up half an octave at the end of her sentence from the force of her cheerfulness.

Rowena's frown dug in deeper. She remained silent.

"You did know that, right?" Julia ventured.

The woman reached into her back pocket and pulled out a letter that appeared soft from repeated folding and unfolding. "Yeah, I suspect I know, seeing how I got this here letter saying I'd been traded. Makes me feel like a baseball card, you know? I've been with Marlene for eight years, and now you is what I get? I guess she needs a break from me is all I can figure."

Inwardly, Julia groaned. Marlene had gone over the clients' profiles with her, but not how the transfers were to take place, and Julia hadn't thought to ask. If only Marlene had picked up the phone and called each person individually to explain the situation and answer any questions, that might have reduced hurt feelings. She could imagine Marlene, precise and efficient, typing out a form letter to her clients, and then swiping each address label onto the envelope in one smooth motion before dropping the letters in the out-going mailbox at Mona's desk. Job done, move on.

"Well, I can see where that would be a surprise to get such a letter, and maybe leave you with a question or two," Julia said.

"One or two," Rowena said dryly.

"Okay, so what questions do you have?"

She frowned and lifted up a meaty index finger. "Who the hell are you?" Up went her thumb. "And why's I picked to be your lab rat?"

Sweat beaded on Julia's forehead as her mind whirled. Those were good questions, because after all, who was she to take on Rowena Horn? A hand clamped down on Julia's shoulder and she jumped.

"Sorry, didn't mean to scare you," Angel said. "We're settled with the cashier. Let's blow this pop stand."

The trio left the store and walked into the blinding mid-morning light before they stopped in front of Angel's car. Julia turned to Rowena. "Marlene must have thought we'd be a good fit."

"Good fit or a good break for her?"

Julia glanced at Angel in a bid for back up.

He shrugged his shoulders in a ball-is-in-your-court gesture.

A billboard behind Angel caught Julia's eye of a vulnerable looking young woman above the caption, "Pregnant? Need help?" A seedling of an idea sprouted, and Julia said, "Rowena, maybe you're assigned to me because of your experience as a client. You're seasoned and I'm new. Marlene may have seen the strengths you bring to the work we'll be doing together because you can help me."

Surprise, then suspicion, flickered across Rowena's face. "I'd *help* you?"

"Sure. You know what works and what doesn't. You have a history with the clinic. You might even be called a ..." Julia struggled to think of a title for Rowena Horn. Drops of sweat trickled down the side of her face.

Rowena glared at her while the corners of Angel's lips twitched as he attempted to stifle a smile. Julia closed her eyes and snapped her fingers several times, trying to pull a word up from murky depths. One floated up. "A veteran!"

"A veteran, huh?" Rowena said, with a trace of scorn. But the grim line of her mouth softened a bit.

"It really would help me if we worked together this summer, Rowena," she said, surprised at how true those words rang for her. A bead of sweat slid off the side of her face and dropped to her collarbone.

Rowena studied Julia before cutting her eyes to Angel to see his reaction.

He had settled his features into a benign Buddha expression with an attentive, curious tilt of the head. "If you're a veteran, Rowena, don't come to me trying to find out how you can get combat pay."

"Shut up, Angel," Rowena said, the heat in her voice reduced to a low, even friendly, simmer. She studied the cracked pavement between her chunky, brown work boots for a bit before she looked up. "Okay, my usual time is ten in the morning on Fridays. Don't make me wait none in your shitty lobby."

She straightened to her full height, which put her an inch or two over five feet. "If you suck, back to Marlene I go. No matter what no letter says."

"Thank you, Rowena," Julia said, before inhaling a deep breath and leaning against Angel's car.

"And this," Rowena said as she snatched a *Vogue* from the stack of magazines in Angel's arms, "belongs to me."

Angel and Julia watched her plod across the oil-stained parking lot, her lower jaw jutting out like the bow of a ship. Sweat glistened on Angel's bald head and he turned to Julia to whistle a long, low note. "She's yours now, but what you got, I don't know. Could be trial by fire or might be tiger by the tail."

"Tiger by the tail?" Julia gave him a half-smile.

The case manager grunted and opened up the car door as a wave of heat rolled out. "With Rowena? Tiger on fire by the tail."

They plunked themselves down into the heat of Angel's car and he placed the thick stack of magazines into Julia's lap. "Here, have some light reading," he said as he started the car and they headed back to the clinic.

The covers of the magazines were crumpled and moist from Rowena's sweaty hands, and Julia eased them onto the floorboard. She stared out the window and caught a glimpse of her glum face staring back at her from the side mirror, which did nothing to improve her mood.

Chapter 17

A chorus of cicadas sang in the towering oak trees that canopied Julia's car as she sat parked on a suburban street two blocks from the clinic. Morning heat curled around her while she wished for a cigarette. Being a non-smoker didn't squelch the urge. She laid her head back and imagined holding the death stick between her lips while she struck a match and brought the bright flame to the cigarette's tip until it glowed as orange as campfire coals.

She inhaled as though drawing in blue smoke deep into her lungs before exhaling a smooth nicotine cloud. Wouldn't there follow the Zen cocoon experience she imagined smokers had, such as the ones she'd seen huddled outside office buildings during their breaks?

Julia sighed and shoved open the car door. A short walk would have to replace a Marlboro as she sorted out the scene she'd had with Nick this morning. She grabbed her satchel and purse, locked the car, and trudged past the shops and smatterings of houses.

* * *

HALF AN HOUR AGO, when she had come out of their bedroom looking for Nick's help with her bracelet's tricky clasp, his voice, muffled and terse, floated in from the balcony. Julia edged closer. Nick held his cell phone pressed stiffly to his ear while he paced from one end of the balcony to the other.

"The capacity isn't the issue. So what if we can fit in more tables? We're not cramming sardines in a can, here."

Oh shit. Nick's mom was at it again. Mrs. Meyer's current focus was to expand the wedding guest list with people Nick called her country club cronies. For the past few weeks, his mom had alternated calls between Nick and Julia with the argument that if the guest list were at two hundred, what's another twenty-five? Plus these were quality people she just knew Julia would love.

With each call, Julia had to haul up the resolve to tell his mom a polite, but firm, "no," which generally was met with a stunned silence followed by a frosty goodbye. Now it was Nick's turn.

Nick stopped pacing and stood still, the phone pressed to his ear and his back radiating an impatient stiffness. She held her breath and found herself edging closer.

Suddenly he shot his hand up like a cop stopping traffic. "Mom, this is not a gala benefit for the symphony. We told you this is our wedding and we don't want it spiraling out of control." Silence followed as Nick bent his head and listened to his mom. "Too bad if Misty Hoffman invited you to her daughter's wedding. Misty and her clan can find something else to do that particular Saturday night. But they sure aren't worth reserving another table and six chairs at the reception. With drinks and meals to boot. Mom, you need to untether yourself from the wedding planners and let me do something productive, like go to work."

Julia backed away from the door as Nick walked into the living room, the cell phone cocked to his ear. His mom's tinny voice came through anyway, rapid and insistent.

Seeing Julia, Nick rolled his eyes, then cut his mom off in what sounded like mid-sentence. "Seriously? You're going to cry about this? Get a grip or take a Xanax. But if you keep pushing up the guest numbers, then don't be surprised if you get a postcard from us postmarked Cancun with one sentence written on it: *We've eloped.*" Nick cut off her squawk from the phone. "I'm hanging up now, Mom."

He clicked off and shoved the phone into his pocket. "Dad's annual deployments overseas make more sense to me. Insurgents can be more reasonable. God, can you believe she's still trying to jack up the guest list? But you can thank me for reining her in for hopefully the last time."

"Well, thank you, I guess. But did you have to be so harsh?"

He frowned and tilted his head at her. "Yes, I did. Soft and fuzzy doesn't make a Sherman tank flinch." His eyes traveled to her hand. "What are you holding? That bracelet again?"

He stepped forward as if to help and Julia backed up. "No, I've got it," she said as she brought the bracelet up, arm across her chest.

A whoosh of brown and yellow wove between them at their ankles. Trixie gazed up with her solemn, amber eyes and gave a questioning meow.

"Your cat's hungry and I'm late." Nick bent down to kiss Julia, his lips barely brushing hers.

She looked into his eyes, which were focused on the front door as though he were already through it.

"I've got a meeting late tonight with the city council, so don't wait up." He stepped wide of Trixie to avoid her swishing tail from brushing against his dress trousers, then was gone.

* * *

AS SHE TRUDGED DOWN the sidewalk toward the clinic, Julia furrowed her brow and tried to push away the last thirty minutes. A fitful energy coursed through her and she jumped when a city bus rumbled by. While it was a relief to have Nick run interference with his mom about the guest list, the manner in which he spoke to her gnawed at Julia.

Sure, Mrs. Meyer was pushy and often barreled straight into the land of overbearing, but she was still his mother.

A worry bubbled up, and it was becoming a more insistent one: If this was how he spoke to his mom, how long before she wound up on the receiving end of such treatment? And given his standard cavalier sharpness, wasn't that already happening? Maybe she would give her friend, Fiona, a call on her lunch break. But with a practiced pivot, she shoved the thought into the things-to-be-dealt-with-later category of her mind.

The edge of her pump caught on the side of the sidewalk and she stumbled before catching herself, which shocked her from her musings. "Woolgathering," her mom always called Julia's tendencies to float away on trails of thoughts. She cursed her new shoes, so much more to contend with than sneakers, before she realized she was in front of the clinic. Walter's Jeep Wagoneer and Mona's ancient two-seater Datsun sat parked side-by-side, the only cars in the lot.

The hinges of the clinic front door rasped as Julia walked in. Mona peered up from behind the front desk glass partition, and then pushed the glass panel aside. A dozen bracelets of purple and aqua slid from her wrist to the middle of her forearm. "Morning, cupcake. I didn't see you drive up. And what's with the long face? That's supposed to be the end-of-the-day look."

"Just tired is all." Julia took a deep breath and straightened her back, as if to affect a perkier stance.

Mona arched her eyebrows and gave her an appraising once over. "Uh huh. Well, seems like you could use some caffeine from the great state of Maxwell. Come on."

Julia rounded the corner into the receptionist's area, where an interlacing of floral perfume and the coffee's deeper notes greeted her. Mona poured two cups, gave one to Julia, and together they toast-clinked.

As Julia sipped the chocolaty-brown brew, it warmed her throat and chest. "Oh, yes, now that's better."

The receptionist cocked a hip and leaned against a filing cabinet. "Just so you know, heads up. There's a busy bee in your office right now and he's packing power tools." Julia poked her head into the hallway leading to the counseling rooms and heard the muffled whine of a drill.

She turned a questioning face to Mona. "What gives?"

"Walter read Angel's report yesterday on you guys' visit with Miss Sticky Fingers at the Gas-N-Go. Seems Walter's not happy with how Rowena's been ..." She snapped her fingers. "Oh, what's that word you people keep throwing around here? Escalating! That's it. Personally, I like 'off their meds' better, but that's just me. Anywho, he comes in about an hour ago with his tool kit, saying something about adding a safety feature to your office."

"Really? What kind of safety feature?"

Mona snorted. "Who knows? But for me, anything less than a cattle prod would be skimpy in that department. But hey, since he's in an industrious mood, see if you can get him to wire together an espresso machine. Old Mr. Coffee here is in serious need of a retirement party." She clicked her nails against the splotched glass carafe.

Julia smiled. "Maybe we can all go in on one of those Cuisinart models. You know, the 14-cup jobbers?"

"Girl, I like how you think," Mona said, brightening. The phone rang and she wagged her fingers goodbye at Julia. "Incoming! Duty calls." She picked up the receiver.

Julia approached her office, where a screwdriver and drill lay beside a splayed-open toolbox. She peeked in the doorway and found Walter sitting cross-legged on the floor in front of her desk, with an opened plastic clamshell package next to him and long scroll of crinkled instructions by his side. His tall frame was bent at an awkward angle as he turned a screwdriver on a bracket under the desk. As Julia's shadow fell across him, he glanced up and smiled. "Morning, there. You're here bright and early."

"There seems to be a gravitational pull for people to crawl under my desk. Mona said you're installing a safety feature?" She dumped her purse and satchel into a corner before she crouched next to Walter.

"Yes, indeed," he said while reaching for a thin black cable and then uncoiling it.

She watched Walter attach the cable to the back of a rectangular black box in his lap no bigger than a deck of cards. In the middle of the box was a raised red button. Julia was aware of Walter's scent of soap and oakwood smoke. She inhaled, caught herself, and made a small coughing sound.

He glanced at her. "Don't worry, this isn't a bomb." With the end of a screwdriver he tapped the box. "It's an alert button, what you'd call a panic button, that's standard issue under our therapists' desks. Or at least it should be. I checked yours, formerly Paulie's old desk, and we must have forgotten to install one when he was an intern."

Her mind bounced between the need for a panic button and knowledge that Paulie had started at the clinic as an intern. "Oh," was all she could manage.

Walter ducked his head under the desk and snapped in a wire. "So I drove into town yesterday and picked up this model from the electronics store. All right, almost done. Here, let me give it a test."

While grateful for Walter's concern about her safety, she worried about the necessity for a panic button. He must have already spent some time this morning on this project. "Oh wow, Walter, you didn't have to go to so much trouble. You must have gone after work to buy this."

A curious thought bubbled up, but before she could stop herself, she added, "I'm sure your family missed you."

Walter scooted back from the desk and handed her an owner's manual. Their gaze held for a moment and Julia's heart sped up as he searched her face.

He averted his eyes. "Duke didn't mind, being a twelve-year-old Basset hound and all. Gave him more snooze time, I suppose." His voice thickened, as though his throat had constricted. He knelt down to her desk and whistled a cheerful tune, giving the bracket's screws a few more tight turns.

Still, her pulse quickened at knowing Walter was single, immediately followed by her mind's shocked voice: *So what? He's your boss. You're engaged, end of story.* She twisted her engagement ring until the solitaire diamond setting bit between her finger and palm.

"Okay, Julia, the panic button is all set up. On the rare case you'd need to use it, just reach under the desk and hit it square center. The signal travels to the relay box on the floor at the back of your desk."

He pointed and Julia peered underneath. A larger black rectangular box rested next to the wall with a short antenna protruding from one side.

"The signal travels from the panic button to the relay box, which then calls 911, the front desk, and my cell phone. There's an audio and printed message letting us know from whose office the call originates. We all have one, and now you do, too."

The red button glowed under the desk. Julia shuddered at the idea of having to mash that button and activate three branches of help. "How often have you all needed to use these things?"

"In the past seven years? Maybe one or two times. Therapists can go their whole lives and never encounter the need for such a back-up system. However, our population here is more vulnerable, and sometimes they act first and think about better options later."

Julia drew back and bit her lip.

Walter put his hand to his chest. "From my lips to God's ears, this contraption will gather dust. But at least these safety features help lower our insurance premiums."

Without even noticing, she had joined him on the floor and now they faced each other cross-legged. Julia considered scrambling up and sitting in a chair for a more dignified pose, but didn't want to break this easy moment where they were just talking. To extend the time, she said, "And the Petersons? You know, the couple with the bullwhip? Did Paulie have to mash his button during that session?"

"Nope," he said with slow shake of his head. "That played out in the parking lot. Not a hair on Paulie's head was disturbed in his office, or outside either, for that matter."

Walter stood up and offered a hand to Julia, his six-foot frame towering above her in the small office. She slipped her hand into his. Unfolding her legs as gracefully as she could manage, she swayed up.

Silence fell between them until Julia blurted out, "Am I getting the panic button because you think I've been given too many tough clients and I can't handle them?"

At once, Julia wished she could swing a net and nab her words back. Maybe talking about her fears to her boss wasn't the best tactic.

He squared his shoulders and a formality descended between them. "Marlene and I had some discussions about your client list. She felt because you were an older intern with more life experiences, that you could take on more complex cases."

"Like Rowena?" she said. The lights in the room appeared to expand and glow. *Breathe, go with it*, she instructed herself. The vein in her throat throbbed.

Walter placed his hand on her shoulder and, despite his light touch, energy radiated across her back. "We would never give you anyone we believed to be a threat. The noisiest clients aren't always the most troubled. You've got to keep your eye on the quiet ones, too."

He hesitated then added, "But Marlene and I decided we would give you extra supervision support. You'll be co-leading her Wednesday Lunch Bunch group therapy starting this week."

"Wednesday Lunch Bunch?"

"If we called it a dialectic process therapy, then no one would come. This is more a social skills group, and to make it friendlier, Marlene came up with the whole lunch idea. Can't argue with success. Some of these group members have been meeting with her for the past five or six years."

Julia winced at the idea of being under Marlene's microscope during counseling sessions on a weekly basis. "Was this your idea or Marlene's?"

Walter stalled, as if choosing his words with care. "Mine. But after some discussion, we agreed. I've put her in direct charge of supervising you and she'll be in contact with your graduate program. It will help if you both work together so that, after each group session, you can use that time to discuss cases with her."

Julia didn't doubt for a minute that "after some discussion we agreed" was code for "after I strong-armed her." She forced her lips into a tight smile. "Okay, then I'll tell Mona about the schedule change."

"No need. I alerted her yesterday and she has the group sessions on your calendar."

Julia stooped to grab her purse and satchel when something red snagged her attention from the corner of her eye. The panic button emitted a steady glow—she shuddered and scrambled up faster. She made an immediate resolution that no way, no how, was she ever going to tell Nick about this part of her morning.

Chapter 18

From the smell of it, the pudgy man to the left of Julia was eating a raw onion sandwich. The acidic stench brought tears to her eyes and Julia tried to breathe through her mouth. *Hadn't such meals been left behind with the Great Depression?*

He gave her a toothy grin and then took another crunchy bite. An oily slice of onion fell onto the wax wrapper balanced on his rotund belly. Julia braved a return smile, trying not to inhale too deeply, and shifted to the circle of five clients crammed into Marlene's office.

Across from Julia sat Marlene, her posture as straight as her highbacked shaker chair with its needlepoint seat cushion. She was dressed in a charcoal, pinstriped shift dress offset by a string of luminous white pearls looped three times around her throat. With her legs crossed and a notepad on her knee, she reviewed her previous memos while a lavender candle flickered on the desk behind her. Next to the candle, a small oscillating fan turned as if on cue and ruffled Marlene's hair, cocooning her in a zone of perfumed air.

The pudgy man tucked into his sandwich again and Julia's eyes prickled with tears from the stink, as Marlene jotted a note in an upper corner of her document with a sharpened pencil. Julia fantasized about pouring hot lavender wax all over Marlene's notepad while breathing through her mouth.

Like people in an elevator, Julia and the group members avoided eye contact as they shifted in their metal folding chairs. No cane-woven chairs with thick seat cushions for them. To Julia's right sat a slender woman who may have been in her early twenties, but had a wizened frailty to her. She hunkered down like a turtle into her T-shirt, which had to be at least an XXL, with Slayer splashed across the front. The woman didn't strike Julia as though she'd have the energy to be your typical head-banger fan.

Next to her was the only client Julia knew, Nadine Peterson. She seemed better than the last time Julia had seen her, when she had been driven off in the back of the squad car as it left the clinic's parking lot. This morning her hair was pulled into a tight ponytail and her khaki shorts and white dress shirt were freshly pressed. She gave Julia a small wave and nod.

The fourth client was a woman in her late sixties, whose reddish-brown hair, without a strand of gray, was perfectly coiffed in a tidy updo. Her chair was angled a couple of inches closer to Marlene's and she kept glancing to her left as though trying to read the senior therapist's paperwork.

Completing the group of five was a teenager, who may have been nineteen, tops. His body language broadcast he would rather crawl through twenty yards of sewer pipe than be where he now sat. Acne glowered from his pale, narrow face as he slouched with arms crisscrossed across his thin chest and hands buried into his armpits. His hair, or lack thereof, made Julia wonder if he had shorn it down to its current blond peach fuzz, or was this the buzz cut courtesy of some county jailhouse? He had a definite orange jumpsuit aspect to him.

At last, Marlene put down her paperwork and announced in a clear, ringing voice, "A happy Wednesday to you all, Lunch Bunchers. As you may have noticed, we've grown by two new members. First let me introduce our new summer intern, Ms. Julia Longley, on loan to us from the local college. And please welcome Morris. He's a tad bit younger than our usual group member, but I'm sure we'll learn as much from him as he will from us."

Morris slid deeper into his chair and focused on the hem of his jeans, which trailed filthy denim strips over the linoleum. He glanced up and said to no one in particular, "That ain't my name."

Unruffled, Marlene tapped her notepad. "And how do you prefer to be addressed? According to your intake papers, it's Morris Pennington."

This pulled the red-headed woman's gaze from Marlene's notepad and she sat back and sucked in her breath.

Morris' strawberry acne blended into a creeping blush that fanned his cheeks. "It's not Morris and it sure as shit ain't the Gas Can Bomber, if that's what you're getting at. Slate. My name's Slate."

The man next to Julia, sandwich gone, wiped his fingers on the wrapper. "Well, yeah. Morris is a name for a cat, or an accountant."

"Very well, Slate," Marlene said, her tone inserting quote marks. "Group members, let's go around and introduce ourselves. Travis will tell us a brief bit about himself." She gave the man on Julia's left a meaningful glance.

"Sure," he chirped. "Name's Travis. Been a member of Marlene's class for the past—"

"Group," Marlene said.

"Group." Travis nodded. "Been coming here for the past three years. My girlfriend, she's a nurse at St. Carmen's shelter where we met—"

"Ex-girlfriend," Marlene said.

His doughy face clouded. "Yeah, ex. I keep forgetting that part. Don't seem possible we're done, you know? First she was my nurse at the shelter. Then we got to be friends, and next thing you know, we agreed to me moving into her house. It was cush all the way before she got all picky and naggy. Felt I couldn't do nothing right. It was her idea for me to come here to the clinic and learn people skills and whatnot. Anyhow, guess I wasn't learning quick enough. She kicked me out and now she's long gone. But I still got you people, so I guess it ain't all bad." His lower lip quivered and he wiped at his eyes with the back of his hand.

Onion breath and all, Julia wanted to give him a hug, but instead gave him a sympathetic smile and patted his knee. Two tears tumbled down his whiskery cheeks and he glanced at Julia before reaching over to pat her knee in return.

"Travis, remember, we ask people if we can touch them," Marlene said, shooting Julia a sharp look.

"But she touched me first!"

"Julia is an intern and she's learning the rules. Much of learning about social skills is about rules, right? Now, let's move onto our next member."

Humiliation burned through Julia and she clasped her hands in her lap as if they'd stray on their own volition. The group members turned their attention to the petite woman who at that moment took on a bird-caught-in-a-net look.

"Uh, hi. My name is Erin and I've been to this group a couple of times, although so much has been going on these past weeks, I've sort of lost track of time." As she spoke, her voice's volume dwindled, and some of the members leaned forward to hear.

"Speak up, dear," Marlene said.

She cleared her throat and said in a louder voice, "Me and my daughter, Chloe … Things hadn't been working out so well back home, so we lit out and ended up here in Elston. Been at the shelter family unit for a few weeks. It's been okay and all. I mean, it's better than couch surfing.

The folks at the shelter are helping us with clothes because I didn't exactly have time to pack when we left. My case-worker, Holly, is helping me look for a job. She got me to finish my GED last week, so at least that's something."

Travis brightened. "Hey, I know Holly. She's not bad-looking for a larger gal."

"Travis," Marlene said in a stern manner.

He raised his hands as if in surrender then fell silent. Erin's eyes were dull marbles as she continued in a mono-tone. "Like I said, we left in a hurry. Had no choice really, my husband Lonnie got drunk again and threatened to kill us. I grabbed my girl and my purse and just ran. Lonnie ain't much for keeping his word, but when it comes to evil acts, I've learned to believe he'll follow on through."

Julia's heart ached for this runaway wife with her little girl to protect. She cut her eyes to Marlene, whose face had softened. She wanted to jump in there and say something but, uncertain, ducked her head and held her tongue.

"Good things can happen one brave step at a time, my dear," Marlene said.

Erin closed her eyes as though a wave of exhaustion had rolled over her. Julia noticed that her nails were bitten down to the quick. "I called a friend of mine from back home and she says Lonnie's been trying to track me down. He calls her and hassles her all the time, but she won't tell him where I'm at. He keeps telling her how he'll forgive me if I come back. Tells me we can pretend none of this ever happened and he'll even let me get that little ole job I was after. That's what started our last fight. I got so tired of being broke all the time and under his thumb. I know Chloe misses her daddy and her toys and own bedroom, but I don't know ..." She stopped there, staring at a spot in the middle of the floor.

"Crackling balls of fire, girl! Don't let that bum back

in!" Nadine hollered.

Erin jumped as if she'd brushed against an electric fence. She glanced up at Nadine, whose eyes had taken on a gleam while her left heel bounced up and down.

"He ain't changed! He's just sweetening up the pot to lure you back in. Then, pow! He'll give you the what-for the minute you walk back through his door. Trust me, I've got one at home stamped from the same mold. Only difference, is you still got your youth, and a kid in the mix." Her ponytail bobbed as she nodded her head.

Marlene's softness evaporated. "Nadine, we appreciate your ability to divine the future, but one of the first rules of group work is we don't give advice." Pivoting to Erin, Marlene said, "Do you know what was the most powerful piece I heard in your brave story? You completed your GED and may soon have a job. Your intuition got you this far because look at what you've already done."

Erin remained mute, motionless, and stared back at her with those dead eyes. Marlene straightened and faced Nadine. "Since you've started your story, would you please continue, Mrs. Peterson?"

Nadine nodded to Erin. "I was her twenty years ago. Married too young to a guy who was the big football star in high school. All the girls were after him. He smelled good, looked better, and washed away all my common sense. I thought it would always be, you know, magical between us. Taking a six-pack out to the lake, dancing by the truck with the radio going until the sun peeked up over the water. I'm not in this group because of Johnny Law ordering me here or because some man is chasing me here. I'm here because I've got this thing called a pattern of behavior, and I'm what you'd call a contributing factor. At least according to Paulie.

Julia scanned the group. They were all listening to

Nadine, even Erin, who peeked through her shaggy bangs. "My current no-account husband, Justin, and I been seeing Paulie for a year, and I've been coming to this group for the past six months. We've had our ups and downs, and you might of heard, a couple of weeks ago we had a scuffle here at the clinic. Big time."

Nadine closed her eyes and swallowed a few times before she continued. "Justin didn't used to be this way, but when he came back from his third tour over in Iraq, he was different. All quiet and balled up. I had warned him after his two tours that God only hands out so much luck, and when you run dry, it can leave you stranded. But he said we needed the money. We had bought some land out by the lake and he wanted to get the scratch to start building our house. The morning, he walked onto that airplane for that last deployment, and didn't turn around to wave at me like he'd done before, I knew he was going for himself and not for us. And nothing good was going to come of it."

Her voice caught and her eyes focused past the far wall, lost for a moment in the memory. Everyone held the quiet and Julia sat very still, fearful of shifting in her folding chair and making it squeak.

"Weren't there but a week before his troop was ambushed on patrol. Seven of the men died and he came back all scrambled from a concussive brain injury. The minute I saw him curled up in that VA hospital bed, I knew my sweet Justin was left in some Middle East alley and I had a whole new guy on my hands."

Slate's scowl slipped. "What kind of dude is he now?"

"Best I can figure, he's gone back to his teenage asshole self," she said with a bitter laugh. "No offense or nothing."

Slate shrugged in a none-taken way.

"It's all about him now. Him chasing skirts. Him pissing our savings away because chasing skirts costs money. Now we're dead broke, even after we sold our land. What keeps us together are the bills. We're too broke to leave each other. But one thing we've agreed to is couple's counseling. Paulie says it takes time for the hurt brain to knit back together, and I need to give Justin more time."

"So that's what happened with your parking lot dust-up?" Travis said. "Saw it on the news with that pretty TV lady talking all about it."

Nadine nodded and massaged her temples with her index and middle fingers.

"Thank God, the judge only gave me a disturbing the peace charge, but I told Justin one more screw-up, even a bounced check, and I'll sell my car to make a cheapie divorce happen. Since then, he seems to be trying harder."

"And a bullwhip constitutes improvement?"

All heads jerked around to the imperial-sounding older woman next to Marlene, her upper lip drawn slightly up in one corner. She had been so quiet that Julia almost forgot she was part of the circle.

Even Marlene seemed taken aback as she said, "Stella, the only people who know the true inner-workings of a marriage are the couple themselves." Frustration rippled across Marlene's face, then, like the snap of magician's silk cloth, her pleasant mask floated back over her features. "Let's be careful not to cross into judgment. Now, for group safety, how might you relate to what Nadine has shared with a similar experience in your own life?"

The two women stared at each other until Stella broke her gaze first. She crossed her sun-spotted hands into a tight X at the wrists in her lap as if to contemplate the question. Julia eased back into her chair, her respect for Marlene grudgingly upped a couple of notches.

"While I may not have used a long leather rope to garner my spouse's attention, I can assure you I fully relate to your frustration," Stella said. She nodded to Nadine, who sat ruffled as though not quite ready to make nice. "And like you, I also did everything right, everything I was supposed to do. Yet, here I am."

She spread out her arms in a sweeping gesture, as if being in this room was a ridiculous bottom of the barrel. "For you new young people, my name is Stella. However, if we should meet on the street, you may address me as Mrs. Schmidt." She gave a nod to Julia to make it clear she was also lumped into this category.

Stella spoke as though she were perched behind a podium addressing the garden club. "In the six years I've been attending this group, I've had to come to the realization that I married a dud. This, in spite of my encouragements and my wisdom. I pointed out the obvious paths he should take, and even at times engaged the not-so-subtle prod."

She shrugged. "Still, my husband of thirty years has failed to live up to his true potential. Not to say he hasn't changed. Why, to look at him now, he's hardly the same man I married. When we met, all he wanted to do was study birds. Birds, of all things! He always had binoculars around his neck and a notepad in his pocket to record whatever flittered by. And if he spied a painted bunting, well, you'd think Elizabeth Taylor had just alit upon a branch, he'd be so beside himself. But we had a business to run, my father's printing shop to be exact, and there was no time for such foolishness. I can't even imagine where his old spy glasses are today."

A flame of irritation burned inside of Julia. She could imagine Mr. Schmidt's hell as he was scolded and molded into a trainable worker-bee, all so he could print catalogs, business cards, and fliers for his father-in-law's business. Just to keep the peace. Sometimes with Nick she felt such suffocation at being squashed into a box, until she convinced herself that four corners were all she needed to live a satisfying life.

"However, I didn't have a head for numbers," Stella said, "and Mr. Schmidt claimed he did, so he took over our investments. Do I really need to state how this ends? Suffice it to say our portfolio was drained by his sloppy investments, which came to light when our credit card was denied at my favorite bistro. I'll never forget the pity in the waiter's eyes as he handed back the rejected card. When I confronted my husband, he admitted we were almost bankrupt." Stella gave a shudder and fell quiet.

Nadine, whose foot had been tapping in impatience, brought it down with a loud thump. "So you're saying you're dead-ass broke? La-di-da. Welcome to that leaky boat. And in case you haven't noticed, the passenger list is full."

"Please, Nadine, that statement is not supportive," Marlene said.

Stella glared at Nadine and inched her chair closer to Marlene as though channeling support.

Julia scanned the rest of the group and winced at the sight of Slate, Travis, and Erin's downcast faces. However, Marlene's attention was on Stella as she whispered something to her client.

Julia's anger rolled from her thoughts and out her mouth. "I believe to insist on what's best for another person comes from fear, not strength. If we don't know our own heart, how can we know someone else's? Does control come from love?"

The room fell quiet and Julia swallowed. *Where did THAT come from?*

A tiny mouse voice on her right broke the silence. "No, it comes from fear," Erin said, pink rising into her cheeks. "Fear makes people want to chase someone down and control them. And not stop until they're smaller."

For a second, Julia and Erin's gaze met and the young woman's mouth twitched into the tiniest of smiles.

Stella huffed and drew herself up. "I'm not trying to control my husband, I'm trying to save him!"

Travis interlaced his fingers behind his head and stretched his legs out. "But ain't it up to us to save ourselves instead?"

Five voices spoke at once, rolling the quiet out of the room like a hot wind. Julia watched in wonderment and awe as the five group members sermonized over each other and to each other, not waiting for Marlene's direction or permission.

However, Julia's scrutiny stuttered to a stop when her gaze met Marlene's. Her eyes glittered like a cobra studying the scurrying rat before the strike.

Chapter 19

As she sat hunched over the phone, Julia doodled squiggles and daggers and square boxes along the edge of her notebook. Her office was dark, except for the circle of light thrown by her desk lamp that spotlighted a stack of charts, an open textbook, and the remains of her dinner, a take-out salad from the grocery store. The blue LED glow of the clock on her desk read the time at 8:44 p.m.

She shook her head. "No, it wasn't like that. I'm telling you, the members weren't out of hand. They were more what you'd call *lively*. I'll admit, after Marlene got the group quieted down and talking in turns, things did flow better. But it felt like the conversation was less real, more stilted, you know, not the same passion."

"Maybe less passion and more thinking things through is what the doctor ordered for these people," Graham said. "Anyhow, sounded rough,"

"Got rougher. One of the members came up to me at the end and said it was the best class he'd ever had."

"You call them classes?"

"No, but this guy did. Too bad he said it in front of Marlene. If she had been considering mercy, then that went right out the window. Off she marched to Walter's office. He's the clinical director. I've felt miserable about it since then."

Graham gave a low whistle. "Man, new at school and already hauled before the principal. So what's the punishment? Clapping erasers, scrubbing out prescription bottles?"

Turning the pad horizontal, she drew tight, whirling

tornadoes in a row. "That would be easier. Let's just say, I'm getting a jump on my group theory class that I'm scheduled to take in the fall."

Julia propped her elbow on the thick text Walter had given her after his meeting with Marlene, *Irvin Yalom's Theory and Practice of Group Psychotherapy*. It was a truly cringeworthy moment when Walter summoned her into his office, where Marlene sat in a chair with her arms crossed and her jaw set. She wasted no time in laying it out straight for Julia: in order for there to be safety in group, there had to be a process so all the members could speak without emotions spinning out of control.

Julia pointed out that, while some of the exchanges were heated, she thought the group members had done a good job of expressing themselves.

Marlene stared at Julia as if trying to decide exactly what kind of fool she was dealing with. In a frosty tone, she pointed out that all group members speaking at the same time was not them expressing themselves, but rather a shouting match.

Walter coughed, stood up, and broke the tension. "You know, I think I have something here in my bookcase that might help Julia get a better understanding of group dynamics." He placed the dusty tome in her hands, assigned six chapters to be read by the end of the week, and escorted her out of his office.

Behind Walter's closed door, Marlene said in a voice that carried out to the hallway, "The idea of having interns to assist is quite altruistic, Walter, but we have to survive their help."

Julia wished she could have melted into the carpet and burrowed her way back to her office.

Motivated through shame, Julia powered through three chapters during the afternoon, including written outlines to show contrition, until she hit a wall of exhaustion. Several times, she called Nick in case he was worried about why she was working so late, but her phone calls all went to his voicemail. Frustrated and needing to hear a friendly voice, she had rung Graham at the paper.

"So what does your boyfriend say about all of this?" Graham said.

In the background, the scanner droned and there was tapping of computer keys—probably someone writing photo captions. Nostalgia stirred in her. She almost wished she were back in the photography department with its low-level dissatisfaction, rather than facing her high-profile incompetence. Almost.

Ever since Nick's phone call with his mom a couple of days ago, things between her and Nick had been strained. It seemed she had crossed an unspoken line by questioning his judgment. Julia weathered his cool politeness and tried joking him out of his pout, but he sidestepped her by being busy or, with increasing frequency, unavailable.

"I've called but he hasn't gotten back. Can you stick your head out and see if he's in the newsroom? He said something this morning about covering a planning and zoning meeting." Julia chafed at asking Graham to be her mole, but Nick's radio silence was worse.

"Wait, you're not at home? Are you still at the clinic?"

"Yes."

"Is that safe? You're not by yourself, are you?"

Glen had been banging around in the break room about an hour ago. Or was it two? Julia cocked her head and all she heard was the low whoosh of the air conditioning. She took a deep breath and said with bravado, "There may be someone in the back. Plus the doors automatically lock at 5:30, so the only ones who have a key are staffers and the cleaning crew." Under her desk and next to her left knee was the panic button, but she kept that tidbit from Graham.

"I'm not your dad, but I don't like the idea of you being

there so late at night. Let me go on a Nick sweep, be right back."

"Be cool!"

"Don't want to look like the psycho-bride-to-be, eh? Got it."

He clunked the phone down and was gone.

She cursed her insecurities for sending Graham off on this silly exercise. As an added bonus, she caught a snippet from the scanner of back-and-forth dialogue between a police dispatcher instructing a cop in the train yard on where kids were reported seen tagging boxcars with spray paint. The officer was searching up and down the train and there was frustrated chatter between the two as to exactly which graffiti-covered boxcar it was. Julia's newspaper nostalgia faded.

Footsteps grew louder and there was a scraping sound as Graham picked up the phone. "No sign of Mr. Marvelous. And city desk's not aware of any P and Z meetings tonight."

Julia frowned and shoved her salad farther away. The smell of the vinegary dressing turned her stomach. "They don't know where he is?"

There was a cautious pause before Graham said, "Well, they assumed he was with you. He took a personal day."

A tinny sound buzzed in her ears and Julia shook her head as if dislodging a noxious insect. "What? No ..." She tried to make sense of Graham's words. Personal day?

"Now, don't let your imagination take you to bad places, Jules. You're both planning this wedding. Maybe he's working on some surprise, right?"

"Yes, probably a surprise," she parroted. She had to get off the phone. "If you see him, don't tell him I was looking for him, okay?"

"Discretion is my middle name. Or at least I wish it was, because Alfonso sure sucks."

Once they hung up, Julia tapped her thumb against her lower lip. Could Nick be on a secret errand to surprise her for the wedding? She let that scene roll around in her mind as she tried to force life into it. Then she stopped and lifted her head.

What was that? Did something drop?

She stood and crept to the hallway, listening to her left, and then to her right. Silence.

She closed her eyes and strained her ears. More silence. Or was there something buried beneath the silence? An undertone, as if someone held their breath and listened back? The hair on the back of her neck rose. She grabbed her cell phone, punched in Nick's number, and once again heard his sexy, baritone voice telling her to leave a message and that he'd get right back as soon as possible.

Where the hell is he?

Chapter 20

Paulie studied the chalk menu on the coffee house wall as though reading each coffee drink line by line. The barista poised her fingers above the register buttons with an expectant look, waiting for his order. Behind Julia, the shop's bell chimed as another customer joined the growing line.

Julia coughed and murmured, "Your first time here?" Which would have been unlikely, given the shop was only two blocks from the clinic.

"Oh, no, I come a couple of times a week. Just checking to see if there's anything new," he said as he scanned the board again.

The barista rolled her eyes. At last, Paulie ordered an iced coffee and asked for a splash of half-and-half and two splashes of non-fat milk.

"Um, how about some two-percent instead? It will amount to the same thing and will take less time to make," Julia said, as the woman behind them muttered, "Oh, brother."

The barista handed Paulie his drink. "It's cool, I saw y'all walk up and started on his drink order. Your usual, right, Paulie?"

Paulie accepted the drink with a nod before threading through the crowded room for a small table in front of the shop's main window. The view overlooked a park ringed with leafy oaks and a few scrubby cedars. Julia ordered a black coffee, paid for their drinks, and joined him.

"Thanks for the coffee," he said before taking a long

draw on his straw. "So you said you wanted to talk about a couple's case? I didn't know Walter assigned you that kind of work."

His glasses were smudged and Julia resisted the urge to pluck them off his nose and polish the lenses. She took a sip of coffee, buying more time as she tried to remember the script she had been playing out in her mind since she'd arrived to work this morning. "No, I'm not seeing any couples. But I do have a client who's having problems with her husband. She's new to the clinic. I don't think you know her."

Julia's voice edged up a few notches and her words rushed together. She forced herself to take a deep breath and hoped Paulie hadn't noticed. He took another draw on his drink and watched her behind a film of smudges.

His drink was already half gone, so Julia jumped back into her story as though his cup were an hourglass with the sand slipping away. "Anyway, my client is upset because the husband's been gone a lot lately. When my client asks where he's been, he gets defensive and tells her he's got the right to not be under her microscope. And he says he doesn't ask what she does all day, which is true, but she wouldn't mind if he did ask. There's a big trip planned and the wife doesn't want to push him and ruin their plans, so she's keeping quiet and hoping everything will smooth over …" Julia finished, her energy drained by this pathetic, watered-down version of her fight with Nick last night.

"Is there a history of this behavior from the husband?"

"No, not like this. Or so she says, I mean. But maybe there's been a distance and lately she's more aware of it. At first it was all so brand new and exciting, but the tension got worse because they were changing, and maybe they discovered they were turning into people who weren't fitting together as well. Then he gets all impatient and critical and she doesn't even know who he is anymore," Julia said, dismayed at how the words kept spilling out of her mouth. *Shut up,* she told herself. *You're babbling.*

An unblinking owl, Paulie studied her, and then shrugged. "Sometimes couples have these patterns where tensions will build up until a fight breaks out over some little thing. Afterwards there's the honeymoon phase where the acting-out spouse will be nicer by promising to change or will give gifts to the victim spouse. But that phase usually ends when the resentments start to build again."

Julia squirmed in her chair at the term "victim spouse." Last night, when she returned home, she'd found Nick sitting before his computer and drinking a beer. His mood was none too contrite. Three empty beer bottles were lined up on the desk.

When she asked him why he hadn't returned her calls, he shrugged and said he took the afternoon off and didn't noticed his phone had died. Besides, he said, after taking a long draw from the bottle, didn't he have the right to take a personal day off without running it past her?

Julia started to say, No, you do not have that right, but stopped herself. *Does he have that right?* The controlling people in her life, like her father and Nick's mom, were cautionary tales, not role models. She didn't want to turn into the nag. And he had always declared how special they were as a couple, so evolved from their parents. Too evolved to nag, anyway.

Maybe Nick sensed how abrupt he sounded. His voice softened and he offered up a carrot: a trip next weekend to a bed-and-breakfast a few hours away, saying it was on his list as a possible location for their honeymoon. He clicked to a site on his computer and a picture of a Victorian house popped up on the screen. The two-story house was painted a canary yellow with a crisp green trim and a wrap-around porch dotted with rocking chairs under a sky-blue porch ceiling. Normally Nick hated B&Bs and called them claustrophobic, bed-bug palaces.

Julia pushed from her mind his previous ugly tone and dived for the carrot. She gave him a hug and dropped the fight.

Except she kept getting snagged by his off-hand comment about his phone being dead. Nick never let his phone go dead. He was rabid about "keeping the channels of communication open." He'd lied, but puzzling out why he lied had kept Julia tossing and turning for hours while Nick snored softly beside her.

Paulie's straw hit air as he finished his drink. Rattling the ice cubes in his plastic cup, he announced, "That's one dead solider."

"What does make a relationship healthier?"

He cocked his head toward the window, where outside stretched the sloping lawns of the park. Julia followed his gaze. Two old men chatted on a bench while a fountain before them sprayed crystal beads of water up into a continual arch.

Paulie turned his head back to face her. "I think you need to start off with friendship and chemistry. And then in the middle years, when things can be the hardest, friendship, chemistry, and community. But toward the end, a healthy couple comes back to their friendship. I saw that with my grandparents. Were you close to yours?"

Julia shook her head. After her parents' divorce, her mother had avoided her family members, maybe thinking it was easier than explaining how her life had become so small. And her father preferred his bubble of work punctuated by restless travel with his new wife, which left little time for family. So with her mother collapsing inwardly and her father always on the run, she had rarely seen her grandparents.

Paulie nodded as though he guessed as much. "I was close to mine and I loved to visit them at their farm. My parents always assumed it was so I could ride their horses or get spoiled rotten by my grandmother's cooking. She was one of those cooks who would either drench meals in butter or smother them in marshmallows. But, deep down, I enjoyed how peaceful it was just being with them. At night they'd sit at their Formica kitchen table playing dominoes while I lay on the couch in the living room and watched them. They were framed in the doorway and I imagined they were on a stage. The only sounds were their dominoes clicking against each other. I didn't have the words back then to explain it, but I knew if I could be that content and quiet with someone, then I'd have a good marriage."

Tears blurred Julia's vision as she tilted her face toward the park. The two old men were now crossing the street to the coffee shop. The shorter of the two wore red suspenders with bright brass clips that winked in the sun.

When was the last time Nick and I just hung out?

She turned back to Paulie to tell him how she could almost picture his grandparents, but he had stood up, pushing the chair back. "Of course," he said, "statistically-speaking, couples who make it past the twenty-year mark tend to be close in attractiveness and education, have similar spiritual beliefs, and shared goals. Oh, and money. That's a biggie. Always helpful if people are solvent. Nothing kills romance like being broke."

"Yeah, well, sure," Julia said, trying to sort through that fact blast.

Paulie glanced at the clock near their table. "I've gotta go. New couple coming in at two o'clock."

Julia watched him retreat before she grabbed her

purse and hurried to catch up. As he swung open the door, the red suspenders guy on the other side reached for the handle. Paulie strode out and the older gentleman had to jump back to avoid being whacked by the swinging door, almost bumping into his friend. He shot Paulie a dirty look, grabbed the door, and held it open with a grand gesture for Julia.

She mouthed sorry to the men before trotting up next to Paulie. Irritability crept into her voice. "So that's it? That's all I need to know about how to make a marriage work?"

He slowed his steps as though puzzling out her words. "Well, no. We can talk reams about any one of those relationship factors. Anytime you want, but …" he said as he tapped the face of his watch.

They walked in silence to the clinic as Julia mulled over their conversation, wondering what Mrs. Paulie thought about her relationship factors with her husband. Still, if Paulie, with his smudged glasses and lack of manners, could be married, then why was it so hard for her and Nick to live together? Marriage had to be harder, right?

When they entered the front door of the clinic, Paulie veered right and disappeared into his office without a backward glance. Julia sighed. *Whatever.*

Mona's baleful stare greeted her in the lobby as she rested her elbow on a stack of magazines. The corners of her mouth were turned downward. "Your two o'clock is here."

"But I don't have a two o'clock."

She shot a glance behind Julia. "Your schedule got updated."

Julia spun around. Rowena Horn glowered from a corner, her beefy arms crisscrossed across the shelf of her bosom, her eyes glittering from Julia to Mona, before settling in on Julia. She opened her mouth as if to speak.

Instead she bellowed out a wail that would have rivaled an ambulance's siren. Tears streaked her face.

Shocked that another human being could even be that loud, Julia turned back to gape at Mona, who was scooting the magazines closer to her keyboard. "What's the matter with her?"

Standing up, Mona said, "Rowena got short-changed at the Penny Pincher. Again." With a flourish, she pulled the glass partition window closed, while Rowena's cries drowned out her bracelet's tinkling chimes. Alone together in the lobby, Julia swiveled her head around, looking for help as her new client's sobs turned back to wails.

Chapter 21

It took Rowena ten minutes to go through half a box of tissues before her sobs wound down to the occasional hiccup. Julia held the box out to her, berating herself for not having a back-up supply tucked somewhere in her office. But then again, it never occurred to her she would even *need* a backup box.

Rowena's nose was red and raw as she honked one more time into her tissue before quavering, "I ain't no dummy and I dang well know what profiling is. And I'm being profiled as a stupid person if they think I can't figure out how to count my own change."

"How much were you short-changed?" Julia said, not even bothering to question if she had been short-changed at the general store. With only half a box of tissues left, Julia didn't need Rowena revved up again.

"Seventeen cents."

Julia fought the urge to reach into her purse, give Rowena a quarter, and call it even. Instead she said, "And you believe this has happened before?"

Rowena's nostrils flared. "I don't *believe* it's happened before—I *know* it. But this time I was ready and counted my change back, right in front of her. I told the lady she'd come up short, but she claimed to have already closed the register and couldn't open it back up 'less I bought something else! I was so mad, just stomped out of there! That's when I heard her laughing with the lady who'd been in line behind me. They was laughing at me, I just know it."

Her large, pasty face crumpled as tears coursed down the lines in her cheeks and slid off the undercut of her jaw. She tugged a fistful of tissues from the box.

A snowy mound of paper balls filled the trash can next to Rowena, as Julia struggled with how to defuse this human time bomb. Her nerve endings still jangled with the adrenalin flush from Rowena's crying jag in the lobby. The fight was absurd, but Julia knew better than to say that to Rowena.

Still, she knew how it felt to be an outsider and so want to belong, only to find social doors ajar but not open enough to enter. Ever since she was a small girl, Julia had known times when she was alone and vulnerable. The times she'd watched knots of girls cozying up together in the lunchroom while she sat at the table on the far side of them, trying to disappear behind her peanut butter sandwich. Or listening to classmates talk about movies and sleepovers or pool parties that seemed to be the birthright of those given the privilege of belonging.

Oh, yes, she knew.

"That really bites, Rowena," Julia said. "Hard." That was probably not the expression Marlene would have used, but it seemed to be the truest word Julia could think of.

Rowena glanced at Julia with a suspicious squint then heaved a sigh. "Yeah, it does. Bites hard."

"The first time we met, you were in a similar situation with the clerk at that convenience store," Julia said, praying she wasn't opening up a new can of worms.

Rowena merely nodded. "I ain't ever going back to that store neither. They pissed me off so bad. Then here I go and get ripped off by this one today! I've gotta make these stores work cause I don't drive, and Mama used to drive till her eyesight got all bad with the diabetes. Now it's up to me to run our errands on foot and I can't even get to the big grocery stores. Not without taking the buses. I hate them buses." Her eyes grew bright with tears again and her lower lip trembled.

Julia jumped in. "Do you see any patterns with these stores?"

Rowena scrunched her massive brow together. "Patterns? These ain't fabric stores, these are itty bitty grocery stores!"

Taking a deep breath, Julia said, "I'm sorry, I phrased that wrong. I mean, do you see where the same things keep happening to you? Like having similar problems with other people, like these clerks?"

"Now if you're setting this all up to being my fault, then I'll haul you up short." A dusky red glow crept up her throat. "Counseling don't mean it's open season on Rowena Horn. And Marlene never told me such things 'cause she knows it's hard for me and Mama. All I have to do is ask …" Rowena snapped her fingers in front of Julia's face. "And Walter will switch me back to Marlene just like that."

Julia sat back in her chair with a sharp inhale. Of course, Walter would switch Rowena back to Marlene, but that didn't bother Julia as much as the superior, I-told-you-so manner Marlene would adopt. Julia could imagine Marlene accepting Rowena's thick file and saying with a doleful shake of her head, "Of course I'll take Rowena back. Poor Julia, but at least we gave the intern an opportunity, right?"

"Rowena, you have the power to do anything you want and I'll support you either way. But may I give an observation?"

She tilted her head. "Depends on the observation."

"Rather than trying to find new stores, how about if we work on new approaches for working with people?"

"You saying it's my fault again!" Rowena cried, her

voice rising.

Julia held up her hands, palms forward. "No, absolutely not! While you can't control the clerks, maybe you can improve the way you say things."

"I talk to people direct. Including that uppity woman who stole my money, so she understood me just fine." Rowena sat back and crossed her arms.

Julia flipped through several responses and each one was painted with bullseyes for Rowena to shoot down. What did Rowena really want, because her hurt wasn't about a few coins. *But what does anyone want?*

An image floated up of Paulie's grandparents as they played dominoes late into the night, their gnarled hands lining up the black-and-white tiles on the kitchen table. Acceptance, she thought. People want to be seen and feel heard and just somehow belong.

And what would Paulie's grandparents say to Rowena? In her mind, Paulie's grandmother glanced up from the game and spoke to her.

Julia sat up straighter, unaware she had been slouching. "Rowena, have you ever heard people say you can catch more flies with honey than vinegar?"

"Sure, who hasn't? What a bunch of hooey. Who wants to catch a bunch of flies anyhow?"

"Totally. What a weird saying, right? But I think it's supposed to mean if we're nice to people, then people might be nicer to us. And if we're nice for long enough and keep on being nice, then maybe people will feel safe around us. We could gain a friend or two along the way."

Although in Rowena's case, Julia suspected it would be a major victory if she made even one friend.

The room grew quiet as Rowena stared at a spot on the wall and worried a piece of tissue into a smaller and smaller ball with her rough-knuckled right hand. At last she said, "Yeah maybe true, maybe not. But I'm nice to people and they ain't nice back." A tremor had come into her voice as a single, slow tear trickled down her cheek.

Julia could imagine Rowena as a young girl, chubby and awkward, as she lurked on the edges of the playground, watching all the kids around her played monkey-in-the-middle, tag, and war, while she rocked from foot-to-foot, clueless and praying for someone to ask her to join them.

When Julia was photographing for the paper, hadn't she always trained her camera on those same outcast kids, the ones who stood away and separate from the rest of the herd? Their very aloneness drew her to them because she had been one of those kids also. Too quiet, too sensitive, as her father used to say. Julia imagined what she could have used as a kid when she was left to knock about to her own devices.

"Two words, Rowena. Social skills. And they're called skills for a reason because we need to practice them. And not just once, but over and over. If you're rusty on how to talk with people, then you and I have the summer to work together. What do you say?"

Julia held her breath, because, within her paltry bag of tricks, this was the only one she could think of to pull out and offer.

"How do I get them social skills you're yammering about? You ain't better'n the other therapists by a long shot, being just some kid off the street they throwed at me."

Julia shrugged her shoulders. "Honestly, I'm going to have to think about this. Do you trust me to come up with a plan?"

Rowena barked an incredulous laugh. "Well, ain't this a pretty picture? The blind hauling off and leading the blind."

It seemed, Julia thought grimly, that she and Rowena were finally on the same page.

Her client honked into the last tissue, glared at the empty tissue box, and then waggled it at Julia. With a sigh, Julia stood up and stepped out into the hallway before she realized she had no idea where the paper products were stored.

"Great," she said to the empty hallway then trudged out to find Mona, once more, and wondered if there would be a time when she wouldn't need others to bail her out, multiple times a day.

Chapter 22

When Julia rapped twice, Walter's door, which stood ajar a few inches, swung open and revealed the clinical director at his desk in front of a table vise with a hemostat clamped in the jaws. He wound a thread around a small curved brass wire in the jaws of the vice.

"Oh, hey, Walter, sorry to bother you … "

He glanced up, and then motioned her in. "I'd pull up a chair for you, but as you can see, I'm in mid-wrap."

"Mid-wrap?" Julia said as she approached the desk. She was careful to avoid the splayed-open toolbox on the floor, which displayed tidy compartments of spools of clear threads, metal wires, feathers, bits of animal fur, and a garish nest of thin tinsel.

Walter wound the thread a few more times before he looped the knot with his square knuckled hands. "There we go, that should hold it." He smiled up at her.

Her expression must have been one of incomprehension, because he nodded to the wire in the vice. "It's a fishing fly."

"But it's so small. I've never seen one so tiny." She stepped closer and examined the hook clamped between the vise's jaws.

"Tiny but mighty. This bad boy isn't for snagging your common catfish or bass. This is a trout lure. Fly-fishing is a game changer, for sure." He reached down into the toolkit and pulled out a spool of wire no thicker than a thread.

"I've never known anyone who fly fishes, much less made their own hooks."

"Flies, not hooks," he said. "If you call them hooks, then fishermen will think you put your waders on backwards."

"Fly fishing in Texas?"

"Why let Montana and Colorado have all the fun? In fact, the fish hatcheries release young trout in our rivers every fall. A big drop is done outside of Elston on the Guadalupe River and I happen to know a few fishing holes too tucked away for tourists to stumble onto. Used to be, after a hard day's work, I'd drink a beer or two to unwind. Once the beer count increased to four to five, I knew I had to find a better way to unwind. So I took up fly fishing. One of the few ways to fish and not drink beer."

He poked through the pile of feathers then stopped and straightened. "Here, you pick out a feather."

Julia stepped closer and ran her fingers through the soft tangle before she pulled out a narrow, curved feather with shimmering colors of brass and emerald. It gleamed as though dipped in Mardi Gras paint. She handed it to Walter.

"Pheasant's tail, great choice." Snipping off an inch of the feather, he said, "Now we know we're making a Pheasant Tail Nymph fly."

He laid it against the hook's back and wrapped the thread in tight, precise loops around the feather and hook until they were bound together. "Let me add some bling here to help catch the eye of my future dinner."

He pulled a crimson curl of tinsel from the box, wound that around the hook, loosened the vise, and then held up the fly for Julia to see. What had been a hook, feather, and a bit of shiny tinsel now came to life in resplendent, deep colors topped by one bright spot of crimson.

"It's beautiful." Julia reached out to touch it. "So charming."

Walter handed her the nymph and their fingers touched. His warm touch snapped electricity through Julia. She fumbled the lure and dropped it.

In a swift motion, Walter scooped it up and let it fall into Julia's palm. "They're sometimes hard to hold onto," he said, but now his eyes avoided hers. At once officious, he pushed his chair back. "So don't let me bore you with my hobby. How's it going with your clients?"

Julia drew herself up and curled her hand around the fishing fly. "Okay, I guess. I'm hanging in there with them. Whenever I get stuck in session and don't know what to say, I ask questions and that jumpstarts the conversation. At the end of the session, they usually tell me they feel better," Julia said, with a shrug. Hearing her paltry technique spoken out loud made her squirm.

But Walter only nodded. "That's how we all start as therapists. By asking questions, sometimes the clients come to their own aha moments. Besides, how often is it we talk with someone who really listens? Just being heard can be therapeutic."

An image flashed into her mind of Nick reading the paper or surfing the Internet while she talked to him. His answers were usually of the uh-huh variety.

"Yes, I suppose." She paused then swallowed and forged ahead. "But there's this one client—"

"Let me guess," Walter said. "Would this be a Ms. Rowena Horn?" He reached down, picked up the toolbox, and placed materials back into their compartments.

"Yes! She came into the office just a mess because she thought she got short-changed a few pennies at a store."

"Rowena has blown into all of our offices at one time or the other with similar emergencies. Let's see. There was the someone-took-my-seat-on-the-bus crisis. The I-was-told-not-to-eat-all-the-cookies-at-the-free-sample-booth-in-the-grocery store crisis. And the I've-been-falsely-accused-of-stealing-magazines crisis. Actually, that particular one has been happening more and more."

Walter snapped the lid of the box closed. "After each episode, Marlene, Paulie, or I listen to her, check to see if she's taking her medications properly, and we go over her coping strategies."

A sodden weight seemed to grow inside Julia's chest and pin her to the chair. She had read through five volumes of Rowena's charts and shuffled through the stacks of progress notes written by the therapists and caseworkers, some of whom had long since moved on from the clinic. It was clear Rowena wasn't a particular therapist's client. She was the clinic's client.

"But does any of that help? Is she any better?"

"Well, she's not in-patient at the state hospital, which happened a lot in her younger years, and so far she's avoided jail for petty theft of magazines. From that yardstick? Yeah, she's stabilized. Better, for Rowena, is a relative term. As you may have read in her chart, she lives with her mom and probably always will. What may not have made it into the chart yet is that the mother's diabetes has worsened, possibly to the point where she may need to get a foot amputated. Rowena's greatest fear is her mother will die someday, and that someday is coming faster and faster. I think that's why we're seeing a spike in Rowena's aggressive, paranoid behavior."

"Well, of course she's scared. What's she going to do?"

Walter tightened his lips and gave a short shake of his head. "That's been our treatment goal from the beginning. Rowena's problem isn't her mother's diabetes—it's her fear of people who aren't her mother. She demands people act in a certain way rather than learning how to go with the flow. Unless she plans to hole up in a cave somewhere and live off the land, she's needs to develop better communication skills. And we've gone over those techniques with her time and again. If she's scared, then that's appropriate, because I'm scared for her also."

Julia chewed on her bottom lip and glanced down at her hands, surprised to see she had been holding the fishing fly between her thumb and index finger. The crimson tinsel glinted as it lay nestled in the pheasant feather. *Rowena will probably never go fly fishing. So much life is passing her by.*

Her frustration with Rowena melted into empathy. If anyone stays scared long enough, sooner or later that fear turns to anger. And there must be a fear of seismic proportions rumbling underneath Rowena's volcanic temper tantrums.

"She's been seen by everyone here. But has anyone taken Rowena out to a location and schooled her on these skills and shown her how it's done?"

"Glen and Angel have taken her to medical appointments before, but she's been doing that on her own for the past couple of years."

"No, I mean has anyone taken her someplace public and coached her on actual social skills?"

"Hmm, no, that's not our normal protocol. Client work is office-based. Why, what do you have in mind?" Walter cocked his head.

"Rowena may need to be shown social skills because she's not getting them simply by being in a session with a therapist. No way could I learn fly-fishing from you just telling me about it. I'd have to be shown." Julia set the fly on the edge of his desk.

Walter's smile widened. "Sure, I get it. Exposure Therapy. Let her face what she's afraid of." He shrugged, looking thoughtful. "Why not? Might be worth a try if you're willing. But, more importantly, if you can convince Rowena. You are signing up for this project, right?"

"What?" Julia gasped. "No, I just thought of the idea, but surely someone else is better qualified to do it. You know, Paulie or Marlene ..."

Julia stopped. Paulie was hardly the person to teach social skills and Marlene would never run that far afield from tried-and-true clinical procedures. Her excellent idea had seemed fine if someone else guided Rowena. *What possesses me to keep opening my mouth like this?* Walter laughed. "No, it's different. Like I've been saying, student interns bring in fresh energy."

Julia frowned as she wondered to whom he had justified the need for an intern. She shook the thought away. "But where would I take her and what would we do? I just can't wander into a store with her. All she knows is how to attack or snub people."

Walter stood and placed his car keys on top of his toolbox, his eyebrows knitted in concentration. He was silent before snapping his fingers. "Chuck Munson. He's manager at the Penny Pincher, and he owes me a favor. I'll explain the situation to him and see if he'll allow Rowena to volunteer as a greeter. She'll have to interact with people because that will be her job."

"What? No really, Walter, you don't understand. That's the place Rowena said she was just short-changed. She hates the Penny Pincher!"

His smile grew into a large grin. "Even better. She gets a chance to muzzle her growl with customers and maybe learn that the store isn't so bad."

Julia struggled to comprehend how her problem with Rowena had become an expedition with her as the guide.

"Please, I'm not the person for this."

"Of course you're the person for it. You came up with idea, didn't you? Sometimes, Julia, you've got to trust your gut." He pointed to the fly. "And keep this little guy as a reminder, okay?"

"What if my gut's wrong? What if she feels pushed too hard and comes unhinged?" Her last session with Rowena was still fresh in her mind.

He reached over and curled her fingers gently around the fishing fly. "Let her self-preservation kick in. Struggling isn't bad—it's at the heart of where we need to grow. Now hang onto your nymph fly for luck because I've got a fishing spot calling my name."

As he strode out the room with the rod clicking against the toolbox, Julia's hand stayed warm where his large hand had briefly covered hers. The pheasant feather caressed her fingers while the pointed end of the hook dug at the center of her palm.

Still, she gripped the fly tighter and wondered whose self-preservation was going to kick in the most. Hers or Rowena's?

Chapter 23

U p until a few minutes ago, Julia thought, Rowena's most surprising behavior the morning of her first training had been her cooperativeness. She had agreed to meet Julia at The Penny Pincher before the store opened and had been civil to the manager. She'd even put on the green polyester apron, which stretched taunt across her shelf of a bosom and donned the cap emblazoned with the store logo.

Yet when she was flanked between Julia and the manager, Chuck Munson, a slight ribbon of a man with a protruding Adam's apple that bobbed above his tie as he talked, Rowena balked at wearing the nametag. Watching the manager cajole Rowena at the front of the store near the line of shopping carts, Julia suspected it had been quite the favor Walter had called in to allow Rowena to try out for the store's greeter job.

A mulish expression, one that Julia was becoming way too familiar with, settled onto Rowena's face like just-poured concrete. "I ain't wearing it, so no need to try and stick it on me," she said as she refused to look at either Julia or Mr. Munson.

There you go, Julia thought grimly. Her question of how long Cooperative Rowena was going to be in the house was answered. Nine minutes.

The manager shot Julia a worried glance then said to Rowena, "Um, Ms. Horn, a name badge is part of the uniform. It makes our guests feel more comfortable to know who in our Penny Pincher family they're addressing." He offered up an encouraging smile.

"They might feel more comfortable, but they'd be the only ones. None of their damn business what my name is, because I sure won't be knowing theirs," Rowena shot back.

His smile evaporated as his Adam's apple hitched. Still, he persisted. "As a greeter, our name becomes part of the uniform. And coarse language will not be tolerated by any Penny Pincher employee. We are a family business."

Her client lifted her chin and started to open her mouth when Julia stepped in between them. "Of course Rowena won't use rough language. She's just new and a bit nervous."

"I can speak for myself," Rowena growled from behind Julia.

Julia spun around and gave Rowena a warning look, but continued in a cheerful voice, "And you will! But we first need to get through this brief training."

Rowena fell into a glowering silence.

Mr. Munson's gaze darted between the two women before settling on Julia. "Um, we can leave off with the nametag during this training period. But if she gets hired, then the nametag is part of the deal."

"Certainly!" said Julia, mentally willing Rowena to be quiet behind her.

The corners of his mouth tugged down. "Anyway, the rest is pretty simple. When a guest arrives say 'Welcome to the Penny Pincher,' ask if they'd like a flier with today's specials, and if they seem a bit uncertain then ask if they'd like some assistance."

Rowena's restraint crumbled. "So now I've got to be a mind reader? How's that supposed—?"

"Like we talked about earlier," Julia widened her eyes at Rowena, "this is all part of the learning curve, right?" She cringed at how she sounded like a game show host trying to sell what was behind curtain number three.

The manager seemed doubtful. "Well, you two work it out. I'll be running the cash register over there." He pointed to a line of checkout lanes to his right. "So I won't be far if you need me."

Once he left, Julia lowered her voice. "Okay, Rowena. We've made it this far. Good job."

"Don't see how there's a we in all this. Unless you've got a frog tucked in your pocket. I'm the one in this get-up, yakking with whoever waltzes through the door," she grumbled.

Before Julia could answer, the double doors automatically swung open and in walked a gray-haired woman in fuchsia slacks and a matching floral top.

"Welcome to Penny Pincher!" Rowena hollered. "Home of down-home savings! Wanna flier?"

The woman jumped as though she'd been tasered and veered to the left toward the hardware section, although she didn't seem to be the hardware type. She cast a quick, backward glance at them and disappeared around a corner.

Julia thinned her lips together and tried to keep her voice light. "You really know the script, but maybe take the volume down a few notches? When a customer comes in, just start with a friendly hello and casually welcome them to the store."

Rowena huffed so hard her bangs lifted up from her forehead, now shiny with sweat. "People don't come in here to be all casual. They come to get their stuff 'n go."

"Yes, but they also don't want to be startled. How you say something is as important as what you say."

At the sound of the door opening behind her, Julia took a deep breath as two teenage girls sauntered in, their purses bouncing against their slender hips from long chain straps. Julia cut a quick glance to Rowena and her throat constricted—Rowena's expression was like that of a cat cornered by two junkyard dogs. Was she imagining it or were the hairs on the back of Rowena's neck standing up?

"Okay, Rowena, just—"

"Welcome to Penny Pincher! Down-home savings! Flier!" Her voice rose with each phrase and she thrust the crumpled flier toward the girls.

The girls jumped back, one put her hand to her chest and the other gasped, "Oh, shit!"

"I'm sorry," Julia stammered, "but there are some really great specials."

The girls interlocked arms and hurried past them, their heads bent toward each other, whispering. Rowena fixed a doleful stare after their retreating backs.

"Rowena, that time you were even louder! Just breathe in and out a few times, okay?"

"What?" she snapped. "Now I ain't breathing right?"

Julia took her own advice and inhaled and exhaled three times to slow her racing heart. "How about if you start with a small step with the next person, like saying 'hello?' You don't have to recite the whole greeting."

Rowena lifted her heavy eyebrows and burned a stare into Julia. "Hello," she intoned in her deep, bass voice that came across more like a threat than a welcome.

The floor under Julia softened. Vertigo wound up from the floor as if to encircle Julia's ankles and pull her down. A metallic taste crept under her tongue as her gaze flickered to the doors. What if she walked through them and away from this impossible person? A voice bubbled up through her fear: Where would you go? Back to the condo? Back to the newsroom? Back to Mom's?

A large shape filled the door as a barrel-chested man walked in the store with "Hoggett Trucking" stitched across his shirt's front pocket. Julia held her breath, not even daring a sideways glance at Rowena, and braced herself.

"Hello. Welcome to Penny Pincher. Wanna flier?" Rowena's tone was flat and colorless as milk in a bowl. She thrust the flier toward the trucker.

He paused, reached out, and took it. "Thanks, don't mind if I do."

When he ambled past them, Julia said, "Hey, you nailed it! Did that feel any better?"

Rowena cocked her head and fixed Julia with a quizzical squint. "What's to feel about handing out a piece of paper?" Yet a ghost of a smile hovered at the corners of her mouth as she straightened her fliers, and then faced the door.

A minivan slid into a parking space in front of the store and a man got out of the driver's side door, stretched, and then reached into the backseat to pull out a drowsy toddler with a purple pacifier in her mouth. From the passenger's side, a woman, whose belly swelled against her maternity smock, coaxed out a small boy who avoided his mom's hand and pointed back plaintively to the van.

"Okay, Rowena. Now here comes a family, so maybe see if one of the parents want a flier," Julia said as the dad pushed open the door.

Silence.

Julia glanced at Rowena, whose eyebrows furrowed together like gathering storm clouds. Her posture had gone board-straight.

What the hell? Julia reached over and touched Rowena's arm. "Hey, are you—?"

Rowena jumped as she flung Julia's arm away, and then took a step forward. "Penny Pincher welcome! Flier!" Her voice rose on each word as she thrust the fliers out from her shaking hand.

The toddler's mouth gaped open and the purple pacifier plinked to the ground as she wailed. The father pulled the baby back in a protective gesture while the mom rocked back on her heels and collided with her son, whose sullen expression switched into one of surprise.

"Why are you yelling at us? You can't just jump out at people and holler!" the father said as he reached down and picked up his child's pacifier.

Rowena fell silent, the pink in her face draining to white. Her Penny Pincher cap sat askew on her head and threatened to topple.

Julia stepped forward. "So sorry. We're just in training here at the store."

She wished desperately for a reset button that would take her back to the moment she and Walter had come up with the harebrained idea of Rowena being a store greeter. She would squash it.

Mr. Munson appeared by the man's side, out of breath and with flushed cheeks, as though he had sprinted from his cashier's post. "Is everything okay here?"

"Not by a long shot, buddy. What's the big idea of hiring people to jump at us? You trying to scare the money out of us customers?" The father fumed as he handed the sobbing toddler to his wife. She shot a menacing glare at Julia and Rowena.

The manager shook his head and pointed behind him. "Please, when you're finished shopping, come to checkout number two where I'll be working. You'll receive a twenty percent discount on your entire purchase."

The child's sobs had downshifted to hiccups against her mother's neck as the parents glanced at each other. The wife said, "Well, that could work. Although I'm warning you, we were planning on buying a lot of stuff."

The husband nodded solemnly at her, but a smile twitched his lips.

Mr. Munson watched the family stroll away with

both parents now pushing their own shopping carts with a kid plunked into each front compartment. He whirled to Rowena and Julia, but directed his ire to Julia. "What in the Sam Hill is going on around here? First, I've got a couple of girls telling me the greeter was rude to them, and while they're complaining, I hear all this racket coming from the front of the store. And you've only been on the job twenty minutes!"

Rowena's hat tumbled to the ground as she struggled out of her apron like a snake scraping off old skin. Material ripped as Rowena flung the apron down and her eyes blazed with fury. "I tole you this job ain't for me! Stupid me for trusting stupid you!"

Mr. Munson stepped backward as she barreled past them and flung herself out the front door.

"This is my fault, sir," Julia said, stooping down and picking up the torn apron and dented hat.

Her apologies were anemic even to her own ears. But the bigger problem was how to repair the damage done to Rowena, whose resiliency was only the thinnest layer of brass rubbed down to exposed nickel.

He accepted the clothing with an impatient snatch. "Let's just call this an expensive lesson, shall we, young lady? Now I've got to get back to the register and wait for this couple who seem intent on taking full advantage of their discount."

Julia dashed out the front door and glanced up and down the sidewalk. Rowena was nowhere to be found. She prayed for a break and turned right, hoping it was the direction Rowena had traveled. She took off at a sprint. At the corner, she spotted Rowena's stocky frame marching into the distance, two blocks away. For someone so heavy, Rowena could move when motivated.

Julia ran and finally trotted up next to her client.

Between pants, she said, "Rowena, slow down and talk to me. You have no idea how awful I feel about this."

Rowena whirled around. "How awful you feel! I got hauled up into somewhere I don't belong, and here you carry on about your feelings." Sobs rose up from Rowena, followed by tears that streamed down her cheeks and left silvery streaks.

Oh, Christ, I can't even apologize right. Julia reached out and touched Rowena's shoulder.

With a hard shove, Rowena pushed Julia back and shouted, "I ain't no lab rat for you to experiment on! But now we know I don't fit in. I don't fit in nowhere!"

The shove shocked Julia out of her guilt. "That's not true! You were doing better. With that one guy you did just fine! But when the family showed up, you got your confidence rattled or something."

With her eyes closed, Rowena shook her head from side to side as if to shoo away a buzzing insect. When she opened her eyes, she took a step toward Julia and said in a quiet, tight voice, "I know you ain't no real therapist— you only some student from that fancy pants school across town. But what you done back there wasn't right. Marlene never asked nothing of me like that. So maybe you best go back and do whatever it was before you took up helping people. Cause from where I stand, you ... you suck."

Rowena wheeled on her heel and barreled away from Julia. Pedestrians veered off on either side of her to avoid being railroaded as she cut a straight swath down the middle of the sidewalk. Julia leaned against a lamppost and watched her client, now probably former client, disappear around a corner.

What have I done?

Rowena's scars from having no friends, no job, no family of her own were now rent open with a fresh, gaping wound, all thanks to Julia's misguided good intentions. And to top it all off, she had to trudge back to the office and write up her report on the whole fiasco.

Marlene's prim face floated up before Julia. With a groan, she patted her jeans for her keys, remembered they were tucked into her purse back at the Penny Pincher, and then closed her eyes to better curse this day.

She dug her hand into her pocket for her cell phone to call Nick and find some comfort in the middle of her self-inflicted storm, but her fingers froze as soon as they touched the hard, plastic surface. He'd just tell her she was delusional to have expected any other outcome. He'd tell her she was crazy to think she could reason with crazy.

With heavy feet she went back to the store. Once she told Marlene and Walter how it went with Rowena, she'd be asked to pack her meager belongings and leave the clinic. Lord knows what they'd say to her graduate advisor.

When would she ever get her life right?

Chapter 24

A light rap on the door startled Julia from her dark musings. The scent of warm roses wafted in. Without looking up from the blank notepad in front of her, Julia said, "So I'm up, Mona?"

"Yes, Chickie J, you're up. Let's get this party started!" The women's gazes met and Mona dropped the jokes.

She sat on the edge of Julia's desk. "Remember, if it gets rough with Marlene, you can always toss a bucket of water on her and see if she melts." She drew her fingers into curled claws and mimicked the Wicked Witch of the West.

The corners of Julia's lips lifted up, but she couldn't get a real smile to surface. Mona had put Julia on the tail-end of Marlene's packed appointment list at six p.m., just before the clinic closed. Because Julia's last client session ended at three, she'd watched the clock's hands inch across its white face for three hours, which allowed her plenty of time to worry about Rowena. She called Rowena's house twice and received no answer (a repeat from yesterday with the same result).

When she had typed up an incident report of the Penny Pincher debacle and saw how it read in black-and-white, Julia prepared herself to be told to grab a packing carton for her half-a-box of possessions, and then turn in her keys. Once Marlene sent the final report to her professor overseeing her internship, the nail in the coffin would be struck. It would be official: she was not the stuff of which counselors were made. And she'd not even been on the job for a month.

As Julia approached Marlene's office, she squeezed past a janitor wearing purple gloves while he mopped the floors. The words, "Cleanin' Up Janitorial Services," were stitched across the back of his uniform.

"Excuse me," Julia said, edging next to the wall to avoid the handle as the man swished the mop in large arcs.

He touched the brim of his hat. His neck was pale as though he'd recently gotten a short haircut. "No problem, ma'am. Mind the wet floor."

Under the Pine Sol scent from the freshly mopped floors, Julia breathed in the scent of burning sage that grew stronger as she approached the open door of Marlene's office. Her supervisor, who waved a cigar-sized bundle of herbs around the center of the room, motioned for Julia to come in.

"Here, let me extinguish this and put it away," Marlene said as she tamped down the glowing embers of the smudge stick into a red clay bowl. She opened up a small drawer in her desk and placed the bowl at the bottom.

"Smells pretty. It reminds me of the desert after a rainstorm. I'm amazed at how people around here love incense and candles." Julia sank into the softness of Marlene's couch and attempted to keep her posture erect.

Marlene lowered her head and gave a half-smile. "You do know there's a functionality behind our incense and candles, don't you?"

Treading quicksand, Julia said, "Uh, no. I mean, other than I thought you liked how it smelled." A tiny voice in her head warned, *Stupid! Wrong answer!*

"No, that would be rather frivolous of us, wouldn't it?" Marlene seated herself across from Julia with her ankles crossed in their customary tucked position. "Part of our clients' mental health issues can be detected by their personal hygiene. Or lack thereof. So after a particularly fragrant client, like my five o'clock gentleman, I find ways to clear the air. Pun intended."

Pieces clicked together and further expanded Julia's picture of how far her ignorance extended. Mona's love of heady perfumes took on a new meaning.

"But that's not why you're here, is it? We're here to talk about your latest encounter with Rowena, correct?"

Well, at least this would be quick.

"Yes, that's correct. My attempt to work on social skills with her went as badly as it could go. I've written up an incident report for you and Walter."

Passing the report to Marlene was like handing her a switchblade while Julia bobbed in an inflatable life raft.

Marlene scanned the pages for a few minutes before she slipped it into a shredder next to her chair and it mechanically chewed the pages into crosscut confetti. Julia's jaw went slack as she stared at Marlene. Had she screwed up writing the incident report on how she had screwed up with Rowena?

Marlene folded her hands into her lap and her face remained as impassive as a cat's in a bookstore window. "I would suggest you change the title from Incident Report to Progress Note, then please resubmit it to me. Because in many ways you did make progress with Rowena. Who, by the way, called me yesterday afternoon and offered the suggestion that you be fired first then hung from the highest tree, if I'm summarizing her request correctly. However, I noted that her presentation was different. Dare I say she was … energized? For Rowena, that is progress. And quite frankly, I have to admire your courage. Taking her out anywhere and asking her to step up and engage with others would not have been anything I'd have done personally, but it seemed to have gone to the heart of her fears. And lo and behold, she survived to tell the tale."

"You mean I'm not fired?"

Marlene waved her hand in a dismissive gesture. "Oh, Rowena's threatened to have us all fired. She even called the governor's office in an attempt to get me terminated a few years ago for something probably neither one of us could recall today. Rowena is scared and has been her whole life. But lately her fear has turned more toward anger. You're challenging her anger and getting to the layers of the terrified young girl buried inside."

Marlene turned her hands palm-side up. "Our goal here has been to keep her maintained and not decompensate further. But you actually reached out and asked more of her. Maybe the results were not what you'd hoped, but Rowena did risk. Risk alone is success."

Julia gaped like a fish.

Marlene sighed and continued, as though she was explaining something elementary and had to use small words. "People are a mixture of strengths and weaknesses, but sometimes you have to encourage them to push into their weaknesses. That's where strengths lie."

"But did I do damage?"

Marlene cocked her head to one side. "My, how powerful you perceive yourself to be."

Julia was caught off balance. She had expected to be chewed out for pushing Rowena too far, instead of being told she was taking on too much responsibility.

"So if I'm still her therapist, what do I do next? She hates me now." Julia slumped back into a couch cushion, all pretense of perfect posture abandoned.

"I have no idea, my dear. Quite frankly, her future at best is murky. But what I do know well about Rowena is her past. The first time I saw her, she was a tiny slip of a girl, you know, awkward in the way twelve-year-olds are before they become teens. I'd been here at the clinic about a month when she came in with her mom, who was my client. I had read in the papers about the railroad yard accident where Mr. Horn was killed, so when I was assigned Mrs. Horn, I knew she was going to be a tough case."

Julia cast back to what she had read in Rowena's charts, but this accident was unfamiliar. Then again, the five fat charts she was given went back ten years, not twenty-five. "Her father died in a train accident?"

"Yes, and it was horrific. A freak accident where Mr. Horn got pinned in between two box cars and was crushed. The worst part was he was conscious while pinned. The paramedics told him that when they separated the cars he was going to bleed out and die. Mrs. Horn had rushed to the railway yard and was a witness to it all. His death went just as they predicted, and Mrs. Horn fainted on the spot. Needless to say, she was traumatized, and poor Rowena, from everyone who knew her before, they said she was shy, but sweet. She withdrew into herself, became reclusive, and increasingly, well … odd."

Yes, the odd part. Julia got that, all right. "So then it was just Rowena and her mom?"

"Pretty much. Mrs. Horn was a teller at the bank for years, but after the accident, her concentration was impaired and she became easily overwhelmed. Today, we'd say she had Post-traumatic Stress Disorder, but back then we only knew she was in shock. I wish we could have used the treatments we have on hand now for PTSD. Still, I believe our therapy sessions, and time, did help her grief." Marlene grew silent and her eyes focused on some middle ground past Julia's shoulder. She shook her head as if coming back from a distant place. "Mrs. Horn was able to find a job at the local cafeteria, the Round 'Em Up. She did simple things, like rolling silverware into napkins, and on her good days she was able to work the serving line. But the few times I saw her there, she appeared to be on autopilot and avoided looking people in the eye. However, working at the cafeteria became its own problem."

"Too boring?" Julia said.

Marlene arched an eyebrow. "Too fattening. I take it you've never been there."

"Oh, I've been there. Twice," Julia said, with a smile and a shake of her head.

"But not three times. Obviously that's how you keep your trim figure."

When working at the paper, Julia had met Graham for lunch at the Round 'Em Up Cafeteria, or as Nick called it, the Let's Round Out Cafe. Most of the patrons were soft and pudgy, and wore sweatpants with stretchy elastic waistbands.

When inching through the long cafeteria line, she scanned the steaming serving trays piled with meat loaf, fried catfish, and planks of breaded chicken-fried steaks. Even the vegetables floated in a buttery-yellow water, and slices of pies topped with fluffy meringues and cakes coated with frostings an inch-thick precision-lined the dessert shelves.

Graham, the perpetual beanpole, heaped his tray high with chicken-fried steak, mashed potatoes and gravy, and yeast rolls with tops so shiny from an oily glaze they reflected the fluorescent lights. Julia settled on a piece of broiled fish and some steamed broccoli. However, she refused the tartar sauce for the fish and melted cheddar cheese for the limp broccoli from the woman serving behind the counter, whose gray hair was capped by a black hairnet while sweat beaded on her brow.

On their second visit, Julia picked at her plate and asked Graham how he could eat such food.

He winked at her while reaching for his pecan pie. "It's brain food."

She rolled her eyes. "Well, that explains a lot." They had laughed.

She didn't laugh now. "So Mrs. Horn brought home some meals?"

"At first, but toward the end, mother and daughter were pretty much living off the cafeteria food."

Julia whistled a low note. "I can't imagine that as a steady diet, but seeing Rowena's size—"

"And when a person is heavy, they get more depressed, isolate more, and then turn to their only comfort."

"Food," Julia and Marlene said in unison.

The older woman nodded to Julia. "So now we have two shut-ins, with Mrs. Horn on disability and her diabetes progressing at an alarming rate. Rowena's on the same path, which is why I believe she's so terrified. Terrified enough to become a store greeter."

"And I let her down."

"You lit her up." Marlene gave Julia a sharp look. "She may be angry at you, but at least there's movement. We've all tried with her … Maybe I'm asking too much of a summer intern, but if she's mad at you then she's connected to you."

"I don't want her. I don't have the training and she needs to go back to you because I know next to nothing." To Julia, the Horn case was nothing but solid brick walls.

Marlene's face grew neutral as she considered Julia. She tilted her chin up and said, "You are absolutely right. I'll let Rowena know that she's to return to me on Monday. This should be a relief to both of you."

Julia opened her mouth to continue her protests, but stopped, confused at this rapid dropping of the tug-of-war rope. For the second time in fifteen minutes, her equilibrium roiled. "Uh, you'll take her back?"

"Of course. She was always coming back to me in August. You were only to be her therapist for what, two more months?" Marlene's face remained that maddening blank slate with little hint of emotion below the surface.

Their conversation died to polite silence and Julia glanced toward the door with sweet escape on the other side. Still, she hesitated as if moored on the couch. Her gaze fell to the bookcase where tucked to the far end of a shelf was a small framed picture of a much younger Marlene standing beside a little girl who gripped the brass pole of a merry-go-round pony. Their smiles shone from the frames and Marlene's eyes were half-moons of merriment.

"What a sweet picture. Is this your daughter?"

Marlene reached over and handed the picture to Julia. "That's my darling girl, Linda. Now she's a mother herself. Daughters are always a blessing, don't you think?"

Julia studied the picture and thought of her own mother, and then of Mrs. Horn—two broken women trying to raise daughters on their own, while struggling to steady their own wobbly gravitational orbits. Maybe once you get past the surface stuff, Rowena and I have quite a bit in common.

She handed the picture back to Marlene. "What if I fail? What if I work with Rowena and I keep mucking things up?" Marlene shrugged. "Not every mistake leads to a dire consequence, but failure takes root the minute you give up. Rowena may not be conscious of it, but I believe she's testing you to see if you'll walk away from her like others have before. Perhaps the real question is, how willing are you to show up?"

Julia remained quiet as she contemplated the real question. Could she survive the summer as Rowena Horn's therapist?

Chapter 25

The cuff button of Nick's jacket dug into Julia's bare shoulder as he draped his arm around her. She resisted slipping out from under his arm and away from that biting piece of plastic because, finally, he was approaching his story's punch line. The other three couples at their table in the hotel banquet hall stared at him in anticipation.

In the past, when Nick draped his arm around her shoulder at parties, Julia was thrilled to be tucked in next to him, all claimed and secure. But tonight his arm made her shoulder sweat and the button scraped against the skin. Her attention narrowed until all she could think of was how to shrug him off.

"So when the police officers arrived," Nick said, "she was still scattering moth balls around her front yard, and mind you, had even gotten into her car and ran some over. They were crushed all over the street."

"Why would she do that?" asked a breathy woman who appeared to be only a few years out of her teens and had barely acknowledged her date by her side. He wasn't nearly as fascinated. Julia bet the woman wished she had a long straw so she could drink Nick up.

He rewarded her with an impish twinkle. "She told my cop contact she needed to crush the moth balls in order to release their smells so the neighbor's dog wouldn't do his business on her grass. She had bought boxes of those things and scattered them on the lawn and the road. He said the street stunk like his grandmother's closet."

The couples broke into laughter. People from other tables turned and smiled. Julia scooted forward with the pretense of picking up her program and Nick's arm dropped to the middle of her back. The program read, "Texas Newspaper Awards," an event Julia had attended twice before as a nominee in the newspaper photography category, but never as only Nick's date.

As the evening dragged on, Julia decided newspaper award ceremonies from the outside weren't nearly as exciting without your story or photograph in the running.

Three wooden plaques with Nick's name etched in twenty-point font fanned out in front of him on the table next to his now empty dinner plate: "Investigative Reporting." "Breaking News Reporting." "Editorial Writing." All first-place awards.

Nick turned his attention to Julia and ran the tips of his fingers down her bare back until he came to the soft blue silk of her cocktail dress. He leaned in and whispered, "You're the prettiest woman here. I can't wait to get you home and take off that amazing dress."

Julia soaked up his praise and pressed against his shoulder. The young woman across the table jerked her chair to one side and frowned across the crowded banquet hall, giving Julia and Nick her sharp profile.

Julia suppressed a smile before turning to Nick. "And I can't wait to—"

A form appeared next to them and a baritone voice jolted Julia into a stick-straight position as though she were a teen caught necking.

"The person of the hour! A beautiful woman by your side and three first-place planks in front of you. Good to be you, eh?"

Nick slipped his arm away from Julia's waist, stood up

and shook the man's hand, giving Julia a good look at the button whose outline she was sure was imprinted on her back. "Life's too short to shoot for only second-best, right?" Nick grinned. "Julia, I'd like for you to meet Steve, the managing editor of the Dallas paper I was telling you about."

Julia gave a quick wave. "Hi, Steve. Nice to finally meet you."

She cut her eyes to Nick for more information—she had never heard Nick mention a Dallas managing editor, but he and this Steve guy were already walking away.

Nick's face was alight as he called over his shoulder, "Let me get you another drink, all right, babe? Cabernet Sauvignon?"

"Pinot grigio." She doubted he heard because the two men were already deep into conversation as they headed toward the bar. Julia sighed and sat back into her chair. She picked up one of Nick's awards and ran her finger across his engraved name, her face a blurred reflection from inside the dull brass.

"Hey, oddball," came a voice from behind her. "You can't shoot laser beams from your eyes and etch your name over lover boy's."

A smile bubbled up as Julia tilted her head up to Graham standing next to her, dressed in a plaid sports coat over a scruffy pair of jeans. "Shopping your closet again?" she said.

Graham unfolded his long frame into Nick's vacated seat and placed his hand across his heart. "You wound me, woman! Up until yesterday, this fine piece of polyester resided on the suit rack at Goodwill. And a bargain at eight dollars, I might add," he said, tugging at the lapels. "But phew, I had to hang it outside last night to air out. I think the previous owner was a smoker."

Julia laughed and shook her head. "Well, you never

were the fashion plate."

"Truer words were never spoken. But Daddy's got to buy some new monolights, umbrellas, and strobes. Current lighting kit doesn't have the punch I need for an upcoming glamour shoot for the Lifestyle section."

The wavelets of nostalgia that had been lapping up to Julia the entire awards evening spilled over. For journalists, award nights and fashion shoots were the cherries on top of complicated cakes.

Graham's face turned wavy as tears welled into her eyes. "I miss you, Graham. I don't know, hearing about the stories tonight and seeing so many people from the newsroom, makes me wish I could come back."

Graham picked up Julia's empty glass and waggled it at her. "Girl, you've got your wine goggles on. Besides, we've already established newspapers aren't for you. I don't even know if they're for me, but unlike you, I lack the motivation to consider anything else."

"No, you're meant for photography. Don't be all modest. And congrats on your awards! Even Tuckus-in-the-dirt won, right?" she said as she brushed aside a tear trailing down her cheek.

"Finally! You got back to talking about me, because it is all about me," Graham said with a laugh. He scanned the room. "Okay, hanging with weepy you makes it obvious my beer goggles are drying up. See a waiter anywhere?"

Julia craned her neck to scan the room. Her gaze stuttered to a stop at Nick talking to a woman with a sheath of shellacked blond-hair that could only belong to Calliope Smythe. Suspicion roiled and coiled and snapped.

"What is she doing here?"

"Who?"

"Calliope. The talking head next to Nick. This is a print media event, not broadcast."

Graham shrugged. "Don't know. Maybe the hotel didn't fill the moat properly with crocodiles. She's probably some poor sap's date. Should I tell her there's a sale on Miss Clairol hair dye at the Piggly Wiggly? That should clear her out."

Julia stared unsmiling at Graham.

He nudged her with his elbow. "C'mon, relax and unclench something. Nick chose you, not some bimbo bombshell."

"You can stop trying to make me feel better any time, if that's what you're trying to do."

"Well, take him off the market. Put a ring on it, or whatever the hell women are saying these days. When is the wedding date, anyway?"

A waiter walked by with a tray of champagne glasses, and Graham stood and swooped up two then handed one to Julia.

Julia set the flute aside. "Nick's pushing for a Christmas wedding, but I kind of like the idea of June, or October. Fall's always pretty with the leaves changing color and all."

"Oh yeah? You got a year picked out? Somehow you don't seem all on fire to book a wedding hall." Graham paused before sipping his drink.

"I want to get married, but between my school and his work … I don't know, things keep coming up."

Graham and Julia stared at each other and the silence stretched. After a few moments, Graham drained his glass, set it on the table, and said in a low, conspiratorial voice, "Listen, I know of this thing they call an airplane. You go to where the airplanes hang out, it may be called an airport, and there you buy this other thing called a ticket. Then poof!" He fanned his fingers out like a magician. "You're gone."

Julia snorted and shook her head. "It's not like that. I love Nick, but things feel so muddy lately."

Graham considered Julia a moment before standing and extending his hand out to her. Puzzled, she took it and he pulled her up.

"Muddy times call for clear action, girl! And by action, I mean dancing."

But rather than going to the dance floor, Graham wound her through the crowd to where Nick and Calliope stood chatting near the bar. As they approached, Nick threw his head back and roared as though something Calliope said was hilarious. In his hand was Julia's ruby glass of Cabernet Sauvignon. Julia tried to squirm away from Graham, but he held her hand in his firm grip.

"Calliope, the fair damsel of Channel Seven," Graham chirped. "You brighten our drab existence with your pixelated effervescence."

Surprise fleeted across Nick and Calliope's faces when they saw Graham. Seeing Julia behind Graham, Nick broke into a too-broad smile and clapped the photographer on the shoulder.

"Graham, my man! Congrats on your awards tonight. I lost count after two."

"Same back atcha, bro," Graham said before turning to Calliope, who thirty seconds earlier had been all but standing on her tip toes while she craned her head up at Nick. Annoyance marred her china-doll face as she stared at the sight of the photographer in his ghastly plaid jacket.

Graham blew through her bitch force field with a cheerful, "Ms. Smythe! It is known from all the far-flung corners of Elston that on the dance floor you put Ginger Rogers to shame."

Her features scrunched up. "Who?"

"You're right, an ancient nobody. Ginger Who? But I

must have this dance with you as I foresee that this song will someday be our song," he said as he gave a short bow, and then offered his crooked elbow.

The DJ had swung from a slow dance into the growling vocals of The Commodores' "Brick House."

The word "no" formed on Calliope's crimson-painted lips when she caught sight of Julia. She hesitated then slipped her willowy arm around Graham's and beamed up at him. It heartened Julia to see that one of her perfect front teeth had a smear of lipstick across its startling whiteness.

"Why, Gordon, I'd love to dance. Thank you for asking," Calliope purred.

Graham gave Julia the tiniest of an eye-roll before he whisked Calliope away.

Couples streamed to the dance floor past Julia and Nick as the bass vibrations from the speakers filled the room. But she doubted music was the reason her heart beat so heavy and fast. She set her jaw and waited, determined she wasn't going to be the first to break the silence between them.

Nick wrapped his arm around her and proffered the glass of wine. "My rescuer! Thank you for saving me from people full of small talk."

Julia drank down half the glass of wine then said, "Oh, yes, lots of small people full of lots of small talk."

He gave her an assessing gaze, as if she were a time bomb and he had to decide whether to snip the red wire or the black wire. He barked a laugh. "You're not jealous of me talking to another journalist, are you?"

She raised an eyebrow at the word "journalist" being used to describe Calliope, but let it go. She threw back the rest of her drink in one gulp. "Funny how you filled in the blanks there all on your own. And I didn't appreciate sitting at the table while you promised to get me a drink, but you milled about instead. I felt forgotten."

She hated how petty she sounded, but she was mad and had decided to just let the truths fly.

"Oh jeez, Julia. This is a social event. Lighten up. You don't see me getting twisted into knots because you were talking with Graham, now do you?"

The sparks of a headache burrowed behind her right eye as she struggled to find the words to describe the worlds of difference between Graham and Calliope. Which she knew that he knew. And what about that man who had approached their table and spirited Nick away? To avoid a messy fight, she seized on that thread. "Who was guy from the Dallas paper? Steve?"

Sunlight broke across Nick's face. "Yeah! I want to tell you about what he said, but not here. Grab your purse and we'll talk on the way home."

They made their way back to the now-empty table to collect her things and his plaques. The music and chatter in the room crescendoed and Julia wasn't sure if her mind was fuzzy from the wine or her anxiety from Nick's excitement. Either was, the feeling in her head had a sharp, needling quality. He hurried them down the elevator and to his car in the underground parking lot.

Once they closed the car doors and the quiet settled around them, Nick swiveled to her and said, "Steve told me he's been following my work for the past few years and thinks I may be a good candidate for a job opening up on news side. He wants me to call on Monday and set up an interview with their scheduler in about two weeks." Despite the dark cloaking them in the car, he seemed to glow.

The word "scheduler" snapped Julia awake and chased away her tipsy feeling. The Dallas paper, with its one-hundred-and-fifty-year-old masthead, had power, influence, and apparently, schedulers. Julia imagined Nick sitting in the center hub of a massive metro newsroom, calling a source and feeling that click of satisfaction at how quickly the person on the other end of the phone hurried to take his call. The entire time she had known Nick at *The Elston Daily News*, he groused at how many times he had to leave multiple messages before someone got around to calling him back.

Knowledge settled like snow. Nick would get the job and that would cement their plans to leave Elston and set up their new life in Dallas. Another image popped into her head of Nick's life being thrust in complicated center stages, but where would that leave her? No crystal ball was needed for her to know she'd be floating on the outskirts as a spousal appendage, reading her husband's stories from the same inky pages as her neighbors.

"Wow. Dallas," Julia said as she struggled to slow her tumbling thoughts. "That is amazing, but it all seems so fast."

"Yeah, maybe fast to you, but next month makes my fifth year here. It's time, Julia. This is our big break and we've got no choice but to grab it."

It was as though a train had suddenly screeched to a stop in front of them and Nick had leaped on board and was pulling her with him.

"But wait. I've got another year of school. And you're working on that exposé. And to move all of our stuff would be …"

She flapped her arms as if she might as well have been trying to sprout wings and fly out of the car. Then it came to her: Nick would hire movers, transfer all his on-going stories to another reporter, quit the paper, and maybe quit her if she didn't get with the program. Finishing her master's degree in Dallas would be on her to figure out.

Nick cupped his hands around her face and gave her a deep kiss. She could taste the oak flavor of bourbon on his lips. "Baby, that's all small stuff. But Steve sought me out and you know that only happens when somebody higher up is interested. You'll love Dallas! We no longer have to drive up there for long weekends. All those restaurants and theaters and concerts are waiting for us, twenty-four seven! And this job will pay better, so you can relax more and take time for yourself. You know, find balance, like that shrink guy recommended."

"Dr. Donovan encouraged me to work. Going to school is how I'm trying to find balance," Julia said. Tears blurred her vision at the thought of letting go of her graduate program at Elston. A mournful tug arose in her chest at the idea of leaving the clinic and this small world she had carved out for herself.

Nick pulled back, as if surprised by her reaction. "Darling, you know Elston is only a steppingstone. Every day I'm here, I feel my energy sapped away by dealing with people satisfied to settle for so little. And anything in the city will trump this dinky college. You'll find a better program and transfer your hours over. Come on—even your internship is just you talking to a conveyor belt of sad sacks. If I can be flexible, then so can you, especially if we're going to start a family soon. Balance is our goal."

"Our goal? You're just telling me I can't handle pressure." And as if to prove his point, her tears betrayed her, more from anger than sadness.

"Okay, I don't need you getting upset and twisting off into another episode." Color rose into his face, but his gaze was level and unwavering.

"An episode! Is that what you thought I had?" She swiped at the tears on her cheeks, wishing she could also bat away his words. "You talk about balance. But what you mean is what's best for you!"

Julia closed her eyes and imagined how they looked from the outside as they squared off against each other in the car—her pinched face versus Nick's stubborn scowl. A twenty-year-old memory flashed through her of a fight between her parents. Her father had stormed out on yet another evening meal to attend a hearing, a meeting, or anything more important than Julia and her mom seated there. They had stared after him as the meatloaf and two side veggies cooled on the dining room table.

But there were so many other memories of her father breezing in on a charged cloud of charisma—tossing his jacket on a chair, spreading out his paperwork over the coffee table, and grabbing the phone. He would speak in a loud voice and punctuate the conversation with short barks of laughter. And just like that, he'd peck the cheeks of Julia and her mother before breezing back out with the door slamming behind him. A hollow quiet always filled his wake.

One time her mom leaned against the kitchen counter with a tea towel dangling from her hand as she had said to no one in particular, "Your daddy's big important life." The message was clear: Daddy was the Problem.

Now, as Nick sat forward with his gaze on some middle distance past the parking garage, his jaw muscles knotted, another thought dawned. Maybe her mom was the other half of the Problem. Her mother sat and stewed and fumed. But she didn't create an action plan, and she didn't stand up and fight for what she wanted. She believed she was helpless, and Julia, the ever-watchful daughter, felt helpless, too. Julia didn't want to be a victim anymore, wandering in circles only to follow in her mom's well-worn tracks.

She let go a shaky breath. "Nick, what are we doing here? We're getting ahead of ourselves and you don't even have an interview scheduled. Can we both just slow down and hit reset?"

Inch by inch, he turned back to Julia, his face a mask of calm. His lips spread into his familiar, sensual smile that could rope her heart, but in the center of his eyes was ice where the warmth didn't touch. "You know, I was thinking the exact same thing." He kissed her forehead and started the car.

As he backed out of the parking spot, Julia understood Nick wasn't thinking the exact same thing, not even close. She was seized by an overwhelming desire to open the door, lurch out of the car, and sprint away.

Julia fingered the seat belt clip above the latch, not compressing the two together. She contemplated the door handle, mesmerized, and could almost feel the cool metal in her hand.

Beeping filled the car and Nick said, "Hey, babe. Buckle up, will you?"

She squeezed the clip and latch together until they locked with a sharp click. The beeping stopped and the air between them fell quiet.

As they slid past the rows of parked cars, Julia considered a hard truth: from a distance, leaving was easy. Like how a cloud bank looked solid from the ground. But in reality, if you stepped out onto a cloud, the unsubstantial mist would flow past as you fell through the shifting layers of gray.

Perhaps she was her mother's daughter after all, and all the insight in the world wasn't going to change that one whit. She exhaled a tired sigh and stared out the window as they drove out of the garage and merged into the moving stream of traffic.

Chapter 26

Julia's mom held two wedding gowns up by their wooden hangers and her arms quivered slightly from the weight. Julia selected a dress of ivory taffeta brocade, embroidered with lace and seed pearls. She, too, sagged under the heft and was amazed her mom had held both dresses up for as long as she did. Running her fingers across the topography of pearls nestled into the stiff lace, she tried to decide between "no way" or "no way in hell."

"Oh my gosh, Mom! How many yards of material are in this thing?" Julia turned to the bridal shop mirror and held the dress against herself. The reflection showed an expanse of shimmery silk cascading to the floor. She shook her head.

Her mother exchanged gowns. "Here, this one is lighter, the tag says it's a crinkle chiffon."

Julia draped the filmy, dusty-rose gown up to her chest and faced her image. Now it looked like her head floated at the top of a pink waterfall. "It's lighter, but doesn't this look more like a fancy nightgown?"

"Well, no nightgown I've ever seen." Her mom scanned the bridal shop lined with rows and rows of gowns under insistent fluorescent lights. "My goodness, I should have worn more comfortable shoes. I thought I saw a chair somewhere when we walked in."

"Oh, Mom, I'm sorry. There's an ottoman, beside the veil display. This is why I thought coming here during my lunch hour would be a good time to look around, so we could, you know, focus our energies. But not take too long."

Julia's mom sank onto the large square cushion and took off a shoe to flex the arch of her foot. "I'm glad you two are deciding to go forward with the wedding plans, but suddenly it seems a bit rushed. Is there something else going on?"

Julia glanced at the price tag on the dress and blanched: Just under $5,500. She placed it back on the rack. "No, nothing really," she said in any airy tone, avoiding her mother's gaze as she busied herself by looking through a row of gowns. "Nick wants to move things forward, is all. We were thinking of June, but he thought it might be too hot. So we might go for April."

Actually the wedding, his job, and her finding another graduate program in Dallas had become competing bargaining chips between them. To appease Nick, Julia had fallen into knee-jerk agreeableness. The reward was less friction between them, and even Mrs. Meyer had been sunnier with her. It all seemed to be a small price to pay.

Still, as the details of the wedding were hammered out, she was becoming less and less attached to the unfolding plan, as though it were an event that belonged to another woman.

Her mother grew still. "Well, sometimes, even if people are careful, things can happen and there's more of a need to get married. Not that there's anything wrong with that and heaven knows you wouldn't be the first bride to push up her wedding date."

Julia laughed. "No, it's nothing like that. We're not shopping for a wedding *and* a baby wardrobe. It's just, I don't know ... complicated."

Her mother's eyes narrowed, but she kept quiet.

A slight man in a paisley waistcoat hurried toward them with several wedding gowns folded over his arms, the silk and satin rustling like leaves. He hung them on a large hook next to the bank of mirrors and clapped his hands together. "Now then, darling, here's round three. With your trim figure, I insist you try on this tulle mermaid gown. The satin lattice really works the dress and will just capture the copper tones in your hair."

The gown's hourglass shape stood out as though someone already wore it.

"Um, wow. That looks like it would be really tight, how would I even be able to sit?"

"Sit? My darling, it's your wedding! You have the rest of your life to lounge around, but on your big day you are the center of attention. Not to worry, though. This material has some give. Here, go try it on then come on out and give us a show." He parted the curtain to the dressing rooms.

Ten minutes later she emerged, sweaty from the effort it took to wriggle into the dress that corseted her torso so much she could only take shallow breaths. She blushed when she saw herself in the triplicate reflection of the mirrors, front and side views exposed. All eyes would definitely be on her rear if she dared to walk the aisle in this number.

Her phone rang and Julia pulled it from her purse that was on the floor next to her mother, grateful for the diversion. "Wait, I've got to take this, it's my … um, fiancé." Her tongue stumbled on that word. "Boyfriend" had been much easier to say.

"Hello?" she said, walking a few feet away from her mom and the salesman.

"Found your dream dress yet?" Nick said. He sounded chipper.

"Of your dreams is more like it. The bridal guy has me in this dress that shows every inch of my panty lines. So what's up?"

Nick chuckled. "Sorry, still imagining that panty line

thing. But I want you to be the first to know, I got a call from the Dallas paper and they asked me to come up for an interview next Tuesday. Let's go together so we can start checking out some neighborhoods, preferably within thirty minutes of the newsroom."

Now she knew why his voice sounded odd—this was Nick happy. He hadn't been this glowing on the night they got engaged. The room took a sharp tilt and the lights grew bright and hot. Sweat beaded her brow as Julia struggled against the dress and walked knock-kneed to the back of the store. She stopped in front of a mannequin sheathed in a slip of lace, tulle, and a dusting of seed pearls. *Not a slip*, she reminded herself. *A wedding gown, probably going for thirty-five hundred.*

"Dallas? This Tuesday?" Her mind was a parrot throwing back the stickier words. A shard of memory pierced the fog. "Wait a minute. I can't go on Tuesday, that's my long day at the clinic and I have at least six people scheduled." Silence flowed and Julia wondered if it were possible to hear a shrug over the phone.

"Well, cancel them!" Nick finally said. "Push them off onto someone else and clear your calendar. Don't you know I'm clearing mine? And besides, what's going to impact us more? One day of your summer job or my interview?"

Her six clients' faces came to mind. "This job is important to me, and I just can't dump people because someone called and asked you to show up! Did it occur to you check in with me first?"

She looked up into the flat, black eyes of the mannequin who gazed nonplussed past her to the plate glass windows at the front of the store.

During the pause that followed, Julia imagined Nick's puzzled face at the thought of her as anything other than a willing appendage. "Honey, my calling you now *is* my thinking of you, because I know you can reschedule those people. Besides, come September you won't have a future there. Even that clinic may not have a future." Nick used the patient tone he'd adopted in the last few weeks that drove her mad.

"What?"

"One of my sources in the mayor's office told me that in the upcoming budget cuts, the Elston Clinic is slated to take a big hit."

"How big?"

"Big. They're funded mostly through Medicaid contracts, but the state budget analysts have been requesting a major restructure. That place has been running in the red for years and your clinical director knows it. Apparently, he's been fighting the cuts, and pretty much alone. My source said the clinic's board hasn't been as strong an advocate as other boards in neighboring counties. This year, the director won't be able to hold back the tide. These scalebacks are hitting other state-funded clinics, too, but they'll probably weather the storms better. Either way, sweetie, if this goes down, the employees may be cut by half and there will be zero chance of a job there for you after graduation. So turns out our move couldn't be timed better."

"But I don't care about a job for me at the clinic in the future!"

Julia thought of the staffers. Angel and Glen couldn't both stay, so one of them would be cut. Mona's job would probably not be considered essential. And Paulie! Paulie would get the ax like a Thanksgiving turkey wandering around a Butterball factory.

Her stomach lurched as she considered the biggest domino to fall: the clients. There were already too few available slots for counseling and medical appointments with the circuit psychiatrist, often booked out for months. Now many of the clients, some of whom were barely hanging in there, would slip all the way through the cracks.

"Of course you don't care about a job there," Nick said, sounding relieved as though Julia made sense at last. "You're going to find a much better job in the city. This could not have been scripted better. What timing, right?"

The city. How quickly Nick was kicking Elston to the curb and embracing Dallas. She willed her tone to be neutral. "Yeah, the timing is something."

"All right, enough chit-chat—I've got to get to a briefing. Look, babe, what I told you is strictly on the inside, okay? Don't tip your hand to anyone at the clinic about what you know because I don't want anyone figuring out I'm your source."

Julia's voice turned to ice. "Protecting sources above all else, right?" Muffled voices of a side conversation came through the earpiece and the low rumble of Nick's response. "Got to skate," Nick said. "Now go pick out a beautiful dress that will show all your assets. Your panty line may be pure bonus. And listen, we may need to go even earlier on the wedding date. Let's talk tonight."

Her knees softened like warm wax and she slumped onto the mannequin's pedestal until the fiberglass figure wobbled above her. The dress cinched around her rib cage and waist, forcing her to take shallow breaths. A thin hand reached up and steadied the mannequin as Julia's mom peered down with a questioning expression.

"Honey, are you okay?" Her mom crouched in front of her.

Julia held her phone out as if the answer were etched on its glass screen. "Nick is going to Dallas for a job interview and he's got a good chance at getting it," she said, spilling the secret she had agreed to keep quiet with Nick until he got a definite offer from the paper. "If this happens we may be moving there in what, early fall? Maybe late August? And what if they need him sooner, then God!"

Julia let the phone fall to her mother's feet. "What if we have to move next month!"

Her mother picked up the phone and handed it back. "This is sudden, but Dallas! Oh, honey, isn't what you two have talked about? And with Nick being so young, those paper people must really see something in …" She hesitated when her eyes met Julia's.

"Mom, he's talking about moving the wedding up," Julia wailed, as she struggled to stand.

Multiple emotions flickered across her mother's face before the worry lines smoothed out between her eyebrows and she gave a shaky laugh. With an airy wave of her hand she said, "You've only got a case of the bridal nerves. It could be a blessing if the wedding is moved up. You'd have less time to be nervous!"

All of a sudden, her mom jumped and cried "Ow!" Julia's hand was clamped around her wrist.

"Mom! Stop defending Nick as if this is all okay. I'm feeling railroaded here just as I've begun to build something for myself."

Pulling herself free, her mother said, "For heaven's sake, Julia, compose yourself!"

She rubbed her wrist and lowered her voice, glancing back at the salesman who was watching them with a puzzled expression near the bank of full-length mirrors. "He's a good man, so don't push him away. Don't do what I did and be afraid to change. Maybe if I had taken more chances, been braver like your father wanted, we would have stayed married. A wedding is something you do in one day. Staying married is far harder."

"Shouldn't compromise be a two-way street?"

"He's asking you to be part of his life. Not everything is

fair, and besides, fair is a child's game. You'll create your own life wherever you go, sweetie. But a home and children can fill your life regardless of a zip code." Wistfulness wound through her mother's words.

A vision came to Julia of a suburban street with dappled sunlight splashed across green lawns as she walked down the sidewalk with a child's pudgy hand held in hers. She rubbed her fingertips against her temples to push back the threatening headache.

Her thoughts were a jumble: Nick wanted a home and family—all the things she wanted. And what her mother said was true and reasonable. So why in the middle of all this truth and reasonableness did moving to Dallas feel wrong in her bones? Some core piece of her flexed a protective muscle so all she could do now was stand rooted next to this mannequin with a thousand-yard stare.

"Mom, I know you're telling me to be realistic, but if I don't ask for what I want and be unreasonable, then how do I move forward? Dad could be a bastard, but weren't there times when you were a pushover because it was easier? Weren't there things you wanted to fight for?"

Julia's mom inhaled sharply and her nostrils flared. "Wait, how has this become about me?" Tears sparkled in her eyes.

Julia's go-to emotion, guilt, tried to muzzle her. But before she could apologize and back down, anger elbowed forward. "Because you were the only one around for me to learn from. You didn't stand up for yourself, and now when I'm trying to find some kind of ..." Clouds billowed in as she struggled to call up the exact word for what she was feeling.

"What, Julia? What more do you need?" Her mother sounded flummoxed.

"I don't know. More meaning?" She met her mother's

gaze and refused to look away.

Her mother stared back, opened her mouth as if to speak, then shut it. Julia imagined herself through her mother's eyes—an entitled child in an adult's body who had so much, but was still clamoring for more.

The salesman fluttered up, glancing between the two women. "Ladies, is there a problem? Being a future bride isn't as simple as deciding whether to wear your hair up or down, now is it, my dear?" He tsk-tsked and shook his head, as if he were in on the conversation.

Julia frowned at him and tried to retrieve her previous urgency to find a dress. All the wedding dresses lined up around them like snowy shrouds.

He clapped his hands as if to stop the lengthening silence. "Now if you desire something a bit edgier, you know, not so traditional, then I can show you a collection we just got in this morning. Still in their shipping cartons."

"What she wants, I doubt your store sells," her mother said, flicking her hand as though shooing away a fly.

Julia shot her a look before turning to the salesman. "What my mother means is this my first time to try on dresses, and while you have a lovely selection—"

The phone buzzed in her hand and Julia glanced at the number. "I'm sorry, but I need to take this."

The salesman, probably sensing a lost cause, stuffed his tape measure into his pocket and walked away.

Julia pressed the receiver. "Hello?"

Walter's voice filled her ear. "Oh good, you answered. Say, Julia, I know you're running an errand right now, but we could use you here."

A loud voice bleated in the background, "Yeah, tell princess to quit her gallivantin' around and come on back here. Tell her to grab a cardboard box so I can plunk her desk junk 'n it!"

Rowena. Oh, Christ.

Sounds became muffled as though Walter had covered the phone with his hand. Rowena's demanding tones drowned out the low murmurs of his voice. Walter returned and said, "Yes, well, as you may have surmised, Rowena is here and requesting a meeting between the three of us to talk about—"

"Gettin' yer candy-ass fired, princess!" Rowena bull-horned in the background.

"Um, the quicker the better, okay?" he whispered. The line went dead.

Standing a few paces away, her mother shook her head. "Let me guess. Trouble at the office?"

Julia's headache punched a root deep into the center of her forehead. She closed her eyes against the bloom of pain. "Not now, Mom. I need to get out of this gown. I'm sorry our outing didn't work out like we'd hoped."

She gave her mother a quick hug before she trundled to the dressing room, the hourglass skirt binding her legs so much she was forced to take mincing half-steps. She fought the urge to take one long, bold stride and tear out the tulle hems of the mermaid wedding dress just to hear the satisfying rip of setting her legs free.

Chapter 27

Julia entered the lobby into a bubble of quiet. Mona gave her a curt nod, then rolled her eyes toward the offices behind her.

Not bothering to ask what she meant, Julia trudged down the hallway to Walter's office until she reached his half-opened door. The director sat at his desk, typing on his computer. She exhaled a held breath. Maybe the crisis was over and he'd already convinced Rowena to leave.

Julia stopped. Just to the right, a battered sneaker bobbed up and down below a chunky calf. She knocked on the door. As it swung open, Rowena, who sat crammed into a corner chair, stared at Julia with her head lowered so that her double chins morphed into a trio above the collar of her faded t-shirt.

Walter looked up from his keyboard. A taciturn "Good, you're here" replaced his usual broad smile.

Julia stood in the doorway, reluctant to walk into the room. "Hi, Walter. Hi, Rowena."

"Tell her she's fired," Rowena barked. "Jus' like the ones I got fired before."

"You haven't gotten anyone fired before and no one is getting fired today, Rowena." Walter sounded tired, as though they'd gone over this point several times already.

Rowena sat up straighter. "I got that Becky woman fired."

"She moved to Portland to be near family. Now let's discuss something more substantive, shall we?" Walter turned to Julia. "Rowena feels your first outing wasn't as productive as she'd hoped for."

"Productive? She set me right up! Took me smack into the middle of the same store where I'd been abused, only so's I could get a second round!"

He shot Julia a puzzled glance.

"Rowena got short-changed at the Penny Pincher the week before," Julia said, tensing for an explosion from Rowena at its mere mention.

"Ah, yes, I heard something about that." Walter's expression remained mild, revealing nothing. "But, Rowena, wasn't that the reason Julia wanted you to go back? To face your fears? I hear the hurt and anger in your voice, but at least you tried something different. Making changes isn't always easy, and what you did was very brave."

Rowena's eyes grew shimmery with tears before she blinked them away. "Marlene pawned me off on this kid here. She's supposed to be helping me with my sad times, not setting up a mess of new things to get all sad about!"

"That wasn't my intention! There are all kinds of therapy out there, and having a job may be one of them. It helps you from isolating."

Rowena gaped at her. "How can I be isolated when I'm up in the house all the time with my mom? And what if my getting a job makes me crack, or something? And don't be trotting out that baby steps nonsense, neither."

Heat rose into Julia's face. "But baby steps is how you ease into—"

Walter's words spilled in between them. "How is your mom doing these days? I haven't seen her in several months now." His tone was calm, even conversational, as he folded his hands in his lap.

Thrown off by the change of topic, Julia closed her mouth, rebuked by what she could only guess was Walter's intervention.

"She's doing okay," Rowena said, but fear seemed to flicker in her eyes, until sahe straightened, as though a thought had occurred to her. "And she says it might be a good idea for me to get on disability benefits. That's the other thing I come to talk to you about. You helped Mom get on it and she says you or Angel or Glen can help me with the forms."

Julia slumped against the door frame. *If Rowena got on disability, it would kill any motivation for her to bother learning new job skills.*

Walter remained motionless, but his focus seemed sharper. From his stillness Julia knew he didn't want her on disability either.

"What makes you think you need disability, Rowena?" Walter said.

"'Cause I need money comin' in. And Mom says I can't hold down no steady work." Rowena jerked her thumb in Julia's direction. "And that one there helped me suss that out, pretty plain. So I need to get a jump on them forms."

"Well, your mother has medical problems associated with her disability, but you are, thankfully, healthy," Walter said.

"I can't keep no job," Rowena shot back. "No jobs I'd like, anyhow. You, or that kid there, has to help explain my situation to the disability people, 'specially after that whole store flop. Mom told me to get that across to you."

Julia took a few steps into the room. "Rowena, that's no way to live your life. You're too young to just give up."

Rowena sent back a flat stare. "Getting on disability ain't givin' up. You people are all the time harpin' on about healthy self-care. This'll be *my* healthy self-care."

"You know," Walter said, stretching out his long legs and crossing them at the ankles, as though they were all chatting around a campfire, "as far as I can see, you do have a job. And it's a job you do quite well. You take care of your mother."

Perhaps sensing a trap, Rowena said with an edge in her voice, "Yeah, I do. Everyone knows that about me. But that ain't something you put on a résumé. You can't fool me on that."

Walter shrugged and glanced up at Julia. "Taking care of people isn't easy. Some might even say it's a gift."

A flame of comprehension sparked and Julia blessed Walter silently. "Actually. Rowena. there's a whole field of jobs where you can care for people. Memory units in senior centers, hospitals, clinics, rehab centers—"

"Like I said, I ain't taking care of no strangers. My own mama is one thing, but a bunch of strangers is whole other ball of wax."

"But they won't be strangers if you give them a week or two," Julia said.

"I've known you for a bit and I can't say I'm wantin' to give you no sponge bath," Rowena said with a dismissive snort.

"That's not my point."

"You got a point? Well, trot it on out!"

Frustrated, Julia fell quiet. Rowena's stubbornness had a way of bringing out the stubbornness in her.

"Wasn't Julia's point to try something different? The store may not be your dream job, but it does get you out of the house and experiencing new things. Remember what you and I have talked about? *There are no happy hermits*," Walter said in his I've-got-all-the-time-in-the-world voice.

"Where the hell did they get all them hermits to poll, if they're all skittish?" Rowena crossed her arms.

"I think Julia and you were on the right track. It's important for you to tolerate being uncomfortable because that is how we learn new things."

"What the heck was I learnin' at the Penny Pincher? How mean people are?"

"No. How strong *you* are. Whether or not people are mean, friendly, or look right through you isn't the point. Creating resiliency is the point. You don't get strong by avoiding problems. You get stronger by pushing through those feelings of giving up, and then discovering solutions."

Rowena's jaw muscles knotted. She glared up at Walter under eyebrows scrunched together into a deep frown line. "I ain't no pushover weakling, if that's what you mean."

"Of course not. That's exactly what we're talking about and I'm glad we're all on the same page here. You're stronger than you think you are and it's important for you to begin your second session of this treatment plan with Julia."

The spotlight swung back to Julia and she felt like an actor who hadn't been given this page of the script. "Uh, yeah. Let's look at my calendar and see what looks good for next week."

"I ain't going back to that damn store, Walter! Let's get straight on that." Rowena stood up, cloaked in fury.

The phone intercom beeped, and Mona's voice broke through. "Sorry to interrupt, Walter, but Charlie from the board is on the phone. He says it's urgent."

"Patch him on through." Walter stood up, his tone all business. "I'll let you and Julia work that out, Rowena. Between the two of you, you'll come up with a plan." He opened the door for them, and they filed out into the hallway.

Julia and Rowena stood face-to-face in the cramped hallway, and Julia became aware of how powerfully built Rowena was. She yearned to take a step back, but Walter's door behind her was close enough to hear his low voice rumbling on the phone. She could only assume the news he was about to receive wasn't good.

While she struggled for something to say, Rowena saved her the trouble by snapping, "Walter can shove me outta his office, but he can't make me do diddly-squat with you."

Julia sighed. "I know that, Rowena, but I've already spoken with the store manager and he said he's willing to give you another try, maybe on a quieter day, as long as you promise to stick with the script."

In truth, the manager had only told Julia when she called that he would consider allowing Rowena back in for a training session. But she was hopeful she might be able to sway him with Walter's help.

Surprise lit in Rowena's eyes, which then clouded with suspicion.

"Give it a try, Rowena. If you're trying, then you're learning, just like Walter said." Julia reached up and touched Rowena's arm.

The large woman jumped as though Julia had sent a surge of electricity through her. "The only thing I need from you is help with them there forms. I need to get before a judge and have you speak up for me."

Christ, back to this again!

A surge of anger wove through Julia's fear. "And all I'm asking of you is to give our job training another session." Julia struggled to keep her voice modulated.

The two women stared at each other, and Julia's hands felt cold and clammy.

Rowena curled up her lip before she spun around and clomped down the hallway. A moment later Mona shouted, "Rowena, put those back right now!"

The front lobby door banged and Julia walked into the lobby to find Mona fuming from behind her desk. She glanced up at Julia, shook her head, and reached into a cardboard box under her desk. Pulling out a stack of well-thumbed magazines, she stalked into the lobby, and from chest high, dropped the stack onto the chipped coffee table with a decisive thwack.

A mother and small boy sitting in the corner of the lobby gawked at them as the mother put a protective arm around the child and drew him closer. Through the lobby's glass door, Julia could just make out the diminishing figure of Rowena, once again, stalking away from her, a brace of magazines under her meaty arm.

All of these sticky threads she'd acquired since working at the clinic, Julia could just snip clean away as she and Nick made their escape into Dallas. Just give up, write the report for Rowena, wash her hands of the whole affair, and chalk the past year up to another one of life's experiences.

She bit her lower lip and willed herself to begin the process of closing her work on Rowena's case, but instead she watched her client until she disappeared around a corner. Gone, but still annoying in Julia's head.

Chapter 28

Julia sat on Marlene's couch, bookended between a neat stack of charts to be reviewed on her left and a spilled stack of completed ones to her right. Marlene sat across from her, ankles crossed and hands folded neatly in her lap. Julia cut her eyes to the left stack and was relieved that it was shorter than the splayed charts on her right, signaling they were over halfway done with this week's supervision review.

The reviews left Julia drained. The act of remaining attentive, and being so alert and ready for Marlene's probing questions, always took it out of her. Still, Marlene's tips and the knowledge she was attempting to transfer must have seeped through, because Julia's sessions with her clients flowed better with fewer of those awkward silences. Nonetheless, Friday afternoon supervision time was hardly fun and games.

Julia exhaled a short puff of breath, grabbed the next chart, and opened it. "Now here's Erin from our group, the young woman with the little girl. I find it hard to get a read on her because she's so quiet. If she wasn't asked a direct question, I don't think she'd say 'boo' the entire hour."

"And they're still living in the shelter?" Marlene asked, her silver reading glasses perched on the end of her nose.

Julia sat up straighter and tried to recall what Angel had told her about Erin and her daughter. "Yes, but I believe they're on the waiting list for a Section 8 apartment. It may take a few more weeks before a unit opens up."

"And her employment status?"

"She interviewed at several hotels as a housekeeper, and she has a lead on a job with that big hotel down by the highway near the Mercer Street exit."

"This information is recorded in the chart?"

Julia fumbled through the pages, scanning her notes and Angel's caseworker reports. "Um, no, I don't see it written down anywhere. It was just something Angel told me in the break room, I think Tuesday or Wednesday."

There was a beat of silence as Marlene continued to peer at her. "If it's not in the case notes then it didn't happen. Remember, therapists have a professional obligation to record, record, record. Continuity is essential in order for us to coordinate services. No one can possibly keep all this information in their heads."

"Yes, ma'am. You're right," Julia said, chastened. Marlene's notes, of course, were perfect. Paragraph upon paragraph was written with her rounded, Palmer-style handwriting that detailed client's statements, their moods, behaviors, and progress toward goals. There weren't even strike-outs due to grammatical errors.

"Be prepared for Erin to go back to her husband," Marlene said. "The pressures on her are high, despite all we're doing to help. The draw to return to her abusive husband may be too much to resist if he's been the only support she's had. Especially if he can locate her and start either his charm or bullying campaign."

"And once he gets her back, the abuse starts all over again."

Shrugging her shoulders, Marlene said, "I've seen this scenario played out too many times. We hope Miss Erin stays the course and creates a new life. Check with Angel before you leave and find out the exact status of her employment and housing, then write an addendum report. Oh, and schedule an individual session with her before our next group." Marlene reached for her teacup with the sprinkle of pale roses rimming the edge. She took a sip then nodded at Julia. "Who do you have next, my dear?"

Julia jotted down the directives in her notepad and inwardly groaned—this made chart change number nine. She calculated how much time these updates were going to take.

Oh man, Nick is going to hit the roof when I tell him I'm working late again tonight.

On the nights she worked late, Nick would shake his head as she walked into the condo, tired and frazzled. She no longer told him about the goings-on at the clinic after he started calling it her "summer job cul-de-sac."

From the heft of the chart, Julia knew without looking that she was holding Rowena's chart and it was next on deck. She settled the tome in her lap and turned to the case notes section.

Marlene didn't bother waiting for Julia to identify the client. "How goes it with Ms. Horn?"

"Crummy. I'm sure you heard about how Rowena wants to apply for disability benefits."

"Oh yes, in the past week I've received at least one phone call a day from Rowena aimed towards that goal," Marlene said, smoothing her skirt across her lap.

"You do? Daily? What do you tell her?"

"Why, that I'm not her therapist, of course. And for her to direct her concerns back to you." Marlene cocked her head to one side. "And, by your surprise, I assume she has not been following through?"

Julia suspected Marlene knew that answer, but she went along with the charade. "No, she's avoided me since she came to the office and spoke with Walter. He brought me into their discussion, but I'm sure you already heard about that." She wasn't quite sure why she added the last bit, because of course Marlene was informed about Rowena's impromptu meeting. The senior therapist's well-manicured fingers stayed firmly pressed on the clinic's pulse.

A stray beam of late-afternoon sunlight filtered through the blinds and fell across the side of Marlene's face. Her silver glasses refracted the light, but Marlene didn't so much as squint. "Disability benefits are certainly an option, but only if Rowena's prospects continue to dwindle. Over seventy-percent of applicants on their first try are refused because they don't meet the criteria."

"So you think she'll be initially rejected, but if she worsens with time then she'll qualify?"

"Rowena's problems have been persistent. If she continues on this path she may qualify eventually. It would be a scraping-along existence, but something is better than nothing."

"But aren't we in the change business? If we don't believe our clients can make better choices, won't they pick up on our attitude and stay stuck?"

Surprise flitted across Marlene's face. "Change business? My dear, how powerful do you think counselors are? We may plant seeds of ideas, but only self-determination takes an idea into fruition. We're here to help them assess their situation, open up to new ways of looking at things, but then step back so they can make their choices. As therapists, we need to grow an objective approach and avoid asserting our will over the client's."

"If Rowena gets on disability," Julia said, "then won't she think of herself as disabled and therefore not try new things? Not even make a stab at having a fuller life?"

"First, who is to say she wouldn't have a perfectly full life while receiving benefits, although it would be a financially restricted one? And might you be over-identifying with Rowena? We don't want to be imposing our beliefs onto the client's. Besides, most of the time, people know the truth deep down before they're willing to admit it." Marlene's gaze took on an assessing quality, reminding Julia of a sharp-eyed crow.

Julia squirmed. *Is this why Rowena gets under my skin, because that woman's fear of not making it triggers my own fear?* She shook away the thought. "But during our meeting with Rowena, I could tell Walter didn't want her to get the disability label either!"

"Did he say that?" Marlene said in a mild tone.

"Well, no ... but I could sense it." As soon as her words left her mouth, Julia knew they were butterflies with wings of balsa wood and paper tissue, flying straight towards Marlene to be pulverized.

Marlene's smile tightened to a thin line. There was no humor in her eyes. "Don't you see, Julia? Putting too much faith in our intuition and believing we know someone's true potential are slippery slopes for the therapist and may be damaging for the client."

For no discernible reason, her face softened. "Just now—how we're talking—reminds me of arguments I used to have with my daughter, years ago. Linda always pushed for more, never satisfied with the tiniest bit of stability I was able to gather together."

Julia raised her eyebrows at this rare disclosure. "What kind of things did your daughter want you to do?"

"Oh, leave the clinic and start a private practice. But I needed to be realistic and focus on maintaining insurance benefits and having a stable salary. When you're a single mother, you look less at what's possible and more for the low-hanging fruit right in front of you."

Julia studied the woman's face. This chronic worry might have etched the deep lines between Marlene's eyebrows and her mouth's downward turn. Maybe Marlene also identified with Rowena, but not toward her potential, but rather her fear. Better to maintain the known than invite possible chaos from the risk.

As Julia thought of the clinic's looming cutbacks, information not even on Marlene's radar, she frowned. "You know, maybe it's smart to never say 'never'," she said with an off-handed air. "Have you thought about starting a private practice?"

Marlene snorted. "At my age? You'd have better luck with Rowena pulling down a full-time job. No, I plan on staying here until I retire. Now let's finish your charts. As for Ms. Horn, the ball is in her court. If she wishes to apply, then she knows she can contact the Social Security Administration and give them her information. But for now, it's best to let sleeping dogs lie."

Julia closed Rowena's chart, even though she knew Marlene was right. She gave a shudder, then tried on the attitude of letting Rowena bat the ball around in her own tiny court.

She wouldn't be at the clinic much longer, but still Julia couldn't shake a feeling of unease, as though she had turned her back on storm clouds brewing past the horizon and just caught a whiff of ozone.

Chapter 29

The wrought-iron balcony railings held the summer's heat and warmed Julia's forearms as she watched the last sliver of sunset wink out over the town. Nick always said he preferred the sunrise with all the promises of a new day, but Julia loved the slow roll of a full-pallet sunset folding into muted dusk.

Tonight, however, her thoughts darted like rasping fish, no matter how many times she focused her attention back to the sunset.

How many more sunsets does she have on this balcony? And in a few months, what would her sunsets look like? When people spoke of Dallas, they mentioned the night-life, sports, shopping, and the bustle of downtown. She had never heard anyone say, "You know, when I was in Dallas last weekend, we caught the best sunset." But she supposed all large cities became the focus, nudging nature back to a smaller, more manicured role.

Rowena still refused to return her phone calls, so Julia's next step was to beat a path to her client's door. She wondered if she should ask Angel to come with her, in case Rowena stayed stubbornly inside. Rowena wasn't angry with him, so he might be able to cajole her out from the other side of a locked front door.

Thinking of Angel reminded her of the rest of the staffers, who, with the exception of Walter, were probably going about their days, unaware their lives were about to be upended. Julia and Walter held the burden of this knowledge, but because of her need to protect Nick, she couldn't reach out and tell Walter she knew.

Every time she'd seen Walter at the clinic this week, his brow had been knitted, or he'd been at his computer banging out a document. She wanted to put her hand on his shoulder and tell him the clinic was in danger of losing half its funds and staff. She imagined giving him a hug and sensing his knotted muscles relax through the blue chambray shirts he tended to wear. Sometimes, when she dropped by his office to ask a question about a client, she stepped closer, no more than an inch or two, and inhaled his woodsy scent mixed in with the clean smell of laundry soap.

A hand encircled her waist and Julia jumped, almost spilling the glass of red wine offered by Nick.

"Whoa! Careful there. Didn't mean to startle you," Nick said as Julia whirled around.

"I didn't hear you come out."

Heat fanned her cheeks from a surge of guilt. Why was she thinking of touching Walter?

She accepted the glass. "Thank you, sweetie. You're spoiling me, again." In fact, Nick had been on his best behavior ever since they had returned from the Dallas interview two weeks ago. One of the editors who'd interviewed him said there were a few more candidates to consider, and then he would get back to Nick later in the month. On the drive home, Nick's mood was ebullient—he had a hunch the reporter's job was his and Julia knew from experience that his hunches tended to be correct.

"You're worth spoiling." Nick curled his arm back around her waist, drawing her closer. Together they looked out over the city blocks of Elston, with the suburban neighborhoods rimming the edges. Everywhere streetlights twinkled.

Julia sipped the wine and the plummy notes melted

down her throat. She relaxed against Nick's chest. "Pretty, isn't it?"

He was silent, and at first Julia wasn't sure if he had heard her. Then he said, "Yeah, it's not bad. For a dinky little place."

"Hmm," she said, letting the comment pass.

He reached up to the top of her blouse and unbuttoned her shirt, sliding his hand to the top of her breasts. Julia closed her eyes and became lost in his touch until the cell phone in his pocket rang the "Ride of the Valkyries."

Nick cursed and pulled it from his pocket, read the screen with a grimace then stuffed it back into his jeans. "Oh yeah. In case you haven't seen your phone messages today, just flash-scroll through the dozen or so my mom sent you and call her back. Something about the wedding invitations and the stationery shop she wants you to use. She's already called me twice about this emergency du jour."

"There are still stationery stores?" Julia sipped her wine and tasted an acidic bite on her tongue.

"Apparently. We could send out emails as far as I'm concerned, but since she's so gung-ho to be a wedding planner, let her have at it. Besides, the more we delegate this stuff to her, the more we can focus on the move."

"You're that sure about getting the job?" Julia broke from his embrace and stepped back to face him.

Nick grinned. "Outside of death and taxes, nothing is a lock. But I've got my ear to the ground in Dallas and things sound promising."

So he was already networking his sources.

"Besides, nothing wrong with also delegating some of our moving stuff to Mom. She's offering to help with that too, so I told her to go at it. She's researching moving companies and said she'll have a spreadsheet cost breakdown ready sometime tomorrow morning."

"So you two have been talking, like now I need help with the move also?" Julia's eyes widened. "I'm not even capable of that?"

"Back down, Joe Friday, nothing like that. But when it comes to this stuff, she's a whiz after years of pulling up stakes and following Dad from one air force base to another."

Nick was managing her as surely as if his hands pushed in the middle of her back. She gripped the stem of the wine glass tighter as she worked to keep her voice even. "It's not cool for you to make decisions without talking to me first. It makes me believe you don't trust me and think I might go crazy again."

"Whoa. I thought the word crazy was verboten. No one said you're nuts, but it is a stressful time. We're in the fourth-quarter with two minutes left on the clock."

Oh, not the sports talk again.

"Are you saying you're stressed?" she shot back. "You seem nothing but happy to be ripping us up out of our home and town."

"Our home and town? Don't you mean our first jobs out college? Christ, I've been here way longer than I intended because of us. Jules, lots of homes and towns may be in our future before we sign up for AARP memberships and take Sandals Cruises. And, hell yes, I'm stressed. But that's when I get busy and just cope." His tone was as sarcastic, as if stating something as fundamentally obvious as gravity.

This was how Nick cornered her, by being so damn reasonable and brushing off her concerns as fluff. And she couldn't argue his point because she had seen him handle highly stressful situations and bully on through them. This particular aspect of his qualities was reassuring on one hand, but maddening on another, because it reinforced his way of thinking and doing things as the right way to think and do things. And if she had a different set of thoughts, they'd often be shot down like so many clay pigeons.

But how could he have invested so much of his life in this paper, this town, and their life together, only to walk away as though he'd been in Elston a minute? Was this what it had been like for his mother, to come to a new town, start to invest and feel safe, and then pull up stakes and watch it all fade in the rearview window? Every friendship and relationship would sooner or later be stamped with an expiration date, so why even bother investing?

Possibly taking her silence for agreement, Nick brushed a lock of hair out of her eyes and gave her a kiss. His blue eyes turned violet in the twilight as he smiled at her. "We have so many changes ahead of us—why don't we just kick the jams out and embrace the change."

"What do you mean?"

"I mean I've been doing the same thing at this dump for five years and finally something big is on the horizon. Rather than fight it, let's push through this move and new job and wedding stuff and just bring it all on."

The brightness that lit up from inside Nick's eyes wasn't a reflection of the sunset's glow. Nervous energy vibrated within her and she wanted to push out of his arms.

"Break out the stops. If we're going into the storm, why not face all the chaos at once and get it over with? Why drag out the wedding? Get this show on the road and let's get married this Christmas. No more back and forth."

Julia made a noise like the strangled peep of a chick gasping under a heavy hen.

"I've been thinking about it and it makes sense. You want the wedding small, I want the wedding small. Let's make it small and invite a few friends and any of the family who can tear themselves away from their yule logs and have the wedding this Christmas Eve. All of my mother's social climbing buddies aren't going to give up the skiing holidays in Aspen for us, so they won't gripe too much about not being invited. Let's make it a churchy thing in Dallas. Everything will already by decked out in red-and-green, so, *boom!* Colors are decided for us. And you," Nick murmured, drawing Julia close, his hips pressed against hers, "will come down the aisle with a sexy wreath of holly in your hair, long veil, and candles all around. You will be so hot." He kissed her and pressed against her until she could feel him growing hard.

She pushed him back, but he seemed caught into his own fantasy as he held her tighter until she couldn't break free.

"I know!" Nick gushed, mistaking her struggles for excitement. "Brilliant, right? It came to me when I was driving home tonight then it seemed, oh, I don't know—"

"Insane?" Julia said. "Why in the world would you want to push the wedding up six months?"

"Because I'm going to be thirty next year, you're only few years behind me, and I don't want to be an old dad."

"What?" She wasn't quite sure she'd heard him correctly. Nick caressed the side of her breast and nuzzled her neck. "Let's not spend this spring exhausting ourselves with a wedding." He reached up and deftly unhooked her bra. "Let's exhaust ourselves making a baby."

Walking backwards, Nick pulled Julia with him from the balcony with the stars peeking out above to the darkened living room. As Nick laid her down on the long, leather couch, all she could see was his face before impenetrable shadows enveloped everything.

Chapter 30

Nadine Peterson's purple lacquered nail shook with a palsy-like tremor as she pointed to each group member before landing on Julia. "What would you do, huh?"

"Um ..." Julia fumbled, debating whether to wade in there or keep silent. She was blurry from the night before. She'd had troubled dreams, all having to do with Nick speeding up their exit out of Elston. She cut her eyes to Marlene, who was in her calm pose, attentive and listening.

Okay, two can play at this.

She took her supervisor's lead and willed her facial muscles motionless. Still fresh in her mind from this morning was her discussion with Marlene, when she had warned Julia to curb her desire to save group members as they struggled. She explained that, when group members talk about their issues, they are often thinking out loud, and therapists needn't jump in there to rescue them.

Now on top of deciding what to say, Julia had to judge if her response was even necessary. Anxiety welled inside her chest like water pressing against a thin membrane, but Julia held her silence and kept her gaze steady on Nadine, who stared flatly back.

Nadine waited a heartbeat and then, much to Julia's relief, she wheeled onto Erin and Travis and put them on the hotspot. "After weeks of your husband promising, begging, for another chance, would you give in and trust the turd blossom? Sure you would! Because Justin is so sincere when he agrees with you about how he's a turd blossom, that even J. P. Barnum would have been suckered. But then, what would you do if you came home, all worn out from work, and found him asleep on the couch with one of those throw-away phones on the floor next to him while he snored like a lord?"

Erin and Travis raised their eyebrows and shook their heads. Apparently, they didn't want to wade in there either.

Marlene broke the suspense. "And what did you do, my dear?"

"Packed a couple of bags and picked up his phone to call my girlfriend. Told her I was on my way to her apartment, seeing as to how she'd offered to put me up, should he ever decide to self-sabotage again."

She made air quotes around another new phrase probably learned from Paulie in the Peterson's couple counseling sessions. "Justin woke up just about then, saw me with his poontang phone, and started babbling excuses. I told him to shut it, I'm applying for a home health job over in San Antonio, and for him not to bother calling me because, oopsy daisies, his phone was now broke."

Nadine made a stomping motion with her foot and Julia could imagine the disposable phone on the Peterson's mobile home floor, cracked and spilling out electronics.

Stella, with her hair a deeper shade of cinnamon today, tsk tsked. "If Mr. Schmidt were to be found concealing a communication device from me, then I too would conclude he was hiding secrets. And in a healthy marriage, there can be no secrets. But after Mr. Schmidt reduced our nest egg to dust, he wouldn't dare keep a secret from me now."

"Yeah, well, does Mr. Schmidt have a single, younger brother? Today I'm in the market," Nadine said, crossing her arms with a disgusted look on her face.

"C'mon," Travis said, "give the guy a break. That phone might not be for booty calls. Everyone needs a private life, otherwise being married is like hunkering down with a Nazi guard ..." He faded under Stella and Nadine's withering stares.

The door handle to the group room squeaked and Julia glanced at the desk clock next to Marlene, which sported flowers instead of numbers for the hours—it read sixteen minutes past a peony. Marlene, Julia, and the three group members turned as the door opened and Slate sidled through, the hair on the back of his head splayed out as if it had been squashed by a pillow.

Seeing their upturned faces, Slate shifted from an underdog slink to a bristle. "Oh, hey. You started without me. Cool."

As he passed Travis, they fist-bumped, then he sat in the only empty chair remaining, which happened to be next to Stella, who picked up her handbag with a pearl double-snap and secured it on her lap. She raised her eyebrows and looked as Marlene, waiting for Slate's comeuppance to begin.

Marlene only gave Slate a beatific smile. "Morris, as always, I'm so glad you could make it. However, it is a firm group rule that the Lunch Bunchers show up a few minutes before noon so we can be ready to bring our full selves to group therapy."

Slate scowled and the corners of his lips twitched up, so Julia wasn't sure if he would snap back or break out in a laugh.

"Hey, Slate, she's calling you that cat name again," Travis said, his folded hands resting on his small, beach-ball belly.

The lanky teen ignored him. "Sorry. Tried to get here earlier but got tied up with my probation officer. He ran over our time." He twitched his shoulders up in a what-can-you-do shrug.

"Yes, Mr. Gomez. My, he did go over on the time, especially since he called me yesterday after your meeting and updated me as to your progress."

Travis guffawed and slapped Slate on the back. "Busted, dude!"

Slate frowned but, to his credit, didn't duck Marlene's gaze. Despite his surly teen act, Julia admired his grit.

"Please remember to get here at noon in the future, Slate," Marlene said, the t flicking off her tongue.

Slate grunted and slid down into his usual slouch in the folding chair.

Apparently, this didn't appear to satisfy Stella, who turned to face Marlene. "You say it's important for us to be open with each other in group, so then I will no longer hold in this secret. I don't feel comfortable having a terrorist in amongst us. And a tardy one to boot." She narrowed her eyes at Slate.

For the past month, Julia had watched Stella treat Slate coolly, but still she was surprised at Stella's unabashed rudeness. Surely now Marlene would jump to Slate's defense. But Marlene faced Slate, her expression placid and questioning.

What was the rule book for when to jump in and when to stay silent? It was as bewildering as watching a game of cricket.

"Hey now!" Slate fussed. "I'm as peaceable as anyone here!"

"If so, then why did you attempt to blow up the clinic with your homemade bomb?" Stella said.

Slate sucked in his breath, held it, then said in a rush, "Weren't no bomb. It was just an old gas can my dad had stashed out back behind the garage. Besides, something the newspaper people forgot to write was that the can was empty, save for a bit sloshing around in the bottom. Wasn't enough fuel to light a campfire, much less torch this joint. I never meant to hurt nobody." He mumbled the last bit.

Stella cocked her head to one side. "Pray tell, young Morris, what were your intentions, if not to blow to smithereens the very people here trying to help you?"

Julia heaved a sigh of relief when Marlene reached over and tapped Stella on the knee, a warning to go no further then settled back and leveled her gaze at Slate's reddening face. Julia ached to tell Stella to quit being such a bully to the kid. Whatever the line was between someone giving an honest truth or being abusive, Stella had crossed it.

The room grew quiet as Slate hung his head and color flushed up to his neck while he seemed to struggle to collect his thoughts. After a few moments, he said, "I don't know. I don't know why I did it. Maybe my old man is right. Maybe I'm just a bad seed."

It was one thing for Stella to be a bully to Slate, but for Slate to bully himself was too much for Julia and her words tumbled out. "Was it because you weren't getting the help you needed and you did something to make people really stop and listen?" Her tone turned ferocious. "Because there's only just so much of people not listening to you that you could stand?"

Marlene raised her head and stared at Julia, a line deepening between her eyebrows.

Squirming in the spotlight with her face heating up, Julia grabbed for a therapeutic fig leaf. "If that is what I'm hearing you say, I mean."

Slate's scowling face relaxed and became thoughtful. "Yeah, that's about right. I wasn't mad at nobody here, just more …" He spread his arms wide. "You know, pissed at my dad for being such a hard-ass and Mom for cutting out and leaving me and my brother. Anyway, that day was the day the old man woke up drunk and started right up drinking where he left off. By noon, he was looking for something to get ticked off about. That's when he walked through the garage and saw the gas can cap was off. He yelled at me, saying I was going to blow the whole house up, and what was I, a fire bug?" He shrugged. "I got to thinking how cool it would be to see something burn the hell up. Like a friggin' bonfire, you know? I found the lid, crammed it on then grabbed the damn can and my skateboard. I wasn't going in any direction and when I rode up to this old raggedy place, I walked on in. Maybe I knew I was carrying the stupid can, maybe I didn't. Honestly, I don't remember. The cops can say all day long that I asked for matches, but that don't sound right. Shit, I could've grabbed matches off my dad's smokes right there on the front stoop, so how serious could I've been?"

Nadine snorted. "Darling, if someone thought you actually meant to start a fire, you wouldn't be sitting here with us having a chat. You'd be talking to your lawyer on the other side of a one-inch plate of glass with a speaker in the middle. And trust me, I've visited Justin in places like that enough to know those orange jumpsuits don't flatter nobody."

Slate was silent then tilted his head back and expelled a long breath. "I thought once I turned eighteen and became a legal adult, things would start to go my way. Shit, now I'm nineteen and legal as hell and I'm still going nowhere. Older don't mean better. Things only suck harder."

His ears pinked and Julia could detect the vulnerable little boy underneath the rumpled teen.

"Slate, I agree with you about how things get harder as we get older," Marlene said. "We take on more responsibility—maybe it's unpleasant and maybe it's exhilarating. It depends on what you tell yourself and the choices you make. We aren't given freedom—we earn it."

He began to intensely study the tips of his scuffed boots, so Marlene swiveled in her chair to Erin. "And now, my dear, how are things with you?"

Erin, who had been sitting folded into her chair like a paper origami crane, straightened and cleared her throat. No longer dressed in the huge headbanger T-shirt, she wore a flowery print blouse, frayed at the collar from too many washings, and shiny polyester slacks cut so short her ankles were exposed. To Julia, she seemed even more delicate and frail.

A blush crept up Erin's cheeks. "So ... uh, my new housekeeping job at the hotel is okay. I get paid at the end of each day and I'm saving some money. My caseworker at the shelter said I ought to open up a bank account. Now that my cash envelope is getting thicker, she says it's no longer safe to keep it tucked in my duffel bag at the family shelter. After our meeting here, I'm going to the bank." A tinge of pride strengthened her voice.

Marlene and Julia exchanged glances and smiled.

"Sweet!" Travis said. "How do I score a maid job like that? I may be back to sleeping in my car if my buddy's wife keeps up her squawking. Which him and I both agree is a damn shame since no one hardly uses their basement couch and he don't care if I bunk there. Gives us a chance to drink a few beers and hang out."

Erin looked doubtful. "I can put in a word for you, but it's not so glamorous. I mean they work you hard and you have to turn over a room in twenty-five minutes. And to keep the job, you have to show up. Every day."

Cutting her eyes to Travis, Julia wondered if the skepticism in Erin's voice would insult him.

But he only shrugged. "You may be right—I'm more the management type. Just can't say I've found my niche."

"Niche. Yeah, that's a good word," Erin said, her eyes

sparkling with tears. "Can't say I've found mine neither. Some days it's like I'm down someplace deep, and I'm trying to dig my way up just to keep from falling more behind."

At this, Nadine interjected her own two cents, "Maybe it ain't high-dollar work and Lord knows it ain't easy, but you're doing it. Each day you're away from that bum, you're feeling stronger, right?"

The tears welled in Erin's eyes. "No, I don't feel strong. I feel weaker since I left Lonnie. Each bed I make and each toilet I scrub, I wonder if I've done the right thing. Chloe has these fierce nightmares and wakes me up every night, afraid there's a monster under our bed. She cries to go home and be in her room and misses her daddy. We're sleeping on bunk beds, so I'll climb down and hold her until she falls back asleep. Then I lie awake and think about my monsters. Like how am I going to feed us, where are we going to live, and what if Lonnie catches back up with us?"

Erin wiped her cheeks with the back of her hands. "Sometimes I do imagine calling up Lonnie and telling him I'm sorry, because part of the problems were my fault. I'm starting to see that better now. Maybe I asked too much of him, like he said." Erin looked around the circle as if searching for answers in their faces.

Julia gritted her teeth. Erin was falling into Marlene's predicted pattern of returning to her husband. Of course, Marlene wanted Erin to make a better life for herself and her daughter, but poverty's grip was tight as a vice. And if those impoverished women returned, Julia imagining that their men would only keep them closer, with their wings clipped short.

"Slate, what you did sounds like what I did," Erin said, nodding at him. "The night I left, it was as if some part of me made a decision to take one step, and then another. I kept following those steps, until eventually, well, here I am. When we ran away, I'd never been so scared in my life. But that one part of me felt like a flame, and I wanted to live and keep my daughter safe. So I kept following it."

Erin sat in silence and the group grew still with her. Marlene said, "What are you thinking right now?"

Erin inhaled sharply and her eyes stared at the wall, as if she was far from the room. "My last night with Lonnie, we had another one of our big fights. But this time was different. He went crazy, with his face all twisted up like a Halloween mask. He punched me so hard in my head I saw stars. I thought that only happened in cartoons. He was calling me awful names and I was crying and we must have woken up Chloe, because she came running up and tried to push Lonnie off of me." Her breath came in jagged spurts and she closed her eyes as if to block the terror of the memory.

A shudder ran through Julia as she imagined Erin being brutalized while her four-year-old girl tried to defend her against the raging man who was her daddy, but not her daddy. He had become a monster. Not knowing what else to do, Julia reached for the box of tissues next to her chair, but Marlene shook her head and motioned for her to be still. She obeyed and wrapped her fingers around the box, the cardboard edges pressing against her clammy hands.

"He raised his fist like he was going to hit Chloe and I screamed for him to stop. Then I pushed him with all my might and he fell and snapped out it, or at least he stopped coming at us. His face was pale and sweaty, and I'll never forget those eyes. Like a shark's eyes. He was going to kill me that night. Maybe Chloe, too."

"Oh, darling girl," said Nadine. "What did you do?"

The question snapped Erin back into the room as she looked around. "Chloe and I held each other, and Lonnie stood over us, shaking. Then he grabbed his keys and wallet and stormed out the door. Chloe she cried that she wanted her daddy to come back. A voice told me, Run! I started stuffing our clothes in a bag, grabbed my purse, picked up my daughter still in her nightgown, and we ran. I didn't know if he was at a bar halfway across town or around the corner of the apartment waiting for us. But I knew we didn't have much time." Erin met Julia's gaze. "I didn't know where I was going either, but my feet kept moving me forward. We walked and walked, me carrying Chloe half the time and making her walk the other. The whole time I was lugging our bag until my arms were shaking and I was afraid I was going to drop to the pavement."

She writhed in her seat, seeming to relive her actions. "At last I saw the lights from the bus station and followed them right into the lobby. I handed the man behind the ticket window all the money I had, except for twenty dollars, and asked for the next bus leaving town. He looked up how far our money would take us, and it got us to here. I'd never even been to Elston. The next day at noon, Chloe and I got off the bus, and well, you all know the rest." Large tears slid down her face and made dark splotches on her shirt.

"Erin, here you go." Julia offered the tissue box, slightly crumpled on the sides from her grip.

Erin gave a tremulous smile, her face now splotchy from crying, and extracted one tissue as though it was all she was allotted.

"You're very brave, you know that?" Julia said. "Even coming to group is a leap of faith."

"Damn straight," Travis added. "You are brave in the triple digits."

The young woman shook her head. "The part of me that cut and run was the tiny bit Lonnie didn't beat down. But now that I'm gone and it's all on me to make it work, I still feel small. Some days even smaller. How do I take care of me and Chloe? In the end, this could all be for nothing and maybe I'll go back to him. He'll give me hell, but I know he'd take us back. What is it they say? Better the devil you know than the one you don't?"

Slate jammed his hands into the pockets of his hoodie pullover and said, "That's how I feel. Only half-grown myself and suddenly now I'm in charge of me. Maybe that's how my dad felt when Mom left me and my brother and he was stuck with no one to take up the slack. But just because we're scared don't mean we're weak and can't make something of ourselves. And it sure as shit don't give us a license to turn into a jerk, like my dad and this Lonnie dude." He rubbed his moist eyes with the cuff of his sweater and waved off the tissue box offered by Julia, keeping his face lowered.

A tiny smile crept across Erin's face as she whispered, "Thank you, Morris. And I think Morris is a nice name. But I'll call you Slate, if you want."

He ducked his head and waved his hand, as if to say it didn't matter to him one way or the other. But he remained quiet, as though he didn't trust his voice to stay steady.

Marlene shuffled her notes. "Okay, that's a nice place to end, since our time is up. Good work and we'll see you all next week."

A quick glance at the clock showed Julia that it was five minutes past a crocus. As the group members filed out, Julia stacked the chairs while Marlene sat at her desk writing progress notes.

This session needled her in a familiar way. It was the same unsettled feeling she had with Dr. Donovan when she told him about her doubts of becoming a therapist. To work with mental health clients, she herself needed to be mentally healthy, or else risk being a hypocrite and a wounded healer.

While she wasn't in as hard a place as the group members, letting Nick steamroll over her was hardly a shining example of assertiveness skills. Erin, Slate, Nadine, and even Travis, each week they came to group, fueled by a dogged hope that if they didn't give up, their lives just might get better. Julia nestled the last chair against the others, and then moved them to a closet next to the file cabinet. "I'm off to lunch now, Marlene," Julia said with her hand on the doorknob.

Marlene raised her head and smiled. "Interesting group today, don't you think?"

"Very. And Slate's making good progress."

Marlene paused. "He is, but he's still has a long way to go before he's stable. But, dear, again do remember to curb your well-intended desire to tell the client what he's thinking or feeling. Let's not confuse our beliefs with their beliefs, even in Erin's case where she might well be brave. We don't know the heart of someone else and we might be wrong. Mindreading is a sticky business and best left at the carnival circuit, okay?"

Julia gripped the door handle and opened her mouth to protest. But protest what? Her hunch against Marlene's years of experience?

Instead, she gave a, "Yes, ma'am" and slipped out the door. On the way to her office, Julia imagined herself walking on a tightrope and with each shaky step she took, it stretched out longer and higher.

Chapter 31

The knock at her office door announced Mona's arrival. Julia swiveled around.

"Oh my God, Jules." Her face glowed. "There's the cutest guy out in the lobby, and he's asking for you! He doesn't seem like one of our clients, but I guess that just goes to show that even being a hottie can come with its fair share of problems. Nothing you and I will have to worry about, right?

Julia laughed and stood up. "No, I guess not. Thank goodness for all that character building we get by being average. But I don't have another client for an hour. Who is it?"

Mona gave a beats-me shrug, as Julia followed her to the lobby.

Nick's muscular frame filled the dilapidated couch and he sat straight-backed as if to avoid close contact with the cushions edged in grime. A small bouquet of flowers lay resting against his thigh. The bright splashes of color from the flowers brought into focus the dinginess of the tiny lobby. He looked so out of place, and it occurred to Julia that this was the first time Nick had stepped foot in the clinic.

Julia forced her lips into a smile. "Nick. Hey. What a surprise."

He stood and gave her a quick hug. "Had to come by and see what all the fuss was about."

"Oh, you're Nick," Mona said in a tone both surprised and confused. She turned to Julia with rounded eyes, indicating her mental picture of Julia's fiancé must have been different from the man commandeering the lobby's space.

"The one and only," Nick said, sounding more confident, as though her fawning had encouraged him. "And who might you be?"

"Mona is our administrative assistant, and Mona, this is Nick." Julia walked past Mona while curbing the desire to elbow her and tell her to cut it out. Besides, the flowers Nick carried made her nervous. He rarely bought her flowers.

As they settled in her tiny, windowless office, Julia shut her eyes to the water-stained ceiling tiles and the closeness of the walls. Even the three lamps could not chase away the darkness in the corners.

Nick gave the place a cursory once-over. "We can say these are the humble beginnings of your illustrious new career."

She pointed to the flowers. "Am I to assume those are for me?"

He glanced down at the bouquet as though surprised to see it there. "Beautiful flowers for beautiful you," he said, handing her a collection of yellow and orange roses interspersed with tangles of baby's breath.

She brought them to her face and inhaled, detecting a faint perfume. "Thank you. They're lovely," she said, and then placed them on her desktop. "What's the occasion?"

"The occasion is our future, because today we're celebrating."

The undercurrent of excitement in his voice rose and she eyed him through narrow slits. "We are?" Her stomach clenched, queasy and uncomfortable.

"I got the call from Dallas today and they offered me the job," he announced, as though he expected Julia to stand and cheer.

So there it was.

"And you said yes." She already knew the answer.

"Hell yes, I said yes!" His grin grew wider. "I've given the paper a month's notice since I figured we'd need that much time to get the condo up for sale, pack, and ..." He scanned her office. "Give you enough time to wrap things up here."

Her office would take all of fifteen minutes to "pack," but still her mind fought against Nick's news.

He did not seem to take notice, but instead pulled out his cell phone and tapped on the screen. "Actually, I think one of the first things we need to do is contact our realtor in Dallas and schedule some viewings this weekend."

"Wait, we have a realtor?"

Never taking his eyes off the screen as he scrolled for a number, "Yes, her name is Brandi. She helped Chuck find his home. He says she's very responsive."

I'll bet she is, Julia couldn't help thinking. "Nick, wait! Who is Chuck? And now we're meeting with someone named Brandi in two days to tour houses?"

He stopped pecking at his phone and cocked his head at her. "Chuck is one of the editors I interviewed with. I told you about him. And I know I mentioned this realtor," he said in a patient voice, as though he needed to slow down his words in order for her to catch up.

Recent conversations with Nick were like tumbling down rabbit holes. She stopped herself from retorting that she had heard of neither Chuck the editor, nor Brandi the realtor, because really, what was the point? The lamp behind Nick cast a pulsating pink aura and Julia's palms turned sweaty. A whoosh of terror washed over her like a wave, as the curl of a panic attack rose up from her gut.

She closed her eyes and focused on what she really needed to say to Nick. It wasn't about Chuck, and probably not about Brandi. Not yet about Brandi, anyway.

"You're throwing the words *we* and *us* around, without actually consulting me," she said, keeping her voice modulated.

Nick nodded, as though in agreement, but his voice grew testy. "Well, why wouldn't I? These are practical steps forward as a couple, not line items to be debated. There is nothing to debate if we're going forward." He paused. "Are we going forward?"

The gauntlet was thrown down as surely as if it had landed at her feet. The question hung in the air: What did she choose?

A queasy wave rolled over her as she flashed through her options. If she stayed in town, then she and Nick would be over, of that there was no doubt. He had been the center-piece of her life, yet she had grown steadily tired of being relegated as a side dish. Still, the idea of his being ripped away from her left her feeling vulnerable and exposed.

An image as clear as a snapshot came to Julia. She would be trudging through next year's graduate program, living alone in a cruddy, efficiency apartment, and all the while wretched with missing Nick. Meanwhile, he would be so busy in his big, important life that she would drift further and further away in his mind until she got lumped into the bin of his former girlfriends. Yet uprooting every-thing meant she would plant herself even more squarely into Nick's shadow.

Walter's voice outside the half-opened door made Julia jump.

He stuck his head in. "Hey, Julia, saw you had a break in your schedule and if you want, we can go over some of these group techniques ..." Walter glanced at Nick's grim face. "Oh, I'm sorry, I thought you were alone. I'll come back another time." He held a thick book with the title,

Theory and Techniques of Group Therapy.

"No, it's okay," Julia said in a rush. "Um ... Walter, this is my boyfriend, Nick. Nick, this is Walter Bridgeman, the clinical director."

Nick sprang up and shook Walter's hand in a piston-pumping handshake. "Nice to meet you, Walter. Julia's told me all about you." His voice took on a booming, baritone quality.

Julia frowned. She had mentioned Walter only in passing to Nick.

Walter took a step back. "Yes, well ..." He studied Nick. "She certainly has become an important part of my staff in a short time."

She had? She dared a glance at Walter, then cut her eyes away because she sensed an odd, jittery energy coming off Nick.

"Nick just dropped by to say hi," Julia said, although Walter had not asked what Nick was doing there in her office.

Nick brightened and picked up Julia's thread. "Yes, and to give her the news." He pointed to the flowers on her desk, in case Walter had somehow missed their Technicolor glow. "My fiancée and I are moving to Dallas at the end of the summer. I need to get us settled before I start my new job."

She wondered why Nick put an emphasis on "fiancée," and then remembered she had introduced him as her "boyfriend." Not only was Nick putting his stamp on her, he was announcing to her boss that she would be moving away. She gritted her teeth at how he, in front of all of them, ripped away her choice of when to tell Walter about the move.

"Yes, this is all very new. I mean, not *new* exactly," Julia said. "It's been in the works for a bit, but it's always a shock when you find out these things are going to happen. New jobs and moves and such." She didn't so much stop as run out of gas.

Both men stared at her before Nick shifted his attention to Walter. "The move will take place at the end of August. The timing should be okay in helping her wrap things up here, right?"

Walter placed the heavy book with a thud on Julia's desk. "Looks like my old textbook will be your going-away present then. It's a bit worn and torn, but still has good information between the covers. I want you to have it for all the places you're going to go."

She dared to raise her eyes to match his gaze for a few seconds and a shiver of electricity ran up her spine. In the dim light, his green eyes appeared to be an emerald shade of sea glass and in them was an intensity that Julia couldn't quite read. Pain, perhaps?

"Thank you," Julia squeaked out and picked up the book.

"Yep, that will come in handy, no doubt," Nick said as he reached into his front pocket and pulled out a business card. Julia groaned inside.

Wanting to shoo Walter out of her office before Nick did what she feared Nick was about to do, Julia said, "And, Walter, I know you're busy."

"Here's my business card." Nick held one toward Walter. "Until we move, I'm still reporting for *The Elston Daily*. I know about the important work your clinic does in saving Elston's most vulnerable population, so I'd like to pick your brain and hear about things from the director's point of view. How about if we schedule a time for an interview?" He pulled out his phone and opened up his calendar.

"Nick, really. This may not be the best time." Julia tried to mask how appalled she felt at his pivot and knew he had no interest in the clinic other than the story of how it was about to be bled financially dry by the upcoming budget cuts. He was grooming Walter as his next inside source.

Then a troubling thought wormed in. What if Nick came to the office to tell her he got the job with the hope of running into Walter and setting up an interview? For Nick to have called out of the blue and ask for an interview would almost certainly alerted Walter that Nick had been tipped off to the cuts, which would have made Walter wary.

Nick shot her a frown. "It's not a good time?" His tone was of the conversational type. But Julia knew Nick and recognized the hard edge underneath.

"No, it's all right. I've always got time to talk about all the things happening at the clinic," Walter said, his face composed into a neutral mask. "Especially with a sympathetic reporter who understands the good we're doing here."

Nick was trying to snow him and Walter knew it.

She wished she could warn Walter. Logic told her she should give up thinking about this place and the people in it, because soon she'd be miles away with bigger concerns. But logic couldn't convince her heart—she wanted Nick to quit pestering Walter and leave this little corner of her world alone.

As Walter walked toward the door, he said to Nick, "Check in with Mona to set up an appointment."

"Mona?" Nick said.

"She's the woman you met up front," Julia said in a dull voice. "Remember, the real cheerful one?"

"Oh, the girl in the cloud of perfume. Yes, hard to miss that one," Nick chuckled, as if expecting them to laugh along with his joke.

Julia winced. Nick might as well have screeched his nails across a chalkboard. Annoyance flickered across

Walter's face before he left the room. He shut the door and left Julia alone with Nick.

As if on its own accord, her hand reached out for the door handle to stop Walter from leaving. Misunderstanding her gesture, Nick plucked up her hand and interlocked his fingers with hers. Julia held still, fearful that if she moved, she'd pull her hand back in revulsion.

Chapter 32

The last client had left the clinic well over an hour ago, yet Julia trailed her fingertips over the manila folder spines in the file room as she pulled out client charts for the next day. A job that normally would take five minutes, she'd managed to stretch out to fifteen.

Nick's visit had left her feeling bruised and vulnerable, and she had gone through the rest of the afternoon in a haze. Now she attempted to stay busy, dodging the fact that she was avoiding going home.

Not that it mattered. Nick had told her before leaving he would be working late tonight on a story and not to wait up. She had called Fiona a few hours ago and left a voicemail, asking if she'd like to get together for a lunch, but hadn't heard back from her yet. Maybe she'd lost her university friend due to neglect. She sighed and brushed aside a lock of hair, reminding herself to call her salon for a haircut.

A lump formed in her throat. This would probably be her last haircut with her stylist, a spit-fire woman who always called her "sweetie." Julia doubted her future Dallas hair stylist would do that. She puffed out a sigh of frustration as she searched again for the last chart she needed, Erin's from group. She flipped through the row of charts again. Still nothing.

A wheel squeaked behind her as the janitor, who wore purple gloves, pushed the cleaning cart into the room. The name Larry was stitched above the "Cleanin' Up Janitorial Service" logo on his uniform pocket, and peeking out from the top of the trash bin were the red and orange petals of Nick's roses.

The janitor, possibly a few years older than she was, stopped next to her, reached down for a brimming trashcan near her right leg, and paused before emptying it on top of the bouquet. "Um, I think these flowers came from your office. Did you mean to throw them away? Looks like somebody spent some money."

"No, I meant to throw them out. Allergies. But you can have them, if you wish," Julia said, her tone frostier than she intended. Just seeing the flowers brought up the earlier scene in her office.

The janitor considered the offer for a moment, and then dumped the trash on top of the bouquet. "Nah, I don't have anyone to give them to." He lowered the empty trash can close to Julia.

She withdrew, and then let out a sigh of relief when he squeaked his cart out of the file room. She flipped through an entire drawer of folders and wondered about how badly she must have misfiled Erin's chart. She was in the process of considering looking under E for Erin when Marlene walked in carrying a stack of charts in her arms. Marlene stopped for a second, then walked to Julia.

"Well, aren't you the busy bee?" Marlene placed the files down on a table. "I thought you'd left ages ago."

"Just finishing up some loose ends, but now I can't seem to find a chart. It's Erin's, for group tomorrow."

"That's odd. I put it away myself last week. Here, let me have a look."

Julia stepped aside as her supervisor flipped through the charts at twice Julia's speed. She stopped two-thirds the way through the drawer and withdrew a chart, flipped it around, and held it up: Erin's name was typed neatly on the left tab.

"Here she is, but how it got turned around is a mystery. Did you pull her chart out earlier this week?"

Puzzled, Julia took it and shook her head. "No. I didn't. Maybe it was Angel or Glen? They were supposed to run by her place for a well-check. It's the second time I've found her chart misplaced."

Marlene shook her head, picked up a chart from her stack, and opened a lower drawer. "Humph. That won't do. Tomorrow I'll address Angel and Glen on the need for attentiveness in filing. What if there was an emergency and we needed the information in her chart? The devil is in the details."

Insistent knocking floated down the hall and Julia raised her eyebrows at Marlene. Before either could speak, Mona yelled from the front office, "Dios mio!"

"What is it, dear?" Marlene called out, as she straightened stiffly. One of her knees gave a pop loud enough for Julia to hear. Despite Marlene's formidable demeanor, every so often her vulnerability peeked out.

"Here, let me help you," Julia said, offering her hand only to have Marlene wave it away.

Mona appeared in the chart room doorway, her purse looped over her shoulder and keys jangling in her hand. Her eyes were bright and color pinked her cheeks. "Big guess who's pounding on our locked front door."

Fatigue washed through Julia. "Marlene, I'm not sure if I can face Rowena right now." She cursed herself for not leaving an hour earlier.

From the front came Rowena's muffled yell. "Open the door, Mona! I seen you turn tail and run."

Mona pointed to the lobby. "See! Can she do that to us, demand that we open up when we're closed? Shouldn't we call the authorities?"

Narrowing her eyes and thinning her lips, Marlene

said with deliberate cadence, "We are the authorities. And Rowena's not choosing this behavior. She's compelled."

She directed her attention to Julia. "You and I will visit with Rowena in the parking lot, however, we'll set a boundary and not let her in the clinic unless it's an emergency. It *is* after hours."

"For sure. Safety in numbers." Mona nodded. "I like this plan."

"Mona, you may continue to your car and go home, please," Marlene said over her shoulder as she stalked down the hall and into the noise of the pounding on the door.

As they followed Marlene, Julia detected disappointment on Mona's face, and it occurred to her that despite Mona's protests and bristling at Rowena's antics, she was drawn to this magazine-lifting client as if by a dark gravity.

Marlene twisted the lock, opened the door, and an exhale of hot summer air whooshed into the hallway. Rowena, whose face was a shiny slick of sweat, with dark stains spreading on her t-shirt under her arms, was planted square center in front of the door. She grudgingly backed up a few paces for the three women to slide out.

From her pocket, Marlene pulled out a small set of keys and clicked the door locked behind her, then she turned and said, "Rowena, are you having an emergency? The clinic is now closed and we're preparing to leave."

Rowena reached into her back pocket and pulled out a crumpled letter. Julia could read the words "Social Security Administration" on the letterhead. This wasn't going to be pretty.

"I mailed out the forms for disability on my own, since there was a bunch of foot-dragging goin' on from you here people. Today I got this letter from them people, tellin' me *no*. Says I'm not disabled enough, but that's a lie. I need you to write me up a letter tellin' them people that I can't do squat. Says here," she said, pointing to a paragraph she had circled several times in scrawled blue ink, "to mail 'em my appeals letter. So that's what I aim to do, and I need you to write it up pretty and sign with all those fancy letters behind your name so they see how bad off I am."

Despite Marlene's directive and the sweltering heat, Mona stayed rooted in the parking lot between them, and Julia doubted if this would help the situation. Rowena might see it as a three-against-one situation. A drop of sweat beaded then rolled down the side of Julia's face and she almost wished Marlene would let Rowena into the cool of the clinic, if only to get out of the oven-blast of the setting sun.

But Marlene's gaze remained steady on Rowena as she said in a calm voice, "You may be giving our credentials too much credit, I'm afraid. The disability board looks at facts, medically recorded facts. Also I do not agree that you cannot do squat. I believe you to be very capable, if you only allow yourself a chance to try."

"Try?" Rowena sputtered. "Try at what? Hangin' out at a store with the kid here?" She hooked a thumb at Julia.

Tired of hearing Rowena refer to her as the kid, Julia jumped in, "Rowena, we've been over this. The Penny Pincher was only a start. Please tell me where you'd like to try job coaching. Any place that you want, and I'll do my best to make it happen!"

"This here place," Rowena said, thrusting the letter at Julia. "I want you to try this here place by you writin' me up something!"

Marlene stepped between Rowena and Julia. "All right, Rowena, let's not get side-tracked. Neither Julia nor I are going to invent stories in order to make it appear you're disabled. That would be fraud and malpractice. But I agree with Julia that you're on the right track by facing your fears and trying on a job."

Julia looked at Marlene, and her eyebrows shot up. Her support on job coaching Rowena had been tepid, at best.

Mona snapped her fingers. "Oh, I know! My first job was at my uncle's bowling alley, the one off Loop 337. I could put in a word for you. Tio Hector would probably start her off with something easy, like giving people their bowling shoes. All she has to do is ask the customers what size shoes they wear then, when they give them back, spray in the foot powder stuff before putting them back in their cubbyhole." Mona grinned. "The bowling alley can be noisy, especially on tournament nights, but after a while I learned to tune it out. In a month, I worked up to concessions.."

The idea of Rowena working in a bowling alley, surrounded by chattering people and the rumbling thunder of bowling balls crashing into wooden pins, would send her running back to her hidey hole at her mother's house. Glancing at Rowena's repulsed expression, Julia wondered why Marlene wasn't shutting Mona down.

Julia said, "Yeah, Mona, that's awfully sweet of you to offer, but—"

"But no way, no how," Rowena said with the finality of a slammed door.

"Mona, dear, thank you for help, but Julia and I need to finish our discussion with Rowena," Marlene said, her faced flushed from either frustration or the one-hundred-degree baking heat.

Why, Julia wondered, as her shirt clung to her sweaty back, did there seem to be so many impromptu sessions out here in the clinic's parking lot?

"Okay, but just so you know, one phone call from me and you guys are as good as in." Mona waggled her fingers at them as she left to cross the parking lot.

Marlene let go a deep breath. "What's really going on here? You seem more determined today than ever to set up a disability case."

Rowena rocked her large frame back and forth, heel to toe, and averted her eyes.

Mona beeped her horn and gave a cheery wave as she drove past. This seemed to break Rowena's silence.

"Mama's sick. Sicker than I've ever seen her. She lays up in bed all the time, and now she's talkin' about some nurse comin' on by to check up on her with the diabetes. Mama's gonna call Glen and have him set all that up." A sob rose from her and she seemed to chock it back down.

They probably should have all gone inside—the baking heat now had all their faces slicked with sweat—but it was as though they were a trio melted and stuck into the sidewalk.

Marlene reached out and touched Rowena's arm. "You have no idea how sorry I am to hear this, Rowena. I will call your mother and arrange to drop by with Glen tomorrow, okay?"

Julia stood, feeling more like a helpless bystander rather than Rowena's therapist. "Um, yes, and if there's anything I can do to help, Rowena, please let me know. I'm here for you, too."

A clacking sound, like sticks rubbing together, made Julia jump. They all turned around as Walter closed and locked the glass-plated front door with one hand while managing two fishing poles in the other.

With a final twist of the lock, Walter picked up his tackle box at his feet and held up his hand against the lowering sun. His eyebrows shot up when he saw the women.

After setting down his gear, he walked over. "Hey, gang, kind of toasty for an outdoor meeting. What's up?"

"Rowena has received some upsetting news from the

Social Security Administration," Marlene said. "It appears she applied for benefits but was denied."

Walter shook his head. "Rowena, I'm sorry to hear you're upset, but that's commonly what happens. I think the denial rate is around seventy percent. There needs to be a strong medical need and clear documentation to show such support is necessary."

"And her mother is not doing well," Julia said, believing this to be the heart of the matter.

Rowena turned a vengeful eye to Julia. "Before you showed up, ain't nobody bothered me."

"Wait, what?"

"All your big, bright ideas, they're turnin' things every which-a-way. None of the clinic people here asked me to do nothing but haul on in and talk about things. Ain't that what therapy's supposed to be about? Just a bunch of talk?"

"It's not just about talk. It's about . . . embracing life." Julia sounded stiff as a textbook to her own ears.

"Rowena, please," Marlene said. "While Julia has engaged with you in a more proactive way, it is what you and I have talked about for a long time. Living independently and not being alone so much."

A glint came to Rowena's eyes and she rocked her head as though shaking away Marlene's words. "Nope. That's not how I sees it. We was doin' okay, then this one here shows up," she said, tilting her chin toward Julia, "with her big ideas on how to run other people's business."

Walter stepped forward. "Julia has been under our supervision and training, Rowena. Marlene and I gave our consent to her treatment plans of your job coaching."

Julia waded in there. "I do see you as a person, Rowena, a fully capable person. And because of that, I'm trying to remind you how strong you are, although I can only imagine how hard it's become with your mother's health problems."

Julia stopped when doubt choked off her words. Whatever direction she took with Rowena, her client would bat her down the way King Kong smashed airplanes circling his head while perched atop the Empire State Building.

"What's the matter?" Rowena taunted. "Don't like bein' all shook up?"

"Okay, stop. Everyone stop. We're getting sidetracked from the real issues," Walter said, an edge in his voice. "Rowena, to me, what needs immediate attention is that your mother is ill and you both need support. However, what's not helpful is if you threaten my staff. Julia will remain your therapist, and personally I agree with her treatment plan."

He clenched his jaw. "And I'd like to remind you that while you and your mom have been our clients for years, we're not the only game in town. There are other clinics and therapists you can go to, many of whom will see you for a reduced fee, and I can help with a transfer. It's your choice to seek services with us and nobody's forcing anything on anyone."

Julia held her breath. She had never seen Walter speak so forcefully to Rowena before, and it was a gamble. Was he pouring gasoline onto a sputtering, angry flame? Still, humiliation burned inside her as Walter and Marlene stood up for her while her tongue lay flat at the bottom of her mouth.

Clouds of emotions roiled over Rowena's face, until she deflated with a sigh and slumped her shoulders. She waved her hand and said to no one in particular, "You tell that Glen to stop by the house first thing tomorrow, okay? I tired of jawing with you people. I have to get home to Mama." She plodded off across the parking lot, the crumpled letter in her hand.

Marlene called after her, "Tell your mom I will drive

over tomorrow morning. Maybe Glen, too."

Rowena trudged on, as though the words bounced off her back.

Spots danced in front of Julia's eyes. The sidewalk pitched slightly fore and aft and her stomach clenched in a spasm of queasiness. She fought against a sensation of swaying.

Today has been too much.

A large hand cradled her shoulder. "Hey, there," Walter said, "you're looking as pale as skim milk."

"It's just the heat, I think," Julia mumbled as she willed herself to stand straight and be still.

"This heat's getting to all of us," Marlene said. "Let's go inside, get a cool drink, and call this day done, shall we?"

Still, Walter's gaze did not leave Julia's face. He said in a low voice, "What do you need, Julia?"

The question was unexpected and rare for her. What did she need?

It sure wasn't to go home, a flimsy concept now. To her horror, tears welled into her eyes as she searched for something to say to make this moment stop.

Walter stepped back and someone took her hand. She looked up into Marlene's concerned face. This kindness unleashed more tears. Fully mortified, Julia waved them away. "It's been a hard day, is all. I'm fine, really. Let me go inside to grab my stuff, and go—"

Her throat closed on the word "home." She had no home.

Bending down, Walter picked up his fishing gear. "Whenever I need a new perspective, I go for a change of scenery." He nodded to his truck parked in the back corner of the lot. "Unless you've got something else to do, how about going for a short ride? Take in some fresh air and clear your head?"

Of course she couldn't go, her mind reasoned. Absurd. How would she explain it to Nick?

Walter's face was open and kind, and as she looked into his eyes, her lips formed the word "no," but instead "yes" came out. The word bloomed in her chest, and before she could talk herself out of it, she dashed back to her office to grab her purse on feet that barely seemed to touch the ground.

Chapter 33

From the bank of the Guadalupe River, Walter cast his seven-foot fly fishing pole out and the line zinged into a swooping arch and then dropped the fly into the center of the swift-moving river with a quiet plunk. In a smooth motion, he pulled the pole up and whipped the line into a back cast, keeping his wrist straight and only bending at the elbow. Each time, the fly kissed the surface of the river to mimic the motion of an insect.

The forward and backward snapping motion of the rod and line hypnotized Julia as a cool breeze blew off the river and ruffled her hair. Walter had told her the small popping noise each time he snapped the line was from the tip breaking the sound barrier. She wound in the line on the much simpler rod and reel gear he'd given her, a piece of equipment he said he kept on hand if he needed a break from fly fishing and wanted to dial down to a slower pace.

As the sun dipped toward the horizon, the western sky was ablaze with deepening ambers and pinks. Julia marveled at such beauty that was less than a half-hour's drive down a twisty county road. She pulled in her line, checked the bait—half-eaten, but still enough to entice a hungry brown trout—and cast again.

After a ten-minute casting lesson from Walter, she was able to hit, more often than not, the center of the calm eddy at this river's bend. She inhaled the deep mineral smells of the river and gazed up into the sheltering branches of the cypress trees, the green canopy swaying with the wind. Calmness seeped into the edges of her thoughts, but still a core of anxiety yammered, keeping her slightly on edge.

Her line tugged and she fumbled the pole in surprise. Her red-and-white bobber submerged and the line in her reel unwound from the strong pull of a fish. "Walter! Something took my bait and the bobber went down. I've got a fish!"

"All right!" he said as he reeled in his line and placed the rod against a tree before walking toward her. "But nobody has a fish until it's in their net, and, by the way, call it a fish indicator. If you ask for a bobber at the tackle shop, they'll know you're a newbie."

"I *am* a newbie! Oh my gosh, hurry up. This one is really tugging on the line," Julia said with a laugh as she watched the line zig and zag in the river's current.

"Don't put a brake on the reel. Let the fish turn around and come back to you."

In fascination Julia watched the unspooling line slow down while she kept her right forefinger on the line and felt the nylon thread slip away as Walter had instructed. "Now?" she asked.

"Yes, but take it slow. You don't want to fight the fish so hard you snap the line or you pull the hook out," he said, moving next to her.

She cranked the reel handle a few clicks and the tension increased as the fish fought back. Bit by bit, Julia reeled in the weaving line until a dark, twisting form came to the surface. Walter pulled a small net from a side gear pocket in his fishing vest and stepped into the river.

Julia cranked back the reel two more clicks, gave a tug, and pulled a flashing, foot-long fish from the water.

Walter swooped under it with his net and nabbed the fish as it thrashed and dripped above the river. He held it up to Julia. "That's how we do it! You've caught a good-sized spotted bass. Not bad for a first-time angler. This one's a keeper for sure."

She peered at the gasping fish. Its sides were resplendent with a row of dotted spots and the top half of the body was a mottled green-and-brown that faded into a silvery-white belly. "When you see them in the grocery store all laid out on the ice, they're so pale and washed out. Look at the colors. She's beautiful."

"Oh, it's a she, is it?" Walter shrugged. "Could be, you've got a fifty-percent chance of being right. I'll know when I fillet her and maybe come across an egg sack."

"Fillet her?" Julia gasped. She placed her hand on Walter's forearm holding the net. "Ten minutes ago she was swimming around without any idea we existed. This is my fish, so I say she goes back."

A breeze curled around them as Julia noticed the gray-blue flecks of color in Walter's green eyes that gave them a dancing light quality. He raised his eyebrows, looked down at the fish, now lying still in the net, and shook his head. A slow grin spread across his face and Julia could imagine him as a little boy, full of mischievous adventure. "Sure, it's your catch and your choice. But we can't just eat the ugly ones."

With gentle tugs, Walter pulled the hook from the fish's mouth, walked a few steps into the river, and lowered the net into the rushing waters. Together they watched the bass dart away with a flick of its powerful tail. "Pity. A little corn meal, a nice tartar sauce with a slice of lemon, and that would have been a tasty meal," he said.

Julia snorted, but held Walter's gaze as he stood in the river's flow. "Thank you for letting her, or him, go. Now I'll guess we'll never know. I'm sure it's feeling better now." She set her rod and reel against the trunk and lowered herself next to the cypress tree, where the canopy above spread out a delicate, lacy shade.

He climbed up the bank and found a hollow between

an outcropping of the water-tree's protruding roots and settled in across from her. Stretching out his long legs, Walter gave a contented sigh and gazed at the river as small crests of waves shone gold. The sun dipped behind the horizon and a purple twilight wound into the grove of cypress and oak trees.

"How about you, Julia? Are you feeling better?" He crossed his legs at the ankles and leaned his head back against the tree, apparently as comfortable on a riverbank as on a couch in his own home. Maybe more so.

With the business of catching and releasing the bass, she'd lowered her guard and forgotten to worry. Not far from the surface, the heaviness returned and she looked away.

"Well, this feels different, being out here by the river. I'm grateful for my impromptu fishing lesson. This spot feels like it's miles from everyday stuff."

She dared a glance at him, but he only nodded. "Everyday stuff can keep us on our toes, but today seemed especially rough for you. Rowena did a good job of transferring her fear to you."

"What she said was pretty awful, but she's in pain. I'm okay, though." She noticed she glanced up and to the left, the classic sign of someone lying.

But she wasn't lying, at least not about Rowena. What had shaken her more to the core was Nick's announcement in front of Walter. No sense going there with Walter, so she focused on Rowena's threat. "I won't stop working with her, but she could do some real damage if she were to report me to my grad program."

"Yeah, she might," Walter said. "But that also would take some work on her end and what would it buy her? Bullies tend to work from either anger and intimidation, or from compliments and charm."

While he sat as relaxed as a woodcut picture of Huck Finn, their eyes met and he watched her with a steely gaze. The air between them turned electric and Julia's backbone straightened. They weren't just talking about Rowena. He was throwing Nick into the mix by describing his behavior today.

She steered the conversation to less dangerous ground. "A guy in our program got a bad review from his internship supervisor last semester and I heard the department head asked him to withdraw. To say Rowena is only a bully doesn't mean she can't do damage. She may have the teeth."

Walter gestured toward the river. "That fish you just caught, once the hook got set in its mouth, it went right into fight, flight, or freeze mode. That's the reptilian brain at work. If you place a fish, or a toad, or a lizard's brain next to our human ancient reptilian brain, which sits at the base of our skull, you'd see how similar they are. Today Rowena got hooked into a fight mode, and when that happens, people can turn ugly. What feeds her fear is she doesn't believe she's capable. That one fear sparks a whole host of connected fears, which lights up her defense mechanism, and then boom."

"Fight, flight, or freeze," Julia said, feeling glum. "But if fight is her go-to mode, what do I do?"

"Your reaction this afternoon was to freeze, and with Rowena there are worse ways to respond. We all have our favorite lizard brain paths. When you caught the fish, your first response was to react to its fear with your aggression, right? So you fought the fish. But once you gave the fish the line it needed to run, you both slowed down and regrouped. See how much easier it was to reel it in after that?"

"Rowena Horn is hardly a spotted bass."

"True." Walter picked up a small rock and threw it into

a quiet section of the river. "But the dynamics are close. When people get scared or angry, sometimes the best thing to do is let them run the line. Eventually they'll calm down and return to more reasonable thinking. Then you can go back in and do something different. But change happens only when we try and not give up."

A rising tide of frustration filled Julia. Every sharp rock dug into her backside where she sat, and her stomach gave a lion's growl of hunger, as lunch was a faint memory. She scratched a bug-bite welt rising on her ankle. "But say someone does try and they're as flexible as a rubber band by trying one new thing after another. Only things get worse, not better! What do you say to them then?" Nick's judgmental face floated before her.

Walter studied Julia, all his laid-back attitude evaporated. "By them, I assume you mean you. Correct?"

A lump formed in her throat so she could only manage a nod.

He stared off across the river at a grove of cypress trees that stretched their limbs into the sky and the roots buried into the sides of the banks. His focus seemed not on the trees, but through them.

When he slid his gaze to Julia, his eyes were filled with compassion and pain. "I know about being lost. When I talk about trying even in the face of so many obstacles, I'm not being glib. It's my mantra and it keeps me sane. Eight years ago when I lost my son to leukemia, I wondered why God continued to punish me by keeping me alive each long day after the next."

By instinct, Julia reached out her hand to Walter, but pulled it back before her fingers touched his. "Oh, Walter, I cannot even imagine. Here I am yammering on about, well, nothing, really."

He shook his head. "No, it's not who has the biggest

loss. In fact, I've found pain is the great equalizer, especially if you live long enough. But the night Luke slipped into a coma, there were still birthday balloons tied to his hospital railings. He had just turned three. A part of me slipped away with him and went numb. The morning he died, my wife and I were holding him in his hospital bed. I can honestly say that was the last thing we ever did together. Luke had been our center and our heart, but with him gone, we didn't have enough between us to keep going."

Walter tossed another small rock into the river and together they watched it blip into the water. In a quiet voice, he continued, "The clinic saved me, actually. People were counting on me, so I kept showing up and going through the motions. As it turned out, I was the one who ended up counting on the staff and they never let me down. They knew when to check in with me and see how I was doing. And at other times, when to leave me the hell alone. But I was never left alone, if you know what I mean. There's never been a finer group of people." His voice was thick with emotion.

Julia knew Walter wasn't married, and had suspected he was divorced, but no one at the clinic had said so much as a word about his loss. She had noticed a loyalty the staffers had toward Walter, and he towards them, that bespoke of deep layers.

They had each other's backs.

The staffers weathered the wars of their clients' problems, but behind the scenes they endured their own as well. She could see how their trust was earned, and with it a sense of family foreign to Julia's patchwork past. Mid-level newspapers could be full of energy, as each edition demanded the pages get filled with stories and pictures. But they were also revolving doors of journalists coming and going for the next big thing.

A stab of regret shot through Julia as she thought of the budget cuts. "You were lucky to have the people at the clinic."

"Yes, but luck can also be made." He reached into a pocket of his fishing vest and pulled out a flat, plastic, rectangular box, which revealed rows and rows of tiny fishing flies, bejeweled in reds, blues, yellows, and greens. They gleamed in the box. "Luke used to sit in my lap and watch me make my fishing flies from little scraps of household items. Rubber bands, plastic bags, bristle from brushes, and bits of feathers. I'd always add a colorful bead at the end and hand it to him. He thought I'd created an actual bug and it would make him laugh."

Julia recalled the first time she'd met Walter, seated in his office in front of his vise and desktop magnifying lens, working on a yellow fly. She smiled.

"Every single time I add the bead at the end for Luke. Remember the fly I gave you in my office that day?"

"The Pheasant Tail Nymph. How could I forget?" Julia said, conjuring an image of the lure's red curl of tinsel jutting out from its back.

Walter nodded. "Those were Luke's favorites, all the deep greens and reds. And when I make them, just for a bit, it reminds me of being with my boy. I guess what I'm saying is that, yes, the clinic sustains me, and coming out here to the river sustains me. Can't say I've trusted faith enough to jump back all the way into life. Funny thing about risk, it runs along a razor's edge, with fear on one side and growth on the other. Can't have one without the other."

With the sun low behind the hills, it had grown so dark Julia couldn't make out what emotion was on Walter's face.

He glanced around. "Uh oh, I've kept you out too late.

Let's get you home before you turn into a pumpkin."

He stood up and extended his hand for Julia, who took it and curled her fingers around his. They faced each other for a few seconds before Walter reached behind her and picked up her fishing pole, which was leaning up against a tree.

Without being fully aware she was doing it, Julia raised her head to be kissed. When he walked past her, blood thudded in her ears and she was thankful he couldn't see the flush fanning across her cheeks.

As they traveled in silence up a trail that snaked through the woods, a deeper darkness closed in. A blink of a light from the corner of her eye surprised her and she stopped as a firefly drifted by and flashed gold again as if to push back the gloom.

"Walter, wait," she said, as she turned in a circle. He took several steps closer to her as she stared in wonder into the thicket, which revealed hundreds of fireflies flashing and twinkling in an ancient dance. Their lights shone bright against the dark.

"Golly," Julia breathed.

Walter smiled down at her and said nothing, but stepped a bit closer. Together they watched the slow circling of luminescence weaving around them, past them, and deep into the woods.

She aimed an imaginary camera to capture the scene, in case she should need to retrieve it in Dallas during the lean times. This one night, she'd experienced magic in the most unexpected place, with the most unexpected man. But the deed was done, or at least imminent: the marriage, the move, and Nick were all on track.

An image came to mind of Walter unhooking her fish and letting it slip away into the green-brown river and into cool freedom. How she envied that fish.

Chapter 34

The low monotone voices of the ten o'clock news drifted through the closed bedroom door, and if Julia focused, she might've been able to make out the story Nick was watching. Instead, she turned her back to the door and stared out the window, where a few faint stars twinkled beyond the gauze of the curtains.

A tiny meow from the floor heralded Trixie's arrival. The cat jumped up and landed neatly beside Julia then flopped down beside her. She flicked the end of her tail, signaling that the petting may commence.

"Hey there, bag-of-tricks," Julia said, scratching the top of the cat's head.

Trixie trained large, yellow eyes on Julia before closing them to stretch out her brown-and-tanned striped legs. When her paws touched the open laptop next to Julia, Nick's computer sprang to life. Pictures of a townhouse interior splashed across the screen, with the realtor's elfin face and cheery tagline, "Call Brandi!" tucked into the corner.

Of course she's a Brandi, Julia had thought after receiving the real estate link from Nick that morning. He would not have gravitated towards a Dan, Tom, or Mike. Julia flipped the screen shut with a loud snap. Trixie jumped up, threw an indignant glance at Julia over her shoulder, and then disappeared back under the bed.

"Sorry, girl."

Silence.

The phone pinged, it was a reply from Fiona to her earlier lunch request, with a curt, *When and where?*

Julia groaned and sat up on the bed, restless and irritable. The last time she felt at peace was on the riverbank with Walter two nights ago, an evening she had considered telling Nick about, but couldn't quite get the words to leave her mouth.

And it wasn't as though she were afraid Nick would be jealous. He'd probably be more curious about why she would battle the heat and bugs while wrestling a rod and reel just to land a fish on the side of a mossy riverbank. Julia imagined he'd view it much like he would going to a monster truck pull—something sweaty and dirty and physical. Okay for others, but not exactly his cup of tea.

She had a memory postcard from the Guadalupe River, and she kept it to herself so as not to cheapen it in an attempt to make Nick understand. The image of Walter sitting across from her, dappled by the sunlight, floated back. His long fingers, squared at the tips and cupped on one knee, were artist's hands. She felt him caressing the back of her neck, and then her eyes flew open.

"Okay, stop," she said out loud. She was not going to let her mind go there. She scolded herself: Walter was her boss and in one month she was moving with Nick.

She padded over to the open window and peered up into the inky sky splashed with thousands of pinpoint stars. They reminded her of scattered diamonds glowing across black velvet. The constellation Scorpio rode low on the horizon with its tail curled behind the silhouette of a church steeple.

Julia traced the tail to the middle until she found the ruby glow of Antares, the scorpion's heart. In high school, her science teacher had shown pictures of Antares and its faint companion star that circled the dying supergiant.

Leaning out the window into the night breeze, she felt a fondness for this ancient star that burned relentlessly, its destiny to collapse within itself.

She breathed in the evening air and tried to ignore the nagging feeling that she had crossed a boundary from spending quiet time in the bedroom to hiding out. Squaring her shoulders, she opened the door into the living room lit by the television's blue flickering light and walked out.

Dead-center in the high-definition screen, Calliope Smythe held her microphone, emblazoned with the Channel 7 logo. An aggressive tilt to her head made it seem as if she were about to devour it rather than speak into it. The lemony yellow of her suit was a shade duller than her waves of cascading blonde hair. Julia squinted at all the brightness.

"And with no end in sight from these triple-digit temperatures, our local farmers struggle to keep their crops from looking like this," Calliope said, brandishing a wrinkled cantaloupe the size of a misshapen softball. She dropped the gourd with a thud as someone from off-camera handed her a plump cantaloupe veined with healthy, dark green stripes. "And more like this!"

She aimed her smile at the camera in a practiced gesture, but with a mischievous glint in her eyes. No doubt this compare-and-contrast stunt was Calliope's idea of a clever way to demonstrate what a drought-riddled melon looks like next to the one obviously bought at the grocery store. Too bad no one had bothered to peel off the label peeking below her thumb.

Calliope swung her microphone to the right and the picture widened to show an older man in overalls with white tufts of hair sticking out from under his sun-bleached cap. He shifted from side to side like someone whose few options for escape had evaporated.

"We are on the farm of Mr. Weitz, a third-generation Elston farmer, who's been struggling this year to barely keep his crops alive from this crushing drought," Calliope intoned to the camera, ignoring the man who appeared to edge out of the frame even though he stood still. "Tell us, sir, what has this scorching drought been like for you and your business?"

"Oh, boy." Mr. Weitz scratched his head through his hat. "It's been no picnic. But neither was the drought of '85. Now, let me tell you what, that one was a doozy. We survived it okay, so I'll guess we'll get past this one."

Calliope frowned and tilted her microphone in closer to the farmer, who shifted his weight back onto his heels. "But these record heat days must be taking a toll on you and your crops. What is it you most need now to get through this emergency drought situation?"

He furrowed his brow, as though considering this to be a trick question. "Um, rain?"

Oh God. Seriously? Julia turned to where Nick sat on the couch and expected to see him shaking his head in wonderment that some editor had greenlighted this segment for broadcast. Instead he stared transfixed at the screen, and when she glanced back at the television, she saw only Calliope wrapping up the segment.

A strangled sound escaped Julia's throat and Nick glanced up, startled. Guilt slid across his face and he sat up straighter and said in a cheerful lilt, "There you are! Come over here and sit next to me. The news is about over." He punched a button on the clicker and Calliope's face went dark.

Julia did not move. "How can the news be over if they haven't even gotten to the weather?" Her tone approached an icy level.

"What's to say about the weather? It's hot and we're in for more of the same. So what did you think of the real estate site? The place on Grover Avenue caught my eye, and that big backyard is a plus," he said, his words slightly rushed.

In the past, she would have ignored Nick's staring at an attractive woman, telling herself looking wasn't doing. But tonight her anger burned. "Nick, you weren't watching the news. You were *watching* the news. What was so fascinating about a badly reported drought story?"

He gave a shrug. "The story seemed fine. How do you mean badly reported?"

"Are you kidding me about that amateur-hour piece? Your ears must have shut down because you were too busy ogling. Do you have a thing for Calliope?"

A blush crept up Nick's throat and a vein throbbed in the middle of his forehead. "What? No! Can't a guy sit down and catch the news without being accused of having an affair?"

"An affair?" Julia said, her voice rising. "Who said anything about an affair?"

Nick came off the couch and he strode over with his hands up in a placating manner. "Wait, wait, wait. This is nuts. Watching TV is not the equivalent of having an affair."

He took her hand and pulled her towards him. In normal times, her body would have responded to the taut muscles in his arms and shoulders, but now all she wanted was to shove him away. She allowed herself to stay in his embrace a few minutes before she stepped back and stared hard up into his face. His expression was composed as he smiled down at her with concern in his eyes, as though she were the problem.

"Are you saying I can't trust my eyes? I saw what I saw, Nick."

He edged in closer and ran a finger down the small of her back. "I don't know what you saw, but I know what is what, Jules. You're just on edge. Change is hard, and it's hard for me, too. But we'll get through this if we work together. Don't make up problems that don't exist."

He hardened as he pressed against her, as though this tug-of-war excited him. Still, her body was wooden.

Her voice trembled but her gaze remained steady. "Nick, I hope what you're saying is true. Because I want to believe you. But if you're lying and making me out to be the crazy one, then that's a whole new ring of hell."

"Theater major." He kissed her on the mouth.

"What?" She blinked hard, pulling away.

"Theater major. Wasn't that on the list of possible careers from your shrink? With all your imagination and fire, that could be your true calling." He reached up the front of her shirt and slowly ran a finger across her breast through her bra.

This time her body did respond, and she relaxed in his arms.

"C'mon, baby. Let's do something real and quit jumping at ghosts," he said, his voice husky.

Words rose in her throat to war with him, but were silenced as a wave of desire ran through her body.

He's manipulating me.

But he also smelled good and she felt protected as he slipped his strong arms around her. She closed her eyes and kissed him back, tentatively at first, then with more passion.

Let me think of only now. Now is real.

As he unbuttoned his shirt, she tried to stay in the moment. But an image came to her of a lighthouse sweeping its beam across a calm ocean surface broken only by the tips of a razor-sharp coastline lurking below the surface.

Chapter 35

Usually before the clinic opened, the only cars in the parking lot would have been Walter's truck and Mona's sedan, but this morning Marlene, Paulie, Glen, and Angel's cars were also parked there.

After climbimg out of her Honda, Julia crossed the parking lot. She eased the clinic door open to reduce the squeal of the ancient hinges and walked down the hallway toward the conference room.

Marlene and Glen sat huddled on the far side of the table, speaking in a low murmur. Across from them, Angel slouched with his hands folded one-over-the-over. His terse nod revealed, however, he was definitely not in his usual bubble of calm.

Julia slid in next to Mona, who was peering into a large compact mirror as she applied a smooth line of liquid eyeliner to her upper right eyelid. Julia was impressed by Mona's expertise; she tried liquid eyeliner a few times and, after drawing blotchy rings around her eyes, had given up and tossed the wand into the trashcan.

Paulie sat hunched over a stack of charts on the other side of Mona, oblivious to her grooming ritual, and was lost in writing client progress notes. Julia considered greeting him, but his studied concentration was such a cocoon she thought better of it and turned to Mona.

"Man, looks like the gang's all here." Julia kept her voice low to match the subdued quiet around the table.

Mona glanced up, her face was mostly bare of make-up

and revealed her youth. Julia had always pegged her to be in her mid-twenties, but now stripped of foundation, blushes, powders, and mascara, Mona seemed closer to nineteen than twenty-five.

She glanced at Julia under the harsh fluorescent lights and managed half an eye roll. "Like we had a choice. Especially when we all got Walter's mystery email last night ordering us for an all-hands meeting. *All hands.* Sheesh, who does he think he is, Admiral Byrd? Are we supposed to swab some damn deck? FTN."

"FTN?"

"Fuck that noise." Paulie didn't bother to raise his head from his writing.

Julia's eyebrows shot up, but Mona's attention was back to the compact as she applied a smooth line on her left eyelid, dark enough to arouse Cleopatra's jealousy. When Walter's email had arrived last night around nine o'clock, Julia hadn't felt irritation at coming in so early, only dread. Rumors could soon be whispers of the past, because things at the clinic were about to change.

At the other end of the table, Glen stopped his conversation with Marlene and said, "Stash the war paint, Mona. Here comes Walter."

All their heads swiveled toward the door when Walter strode in, his face a mask. Julia's heart thudded in her chest. As he went to his usual seat at the table next to Marlene, Julia realized they were all sitting in the same spots as the day of her interview three months ago.

How could it be that only a short time ago all these people were complete strangers to me?

Glancing at each somber face awakened a tug of connection to each of them, as if she were a thread woven into their tapestry. Julia puzzled at what she was feeling, until a word a floated up: family.

Walter eased his tall frame into the chair at the head of the table and his gaze swept their faces, pausing briefly on Julia's. Her neck and cheeks grew warm. She ducked her chin, hoping nobody had noticed.

She realized right away that she needn't have worried. All their attention was on Walter and the only sound in the room came from the wheeze of the ancient air conditioner.

He cleared his throat as if it were dry. "Sorry for the early hour, but I wanted to get ahead of the news so you'll hear it first from me. And not from some media source." Contempt frosted his voice.

At the sight of Walter's drawn face, Julia wished Nick could understand the pain that often flowed beneath the facts of his tightly composed stories. For once in his life, he might be at a loss of words.

Walter hesitated. "As you all know, we've been working on a bare-bones budget for the past five years.

"Yeah, that sounds about right," Angel said. "Five years since the last time I had a raise."

A murmur of assent circled the room as Julia sat back in disbelief. "You guys haven't had a raise in five years?"

Marlene lifted her chin up a notch. "Well, it's certainly not something one advertises, but concessions had to be made for the clinic to continue operating."

"Sure," Glen said. "You're the first new therapist here in a couple of years. Even the pointy-headed accountants over at the state budget office couldn't say no to a free intern." He winked at Julia and said in a loud, conspiratorial whisper, "Not that you aren't worth every penny, Ms. Longley."

Walter held up his hand. "This is not about raises or new hires. I'm afraid we're going down a new road. The state has proposed budget cuts in our funding, and frankly our clinic's board hasn't fought back as hard as I'd hoped.

We will sustain deep and substantial cuts."

"How deep?" Suspicion tinged Mona's voice. "Because I've got to buy a car, and those payments don't grow on trees."

"Our operating budget has been cut by over fifty percent," Walter said.

Stunned silence rolled through the room. To hear the words out loud was even more terrible than Julia had imagined. She glanced at each of the staffer's faces as they absorbed this news and jumped when an angry voice to her left declared, "Well, what the hell!"

Paulie's face reddened and his eyes were ablaze. "Fifty percent? How can we survive? What is the county expecting us to do, live off air? My wife is already threatening to leave me if I don't get a raise this year. I was going to ask you if I could work some overtime!"

Glen blew a low whistle. "Would you even be allowed to do couple's counseling if you're in the middle of divorce, Paulie?"

"Shut it, Glen," Paulie said, slumping back into his chair.

Everyone swiveled their heads back at Walter, who appeared haggard, with purple smudges under his eyes as though he hadn't slept well in days. Still, he held Paulie's gaze.

"For some of us, the state expects we take significant pay cuts. But for others they recommend termination from their jobs. As an agency, our clinic is expensive because of how many services we provide. Because of that, we've been running in the red, with increasing deficits each year. The state compensated for years and floated us, but our last four quarters were just too burdensome, so they slashed funding. We have thirty days to comply."

Reaching out her hand, Marlene rested it on Walter's

arm. "Comply how, dear?"

He swallowed hard and said in a quiet voice that carried all the way down the end of the table where Julia sat clenching and unclenching her hands. "I've got to terminate half the staff in the next four weeks."

Marlene drew her hand back to cover her mouth, her eyes searching his face.

There was a shocked silence before Angel said, "Boss man, can we transfer to the Wildwood Clinic in Comal County?" He ran both his hands over his bald head.

"Sure, that's an idea," Paulie said, a bright gleam of hope in his eye. "I don't mind the drive and maybe some of my clients can follow me—"

"No, Paulie," Walter said. "That's impossible. Wildwood will be completely shut down before the end of the year. They're in it worse than we are."

Paulie stared, his mouth opening and closing, but with no sounds coming out.

Julia could stand it no more. "What about the clients? What's going to happen to them?"

"Some will flood the emergency rooms at every hospital and walk-in clinic," Walter said in a flat tone. "They'll take up the beds at the shelters, until they're at overcapacity. Others may get arrested for erratic behavior, trespassing, loitering, public sleeping, stealing, as well as from people's general fear of mental illness."

Walter spoke to the group, but his eyes never left Julia's. "And some may commit suicide."

Her heart constricted as Julia thought of the clients who had sat across from her in counseling sessions and the ones she'd seen in the lobby, waiting for their sessions.

"And these budgeting people know this and don't care?" As soon as Julia asked the question, she knew the answer. Of course, Walter had warned them about probable outcomes, no doubt pushing and pulling every lever he could with the budgeting committee.

"Oh, yes. The state knows," Walter said with a rueful half-smile. "Every year our budget threatens to be slashed, and every year I've been able to stave it off."

"And how do you pick who gets let go?" Paulie shoved back the stack of charts in front of him. "I mean, what do we do, draw from a pack of straws and hope someone else pulls the short one?"

For Julia, seeing an angry Paulie was nothing short of surreal. She hadn't even known he was capable of such an emotion.

Walter considered him, then let go a deep breath. "The committee doesn't care how many years you've worked here or how glowing your annual reviews are. People with higher caseloads may have more protection, but I am being directed to let go of at least one therapist and one case manager."

"Oh, man." Paulie buried his head into his hands. Mona reached over and put an arm around him.

Something wet slipped down Julia's cheek, and she touched her face, surprised to feel tears on her fingertips.

Paulie was going to be let go.

While he was as steady as a clock, Paulie tended to plod through each session, often going past his scheduled fifty minutes, which made his following sessions start late. Compounding the problem, afterwards he would spend an inordinate amount of time crafting meticulous treatment plans notes. He saw fewer clients than Marlene, but his clients were loyal to him and would usually wait in the lobby. Walter prodded him to speed up and Mona chided him for letting the lobby fill up with his clients, but he was unwilling, or more likely, unable to work any faster.

"Paulie, nothing has been decided yet," Marlene said,.

"I'm at a greater risk than you because I've been here the longest, and as small as my salary is, it's probably higher than yours. In fact ..." She turned to Walter. "Let's stop all this hand wringing and get on with it. I'm the obvious choice to be terminated. Let me tender my resignation, with say, the usual two-week notice?"

Walter's jaw muscles knotted as he stood and addressed the entire room. "We are *not* doing this! Yes, decisions have to be made, but I am responsible for these decisions. And as much as I appreciate you trying to save me the pain of having to choose," he said, his voice softening as he nodded to Marlene, "it's not your responsibility. As director, it's mine. We're a business, but in my heart, you're all more than employees. So let's not allow some budgeting committee to take that away from us, too. We'll find a way to continue to support each other."

In silence, Marlene gazed up at him, her eyes brimming with tears. The distant squall of the front door opening, followed by plodding footsteps broke the quiet.

"Who has an eight o'clock client?" Mona said.

An answer came in the insistent dinging of the lobby desk bell. Groans went up and down the table as Glen said, "Cue Rowena."

"But we don't have an appointment," said Julia. "Is she here to see someone else?"

Heaving a deep sigh, Mona jabbed her make-up back into her purse and said through gritted teeth, "Mija, I think we all know the answer to that. But when I get let go, and believe me—I know I will—Ms. Horn will not be a part of this familia that I'll miss."

Mona disappeared down the hallway calling, "Hold your water, Rowena! I'm coming." And she was gone.

Chairs scraped back as the staff around Julia gathered their belongings in numb silence. Was this the last time they would all be together in one room?

The terrible secret Nick had given her, like a poisoned apple, was now everyone's reality. Being released from the burden of her knowledge gave her no relief.

No matter how cute a house Brandi could find for them in Dallas, in Julia's heart, Elston would always be her home. She considered now an excellent time to put her head down on the table and cry, but a barrage of insistent rings from the lobby bell interrupted her.

"Oh my God!" Julia gasped to Glen's empty Coke can in front of her. She grabbed her keys and purse and almost dared the day to get worse as she hurried to the lobby.

Chapter 36

Like a burlap sack filled with stones, Rowena plopped down across from Julia and gripped both chair arms with her meaty fists, as though anticipating some kind of rocket thrust propulsion. "So?"

Patience.

"What a surprise to see you so early in the morning, Rowena. If we had an appointment, I'm sorry, I wasn't aware of it."

With exaggerated slowness, Rowena swiveled her head left and right, as if taking in the small room, the leveled her gaze back at Julia. "Sorry to get all up 'n your busy morning and all. Should I take a number and head back to the lobby?"

Julia counted to five. "You're not disrupting, I just didn't expect you. How are you doing?"

"Best if we quit with the chit chat." Rowena bent down, grunting from the effort, and reached into the battered backpack at her feet. She pulled out a rolled-up sheath of paper with the word "Appeals" visible on the title page, and handed it to Julia. The disability application packet was dog-eared and stained. Rowena had attempted to answer some of the questions, and her script was surprisingly elegant and looping.

"Here. I'm bringing it in like you told me to. Now fill in the parts them people said they need and mail it today. Please."

Taking the application, Julia slid it face down on the

desk. "I'll see what I can do with it and I'll run the whole packet by Marlene to make sure I've filled it out correctly. But that still leaves the last part of our agreement. One more try at job coaching?"

"You can't make me do nothing I don't want to," Rowena said. "I can haul this right across the hall there and have Marlene put a rubber stamp on it, since it sounds like she's going to be doin' all your work for you anyways."

A fair observation. After Walter's announcement not even fifteen minutes earlier, plus her own time here down to the wire, really, why should she care that Rowena was signing up for a life of merely eking out a living? It was like caring for a dripping snowman at the tail-end of February. By any logic she should give up, and lord knows her life would be so much easier.

As Rowena sat with her arms crossed and her face stony, Julia was struck less by the walls her client had built around herself than by the tiny cracks of vulnerability that shone through. A row of sweat beaded on Rowena's top lip, betraying her bluster as a way to protect her fear.

Julia paused. "You're right. I can't make you do anything you don't want to. And I don't want to. But sometimes we do things because staying stuck is its own misery, right? If you're trying new things, it's not a guarantee everything is going to be okay, but at least it's something different."

Rowena's granite face remained unchanged, but her crossed arms relaxed a bit around the elbows. Silence stretched between them and Julia willed herself into quiet.

"Okay," Rowena said after several moments. "But last time to be your lab rat, okay? Don't want nobody saying Rowena Horn's word is no good. Where's you want to meet? That same place?"

Julia didn't dare speak the name Penny Pincher out loud for fear of bursting their small bubble of detente, but instead nodded. "Let me call the manager and get it all set up, and then I'll call you. Okay?"

"'K," Rowena barked. She stood up then swept out the door.

Exhaling a long breath, Julia said to the empty room, "Lab rat. Yeah, right."

She rested her chin on her cupped hand and knew this was going to be her last time to work with Rowena. No other staffer would have the time—or the inclination—to encourage Rowena enough to go out into the world to make a difference.

A month from now she and Nick would be settling into their new home, undoubtedly to Rowena's relief. But with the reduced help from the clinic, Rowena's path as the town's reclusive shut-in would narrow down to an eventuality. Julia sighed, uncapped her pen, reached for the application, and tried to focus on its instructions.

Chapter 37

After Rowena left, a shell-shocked quiet draped the clinic as the staffers retreated to their own corners of the office. Julia's nine o'clock client, a single guy in his late twenties who had never had a girlfriend but claimed he desperately wanted one, spent the majority of the hour explaining the medicinal benefits of pot.

She tried to focus on their conversation but her mind drifted as he went deeper into the intricacies of how he'd rigged up grow lights in his bedroom closet for his new hybrid marijuana plants.

"And after a couple of tokes off a spliff of my own personal blend, man," he said, "I'm flying so high that half the time I don't even remember to take my Prozac. Do you think that's a sign I don't need it?"

Voices in the hallway grew louder and Julia could almost make the words out. The session ended with Julia urging her client to keep taking his medications and explore how being stoned most of the time might not exactly be making him boyfriend material as she ushered him out the door.

Once outside her office, she glanced to her right where Paulie stood down the hallway talking to an older woman who clutched a pocketbook to her chest, her scrawny collarbones jutting out like commas.

"But I've been seeing you for four years!" the woman said. "I don't want to start with someone new. What am I going to do? Are you sure about this?"

Paulie shook his head. "Yes. I mean, no, Doris. I'm not totally sure about when my last day will be, but I want you to be ready, in case."

"What are you going to do? And that sweet wife of yours, are you two going to move away?" She twisted her hands with knuckles large as marbles. "Will you start someplace in town? Or even close to town? Why, I could follow you!"

He shook his head with even more vigor. "I'm not sure what I'm going to do, but I want to help you get used to the idea of transferring to a new counselor. I know how hard it was for you to adjust to coming to see me, but I believe I can get you in with Marlene Foster here at the clinic. Ms. Foster has many years of experience."

Doris pulled a tissue out of her jacket sleeve and dabbed her eyes. "I'm sure she's a corker, but you're the one I'm used to. I don't want to break in someone new. You've helped me so much and now I'll have to tell my stories all over again to a stranger. You'll let me know if you can stay, right?"

She peered up at him with such intensity that Paulie could only nod as the color rose from his neck to flame across his cheeks.

The woman walked past Julia, glanced up at her, and said, "Wickedness is afoot."

When she went around the corner, Julia noticed Walter standing there. Julia startled at the sight of him then glanced back, but Paulie had already slipped into his office. Walter held his silence as she walked up to him.

"Why did Paulie tell this woman he's being let go? Nothing's been decided, and what if he's wrong and needlessly upsetting her? You must have heard part of what he told that Doris woman and you didn't stop him."

Her indignation propelled her forward until she was but a foot from him. They stared at each other for one beat, maybe two, and Julia wanted to shake him and kiss him all at once. His green eyes held hers until her heart thudded inside her rib cage like a bird, confused and trapped.

Walter stepped half a pace backwards. "No, I didn't stop him."

She blinked then understood. Everyone understood what was going to happen, except for her. She slumped against the wall and wished Walter would reach out and wrap her into his strong arms.

Julia pushed this wish aside to clear her mind. "What's he going to do? Paulie's not exactly the kind of guy to go and make something happen. He seems better at—"

"Maintaining an even strain," Walter said. "Yes, I know. But Paulie will have to figure this one out. It might be a challenge for him to fit in with the few private practices we have in Elston, but there's also hospital and rehab work. Monkey wrenches are being thrown into the works for all of us. Luckily for you, your exit plan is set, right? I believe Mona said you and your fiancé are planning a wedding in December?"

At the idea of Walter slipping away, her heart slowed as if it tried to pump molasses. Her mind clung to a fragment: he'd asked Mona about her, but she shoved the thought away. Of course he did. It was his job to think about everyone, but as a summer intern, she should have been low on his list of concerns.

Julia lifted her chin. "Looks that way."

What else was there to say? Moving away had morphed from idea to fact in a matter of weeks. Following Nick's dreams made her feel flat as a sheet of paper, and if she got any flatter, he could simply fold her into a small square, stuff her into an envelope, and mail her to their new house, where she could be easily slid under the door.

Walter tilted his head for a few seconds while he

observed her, and their silence stretched.

"Right," he said at last. "Well, meanwhile, in the time we have left, we still have plenty to do. Marlene is in the back, culling out some old files. We'll need to do a huge file transfer to a medical storage facility, but we might as well get a jump on it now. How about if you give her a hand?"

"Sure." Julia fought the urge to grab him by the shoulders and shout, "No, I don't want to pull files, I don't want to move to Dallas, and I don't want to walk away from you."

She pulled away, astonished at her need to feel his lips on hers, and headed for the file room before one of those treacherous thoughts blurted out. Yet her mind cast and spun for a way to retrace her steps to Walter.

Julia turned—he stood watching her—and the words "save me" almost formed on her lips. But save her from what? Dallas could be her whole new beginning or a colossal mistake, but either way, Elston was a closing door. Still, anyone from the outside would say she'd be a fool to walk away from Nick and their future together for a man at the helm of a clinic in chaotic free-fall.

She swallowed and willed her feet forward, away from Walter.

Walking into the dimly lit back room, Julia found Marlene in front of an opened drawer of an industrial-gray file cabinet, with other cabinets lined up on either side of her like dusty sentries. Marlene startled and spun around, a file in her hand.

Julia's eyes widened at the sight of her supervisor crying, as tears cut clean lines through the powered foundation on her cheeks.

"Oh, you gave me quite the fright." Marlene faced away and made secretive swipes at her face. "Darn allergies," she said in a muffled voice.

"Yeah, cedar's pretty high," Julia said, naming the

first pollen that came to mind. She cleared her throat and plowed on, "Um, Walter sent me in here to help you pull some files that need to go into storage."

She came up beside Marlene, whose head was bent as she stared into the open file drawer. The manila folder she grasped trembled. With a gentle stroke, Julia removed the file from her hand and gave her a shoulder hug.

A wall between them crumbled and Marlene dropped her head on Julia's shoulder, covering her face with her hand. "It's just a job!" she cried. "Why do I care? I mean, I'll find another one, right?"

"Right! Of course you will," Julia whispered, catching a whiff of Marlene's lilac perfume, amazed at this turn of events.

Marlene whipped her head up. "No! No, I won't. Of course, that's what I tell myself logically, yet realistically? At my age! Who am I kidding?"

A vulnerability arose between them, as though for the first time Marlene saw Julia as a whole person.

"But if you haven't even tried, who are you to say what's realistic or not? How many years have you been here? I mean, a bunch, right? You can try another clinical setting. Or you can set up your own private practice. All you need is to figure out how to do your own billing, right?"

In slow motion, Marlene raised her head and gazed at Julia, her icy-hazel eyes rimmed in red. She seemed to be assessing, as though her mind was an abacus sliding the beads from one side to the other.

"A bunch?" Marlene laughed. "Yes, I've been here more bunches of years than I'd like to admit. But it will take more than learning billing for me to make an independent living as a therapist. The clinic has always handled the business side, which is an asset, but maybe made me weak. Exactly what my daughter kept warning me about.

But we're always so busy here, that the idea of running my own practice was not on my, as they say, radar screen. Now, well, here we are. And really, who do I have to blame but myself? I tell my clients about how to be self-sufficient, yet I'm the biggest hypocrite of them all."

She paused and inhaled, more of a gasp. "I need a break." She walked to the end of the room, opened a door beside the last filing cabinet, one Julia had never noticed, and disappeared.

Sunshine streamed from the open door, lighting a path for Julia as she followed Marlene out to the alleyway. After the dimness of the file room, Julia winced in the bright light.

At a window ledge, Marlene picked up a loose red brick and pulled out a neatly folded cigarette pack, plucked out a cigarette and pink lighter, and lit the end until it glowed.

She threw a glance at Julia. "Yes, I smoke. Or rather I've picked up the nasty habit in the past few weeks. After a twenty-year hiatus, I might add. I'd ask you not to judge me, but that's probably another ship of mine that's sailed." She took a deep drag and exhaled a thin stream of blue smoke. "Damn coffin nails, but one cannot deny the medicinal calming effects of nicotine."

Marlene's fear snaked into Julia's gut, paralyzing her. First Paulie, now Marlene. It was all overwhelming. Still, a burrowing thought broke the surface.

"You know, Marlene, we talked before about starting a practice in theory. And while I also wouldn't have a clue where to start, what with your knowledge and experience, maybe we could figure it out together."

The idea shimmered and took shape in Julia's mind, and her pulse quickened. *What if Marlene and I started our own private practice?*

Fresh energy surged into her heart as the vision gained

more color. In a flash, she imagined a wooden sign planted in the front of a tiny bungalow house with their names etched on a wooden sign and embossed in gold paint. The walls were painted a deep plum and through the open windows a mild summer breeze wafted in as she sat in an armchair, thick and soft, with a client across from her on a matching couch. A yellow candle burned in the corner. She was anchored in, doing good work, around loving people, and a feeling of right descended.

Her voice grew stronger. "We could do this, Marlene! I don't know how, but together we can figure out the details, don't you see?"

For a second Julia's hope leaped between them, and the older woman's worried creases between her eyebrows relaxed.

Then Marlene's expression changed to puzzlement. "But my dear, aren't you and your young man moving away? And let's not forget that you've still in the midst of your graduate school program. While your idea is intriguing, you and I starting a private practice is not exactly executable, is it?"

The soap bubble burst and Julia sank back into reality where she and Marlene stood in an alleyway behind the clinic with a view of a dented dumpster. The image of their own office was stripped of fairy dust and candlelight as the sunlight cast shadows into the etched lines around Marlene's eyes and mouth.

Julia's eyes teared up, and she wasn't sure if it was from the deep bitterness of how her life had risen up to wash her away from Elston, or from the frustrated way Marlene had tossed the cigarette to the pavement and ground it under her patent-leather pump with the one-inch sensible heel.

Chapter 38

E ven the worst of weeks must come to a merciful end, and Julia let out a sigh of relief when the hands of her desk clock swept to five. She signed her last progress note. After collecting a small stack of charts, she wandered up to the front desk.

Mona was applying a dark lip liner around her fresh coat of a corral-colored lipstick, this time sans mirror, another one of her skills that Julia marveled at. She glanced up. "Hey, chica, thank God it's Friday, and all that. If you're done, let's go to the Cedar Door. Angel, Glen, and Marlene are already there."

"Marlene's at the Cedar Door?" Julia tried to imagine such an improbable sight.

"Crazy, right? I wonder if she made the manager bleach their table down first. Bet you she brought along one of her crocheted chair cushions to sit on."

"My, the times really are a-changing." Julia shook her head. What was next? The sky opening up and raining frogs?

"So c'mon," Mona said with a conspirator's smile, "give me five minutes and let's go in your car. Someone needs to be the designated driver, and after all this awfulness, better you than me."

An image came to Julia of Nick at the condo sorting through his bookcases, deciding which of his historical non-fiction tomes to pack and which to dump at the used bookstore. He'd already called her at lunch and asked her to stop by the moving van center and pick up more boxes. "I should probably be getting home—"

"How many more days do you think we all have together here? Besides, Walter mentioned he might drop by," Mona said, all at once preoccupied with rooting around in her purse.

"So what? I mean, of course he would. He wants to support all of us." Julia's voice had risen with each word.

"And what better place to support us than at the diviest bar in Elston?" Mona's eyes widened with innocence. "FYI alert, before he left he told me to make sure you knew you were included. So come or don't come. But if a fine man like Walter asked about me, and it might be the last time I could hang with him …" She rose and slung her purse over her shoulder. "Let's just say, my mama didn't raise no fool." She dangled her keychain, fat with a fist of keys, before Julia. "So who's driving?"

In her mind's eye she was walking out with Mona, getting in the car, and calling Nick along the way to the bar, to say she was going to a work happy hour. And as long as she brought him moving boxes a couple of hours later, he probably wouldn't care.

Julia closed her eyes and pushed the thought away. "No, Nick and I need to pack tonight, I promised him."

Pity softened the contours of Mona's face as she shook her head. "Don't take this all wrong and all, but sometimes you're just plain dumb."

"I have a boyfriend, remember, Mona?" Julia's words sizzling like fat raindrops on hot pavement.

Mona stopped short and spun around. "No, Freud. You have a fiancé, remember? And yeah, he's fine. He'd be all kinds of honey for all kinds of buzzing bees. But Walter is fine, too, both inside and out. I've never seen him look at anyone the way he looks at you. And know what, Julia? I've seen you looking back. If I was you, the last thing I'd be doing is packing boxes to move away with Mr. Arm Candy and leave behind a good man who, right this damn minute, is waiting for you."

"It's impossible!"

"Why?"

She sputtered and her mind whirled. *Why is it impossible?*

"Because it's too late," she said. "Nick and I are engaged. And besides, Walter is my boss!"

Mona's eyebrows made perfect tents above her incredulous eyes. "Yeah, right. Like no one's ever dated their boss before. But you know what, girl?" She slung her purse over her shoulder and started for the door. "Not once did you ever say you loved your guy. Just that it was impossible. Think on that, counselor."

Julia lowered herself into Mona's still-warm chair and watched the front door close behind her with a decisive swoosh and hinge rasp. Loneliness crept into her bones. Was this is how it felt to be stranded at sea and bobbing in a lifeboat that had once been packed with panicked, bedraggled passengers, only to dwindle down to being the last soul?

Would the only sound be the lapping waves against the hull?

She picked up the office phone and dialed Nick's cell. It rang twice before going to voicemail. Julia slammed the phone down with such surprising force that she winced. Nick wasn't answering again.

She frowned at the word *again*. It used to be that whenever she called him, he'd pick up on the second ring, or call her back soon afterwards, his voice warm as cinnamon-laced honey.

Now it might take him hours to get back to her, or

sometimes he wouldn't even bother to call back. She'd ask him where he'd been, or why he hadn't called her back, and he'd shrug and say he was busy on a story.

When they worked together at the newspaper, they were so plugged in as a couple, she never thought about where he was because she knew. Plus all the reporters and photographers kept up with everyone's schedules since their assignments were posted on the paper's online calendar.

Staring at the silent phone, a thread of worry wound around her heart and pulled tight. Had she confused their proximity in the newsroom with real intimacy?

"He just muted his phone where he can't hear it," she informed the empty front office. Her cell phone pinged a text message and with relief she snatched it up and punched open the file folder.

It was from Mona: *Get your ass down here. W's truck is parked in front of the bar.*

Disappointment descended, followed by anger. Dizziness nibbled on the edges as her breaths became shallower and the walls seemed too close. The cluttered desk was sharp with details.

Julia shut her eyes, but instead of relief, her mind lit up a picture of Mona striding into the bar and heading to one of the dark, scarred round tables with the staffers ringed around it. Their faces were lit by the single candle nestled in a red globe at the table's center, greeting Mona as she drew up a chair.

Someone would ask if Julia was coming and Mona would only wave her ring-bejeweled hand to say she had gone home to pack. They might nod or shrug, because after all, Julia had never been one of them. She was a future ghost who, for the next few weeks, would float along their edges.

But might Walter's eyes darken with disappointment? Maybe he'd grip his beer handle a little tighter and sit back in his chair away from the candle's telling light?

Julia closed her eyes and rubbed them hard until starbursts splotched across the back of her retinas. The pain forced back rising tears.

Good. She wanted to feel only physical pain. That she could tolerate better than the pain in her heart.

Numb, she went to her office, grabbed her purse, and stopped to activate the security code near the clinic's front door. The sun dipped below the horizon as she inhaled fresh air, which helped to clear her head as she walked toward her dusty red Honda shrouded in shadow. Only the hood and driver's side of the car were weakly illuminated as a streetlight flickered on.

Julia cocked her head, puzzled. The trunk was lower than usual, and the car listed at a slant. As she drew closer, she could just make out a hissing undertone. Her rear tires were flattened to the point where the rims lay flush against the oil-stained pavement.

She glanced to her front left tire and something shiny stuck out from the top. Taking a few more small steps, she was able to make out a knife handle driven to the hilt and buried into the rubber and the steel belted layers. Air hissed as it escaped from the ragged tear.

A startled gasp caught in her throat and came out as a moan as she stumbled backwards. Past her car squatted the clinic dumpster curtained by scraggly bushes. From the corner of her eye something slithered between a bush and the dumpster that may have been a cat. But the bulk seemed wrong and too big.

Praying this wasn't the knife's owner who would burst out and pound in pursuit behind her, Julia fled to the safety of the clinic, imagining footsteps were seconds behind her.

Chapter 39

Once back inside the clinic, Julia locked the door, called Nick, the police, and finally Walter. Her call again went to Nick's voicemail, but within five minutes a patrol car swung into the parking lot, followed at close range by Walter's roaring truck.

While the patrolman approached her car, Walter hurried to Julia as she unlocked the door and emerged from the clinic. He gave her a hug, peered into her face, and asked if she was okay.

Anxiety seeped from her body and she trembled with relief until she saw the approaching figure of Nick. When she stepped away from Walter's hug, Nick hesitated then quickened his stride toward them. She gripped the strap of her purse with both hands.

Nick halted a few paces before her, as though there was a forcefield between them, and then glanced back at her car. "When did this happen? Did you see who did this to your car?"

Before she could stop herself, she shot back, "Who's more important here? Me or my secondhand Honda?"

A frosty moment passed between them, broken by Nick telling Walter, "Let me ask what Sergeant Morales has found so far." He strode toward the patrolman, leaving them in the wake of an awkward silence.

After the officer finished his report, and the tow truck hauled her car away, she and Nick exchanged not more than a dozen words as he drove her to the car rental lot.

At first Julia was too numb to care whether or not she had been dismissive earlier to Nick, but later she wondered where he had been when she called. Had he ignored her calls, but only responded to the obvious emergency? The question formed on her lips, but when she turned to him, the streetlights slid across his glowering face, with knitted brow and downturned mouth, and the breath with out of her. She swallowed her bitter question instead, and like Nick, faced the road rushing up to them.

* * *

THAT NIGHT AS THEY lay in bed, close but not touching, Nick said, "So, which of your crazies shivved your tires? Any top contenders?"

Julia had been waiting for that question all evening, but still she sputtered, "Don't say that. Never call my clients anything but clients, and none of them would have done such a thing."

"Seemed pretty intentional and personal to have every one of your tires slashed. Maybe it's not someone you know, but they seem to know you. And your schedule. Two years at the paper and you never had so much as a keyed door or busted headlight. Two months here at this nuthouse and I'm forking over a thousand bucks to get you new tires."

"Don't call it a nuthouse! And I'll pay you back."

Nick narrowed his eyes and gazed at her levelly. "No charity work for you in Dallas, Julia. This job needs my full attention and I can't do that while rescuing you from sleazy parking lots."

She glared at him, or rather at his back. He had turned away and snapped off the lamp on his bedside table, cloaking them in darkness.

* * *

THE NEXT MORNING JULIA sipped her second cup of coffee, winced at its bitterness, and stared out the kitchen window at the compact black rental car parked next to the condo's curb. She sighed. A bruiser of a headache was building behind her eyes as it roiled and spun out splinters of pain.

After placing the coffee cup in the sink so it wouldn't make a clinking noise and set off a migraine, Julia wound her way past several partially filled moving boxes in the living room and picked up her laptop. One email caught her eye, a group email sent from Walter last night to the staff informing them that Julia's car had been vandalized the night before and no one should go to their cars after dark unescorted.

"Great," Julia said. Her left temple throbbed.

A beeping noise cut through the silence and sounded as though it were in the front yard. From the balcony, she watched a commercial truck back up into the condo's postage-stamp front yard and its mechanical lift lower a metal storage unit with "PODS Moving & Storage" stenciled on the side.

Nick stood in the driveway instructing the driver, who settled the unit down with a hollow thud. He gave an enthusiastic thumbs up and went to the driver, who handed him a clipboard and pen.

Julia threw on a robe and hurried downstairs as the truck rumbled away. "What the hell is this?"

"A portable, on-demand storage container. We have it for two weeks, which gives us plenty of time to pack." He stuffed the contract into his back pocket.

She gestured at the hulk of steel. "I know what a PODS is. You didn't tell me this was coming."

"You'd rather trip all over the boxes in the house? Best

part is, this is courtesy of the paper. All we have to do is pack our stuff in and the driver comes back, loads it up, and we all head to the new house."

He went over to the container, swung open up the door, walked in, and frowned. "I'm not sure if this one is going to be big enough. Maybe I'll request a second one."

Fifteen minutes later after her rushed shower, Julia's hair dripped droplets onto a rumpled shirt she'd pulled out of a box and thrown on. She slid behind the unfamiliar wheel of the rental car and glanced in the rearview window filled with the bulk of the PODS. Her foot hit the gas pedal and she sped away.

Because she was running late, she didn't bother stopping by the clinic, but instead drove straight to the Penny Pincher, where she was scheduled to meet Rowena. Once inside the store, she wandered the aisles in search of her client before asking the manager if Rowena had checked in with him. He gave a sour shake of his head. At last, she waited outside next to a display barrel stuffed with pool noodles, while scanning up and down the sidewalk.

Julia cursed herself for a laundry list of sins, with the top contender her lack of imagination in not foreseeing being stood up by Rowena. A lump formed in her throat and the passing traffic blurred with tears as she inhaled a shaky breath.

No, I'm not going to feel sorry for myself. Maybe tonight I'll lock the bathroom door and cry in the shower, but not now.

She went back inside the store, explained to the manager that Rowena had been unable to make today's training session, and noted his undisguised relief. She called Mona for the Horn's address, then pointed her car toward Rowena's house and roared off, her thoughts veering between worrying that something had happened to Rowena to a desire to throttle her no-show client.

As she bumped down a thin ribbon of a road, she steered around the potholes while trying to read house numbers on the shotgun-style homes fringed with crabgrass. Rowena's wooden house was painted a faded Pepto-Bismol pink that must have been vivid twenty years ago, but now looked spent. Two towering mountain laurel trees flanked the front porch, intertwined in the middle, and swayed over the roof in their own tangle of wild growth.

The front door was open, save for the latched screen, as Julia rang the doorbell. The inside of the house was murky, and she could just make out the edges of a couch and a card table.

Hearing nothing, she rapped several times, glanced around the porch, and noticed a gray lump against the trunk of the mountain laurel. Closer inspection revealed a foot-tall concrete lawn ornament of a little girl sitting on a bench and holding a woven basket. Crammed inside the basket was a blue ashtray overflowing with cigarette butts.

A noise came from behind the screen and she spun around to glance up into the eyes of an elderly woman in a housecoat so large the collar gapped and exposed her turkey wattle of a neck.

"Hi, hon, what can I do you for?" Her voice had a scratchy quality, as though she wasn't used to talking much.

All the moral certainty that had propelled Julia from the store to the Horn's house drained away. Good question. Why was she here?

"Um, Mrs. Horn? I'm Julia from the clinic here to see Rowena. We had an appointment this morning, and when she didn't come, I wanted to make sure she was okay."

The woman frowned, and for a second became an older version of Rowena—Julia knew she was indeed talking to Mrs. Horn.

"Oh, me. That child. Every gray hair on my head has her name on it. She's here, come on in out of the heat and I'll round her up.'"

Darkness permeated the living room as all the shades were drawn down to the windowsill and it took a minute for Julia's eyes to adjust to the gloom. An over-stuffed armchair butted up to a matching, over-stuffed sofa, and both faced a thick, jutting television. On top of the TV, school portraits were placed in a row of Rowena as a grim-faced child who stared down the camera with a defiant lift of her chin from each frame as, year by year, she grew older.

A thin coating of dust on the surfaces gave a fuzziness to the room. The only clean spot was on the coffee table, where a dozen medicine bottles sat next to the TV Guide. They were as neatly lined up and attended as candles on a church altar.

Mrs. Horn rested a hand against the couch, as though standing sapped her energy. "Angel, Glen, and Marlene has all told me about the extra interest you've taken in my girl. I know you don't have to do so, and because of it, I want to thank you. She's a pill, that one. Nothing comes easy."

"You're welcome," Julia said, uncertain of a better response. So the staffers had been watching her work with Rowena that closely?

Mrs. Horn's skin carried a loose quality, as if she had once been a lifelong heavy woman and now her flesh draped off her bones. "That girl was never what you'd call a social butterfly, but she did have her a girlfriend or two when she was younger. When Wena's daddy died, she was only an itty-bitty kid, and afterwards she just shut herself on up inside her room and wouldn't let nobody in but me. Tried to get help at the clinic with Marlene, who was a comfort, for me anyways. But Wena just wouldn't talk to nobody. See, her and her daddy'd been close as biscuits in a basket, those two."

She shook her head. "But you knows how kids change, and around sixth grade them girls at school got all stand-offish and into boys and clothes, and somewhere along the line, Wena got it into her head that all the world's unfair and she ain't welcome to join on in. She twisted up like a slug on a hotplate every time she saw one of them girls with their daddies. I kept tellin' her it's up to her to make a life, even with no daddy in it. Marlene's told her likewise. And same with our church's pastor. But nothin' gets in. So here she stays, all holed up in her room."

Mrs. Horn closed her eyes and took a long breath, swaying a bit. She opened them and regarded Julia, before laying a frail, cool hand on top of hers. "Me ailin' and all makes us both sick with worry, but my girl's the one who's got to live on. You showin' up today to fetch her, I'm grateful. Just can't say she'll feel the same."

Her words fell into Julia's heart as Julia reached over and hugged the dying woman. Under her voluminous housecoat, Mrs. Horn was no more substantial than tinker toys wrapped in chenille cloth.

Julia followed Mrs. Horn down the short hall where she stopped at a door on the left. She gave a brief knock and, not bothering for a response, swung open the door to reveal Rowena sitting on the corner of a neatly made, queen-size bed covered with a bedspread patterned in a riot of pink roses. In her hand she held a pair of large silver scissors and scattered in front of her were stacks of magazines and a small heap of cut-out pictures and headlines.

But Julia's gaze went to the walls, which may have been painted a canary yellow or a grape purple. Every square inch was covered in layers and layers of pictures and words. Her breath caught in her throat as she took in this kaleidoscope.

With a roar, Rowena stood up, scattering magazines and clippings. "What you doing here? Mama, tell this one to leave, this is *my* room. Nobody comes inta my room!"

"No!" Mrs. Horn barked. "She's here 'cause you didn't show up where you was supposed to. So she's come to fetch you. Besides all that, it's time you had a bit of company."

With surprising strength, Mrs. Horn grabbed Julia by the arm, pulled her into the room, and then left, closing the door with a small bang. From behind the door she called out, "I'm goin' into the kitchen and mix up a pitcher of Tang for both of you. Come on out when you're ready to fetch it. I ain't your waitress." Her unsteady steps faded down the hallway.

Rowena's face turned the color of the roses on her bedspread as she lowered herself down on a corner of the bed and glared at Julia. "You can leave now. I don't care what Mama says."

The doorknob was a foot away, and Julia could almost feel the metal between her fingers and the freedom outside the room. But her eyes were drawn to the walls, as images stood out one by one: clipped pictures of people smiling, hugging, walking down country roads, painting on easels, kissing, playing the piano, clapping in theaters, reading books, holding hands, lounging on thick Persian rugs, making sand castles on the beach, dancing, pulling pies out of ovens, taking notes in classrooms, drinking coffee from oversized mugs, and on and on and on. Interspersed were carefully trimmed words.

You're all set, fresh, outstanding, love your smile, a new you, the taste of success, leads to an adventure, sweet spot, different, get away, magic, explore …

This solved the mystery of Rowena's magazine fetish,

Julia thought as she stepped closer to one of the walls and admired how cunningly Rowena had placed a couple swing-dancing on top of a five-layered wedding cake with the word "Swirl!" underneath.

"These are really good, Rowena. I mean really good. Do you realize that?" Julia said as she walked in a small circle to the other walls, where not an inch of blank space peeked through.

"Yeah, well, this ain't no damn art gallery, so I'd appreciate it if you git now." Underneath the heat in her voice crept a note of uncertainty.

"I'll leave in a few minutes, Rowena. I'll be gone."

Rowena's face flinched under the scowl.

"But like your mom said, I came to check up on you because you didn't show up at the store and you didn't answer your phone. I was worried. But I'm glad I came so I could meet your mom and see your art."

Rowena's lip curled up as she hunkered down in sullen silence. The contrast was vivid. Rowena poised and coiled like a snake, ready to strike and protect her lair against her backdrop of a life she had cut and pieced together from stolen glossy magazine pages. This was Rowena's spliced-together wish list she dared not talk about, show anyone, or risk attempting to live. How many days and nights had she lain on her bed and dreamt about dancing, going to classes, having coffee with friends, traveling, and being kissed? All within reach, if only she'd risk it by stepping out of the house and trying something different.

"Do you have a favorite part of your collage?"

"My what?" Rowena growled.

"Your wall art. Is there a part your eye keeps going to?"

She snorted, but her face softened. "Yeah, I guess. Over there's a part I guess I look at more." She pointed to corner close to the foot of the bed.

Julia was drawn toward a picture of a kitten and puppy who sat side-by-side in a box as they stared straight into her eyes. Next to that image was a picture of a young girl braiding the forelock of a massive Clydesdale horse whose eyes were closed in contentment. She stepped back and took in the picture of a woman walking a dog along the beach, both of them silhouetted against the setting sun. The images overlapped into a whole as she viewed the room in one artistic landscape. An idea sparked. Julia asked Rowena, "How about if you and I go for a ride?"

"You can't trick me, I ain't goin' to that damn store."

Julia shook her head. "Agreed. I think our Penny Pincher days are over. But Rowena, do you trust me? Just a little? I'd like to take you someplace I'll bet you've never been before, and looking at your pictures, I think you just might like it."

Rowena narrowed her eyes under her shelf of greasy bangs. Neither woman blinked, and Julia held her breath.

* * *

ONCE JULIA TURNED OFF the engine, the only sound was a clicking noise as the engine cooled. Rowena hadn't spoken a word the entire trip, nor uncrossed her arms over her seat-belted girth.

Her client squinted up at the sign on top of the building. "What's this place?"

"The Elston Animal Shelter." Julia opened up the door so as not to lose any of their forward motion. "I take it you've never been here before?"

"Damn straight I never been here. What're you up to? If you think I'm goin' to start gassin' animals then turn this here vehicle right on around and get me back home."

After closing her door, Julia walked around to the passenger side and opened up the door before Rowena could think to hit the locks. "The EAS is a no-kill shelter and all we're going to do is take a tour."

Rowena's arms crossed tighter across her bosom.

Julia knelt down and her knees popped in protest. She said in a quiet voice, "We'll stay just long enough for you to take a walk around and see the layout of the place. Five minutes and we're back in the car and I'm taking you home. I promise."

"I knows about you and your promises," Rowena hissed. Her expression darkened like a summer storm and Julia's heart sank. This was her last chance, of this she was certain.

A shaft of flashing light distracted them, and they both turned as a man walked out of the shelter carrying a small animal carrier. A young boy trotted beside him, his face lit with joy, as he kept a protective hand on the side of the carrier. The child spoke to whatever creature was in the box, "And we've got you your own pillow, and a scratching post, because mama says you can't go tearing up her new couch."

A tiny black triangle of a head looked out from the front bars of the carrier, and it stared right at Rowena with lemony-yellow eyes. Then the trio was gone.

Rowena blinked and fell silent. Slowly she reached over and unbuckled her seat belt. "Okay, five minutes. Then we git."

A bell chimed as they entered and the burly employee, Jerry, still there from her days at the paper, popped his head out of the side office with a half-chewed apple in his hand. "Hey there, stranger. Haven't seen you in a while. Your buddy Graham told me you were out of the photography business."

"Yeah, that's right. Just thought we'd take a quick look around, if that's okay with you," Julia said, half-blocking the door in case Rowena made a run for it.

He shrugged and took a noisy bite out of the fruit. "Sure, go for it, dude. You know the drill. I'd take you around, but we're kinda shorthanded here, so let me know if you have questions about any of the inmates."

Glowering, Rowena trailed Julia as they went to the back door with the word "kennels" painted at eye-level. "What's he mean by inmates?"

"Gallows humor," Julia said, pushing the door open.

"Now what does that mean?"

They stood at the entrance of a long building with concrete floors, walls, and low ceilings. On both sides were rows of individual kennels. Some of the dogs gazed up at them silently from behind chain-link enclosures while others yapped and barked and whined in an escalating cacophony.

Rowena clapped her hands over her ears. "Turn 'em off!"

Julia pulled a hand away from Rowena's right ear. "If we're calm, they'll be calm." She forced her voice to be low, not knowing if this was true or not, but somehow it seemed right.

"So these two rows are the dog kennels, and in the back are the cat and kitten areas. There's also an area in another building with enclosures for rabbits, ferrets, and exotic snakes. Sometimes even chickens. You'd be amazed what comes through these doors."

Bit by bit, Rowena lowered her arms and followed Julia, swiveling her head from left to right as she took in all the dogs. There were the usual variety of mixed breeds, but they passed a golden retriever with a gray muzzle who thumped his heavy tail on the ground from his bed. A pair of Chihuahuas yapped and jumped over each other, and a bedraggled, forlorn poodle stood up on her hind legs and trembled at them.

Rowena's expression of suspicion gave way to shock. "There's so many of them. Some of them are expensive dogs that was just let go." She pointed to a brindle-colored boxer. "Like nobody cares about them no more and just throwed 'em away like trash."

At the end of the row was a mother dog, so thin her ribs showed through her dull coat, who lay on her pallet while a half a dozen puppies snoozed by her side. She glanced up at yet another pair of humans passing by her kennel before lowering her head to stare at the wall with a deep sigh. One puppy dislodged itself from its knot of siblings and tottered over to them.

"He's a comin' towards us!" Rowena gushed, dropping to her knees.

The puppy, a male, chewed on the chain-link fence with his tiny milk teeth and made fierce growling noises. Julia eyed the mother, who appeared too exhausted to care, and took a chance. In a flash, she opened the gate and whisked the puppy out, still warm from being so bunched up with the others, and placed him in Rowena's hands.

Rowena's face transformed into an expression Julia had never seen: a smile. Her features softened as she held the puppy close to her chest to pet it then turned it over and tickled its belly. The puppy made joyful growling noises and chewed on her fingers.

"Mama and me couldn't never have a dog, 'cause of the expense and her being gone at work so much. She said it wouldn't been fair and all." Rowena held the puppy up to her face and he licked her nose.

"You seem to have a way with dogs, at least this little guy here thinks so." Julia wished for the first time in a long whihle she had her camera so she could capture this moment. She'd like to make a print and give it to Rowena to add to her wall collage to show her doing something picture worthy.

"A way with dogs?" Rowena said, surprise in her voice.

Julia reached out and touched Rowena's arm. "Yes, and you know what? They have volunteers here at the shelter that all they do is walk the dogs or play with the kittens. Sometimes the volunteers become employees and they do things that maybe aren't so glamorous, like clean up kennels and feed the animals. But they give the animals, like this guy here, a safe life until they're adopted into forever homes."

A yelp drew Julia and Rowena's attention. Five puppies crowded the gate, wagging their tiny, crescent moon-shaped tails and staring up at them with blue-brown eyes.

Rowena's grin stretched wider, transforming her face until she looked almost pretty. "So what's you saying is, for this here job, the hardest part is shoveling some shit? Well, if that's the worst of it, then I suppose it could be tolerable."

While cradling the one puppy, she flipped open the gate and let the five others out, allowing herself to be swarmed by all their kisses and bites and paddling paws.

The sight warmed Julia. A quiet voice in her head said, *Love is thawing her heart.* Then the voice added with a knife's turn, *Good medicine for those brave enough to take it.*

Chapter 40

The drive from the animal shelter was as quiet as the ride to it, except the tension between Julia and Rowena had smoothed into a companionable silence. Julia glanced over a couple of times at Rowena, who sat in the passenger seat and gripped the one-page volunteer application form while the ghost of a smile hovered on her lips.

After dropping Rowena off at her house, Julia rushed to the office and calculated she'd be about five minutes late for the Lunch Bunchers group. Not good. But once she explained her tardiness to Marlene, she knew she'd be in the clear.

And with her breakthrough with Rowena, for the first time in a long while, Julia felt cheered. Even though she would be leaving, at least she'd helped Rowena move the needle forward a few ticks. A smile broke across Julia's face in anticipation of seeing Marlene's reaction when she told her about Rowena applying for a volunteer job.

As Julia pulled into the parking lot, the sight of Mona pacing in front of the building with a cell phone in her hand and a worried expression on her face greeted her. Relief washed across Mona's face when Julia emerged from the rental car. She beelined across the parking lot and reached the side of the car before Julia could even open the door.

"Where have you been?" Mona howled. "I've been calling you for like forever!"

"Jeez, where's the fire? I'm sorry if I'm late but I'm here now, okay? I must have had my phone muted." Julia eased the door open so as not to bump Mona, who backed up a few steps.

"The fire is in the group room."

As the pair hurried toward the clinic, Julia said, "Marlene can handle them for a few minutes without me, can't she?"

"She's can't handle them if she's not here. With you both AWOL, I wasn't sure what to do. After I give your people coffee and magazines, I pass the 'em on to you guys." Mona opened the front door, and all but pushed Julia through it.

Julia came to a stop and put a hand to her eyebrow. "Marlene's not here?"

Angry voices drifted from Marlene's office and Mona cocked her head. "Hello. Welcome to my world. Now go in there and deal with those people. They've been cooped up in a small room by themselves while I've been calling everyone. Paulie and his wife are at another one of their couple's sessions. I couldn't get ahold of Walter because he got called away to some emergency board meeting."

The last bit caught Julia's attention, but she shoved it aside and hurried to the office. The door was half-open and Travis's voice floated out, "Hey, now. No sense in getting all harsh. If I didn't know any better, I'd say you two ladies was all jealous."

"Jealous? Hardly," Stella said with a frosty snort. "I just don't advocate anyone taking advantage of the system."

Nadine and Erin, their faces flushed and eyes bright, glanced up at Julia as she came in, then turned back to Travis and Stella, who sat grimly across from each other in the circle.

"What's going on?" Julia took her seat. "Oh, and sorry I'm late."

"The clinic bought me a bus ticket, and when I told these guys, I thought everyone here would be happy," said

Travis. "But no! They're acting like I'm making off with the Hope Diamond or something."

He crossed his arms above his rounded belly. "Like I was telling these people here, I got kicked out from the place where I was staying. I asked Walter if the clinic could help me find housing. He asked me where I wanted to go, just so's I could get on my feet and all, and I says I wanted to go to my cousin's out in Lufkin, who said he might have a job for me. So he bought me the ticket! Now I'm happy and I'm guessin' Walter's happy since I'm moving on. What's wrong with that?"

"Um, I didn't know the clinic purchased bus tickets," Julia glanced from face to face for guidance.

"I've never heard of it," Stella said. "Apparently Mr. Bridgeman has decided to reward Travis's lack of initiative with free transportation to be with family members in the cooler climes of East Texas. Maybe we should all ask for special gifts. I myself would love to go on one of those Alaskan cruises Mr. Schmidt has so often promised but failed to deliver. Perhaps I should expound to you how it would improve my mental health and you can petition for my request."

Julia struggled to keep up with the changes, but the center of the clinic appeared to be unraveling at a dizzying rate. Forcing her voice to sound braver than she felt, she said to Travis, "So then it's a fresh start?"

He perked up and straightened in his chair as if ready to launch into the story of his fresh start when the door swung open and in walked Marlene and Slate. Or rather Slate took small steps while cupping Marlene's elbow as she hobbled by his side. His ears and cheeks were sunburned a radiating red and his clothes were layered in dust.

A murmur went through the group as Julia gasped and stood up. "Are you okay?"

With a distracted, irritated wave, Marlene said, "I'm fine, I'm fine. Just twisted my ankle getting out of the car. Young Morris here saw me on the ground and came to my rescue." She reached her seat and collapsed onto her chair, rocking it to one side.

"Good landing," Travis said.

Slate shot Travis a warning look, then took the remaining empty seat next to Julia.

The twisted ankle wasn't the only thing off about Marlene. A looseness about how she settled her legs and arms belied her usual, starched crispness. Her shirt was untucked on one side and her left earring was missing. Nadine narrowed her eyes at Marlene, leaned ever-so-slightly toward her, and sniffed.

Julia struggled to mask her shock. *Oh God. Has she been drinking?*

Nadine swiveled her head slightly and gave Julia a wide-eyed expression, answering her question. Julia swallowed.

Should I plow on and hope for the best, or escort Marlene out to the kitchen and set her in front of a cup of black coffee?

Stella's voice rang out. "Have we taken a holiday from the rules? Punctuality has always been strictly reinforced in the group, right, Marlene? Of course, an exception must be made in regard to your injury. But we can't all just wander in and wander out, willy-nilly!"

"Willy-nilly?" Marlene snorted. She threw her head back and laughed. "Oh, this is just the start of willy-nilliness! Before it's all over, we'll be up to our necks in hijinks and shenanigans." She picked up her purse and set her mouth in a line of grim determination as she rooted through it, done with the discussion.

Stella said in a low, conspiratorial voice, "Are you doing some new therapeutic intervention? The one where the therapist produces anxiety to promote the adaptation of coping tools? I think I read about this in last month's *Psychology Today.*"

"So!" Julia attempted to steer attention away from bleary Marlene. "Promptness is important, Stella, you are absolutely right and I myself apologize for being late. How about you, Slate? Why were you late?"

He ran a hand through his dirty hair. "Finishing up my last shift of picking up trash for the county. Took me awhile, but I got my hours signed off." He pulled from his front shirt pocket a folded paper. "I'm free and clear of my community hours, and after today I'm done with my therapy hours, too. If you wouldn't mind, I need for you to sign off for me." He pointed to a blank signature line on the form.

Julia nodded, extended her hand for the paper. "Congratulations, but you know we're going to miss you."

Slate had asked *her* to validate the form, not Marlene. Anxiety fluttered in Julia's chest at the idea of Marlene being reported to the licensing board as an impaired therapist. While it wouldn't be a disgrace if she lost her job because the clinic closed, losing her counseling license, especially at her age, would be devastating.

"That's awesome, Slate," Erin said, her eyes bright and posture erect. "Remember when you thought you couldn't do it? But you plugged away and didn't stop and now you're graduating group." There was strength in her voice, her coppery hair was pulled into a glossy bun, and her hotel uniform was spotless.

Slate ducked his head in embarrassment, but a smile curled at the corner of his lips.

"You know, I thought of quitting the hotel, getting me and my daughter out of that noisy shelter, and just crawling back home to Lonnie. Those first weeks, I wanted to leave every day. No, every hour. But then I wouldn't have been able to come in here and tell all of you how I made it through another week. And if I went back to Lonnie, he would punish me to the end of my days. I wouldn't have any of you to talk to and I couldn't hear your stories and know how you guys came out." She inhaled a shuddering breath, then blinked back tears, which fell anyway.

Nadine knelt down next to Erin and wrapped her arms around the young woman, who heaved a sob and let herself be rocked back and forth.

Julia's throat tightened and she placed her hand over her heart. She glanced at Marlene to see her reaction. Her head was cocked to one side with her mouth slightly open as she slept.

God Almighty. Julia scrambled to think of an excuse to end the group right away before Marlene either snored or toppled over.

Travis slapped both hands down on his thighs. "Since Slate and I are saying our goodbyes here, I'd be amiss if I didn't say how I appreciate all what the headshrinker's brigade has done for me, too."

Julia laughed in surprise. "Headshrinker's brigade? That's what you call us?"

"Why, yeah! And I don't just mean, thanks for the bus ticket neither. I mean for all of you headshrinkers here at this place. I never believed much in griping about your problems, never saw how that helped anyone. But when you see people, I don't know ..."

Travis looked up at the ceiling, as though the right words were written among the stains. He snapped his fingers and said, "Get their shit together. Why, it gives a guy something to hope for. Just because things are going downhill don't mean you have to ride it all the way down until it crashes. Even my brother on the phone yesterday told me I sounded different. I guess when you're changing, it happens all slow-like until one day you look up and go, 'Whoa, now that's different!' It's like, I'm growing tired of just getting by. Know what I mean?"

The rest of the group, even Stella, nodded. Travis's words hit Julia square in her chest with a thud of truth. She knew exactly what he was saying. Bits of change can take hold and slowly make an old habit less of a comfort and more of a stranglehold.

Even though fifteen minutes remained in the group session, Julia announced their time was up. She discretely shook Marlene's knee until she woke up with a start and blinked like an owl. Julia signed Slate's therapy completion form, and gave him, and then Travis, a hug goodbye.

Erin lingered and beckoned Julia out into the hallway. "There's one more thing I wanted you to know. I got a new job at the hotel and they're starting me tomorrow with training on how to run the reservations desk. Seems the manager saw how hard I worked, and sometimes she'd ask me about my girl and my plans and stuff. Last night she said I reminded her of when she was young and she had to provide for her two boys with next to nothing. That's when she told me about the opening if I wanted it. I told her yes before she could change her mind!"

"That's wonderful!" Julia hugged Erin. "You've earned your promotion."

She beamed. "But you were with me. When I was bone-tired, and my back ached, and my daughter cried at night to go home and sleep in her own bed, I imagined what you would do, what you would tell me."

Julia stepped back. "Me?"

The color high in her cheeks, Erin nodded. "Yes. And I could almost hear you say, 'Just be brave, show up, and don't quit.' I could imagine you talking to me, plain as we're talking now. Things aren't getting easier, and for sure in some ways they're getting harder. But it's like I'm stronger, tougher than I thought I could ever be. You taught me that because you didn't quit me."

Erin peeked at her watch. "Uh-oh, gotta run or I'll be late for my shift. See you next week!" And with a wave, she was down the hall and around the corner.

When Julia walked back into the office, Marlene was scanning the floor. She glanced up. "I've seemed to have lost my earring. Be a darling and see if you can help me find it."

Julia cupped Marlene's elbow and guided her toward the door. "Sure, but how about if we first share a cup of coffee together in the breakroom? Seems like we both have crazy stories to tell."

Marlene swayed before grabbing the back of a chair to steady herself. "You don't know the half of it."

Julia exhaled a deep breath and put an arm around Marlene's waist. "No, I probably don't. But I'm willing to listen."

She glanced back at the empty room with the folding chairs in their uneven circle and knew in her heart this was her last group with the Lunch Bunchers. She felt a pang of loss just as Marlene stumbled and Julia caught her. Together they made their way down the hall.

Chapter 41

Julia slid the third cup of coffee across the breakroom table to a sobbing Marlene, who talked about her futile job searches at Elston's short list of clinics and the one middling-sized hospital. Walter walked in, assessed the situation and pulled up a chair next to Marlene. She finally wound down and Walter gave her a one-armed hug around her thin shoulders.

"How's about you finish that coffee and I take you home?" he said to Marlene. However, his gaze was on Julia, searching her face. His blond hair threaded with silver tumbled into his eyes, and Julia willed her hand to stay in her lap and not brush it back from his forehead.

Marlene could only nod in misery while sipping her coffee.

As the three left, Walter escorted Marlene to his truck, and then insisted on walking Julia to her car, an uncomfortable reminder of the tire slashing. He opened her car door and a whoosh of trapped summer heat enveloped them.

"How about you, my friend? Your spark also seems dimmed as of late," he said.

They stood next to each other so close that someone driving by them might glance again to see if they would kiss, or at least embrace.

This time Julia did not shy away from the energy humming between them because she needed to remember this feeling. She closed her eyes and took a deep breath, drawing in his clean scent of pine needles and imagining his lips, strong and sensual, on hers. The photographer in her kicked in and she took a mental picture. She wanted to remember this, for later, should she feel desperate. She felt like a drowning person watching a life preserver ring float within reach to only be tugged away by an insistent tide.

"It's all happening so fast. The move, the changes in the clinic ... and saying goodbye. I'm going to miss ..." She grew aware that her hand dangled inches from his. "Everything."

Walter studied her face, opened his mouth as if to say something, then waited a few seconds. "I'll miss everything, too. But things change, they always do, and it's the one thing you can count on. Just keep doing good work and you'll find your way home."

The word "home" fell into her heart like a small pebble dropped into a pond that spreads rings out larger and larger. All Julia could do was watch Walter cross the parking lot to his truck, where Marlene sat waiting for him, a tiny figure alone in the passenger seat.

* * *

WHEN JULIA GOT HOME, Nick greeted her, fresh from his shower and wearing only a pair of jeans. He nuzzled her neck and inquired if she wanted a glass of wine. Before she could answer, he walked into the kitchen, asking over his shoulder how her day had been.

"I'm worried about Marlene. We spoke after group today and she started to cry. She's been looking for another clinician job, but so far she's not been able to find anything. She told me she's afraid she's too old."

Disdain hardened the chiseled planes of his face and Julia right away regretted opening up to him. Nick detested tears. And women who cried sent him over the edge, a lesson she had learned early in their relationship.

She could only imagine his disgust if she told him the

part where Marlene had come to the office after diving into a chardonnay bottle at her home.

His upper lip curled and he pushed a moving box aside on the counter. "So? Does she think the state owes her a job? People lose jobs every day of every week."

Nick's loud voice echoed in the half-empty kitchen. Julia wished she could hit a rewind button and take back her words. But a stronger desire welled up to take him by the shoulders and shake him and to scream and tell him that she's already missing this little clinic with its rag-tag staffers and rag-tag clients. She'd taken for granted her life here, like a comfortable, pilled sweater shoved to the back of a closet.

But most of all, she needed for Nick to sit down, quit packing her life up into boxes, and just listen.

His blue eyes bore into her, flat as a shark's, and Julia's righteous energy wavered. Nevertheless, she took a deep breath. "All you ask is, 'So?' I care about her and I care about these people. And this little town has been my home since I was a kid. I used to dream about leaving it, kicking off the dust, and checking out newer, bigger, better. Even a year ago, I may have been as excited as you to go anywhere."

"Well, there you have it. You can't trust a flimsy feeling—those come and go. You've got to rely on the big picture and what is logical. If you were excited before, then you'll be excited again once we're on our way." He pointed to the kitchen table where a pile of folded boxes were stacked. "How about if you start packing the pantry and I break down the entertainment center?"

From the refrigerator, he pulled out a beer while Julia stayed rooted, amazed at how easily he brushed her words aside like an annoying cobweb. The hiss of the beer opening snapped her awake.

"Are you not listening to me? I'm telling you, something's shifted. When I lost my vision, my God, I thought I was losing my mind! But since then, I've been facing scarier things, and doing braver things, and even letting people in. I think I used to remove myself to keep safe, and now I'm finding out that if I push myself, I get stronger."

Julia trembled at saying words she had never dared think, much less say out loud.

With a sharp crack, he banged the beer down on the granite counter and Julia jumped. "What am I supposed to say? Congratulations for joining the adult world? No shit, you have to push to make something happen."

He threw his arms up. "Have you not seen all the hard work I've done here for five years? Slogging through reams of ridiculous small-town political red tape to piece together some kind of cogent story that won't bore the reader to death? Covering local-yokel news of some lifestyle feature that baffles me as to why we waste the paper and ink to publish? And every year, I turn the boring, the mundane, the absolute crap, into gold. Every award I have earned is because I've busted my ass and went at it harder than anyone around me. Finally, I'm moving up the food chain." His eyes shone bright and his face was flushed as he stared her down. "And you're not going to moon over some mental cases you've bonded with over a summer. This time next week we'll be in Dallas, and Elston will be a chapter we'll look back on and wonder how we ever survived."

Before, Julia's normal reaction would have been to spiral into submission in the face of such anger from Nick, and part of her brain clamored to fold and appease, anything to make his fury stop. Fear rattled through her body and her fingers lost all their warmth as her legs trembled.

But something he'd said snagged her attention.

"Wait. When you talk about a food chain, you don't see Dallas as long-term either, do you." She meant it as a statement, not a question.

A light flitted into his eyes and he reached out and tapped her temple with his index finger. "Atta girl. Now the train has arrived at the station. I'm at the beginning of my career, Julia. Why would Dallas be it? Do you know where metro reporters go?"

From far away, Julia's own small voice said, *Anywhere they want.*

Her fiancé, who had been swinging on a thin rope of control above a lake of rage, grew still. His lips parted into a smile. "Yes, anywhere. New York, Washington, L.A., London, Paris."

He looked out the window for a moment, but snapped his gaze back on her. "Elston will be our humble beginning and you'll be my sexy, hometown bride." He gave her what he may have thought to be a rakish grin, but instead all she saw was the sharpness of his perfect white teeth.

Wide-eyed, Julia stepped back. "So the narrative is all set, complete with the happily-ever-after tag line? Except while you're off being Edward R. Murrow, how am I supposed to finish school or establish a career? How can we make roots if we're wandering like gypsies?"

"Roots? What are you, an azalea shrub? You'll make your buddies along the way, but friends come and go. I learned that as a kid, when we went from one air force base to the next. Best not to rely too much on other people, because they'll just drag you down." He opened the fridge and drew out another beer. When he closed the door hard, the condiment bottles in the rack rattled against each other.

The walls drew in close. The unpacked dishes, cups, and pans stacked on the countertop bristled with detail. Julia's breathing shallowed out as she struggled to draw in air that had grown thin, and she couldn't trust her legs to hold her up while she fought against the mounting force of a panic attack. This move wasn't simply a transition to a new city, it was the beginning of perpetual moves fueled by Nick's hunger for greener pastures.

Julia imagined the years unrolling in front of her as she waited for her husband to return from the wars. And with Nick, who knew? It could be a literal war front, if that was where the story took him. But in the midst of them pulling up tent stakes and rolling to the next assignment, how was she to craft a life? Would she be the perpetual volunteer? The temporary administrator who never allowed herself to care too deeply for anyone or anything?

Nick's mother, bitter and judgmental, flashed into her mind, but now she saw her behavior as a survivor's tool, forged from trailing after her military husband from state to state, then continent to continent. A wave of empathy filled her for Nick's mom, but fresh fear bloomed for herself. If they had kids, would she be setting herself up as a single parent while Hero Dad floated in and out? Just like her own mom's script?

"I can't go," Julia blurted out. A wave of dizziness fell upon her and she dragged a kitchen chair out from a corner. Her knees buckled and she plopped down. The world blurred on the edges, but at least she wasn't struggling to stand.

"What?" Nick yelped. "Go where?"

"With you. To Dallas! I just can't go."

This is how an animal caught in a trap must feel, ready to gnaw off its paw if necessary, if it means escape.

Nick knelt down beside her and took her hand, stroking the back of it with his fingertips. "Why?" Then he encircled his fingers around her wrist. "And more importantly, what else would you do?"

The trapped animal fear fluttered inside her chest. "I

don't know."

He tapped her temple again. "Think, Julia. You've burned your bridge at the paper, your bleeding-heart clinic is going to fold, and I'm being offered a job at three times my current salary. You can work or not work, go to school or not go to school. What's not to love about our future? Wouldn't it seem crazy for you not to come with me? Say you have another episode and you're stuck here on your own. How does moving back in with your mom sound? Or better yet, dear old Dad. Is he a possibility?"

His words were cruel nails driven through her heart as he played her worst fears against her. And had she burned a bridge at the paper?

She tried to draw her hand back. "Wait, I don't even want to work at the paper. That's not the point."

Nick's grasp around her wrist tightened as he continued in a conversational tone. "The point is we're a team, right? You and I are going to be out of here in a week, so don't let a case of cold feet confuse you about what's real."

Julia forced herself to meet his steady gaze. His face was composed and his head tilted as though he was merely being quizzical. But his grip tightened around her wrist and pain shot up her arm until her fingers throbbed from the trapped blood as her circulation restricted. Julia pulled her arm away from him harder, but he dug his nails into her soft flesh.

"Let me go. You're hurting me and you're scaring me." She twisted her wrist back and forth, somehow daring to confront his ferocity while she stared into his placid face.

He loosened his fingers a bit, but his gaze never left her face. Her heart hammered in her chest.

Is this really happening?

With one strong tug she yanked her arm back. "Let go, Nick!"

He tightened his hold instead, narrowed his eyes, and opened his mouth to speak when from her pants' pocket her cell phone rang out Vivaldi's "Spring" from The Four Seasons.

The trance was broken, and Nick released her. Julia backed away from him and dug out her phone, desperate for contact from a third person outside of this room.

"Hello," Julia said in a shaky voice as Nick grabbed his keys off the counter.

"Hey, Jules, it's me, Mona. Sorry to bother you at home, but Walter's having me call everyone." Her usual chirpy voice was gone, replaced by an almost unrecognizable somber tone.

Julia watched Nick's retreating back as he stalked into the living room and she let out a deep breath. "Why, what's up?" Her voice was tiny and distant in her ears, as though she spoke from the end of a long hallway.

A few seconds of silence passed before Mona said, "Rowena's mom died. About an hour ago, at the hospital."

"Oh, God." Julia put the palm of her hand to her forehead.

"You know when someone's sick and you know they aren't going to make it? Then why's it a shock when they actually don't make it? Anyhow, Rowena's losing her shit and Glen needs for you to head out to the hospital and help talk her down. Like, now."

The front door slammed and Julia fell back in the kitchen chair with a heavy thud. She closed her eyes and let the black clouds of silence in the condo roll over her. From a far distance she heard herself say, "Okay."

Mona wished her luck and Julia snapped the phone shut. She wanted only to sit still among the boxes and the clutter and not be propelled in one direction or the other. But Rowena needed her.

Chapter 42

The automatic sliding doors of the Elston Medical Center whooshed open as Julia and Glen emerged, drained and somber. When Julia glanced down at her shirt, she registered the blotch where Rowena had soaked her shoulder with tears and snot.

Glen stopped at a bench, plopped down with a groan, and pulled out a paper from the folder he carried. He scribbled while shaking his head. "Dammit, why couldn't Angel have been on duty today when Mrs. Horn did the big check out? I hate hospitals, really hate being around dead people, and the worst—being around dead people with a hysterical family member losing it. Trifecta of a real shit show back there."

He pointed his pen at Julia. "Give me a psychotic holed up in a lake house listening to messages from the toaster any day. At least the drive is scenic."

Julia found a tissue in her purse and wiped beading sweat from her forehead. The late afternoon heat sweltered into the triple digits as the sun glared down and bounced off the industrial white of the sidewalk.

"But you were brilliant in there, really, Glen," she said, squinting. "You got Rowena calmed down enough for the nurses to administer a sedative. Thank God they're keeping her overnight for observation. I don't see how she could have handled going back to her house today."

Mrs. Horn had suffered a massive stroke at home while watching her favorite afternoon soap opera on television. Rowena was in the kitchen making them sandwiches, and when she came out with a plate in each hand, she'd found her mom slumped over and unconscious. She called 911 and EMS arrived five minutes later, but by that time Mrs. Horn's heart rate was high and erratic, and her left eye partially dilated.

More than likely she died while en route to the hospital, so it was left to the doctor in ER to deliver the news to a pacing, wailing Rowena. Forty-five minutes later, the same doctor called the Elston Clinic because he and the nurses couldn't tear Rowena away from her mother's cooling body splayed on the examination table.

When Julia met the physician outside the ER bay, his tie was askew and a frown etched his face. In a low voice he said, "I understand the daughter works with you, so I'm sure you know best how to handle her. But we need to move the body to the morgue and get this bay opened up as soon as possible. The daughter is upsetting the other patients and staff."

With the baton passed, Julia nodded as he marched off while Rowena's wails echoed off the walls. She had squared her shoulders, then pulled back the privacy curtains to comfort Rowena.

Glen signed the note and clicked his pen closed. "Well, that's done, but I need to drive this out to Walter's house and have him sign-off on the report, 'cause I talked the admitting staff into keeping her overnight. She's in no shape to stay by herself, and could be a threat to herself. The hospital needs to have my report in Rowena's chart ASAP so insurance'll cover her stay."

At the mention of Walter's name, Julia said, "I'll take the report to him and bring it back to the hospital. I mean, you've already done the hardest part today, so let me handle this bit."

His face broke into a grin. "You're a doll. I'm going to say yes before you change your mind. A charming young thing has agreed to meet me at the Broken Spoke in Austin, and if I leave now, we'll be able to catch the first band for some boot scootin'. Can't think of a better way to shake off this afternoon."

A pang of guilt shot through her because Glen thought her favor was altruistic. Still, she shoved it aside and wrote down Glen's directions to Walter's house on the back of a grocery store receipt she scrounged from the bottom of her purse. Glen assured her the house would be a cinch to find, which she understood was code for, "Head's up! Get ready to get lost!"

After driving multiple passes up and down the same stretch of a two-lane blacktop, Julia considered calling Glen for more directions. She slowed the car to a crawl and was rewarded by the sight of the can't-be-missed landmark of Walter's mailbox, halfway tucked into a blackberry bush with the faded name, "The Bridgemans," hand-painted on the side.

Opposite the mailbox lay a pitted, dirt road, partially hidden by thick overgrowth, and she hooked a sharp left. As she bumped down the road, ancient live oak trees crowded the sides and fanned their gnarled branches above her. The profusion of the oaks' tufted, spear-shaped green leaves arches overhead, and Julia traveled down a shadowy tunnel splashed with ochre sunlight.

She took one final sharp turn to the right and Walter's home slid into view. Julia smiled at the farmhouse, painted periwinkle blue and trimmed in creamy yellow trim, topped with a weathered, silver metal roof. A door inside the screened-in porch opened up and Walter emerged, a wineglass in his hand.

He cocked his head to one side until Julia stepped from the car with the report in her hand, and then his face lit up.

"Well, hey there. Didn't expect you. I thought Glen would be running Rowena's paperwork on by."

As Julia crossed the shaded yard and mounted the heavy wooden steps, a weariness, something she wasn't aware she carried, lifted. Jasmine vines draped either side of the porch and perfumed the air as Julia inhaled deeply. "How did you ever find this jewel of a place? I believe Mark Twain would have approved. Shouldn't someone be white-washing a picket fence or lining up frogs for a race?"

"It may look like country living, but you can still hear the traffic from the highway when the wind is still. Civilization's around the corner, if you want it. These days I'd just as soon as keep it at bay, present company excluded, of course."

He opened the door and Julia walked into a great room with two large, horizontal windows that overlooked a meadow dotted with orange-and-red Mexican hats and purple foxgloves. Built-in bookcases lined an entire wall while the spines of the books created a colorful tapestry. A Native American rug spread across the dark wooden floor and a worn armchair nestled in a corner with a brass floor lamp standing by its side.

She imagined settling down into the chair's cushions with a cup of tea nearby and a book in her hand, lost in the pages. With regret, she turned away, handed Walter the report, and gave him a quick rundown, ending with Rowena being admitted to the hospital for suicide watch.

While reading Glen's notes, he listened to Julia and nodded. "Sounds like Mrs. Horn may have lost consciousness at home before EMS got there. Probably was how she wanted to go."

He co-signed under Glen's signature and handed the paperwork back to Julia. "Thanks in advance for dropping this off to the hospital's administrative office."

Julia paused a moment before making a move toward the front door, but Walter wandered into the bright kitchen and slid a blue wineglass from a shelf above his head. "I've got a nifty little Pinot Noir here, if you'd like a glass." He poured a dusky-red stream into the cobalt blue stemware.

"Oh, I don't know, it's getting late," she said without conviction, drawn into the kitchen as if pulled by a cord.

"I'll pour you half a glass, since you're driving, but you may want several glasses after I tell you about my earlier visitor." He handed Julia her drink, then picked up an eight-by-eleven envelope that lay on the kitchen island. The City of Elston Police Department seal was stamped in the left-hand corner.

She took a sip and the wine was warm sunshine, as traces of blackberry and almond ran across her tongue. When she set her glass down, a glint of light reflected off a framed picture propped against the back of the counter. It showed a smiling Walter with his arm around a woman with a sheath of strawberry-blonde hair who held a laughing toddler in her lap. The boy's eyes shone at Julia and beckoned her with his infectious joy. So much happiness was captured within the three-by-five-inch frame. Her eyes lingered on the photograph for a moment, not yet ready to hear what Walter had to say about what she assumed was bad news.

Julia glanced back at Walter, whose real-time face was more lined than in the photo, but had the same kind eyes. She felt awe at his heart's resiliency to make the daily choice to go on.

He extracted a page from the envelope and held it out to her.

"You had a visitor?" Julia hoped he hadn't noticed her looking at his former family's picture.

"Yeah, it's been a busy afternoon here at the homestead.

A friend of mine at the police department dropped this by to give me a head's up before the story hits the five o'clock news. Seems the young woman in your therapy group was being stalked by her husband, Lonnie O'Connor. According to this report, he's one seriously disturbed individual. Mr. O'Connor waited outside the hotel and grabbed Erin when she exited out the back employee door early this morning. He attempted to wrestle her into his car, but she went wildcat on him and fought back."

"Oh God, is she okay? Where was her daughter?" Julia scanned the report until the stark black-and-white mug shot of sullen-faced man stopped her. His eyes were lit from within by malice. Three long scratches ran down the left side of his unshaven face, a man who may have been handsome if not for his brutish glower. Disturbing alarm bells went off in Julia's head—he looked somehow familiar.

Walter set down his wine glass. "Erin's a little bruised up and her wrist is sprained, but she was saved from more serious injury—apparently, the night manager jumped into the fray. He'd heard her screams and came out. He was able to wrestle this fine citizen down to the ground while Erin called the cops. Seems Mr. O'Connor traced her to Elston soon after she got here, but because Erin was in the shelter, he couldn't get easy access to her or their daughter. Shelters aren't luxurious, but they do offer twenty-four-hour security."

"But why would Erin's husband try to kidnap her? How was that supposed to work out?"

"He sounds criminal to the core. With those guys, their overriding need is for control. Every day she was gone probably ate at him. His wife and child were living on their own against all kind of odds. All of it stoked his obsession. Can you imagine the seismic shock waves that rocked this character when she didn't buckle under and allow him to just drag her into his car? The wheels of karma can turn slowly, but they do turn."

Julia picked up the mug shot again and went to the kitchen window. Holding the picture up into the slanting afternoon light, she studied Lonnie's wary eyes and his nose that bent a few degrees as if from a long-ago injury or fight. But she knew this face. She also knew his voice was soft, with a southern drawl. A memory flashed through her mind like a darting minnow then vanished.

She put the picture back into the folder and closed it so sLonnie's eyes couldn't follow her. "Will Erin and her daughter have to move again, once this guy gets out of jail? Erin told me he'd walk right through any restraining order like tissue paper. Because he's not exactly afraid of the law, that's another reason why she ran."

"His rap sheet is impressive, but so far he's only racked up a long list of misdemeanors. Trust me, I'm sure he's done felony crimes, but he's flown under the radar."

Walter walked toward Julia and for a minute, her heart raced as she held her breath. He tilted the wine bottle into her empty glass. She hadn't been aware she had finished her first drink. A shaft of sunlight pierced through her blue glass and into the red wine, refracting a beam of amethyst against the white countertop. Gooseflesh prickled on the back of her neck and an image of purple gloves swam up.

She spun toward Walter. "This guy is our evening janitor at the clinic, I know it! I've seen him a couple of times when I worked late and something about him always gave me the creeps. He was nice, but like, too nice. And he always wore these purple gloves, I assumed for sanitary reasons."

The crease between his eyebrows deepened. "You mean the new guy?"

"New? I thought he'd been here for a while."

Walter closed his eyes and lowered his head as if calculating. "No, this guy came on board about six weeks ago. Maybe seven." Walter's eyes flew open and he stared at Julia. "When did Erin come in for her assessment?"

"About two months ago, a few weeks after I started," she said then stopped. Another dot connected, and she snapped her fingers. "Wait, Erin's chart had been misfiled! And more than once. I remember being in the chartroom with Marlene and searching for it. I thought I had made the mistake, but I didn't. I *know* I didn't. It was taken out and refiled wrong." Her words tumbled out as her conviction grew.

A thunderous look crossed Walter's face. "I'm calling the janitorial service. This would be a catastrophic breach of privacy and security if Erin's husband's been working inside the clinic all this time."

"Catastrophic because he was trying to find out where she was staying?"

"For starters, yes. But if he was able to jimmy the locks on the file cabinets and read your progress notes in her chart, then he'd seen the work you two were doing and how Erin was trying to move on. You were supporting Erin's independence, but to a guy like Lonnie, you're controlling his woman. And controlling Erin is his job, not yours. If this scenario is true, Julia, then we have an exceptionally motivated criminal who knows too much about both of you."

"And criminals love to control," she whispered, thinking of Nick trapping her wrist with vise-like strength, as a shiver ran up her spine.

Not the same thing, she told herself. *Nick was no Lonnie.*

"Almost as much as they love to terrorize and vandalize." Walter pulled his cell phone from his jeans pocket.

"He didn't vandalize Erin," Julia's eyes rounded. "But

wait, my tires got slashed."

"All four. And that, my friend, is a very determined actor. Top it off with stalking and attacking Erin. This guy may have strayed squarely into felony territory."

While Walter called the janitorial company and asked to speak to the manager, Julia wandered to the bookshelf-lined corner of the living room. She clicked on the brass lamp with tremulous fingers and sank into the armchair's softness. Her body tucked perfectly into the contours of the cushions rounded by Walter's frame. She could see him reading here for hours on end, and imagined it was a balm.

She took a measured sip of her wine and tried to deep-breathe away dark, encroaching thoughts. Still, a picture came to her of how gleeful Lonnie must have been the night he slashed her tires. Had he smiled at her distress when she saw the flattened tires from his hiding spot only yards away? Had the knife in his hand grown slick with sweat while he gauged his odds of getting caught if he jumped up from some tangle of shrubs and pressed the blade's tip against her throat?

One piece of Nick's argument she knew to be true: moving would be an escape from her problems here at Elston. A lump grew in Julia's throat, and no matter how hard she swallowed and tried to will it away, it wouldn't budge.

Finally she set her wine aside as the taste turned sour in her mouth.

Chapter 43

The next morning Julia pulled into the clinic parking lot and killed the engine. Right away the heat began its incremental climb inside her car. She was stiff from sleeping most of the night on the couch, too angry with Nick even to consider sharing the same bed with him. He had nudged her awake before dawn, pulled her up from the cushions, and led her to bed. Her heart felt bruised and she didn't have the will to protest. She even found a small measure of comfort being in Nick's arms.

They remained silent, their détente too delicate for either side to risk broaching, until the morning sky morphed into a pearly white and Julia slipped away to dress for work.

The 'o' in Elston Mental Health Clinic still had the same faded, sad face drawn in its center, but now Julia smiled. The day she'd first noticed this seemed a lifetime ago.

Then she only had seen a symbol of dysfunction, some editorial graffiti from a dissatisfied client. Now it seemed hopeful, with the clinic's name embracing the sad face and keeping it connected to all the other letters.

When she walked into the lobby, Mona glared at her. At first, she wondered if Mona didn't recognize her. Julia herself had a hard time recognizing her friend as Mona wore neither make-up nor jewelry, which made her scowl rawer. Mona snatched up a newspaper next to her and pointed to a headline above the fold.

Julia was too far away to read it. "What?"

"What do you mean, *what?* Are you so busy packing you

can't give us a heads-up?"

"I haven't even seen the paper today. What is it?"

Mona wagged a bare finger at her. "Ha! You don't need the paper. Ask the reporter. I'll bet he's the first thing you saw when you woke up this morning."

Rather than wait for Julia's reply, she spun around and disappeared down the hallway toward the conference room.

What was she talking about?

Julia trailed behind, calling, "Mona, wait!"

All the staffers were there—Glen, Angel, Marlene, and Paulie—and their greetings were as chilly as Mona's. Only Walter's seat at the front of the conference table was vacant.

Glen tilted back into his chair and regarded her. "Girl, why'd you even bother showing up today? Just to rubberneck?"

Julia gaped as her words failed, departed before she could exhale.

"She's here because she's one of us," Walter said from behind Julia as he closed the door. "Julia, please take your seat."

She lowered herself into a chair, thankful Walter wasn't also acting as though he'd lost his mind.

Glen pounced, having none of it. "One of us for a week. Maybe." He slid *The Elston Daily News* across the conference room table towards her. "Every Friday I go to my favorite taco stand and get my favorite order from my favorite taco lady. But this morning, she hands me my order and asks if I want red or green salsa, and, oh by the way, have I found another job yet? I must have just stood there like I had pudding for brains. So she hands me that paper. From the head of a taco line, I find out I'm canned." Glen clucked his tongue. "She musta felt sorry for me because she told me to keep the paper. Hell of a way to get a free paper."

Julia spun the rumpled paper around. The headline read, "County Mental Health Clinic to Close in Thirty Days." The byline read, Nick Meyer.

Oh, say it's not true.

She sped through the first three paragraphs of the story and got the gist, thanks to his impeccable ability to cram the majority of facts into the top-third of a story. The state budgeting committee had reviewed their original cuts, crunched more numbers, and saw there wasn't enough money to keep the clinic afloat for even the next six to nine months.

With much regret, they announced they had no choice but to shutter the entire clinic and redirect the clients to neighboring facilities in the next thirty days.

Bastard! Nick wrote the story last night, and then cozied up to me this morning. His silence this morning wasn't contrition, but retribution.

She wished she had also learned the news from the taco lady, which was preferable to facing a table ringed by angry faces.

Julia held up the paper. "I didn't know a thing about this. Honestly."

Glen, Angel, Paulie, and Marlene stared back with suspicion pasted on their expressions. Except for Mona, whose face softened into pity. She shook her head and her eyes never left Julia's.

Julia got the message: *You poor sap.*

A warm hand pressed upon Julia's shoulder and she swiveled to find Walter standing behind her. He looked at her and gave the slightest of winks.

"All right," Walter said, "let's not take pot shots at a bystander here. The paper must have an inside source because when I called the state senior analyst this morning, he said the decision had just been made late yesterday. He was surprised to see the news broke this quickly, too."

Julia glowered. *Nick and his damn inside sources.* She let the paper drop to the table.

Walter moved back to his chair and sat down. "While this news of the clinic closing caught us by surprise, regardless of how we found out, the facts are real. We've got to coordinate with our neighboring clinics and local therapists to get our clients transferred. And we've all got to do it double-time, folks."

Marlene hugged both of her elbows and her pinched face seemed thinner. "Of course, Walter. The clients are the first priority, but what considerations are we given?"

"I've got a phone meeting scheduled today with the San Antonio clinical director. I plan to talk about transferring some of the clients and seeing if they have openings for any of you—the state's best therapists and case managers, bar none." Walter's voice cracked and grew thick with emotion.

"Oh, San Antonio. That's far away," Marlene said. She hugged herself tighter. "For the clients, I mean."

Making a strangled noise, Paulie stood up. "The clients, the clients, the clients! All I do is think about the clients! I work for them, beg them to show up, all so I can think about and work for them more. What about *us?*"

He whirled toward Walter and blurted, "I found a divorce attorney's card on the floor of my wife's car this week. Maybe it's nothing. Maybe one of her friends dropped it. Or maybe, I don't know, she's going to divorce me. Gee, why does that have the ring of truth?"

Walter said in a soft voice, "Paulie, we're going to figure a way out of —"

"Ha!" Paulie's voice twisted up several notches. "I'm packing my stuff *now*. I've got to find another job and do something besides wait to be evicted in four weeks and get served divorce papers."

"There's some empty boxes in the file room, boss," Glen said in a helpful tone.

Paulie stared at him, the fluorescent lights punctuating a higher than usual number of smudges on his glasses. His face clouded, he made another strangled noise, and then wheeled out the conference room.

With raised eyebrows, Walter turned to Glen. "Really? That's your idea of helping in a crisis? Please, go get Paulie and bring him back in here."

"Nope, that dog don't hunt no more. Find another errand boy."

Angel rose in a stiff jerk. He threw Glen a disgusted glance and announced to the room, "Man, this had better not be what I have to put up with for the next month." Angel followed Paulie out of the room, calling out to him.

With a shaky elegance, Marlene made her way over to Glen, and put a bird-like hand on his stubbled cheek, as if to stroke an errant child. "Darling, this is not a time to be, in the parlance of your generation, a shithead. Save your sulk for later and go help Paulie and Angel."

Outnumbered, Glen lumbered out of the room, but not before beckoning to Mona. "C'mon. I'll take all four of us out to my taco lady's stand for breakfast. My treat. It's the one place I can go and not have the news thrown at me twice."

Julia said to Walter and Marlene, "I am just so sad about all of this." Her words sounded paltry spoken out loud, when compared to her inner dismay.

Marlene managed a tiny smile and picked up her purse that hung on the back of the chair. "You know, when things look their absolute worst, a chorizo breakfast taco may be the best medicine. You two coming?"

Julia and Walter shook their heads, and when Marlene left the conference room, silence settled like snow.

She swallowed hard and faced Walter. "I would have told you if I'd known."

"Of course you would have. And it wouldn't have changed a thing." He paused and regarded her. "But I did receive two phone calls this morning that might brighten your day. The hospital said Rowena has stabilized and they're releasing her at noon. She's even made a phone call to Wilken's Mortuary to start planning the funeral service."

"Oh, thank God. I'll call her and see if she needs a ride downtown."

"And Lonnie was questioned by the police last night about working here as a janitor. Not only did he admit it, he even boasted about getting access to Erin's records exactly as you guessed. He even bragged to the officer how he wore those purple gloves so he wouldn't leave behind fingerprints. But when they asked him about your tires, he clammed up and asked to speak to his attorney. In his mind, destroying tires is a worse crime than impersonation with intent to breach confidential mental health records."

"It *was* him! I knew it!" Julia cried. "But what about Erin? How is she doing?"

"Well enough to press assault charges. I called her this morning and offered to drive her to the police station to meet with the deputy. Lonnie will lawyer up, but I think his days of wife-beating and tire-slashing are about to be sharply curtailed."

"Good for Erin!"

"Oh yes, and for Rowena too. Maybe it's a coincidence both your clients are really stepping up, but I don't think so. I believe you helped them find strengths they couldn't even imagine they had. After Friday, you and I will go our separate ways, but I want you to know I believe you're a gifted healer, my friend."

Julia's heart overflowed, and she managed to say, "Thank you, Walter."

His gaze sharpened. He reached for her hand and turned it over. He traced the inside of her wrist where four smudged bruises fanned out, evidence of where Nick had dug his fingers into her flesh two days before.

Walter thinned his lips. "Is everything okay with you?"

His tenderness was a sharp rebuke to Nick's controlling grasp and she wanted to cry, "No, everything is not okay!" Instead she pulled back her hand from his and avoided his eyes. "Just a moving injury. I'm such a klutz."

Anger flared in Walter's eyes. "No matter where you are, Julia, if you need me, all you have to do is call. I'll be there for you."

Any energy she possessed to fabricate lies evaporated. She stared up into his eyes, which had grown flinty. Walter was so close, but had never felt farther away.

From his front jeans pocket he brought out something that glinted a tip of gold. "I debated whether to bring this today, but I'm glad I did."

He picked up her hand again and placed the soft and feathery object into the center of her palm. A fishing fly with purple iridescent feathers and two brass beads for eyes shone back, and from its center the curved hook pointed upward.

Julia stroked the feathers with her index finger, careful to avoid the sharp needle of the hook. "It's beautiful. One of yours?"

"I had some help. My son and I made it. Actually, it was the last fly we made together. Luke was already getting sick, so I did most of the work, but he picked out the feathers and the beads. He told me this little guy would give me luck in catching the prettiest fish." With care, he folded her fingers around the fly.

"No, I couldn't possibly take this."

Walter cupped her chin and raised her lips to his and kissed her. Warmth spread from his soft lips into her heart, which beat wildly. It was as though her chest had been frozen and now a bright sun shone from within.

He stepped away from her. "I've wanted to do that since the first time you walked in my door. Also I wanted to show my son he was right. For just this minute, I caught the prettiest fish."

Tears streamed down Julia face. "Walter, I don't … I mean I can't—"

"I know you can't, Julia." He beckoned her to follow him into the hallway. "This time next week you'll be gone and I have to keep reminding myself of that. And next month, our clinic will be gone. But right now my job is to get to the shelter and pick up Erin."

They stopped outside of her office and faced each other, and Julia said, "I'm not sure if we'll have a chance to talk alone again, so I'm saying this now. Thank you for letting me be part of something that felt like a family. I didn't know that was possible and I … I had forgotten the feeling."

His gaze was a prayer to her, and Julia knew he was about to kiss her again. She hoped he was going to kiss her again.

Instead he took a step backwards. "You're an amazing woman who is going to go out there and do amazing things." With his quiet grace, he turned, went down the hallway and, when the lobby door opened and closed, she knew he was gone.

Dazed, Julia staggered into her office on wooden legs and sat on the edge of the chair. It felt as though her core was scooped out. With trembling fingers, she placed the fishing fly on her desk.

Go after him, her mind insisted.

She snatched up her phone to call Walter, but paused when she saw a screen notification flashing that Nick had called and left a voicemail.

Julia punched in the code and Nick's voice rumbled in her ear. "Hey, Jules, I'm looking at your damn bookcase and there is no way in hell we're dragging all these books to Dallas. Most are covered in an inch of dust anyway, so how important can they be? I'm working late tonight, so use that time to purge, okay? Just toss them in the dumpster out back. I'm too tired to drop them to Goodwill tomorrow, but you can if you want."

A click and the message cut off.

With vicious intensity, she threw the phone and it skidded across the desk, taking the purple feathered fly with it. They both hit the wall and disappeared behind the desk.

Julia gave a sharp cry, got down on her hands and knees, and crawled under the desk. She retrieved her phone, which had landed on top of a nest of phone and computer cables. But she could not find the fishing lure, even after three tries of lifting and uncoiling the cables.

She trotted out to the parking lot, praying that maybe Walter was still there. But the lot was empty, save for her lone car, waiting to carry her away.

Chapter 44

The last funeral Julia attended had been her grandfather's when she was eight years old. He was cremated, and because it was a memorial service, she assumed her grandmother had brought her grandfather's ashes in the large tapestry purse nestled next to her hip on the pew. It certainly seemed big enough to accommodate two urns of the old man's ashes.

Propped up on an easel at the front of the church, next to the pastor's lectern, was a large photograph of her grandfather, smiling from the confines of his carved frame. Julia remembered feeling warm and loved when she saw his beloved face and cottony curls that formed a half-ring around his otherwise bald head. His younger self beamed across the packed Presbyterian congregation while the pastor had spoken of all the good things her grandfather did in his long life.

However, when Julia entered the church the morning of Mrs. Horn's funeral, she realized right away this was going to be a different affair. For starters, it was held in the Cowboy Church of the Lower Valley, a clapboard house so dinky and tucked away she had never noticed its existence. It sat on the flat outskirts of town between a mobile home park and a cornfield, with no lower valley in sight.

Despite the church's petite size, only the first few rows of pews were filled. Julia followed the slow-moving line of mourners past the open casket and let her eyes roam around the building rather than see Mrs. Horn laid out. Julia was afraid Rowena's mother would appear exposed and vulnerable, but when she gave her respects at the side of the casket, Mrs. Horn looked peaceful, as though she had fallen asleep after applying a generous amount of make-up. Rowena had selected a simple navy blue dress with white piping and at Mrs. Horn's throat glowed a gold cross.

With a sigh of relief, she went back to her seat, where Nick sat in stony silence. His shoulders seemed knotted through his suit jacket and he stared out a window with a view of the parking lot.

Julia wasn't sure why she had insisted he attend the service, except to serve as payback for his writing the story about the clinic closing and not warning her. So this morning when she pulled his suit out of a moving box and stood holding it in front of him, she'd believed he owed her that much.

Now, any payback she hoped to extract fizzled in the face of his complete disconnection. Nick often checked his watch and glanced at the door, freedom so close, yet so far away.

The minister, a young man with a thin, reedy voice, read the sermon from his prepared notes on the lectern. Several times, he referenced Rowena as the devoted daughter who lived only to serve her mother.

For Rowena's part, she kept her gaze focused past the minister and onto the stained glass window depicting a cowboy kneeling before Jesus while holding a calf. Next to her sat a heavyset woman who looked like a younger version of Mrs. Horn. The woman cut her eyes toward Rowena and every now and then offered up a tissue from a small packet.

But Rowena, whose face was puffy with grief, remained dried-eyed and ignored the woman like she ignored the minister. Julia wondered if Rowena even heard his words.

Walter sat in a pew behind Rowena and the seat next to him was empty. Had he kept the place next to him open in case Julia had wanted to sit there?

At one point he scanned the small congregation. Their eyes met briefly, and Julia found it hard to breathe. He gave her a smile before his gaze traveled to Nick. Walter's face turned into a neutral mask as he turned his full attention back to the minister.

The inside pocket of Nick's jacket buzzed, and he reached in to check his phone. Julia leaned in to read the text, but he darkened the screen in a swift motion.

"Gotta go," Nick whispered. "Breaking news."

"What? Now?" Julia said, trying to keep her voice low. The minister asked the mourners to rise for the hymn, "When the Roll is Called Up Yonder," and Nick used that time to shrug in a what-can-you-do gesture, before sliding past her into the aisle.

Flummoxed, she stared after him, then she snatched her purse and followed him out of the church. She caught up to him in the parking lot as he strode toward his car, talking animatedly on the phone.

"Wait!" Julia called, running up next to him.

Eyebrows shooting up, he ended the call. "What?"

Julia held up her index finger. "All I asked of you was this one thing!"

"And I delivered! I was there. Met your therapy buddies, saw the old lady in the coffin, made it through that god-awful solo, and the minister's wrapping up his spiel. But city desk says there's a water main break downtown and that takes precedent. Let's not go through this again on my last day of work, okay? Try and tamp down the drama."

He moved to go around her and Julia laid her hand on his forearm. Nick looked down at her with a stunned expression. "Are you grabbing me?"

"No." She pulled her hand away. "Can't you stay until the end? Have the paper send someone else. No one here will understand why you bolted from the funeral."

"You can't get all mushy about these people. And you have to get your head out of the clouds."

"I'm at a church, attending a funeral. How real is this?"

"Those people aren't important to us. Do you know who they really are? They're not friends or family. They're strangers you spent some weeks with."

"I've known them all summer! This is only your first time to meet them."

"Yeah, that's right, so let's review. I met the little bald-headed guy with the tattoos and his chunky buddy, Country Boy Joe. And was that old lady the Marlene you've been quaking about? C'mon, Julia, I thought she'd be more than a scrawny scrap of a woman."

"These are my friends, Angel and Glen!"

"Fine. Then drop your friends a postcard on Tuesday because we're moving Monday."

"Monday! What happened to next Friday?"

The phone in Nick's pocket buzzed again and he checked the number. "Now I really have to go."

"Why Monday?"

"I spoke with the manager of the PODS and he's got another load going to Dallas. If we piggyback with that truck, we get a discount."

"We're not paying for this, the paper is. How much is being saved?"

"About four hundred bucks. It shows my new boss I'm thinking about their bottom line."

"For four hundred dollars, I'm rushed four days?" Julia's stomach contracted as if she'd taken a fist in the gut.

"Process it, Julia," he said, making air quotes with his fingers. "Four days just means fewer days for you to moon around Elston. The money's the least of it. I'd pay the movers double at this point if we could stop the torture. Come Tuesday, you'll be waking up someplace better. Goddammit, cats are easier to move than you. I've got to go."

He hurried toward the back of the parking lot and she lost sight of him. A honeysuckle bush covered in a riot of yellow flowers was behind her and she caught a whiff of its sugary sweetness and a wave of nausea washed over her.

She made her way back to the church with heavy legs, as though weights were strapped to her ankles. Inside the doorway she found Rowena standing there, watching her.

Rowena inhaled a deep breath. "Couldn't stand to hear another word in there about Mama. And if I get patted on anymore by my aunt I swear I'll—" Rowena's face crumpled and sobs choked her words.

"Rowena, I'm so sorry."

Julia took a step but paused when Rowena held up a large hand. "Now don't you start on up, too."

Rowena dabbed her eyes on her sleeve before she exhaled a shuddering breath. Nick's car roared to life and she squinted in the direction of the noise.

Without a glance toward either Rowena or Julia, who stood rooted on the church steps, he drove past with his cell phone pressed to his ear as he steered his Jeep one-handed. Once he got onto the road, he accelerated so fast his wheels squealed. Both women jumped from the sharp noise.

"That was my fiancé," Julia said into the following awkward silence.

"Uh-huh. Never had no boyfriend, much less one those fiancé fellows." She threw Julia a sideways glance. "Can't see as I'm missing much."

Julia only nodded. Nick was beyond defending.

Another hymn started up and Rowena sighed. "I got

to get back in there—that's the last song on the program they put together. I suppose all the pattin' and tellin' me mama's in a better place is about to start back up. But you know, that's a chicken shit thing to say, and I don't care if God's listening or not. Wherever it is that she's at, I know she'd rather be with me."

Rowena paused and dragged her gaze up to Julia's. "And while I'm in the truth-saying mood, seems you'd be better off on your own than with that pretty fella. Back there in the church, your face was near as long as mine."

Rowena disappeared into the foyer and Julia followed her, but then stopped. She remembered Mona had sent a group email inviting the clinic employees to meet at the Cedar Door after the funeral service. It was supposed to be a wake for the staffers and a going away party for Julia, which Mona called a bummer combo.

At first when Julia read the email, she was grateful Mona had set the event up and was glad to know that they could all be together. But with her leaving in three days, it had taken on a darker tone. Today would be the last time she and the staffers would all be together.

She wheeled and made her way down the steps, tears blurring her vision as she went to her car. She wanted to make it inside before she cried in public.

Her hand was almost on the car's handle when she hesitated by the driver's side window. She squinted and couldn't make out what she was seeing. Roughly she swiped at her eyes, then peered in closer.

In the gray dust coating the driver's side window, someone had written, "Get out now!" The exclamation point was slanted to the right as if hurriedly scrawled.

Julia gasped and stepped backwards from the words. She whipped her head around. Only empty cars sat glittering in the noon light in the funeral home parking lot.

She was alone and felt that to be true.

Is someone still stalking me?

Lonnie was in jail, so he couldn't have written the message. Dread rose up in Julia and her body shook. Maybe she should pack a suitcase and tell Nick she was leaving this afternoon ahead of him. Not breathe a word about her window, but shoot up the highway and leave all this madness behind.

A spark of anger pushed back her fear a bit. *When am I going to stop running?*

With the flat of her hand, Julia wiped the words away and left a clean swath across the dusty window.

Footsteps approached from behind and she spun around as Mona and Angel walked up. Mona waggled her index finger back and forth. "No getting to the Cedar before us!"

When Julia didn't respond right away, Mona cocked her head to the side. "Unless you're ditching us to go to the graveside service or go home to pack pots and pans."

As if, Julia thought.

She opened up the car door and called out over her shoulder, "First round's on me."

"Hell, yeah, chica!" Mona said as she beamed, and Angel nodded while reaching into his dress slacks for his keys.

Hell yeah, indeed.

Julia gunned the Honda and swung out of the parking lot, as she planned to buy not one round, but two.

Chapter 45

J ulia didn't expect the bar to be so crowded on a Friday at noon. She found at seat between Mona and Paulie at a large round table. Waves of cheery conversation and laughter lapped around them, a startling contrast from the funeral service.

Glen seemed nonplussed as he threaded around the clusters of patrons and dodged harried wait staff while holding a pitcher of beer aloft. Angel wove a similar path behind him, clutching multiple beer mugs in each hand. With a thud, Glen landed the pitcher in the middle of the table.

A slosh of beer ran down the side of the pitcher and Glen said, "Well, hell. There goes my tip."

Angel set the mugs down, filled them, and then glanced around the main room. "I guess people are getting a jump on the weekend."

Everyone except Marlene reached for a glass.

Walter raised his mug. "I'd like to propose a toast to Maggie Horn, a woman who fought the good fight and is now at rest."

Tears welled in Julia's eyes and she noticed she wasn't the only one. They clinked their glasses together.

Despite the distraction all around her, Julia couldn't shake the memory of the words scrawled on her car window. When the group broke into conversation around her, she caught Walter's eye and said in a low voice, "Walter, when you get chance there's something I need to tell—"

Their waitress rushed up. "Sorry, y'all. Couldn't get to

you sooner, we're slammed today. I see you got your beer—what else would you like?"

"An iced tea for me, please, and two orders of your largest plate of nachos," Marlene said. After the waitress disappeared into the crowd, Marlene added, "I think I'll leave my drinking days behind me for now."

Glen, halfway through his mug of beer, waved his hand at her. "You keep your teetotalling notions on your side of the table, okay? Getting laid off means I get to exercise my God-given right to lift sixteen-ounce curls. At least until I find another job, which by the way, might be next week."

"Oh yeah?" Walter set his mug down. "Got a lead?"

"More than a lead, boss man. You know the cutie in Austin I went dancing with at the Spoke? Now that one's a keeper, for sure."

Angel snorted into his beer mug, but Glen ignored him. "It's a double score because her brother works for the Samsung plant up in north Austin and she heard they may need an electrician's helper. Pay's pretty good."

"Electrician's helper, seriously?" Angel wiped foam off his upper lip with the back of his hand. "We'd be sitting in the dark at the office if it was up to you. You're the guy who can never remember where the light bulbs are stored and now suddenly you're wiring high voltage lines without getting fried?"

"Oh, ye of little faith, my hair-challenged friend. I got online last night and signed up for a trade school in Austin. Besides, every electrician I've known is half crazy. The way I see it, my work here at the clinic was a warmup for this next gig."

Everyone congratulated Glen, who beamed as he filled up their mugs, and then left for the bar for another pitcher. Julia smiled for the first time in what felt like a long while. The noise in the bar doubled as more lunchtime crowd filed in. She sneaked a peek at Walter, who leaned in closer to Paulie as if to hear him better as they talked.

He cut his gaze toward Julia and smiled, which made his eyes crinkle in a charming way. Julia had sat away from Walter to create distance, but from across the table, now he was all she could see. Running her index finger through the condensation on the side of her glass, she thought about the words written on her car window.

What's the point of bringing it up if I'm leaving in three days?

Julia sighed and decided it would be better to tell Walter before she left the bar that today was her last day. She'd then go the clinic to gather her few paltry possessions and be gone.

She sensed someone watching her and when she raised her head, she stared into Walter's eyes, which never wavered. A bloom of heat spread into her chest, and for a moment she wondered if he had read her thoughts. They were so close, only a few feet from each other, but for Julia it might as well have been a thousand miles.

She closed her eyes and turned away, deciding she'd write a group email to the clinic and tell them goodbye. There was only so much her heart could take, besides, everyone was scrambling with their own problems and exit plans.

The waitress settled the two heaping platters of nachos into the middle of the table and gave everyone small plates. Julia had eaten nothing all day and she should have been famished, but she pushed away her plate, sickened by the smell of the food.

Glen appeared with the second pitcher. "Channel 7 is on the tube right now. There's some big main break flooding Third and Burleson." He chin pointed to the flat screen television mounted on the wall above the line of beer taps at the bar.

The news showed a video of police officers standing in mid-ankle water while directing traffic around barriers erected by orange-vested water utility employees. On the right hand of the screen, Graham loped by with one camera in his hand and the other bouncing off his thin chest. He stopped to point his camera at three workmen gathered at a corner consulting a map. Julia imagined what the shot would look like and the sight of her friend warmed her.

As the reporter squinted in the noonday sun and warned the viewers which roads to avoid, behind him other press members gathered around a man Julia recognized as the city manager. Towering over him stood Nick, jotting notes.

A figure sheathed in a fuchsia-pink dress, more spray-painted on than zipped or buttoned, slipped through the crowd and settled next to him. Calliope. Always dressed as though she was either going to or coming from a cocktail party, she almost matched Nick height-to-height, thanks to her three-inch heels. Her runway model legs seemed even more endless.

The knot of reporters parted when Calliope approached, as though they knew their spot was at the edge of the pack. A man in the back of the bar gave a long wolf whistle and pockets of laughter erupted around the bar. Julia started to roll her eyes, but then they widened and she grew still.

Calliope reached up and cupped Nick's elbow. He turned, as if surprised, until he saw her and then he lit up in a way that Julia recognized. Nick used to smile at her like that when they'd first dated. She had once been the recipient of his rapt attention and felt flooded with Technicolor joy, when all things shimmered with possibility.

Until now, she had almost forgotten that smile.

Nick bent at his waist and whispered something in Calliope's ear. She in turn laughed and blushed.

Julia's heart hammered in her chest and her lungs were leather, incapable of exhaling. Such intimacy was born from knowing layers and layers about each other, and in an unguarded moment, they had let their masks slip.

The truth slammed the last remaining air out of Julia: *Nick was having an affair with Calliope.*

There was no need to smell an unusual floral perfume on his shirt collar while doing the laundry, nor to drive by Calliope's house to discover his car parked discreetly in an alley. For herself, and anyone else watching from the bar around her, their gaze was the smoking gun.

The scene switched back to the station where the anchor moved on to the weather report.

"Man!" Glen bellowed, and Julia closed her eyes to brace herself. "Can you imagine jackhammering through that pavement to get to a busted line in this oven? I feel a heatstroke coming on just thinking about it. Better hydrate myself with a pale ale." He reached for the pitcher.

The walls crowded in and the cacophony of voices grew into an insectile roar. Her panic and questions rolled in at the same pace.

Did I see what I really saw? How long has this been going on? Oh God, are they having sex?

The last question punched the biggest wallop as her mind served up a vivid image of Nick and Calliope in bed with her blonde mane flung back and settling around them like a spider's web.

A voice cut through her rising panic. "Julia," Walter's voice was low as reached out his hand toward hers. His concern, his gesture, and his tone were all confirmations that Walter saw what she did and understood.

Julia scraped back her chair as her vision darkened. She had the presence of mind to grab her purse before blurting out to the group, "Have to go. I just remembered an appointment." She stumbled toward the direction of the door and wove through a knot of people gathered in the foyer waiting for table, then heaved herself outside.

The horrible, tea-stained quality of light returned and she let out a sob of frustration and fear. It was as though she'd been flipped back to the time she'd first lost her sight, but this time was worse. Then she'd had a home, a job, and Nick's support. Now all those things were as tattered as her vision.

Julia wished only to get to her car so she could sit down and try to breathe, even though by now the heat would be stifling in that metal and glass box. She stumbled down the sidewalk and made it from parking meter to parking meter, as each one swam up like a buoy in the gloom.

A hand settled on her shoulder and Julia startled, almost tripping. Marlene was beside her and Julia was torn between a desire to push her away in shame at being seen so broken or to hold onto her and wail her misery.

Julia stammered, "Really Marlene, I'm late and—"

"I caught them, too. Julia, I saw what you saw. And it was wrong. And you, dear sweet child, deserve so much better, especially from a man who is supposed to love and cherish you."

Relief flooded through Julia, in all its terrible truth. Marlene recognized the exchange between Calliope and Nick also, so she wasn't imagining things.

And I deserve so much better.

Marlene's words unclenched the shock that squeezed her heart.

"Nick's having an affair. With that ridiculous—" Julia's mind scrambled for a word low enough to plaster onto Calliope.

"Trollop," Marlene finished.

Julia nodded, and then burst into tears. Racking sobs shook her as the reality of her miserable situation settled upon her: *Nick and I are through.* She was not going to move to a house in Dallas, and come Monday she would be homeless. She had no paying job.

And to top it off, she'd already withdrawn from her college graduate program, which was starting the fall semester next week. This new hard wall of reality was rising up and speeding towards her at an alarming rate.

Marlene held Julia and rocked her back and forth. The sun blistered down all around them and both women were sweating. In some far reaches of her mind, Julia was mortified to be crying in public and being comforted like a child. Still, the sobs came as she gave in to her grief.

After several minutes, Julia caught her breath and Marlene led her to the blessed shade under a jutting green canopy of an insurance building.

Marlene waited until Julia's gaze met her own. "My husband had an affair during our marriage, and when I discovered it, I believed my life to be a devastation. It was as though our marriage was a vase thrown to the ground and shattered into tiny bits. That wasn't the only reason I left the marriage, but it gave me a defining reason to pick up the phone and call an attorney."

"What? I'm sorry. For some reason, I thought you were a widow." Julia took a shuddering breath.

"Oh, there were days I wished him dead, if the truth be known. But I don't feel that way about him now. He's become simply my daughter's father and I'm grateful for his part in providing me with our child. But," she said, her voice taking on a firm tone, "discovering his affair was one of the worst days of my life. I thought if I had done more, loved him more, been there for him more, he never would have strayed. And he was low enough never to disabuse me of such beliefs. I've grown to forgive him, but there are days when the grudges resurface."

Something shifted for Julia as she remembered Marlene's occasional clipped and frosty behavior. A piece of understanding slipped into place as to the seed of her supervisor's anger.

"But that's my question, too, even though I know it sounds dumb." Her voice was barely above a whisper. "Why wasn't I enough?"

"No one's enough for people like Nick. Just like no one would have been perfect enough for my husband to keep him from straying. They're terrified of commitment, so they find someone fun and light and believe the magic bubble they concocted will float from one carefree day to the next. The fools. But eventually the bubble bursts, and when it does, good people get hurt and the careless people concoct excuses for how it wasn't their fault."

Marlene placed her hands on Julia's shoulders and gave a gentle shake. "It's not your fault, dear."

A band loosened from around her heart. "But what am I going to do? I mean, come Monday we're supposed to move to Dallas!"

Marlene raised her eyebrows. "I don't know. I have no idea what you're going to do. Perhaps the immediate question is what are you *not* going to do? Where do you draw the line and tell yourself you allow only those in your life who are truthful and kind? Until you stand up for yourself, fear will be your compass."

A lanky figure approached, and Julia's reflex made her step back at the outline of Nick. But the man's relaxed, rolling gait came into view and his face was open and he was in need of a haircut.

"Hey, gang, is this a closed meeting, or can anyone join?"

Walter spoke to both of them, but the question was to Julia. Marlene stepped aside, glancing between Julia and Walter.

In that moment, Julia knew two things: within Walter's arms lay a circle of comfort, and all around her an ordinary Friday afternoon ticked along as traffic drifted past them under a sky of crystalline blue. Standing beside Walter and Marlene, she sent out a prayer of gratitude that her vision had returned.

He stepped forward. "What was it you wanted to tell me back there?"

At first Julia was confused, and then she remembered the scrawled message on her car window. She shook her head, "Nothing. I mean, it was something then, but now I have to ..."

A wave of anxiety washed over her. She took a deep a breath and said, "Actually, I have no idea what I have to do anymore. Everything is all up in the air."

She placed her hands on either side of her head as if to drown out the noise from her maelstrom of thoughts.

"Sometimes up in the air means all things are possible. You've just got to tolerate the heights."

"And what if I make the wrong choice? Do the wrong thing?"

He drew closer, enough for her to see the blue flecks that lit up his green eyes. "Then do something else. Try. And keep on trying. I'm here. Marlene's here. And that steely part of you, right there," he said as he gently touched the center of her collarbone. "That part of you that wants to survive, that's your life force disguised as fear. It all comes from the same part of you that wants to thrive."

Marlene hooked her arm around Julia's waist and Julia closed her eyes. The warmth radiated where Walter had touched her skin inches above her heart and she'd never felt so loved and terrified in her life.

Still, the question bubbled up. What was she going to tell Nick, and after that, what was she going to do?

Chapter 46

Six hours had crawled by since Julia let herself into the condo. She sat on the floor and rested against the living room wall with Trixie, who was curled up and asleep in her lap. Alone, she surveyed the remnants of her life with Nick.

A few moving boxes were scattered here and there, half-filled with their clothes, books, and indecipherable shapes wrapped in newspaper. The majority of their possessions were packed and waiting in the hulking metal storage container outside on the postage stamp of a front yard. Puffs of gray dust bunnies skittered across the floor and the only witness to her contemplation was a lone broom propped up in a corner.

She would have preferred the deep comfort of the leather couch, but it, along with the ottoman, end tables, and lamps had been carried off. Their only traces were squares and rectangles of clean floor. A card lay where the ottoman had been, and when Julia picked it up after entering the condo, she found it was her Elston College library card. Julia considered chucking it into one of the boxes, but instead opened up her purse and dropped it among her pocketbook, keys, and a stray lipstick.

Her back ached and her legs complained as the hours inched forward, but she remained still on the living room as she watched the sunlight morph from a burnished afternoon into the deepening lavenders of evening.

Memories washed over her. She had moved in with Nick against the backdrop of a January chill. He'd dropped the house key into her hand and the cold heaviness of the metal hitting her palm was a kiss of promise, as though he had unlocked all of their future days together. While she busied herself with unpacking, she hummed and sang. She brought home a brass floor lamp she found at a garage sale, a real steal at ten bucks.

Nick plugged in the lamp, snapped it on, and the room was transformed within its warm circle of light. He pulled her into his arms and nuzzled her neck. "With you here, everything is perfect."

That night they had made love on the couch, one of many such nights, and always with the lamp burning.

When her watch read 11:15 p.m., the newspaper's witching hour for deadlines, she knew the stories had all been filed and the presses were warming up for their print run. As she heaved herself up, her legs muscles cramped and complained. Trixie jumped out of her lap with a cranky meow and walked off with a offended air, her tail a question mark. Julia grabbed her purse and keys, and with one last look at the condo, left for the newsroom.

Out of habit, she parked in one of the photo department spots, went to the side door, and punched in the security code. The door did not click open, so she punched in the code again until she remembered the newspaper changed the code every six months. Had it been that long since she'd come by the paper? She pulled out her phone and texted Graham to let her in.

A dark shadow grew larger in the door's frosted window before Graham opened it and stuck his shaggy head out. "You been reading my mind, Longley? I was just going to shoot you an email tonight and see if I could take you out for a goodbye lunch this weekend. But here you are, lurking in the alleyway."

On impulse, Julia reached out and hugged Graham. "No one calls me Longley anymore. I forget how much I miss hanging out with you!"

"Whoa, a beautiful woman throwing herself at me. When my horoscope said I was going to have a day filled with adventure and surprises, I thought it meant when I waded through a pipe break." He laughed as he hugged her.

Julia burst into tears against his chest, and Graham stepped back and put his hands on her shoulders. "Hey, hey, oddball. What gives with the waterworks?"

Julia paused, but then blurted, "Nick's having an affair with Calliope." The truth cut into the fresh wound.

Graham studied her, then nodded. "Yes, I guess he is."

"You knew and didn't tell me?"

He shook his head. "No, I didn't know, but I didn't like the vibe between those two either. I wasn't sure what was going on, but whatever it was, I hoped it would all be in the past once you guys left town."

"Nick probably thought the same thing, but his timing was off. He should have hauled us out of Elston sooner," Julia said as a fresh spike of anger ran through her. "I need to talk to him."

Alarm crossed Graham's face.

"Don't worry, I'm not going to cause a scene."

He held the door open for her. "He's not in the main newsroom. You might check the conference room. He headed out there after he filed his story."

Julia nodded and entered the newsroom. From the back of the building came the whirl of the offset presses warming up to print the Saturday newspaper. An acidic smell of ink wafted in the air as she walked through the nearly deserted newsroom and the few remaining reporters and editors greeted her. When she passed Nick's vacant desk, his laptop computer was missing and in its place was a packing box filled with files.

Climbing the stairs, the light and conversations from the newsroom faded behind her with each step. The entire

upstairs floor was dusky except for the glassed-in conference room, which was brightly lit from a row of fluorescent
light bars above the long table. When she stepped on the
landing, she saw Nick as if he were a character on a stage.
His laptop computer was open before him and he swiveled
his body at an angle, with his feet crossed at the ankles and
propped up on the table, while he talked on the phone.

Judging from how relaxed he was, stretched out in
his chair, she guessed he'd been on the phone for a while.
And whomever he was talking to, Julia put Calliope at the
top of her short list. Her pulse pounded in her ears as she
approached the glass wall across from Nick and rapped twice.

Nick snapped his head up and stared directly up into
Julia's eyes. Their gaze locked for a few seconds, just
enough for her to register his surprise flash into guilt. He
murmured something in the phone, ended the call, and
stood up.

Julia came to the door and he said, "What are you doing
here? I told you I'd be late." He spoke fast and avoided her
gaze as he snapped his computer shut. He seemed to recali-
brate and straightened. In a smooth tone, like oil sliding
over water, he said, "But since you're here, let's go downstairs and you can help me carry some of my stuff out to
the car. Maybe we can go and get a bite to eat at the diner?"

Nick walked toward her, expecting Julia to step aside.
She stood fixed in the doorway.

Irritation flashed in his eyes, "C'mon, Julia. It's late
and I'm tired."

He tried to go around her, but she stepped in front of
him. "I'm tired, too. It's been a long day that started with
you ditching me at the funeral. Then someone wrote a
threat on my car and now I find you tucked into a corner of
the paper in not too much of a hurry to come home."

Nick swept his hand toward the empty conference

room. "It's called working. Between attending funerals of strangers, meeting multiple deadlines here, and the move on Monday that, I might add, I'm pretty much handling by myself, I have zero time for one of your meltdowns. If you don't get a grip, I'm calling Dr. Donovan to have him put you on some happy pills."

All of Julia's barely corralled anger, humiliation, and betrayal roared to life as she exploded, "Your happy pills seem come in the form of Calliope! I watched you flirting with her at the water line story. From a bar TV across the room it was obvious to me, and anyone else who cared to notice, how you two are together! You were literally on a street corner and didn't have the courtesy to even try to hide it. Too bad it didn't occur to either of you that camera crews tape their reporters. And live, for that matter!"

He rocked back as though slapped. "That's bullshit," Nick barked, his face reddening. "Do you know how crazy you sound right now? Calliope and I are just friends."

Julia grew very still. That line rang an ancient bell.

She took one step toward Nick and he took one step back. "My father used to say that to my mother when she confronted him about his affairs. You know what he would tell her? The same damn thing. He'd tell her his mistress was just a friend, or just a distraught client, or just, just, just! If it's an honest relationship, you don't use that word just in front of their name."

An expression crossed Nick's face that Julia had never seen before: uncertainty. Then he threw his shoulders back as if to cast cumbersome doubts aside. "I'm not going to argue semantics with you. We're going to go home and you're going to get past this version of your nutty phase. Because this time next week, my new job starts. It's late."

The strong lighting chiseled his high cheekbones and spotlighted his sensual, full lips, and Julia wondered how she could have ever allowed herself to love anyone so tightly wrapped up into his own self. She felt shame at her own shallowness. "Yes, it is, but I'm not going."

Up until that moment, she hadn't known what her decision would be. The previous hours spent at the condo she had thought and prayed for a clear answer, but got only swirls and snippets of possibilities. Now something true emerged.

"Maybe I'm crazy and maybe I'm not, but you're lying to me. You're probably lying to Calliope also, but that's her problem. And our problems are bigger than even that." Julia pulled her engagement ring off her finger and handed it to him.

"Put it back on, Julia!" Nick said through clenched teeth, as his voice rose.

Fear ran through her veins like an ice bath, but Julia held her ground. Even though her voice shook, she lifted her chin. "No, because marriage to you would be a terrible mistake. You can have Calliope, even though really, deep down, you don't want her. All you want is for me to be the wife while you're having fun with the girlfriend on the side. And tomorrow you want Dallas. Until you decide to want the next gig or girlfriend. And who would I be but your Steady Eddie, dragged through it all."

Tears ran down her cheeks as she held the ring up to him. "But it'll never be enough, will it? I'm not enough now, and nothing magical is going to happen between us, even if I spend my life doing exactly what you want. You'll always have some deadline or someone calling you away and I'll be stuck playing the pick-me game."

He clenched his fist and stepped toward her. "Goddammit, Julia, I'm warning you—"

"Hey, kids," a voice behind them said.

Julia spun around to spot the head and shoulders of Graham, who stood halfway up the stairs. "Just wanted to tell you, Julia, you left your headlights on." He came up the rest of the way to the landing, his tone casual. "I'll walk her to her car, Nick. I know you've got some things to tie up here."

In a low but commanding voice, Nick said to Julia, "Stay. We need to talk."

They stared at each other before Julia went to the conference table and laid the ring down next to his cell phone. A call lit up the phone screen and his ringer was on mute. She pointed to the phone and her former engagement ring. "Those are both for you." Then she left the room.

Neither she nor Graham spoke as they hurried across the newsroom. When Graham opened the side door, Julia's dark car waited in the parking lot.

"Thank you for coming and rescuing me."

"Hey, what are former lab partners for?" he said, but his voice was serious. "Jules, look, you can stay at my apartment if you need to. You know, in case things get hairy at your place."

Julia let out a long breath. "No, I don't want to drag you into this. And I'm not going back to Nick's. I'll deal with him tomorrow when things have settled down. How much did you hear back there?"

"Enough to offer you a safe place to crash. No one likes breakups, but it's the actual leaving that is the most dangerous, especially for women."

Footsteps echoed through the empty newsroom. Graham grabbed Julia's arm and said, "Call me if you need me, but right now you've only got one job and that's to make yourself scarce."

Julia stood up on her tip toes and kissed Graham on his stubbled cheek, pulled out her keys, and ran toward her car, praying she had at least two minutes on Nick to melt somewhere into the darkness of Elston.

Chapter 47

The gloom of her office whisked away as Julia snapped on the overhead lights to reveal the shabbiness of the sagging couch, chipped desk, and thin nappy carpet. She dumped her purse on the desk, surveyed the windowless room, and was racked by two simultaneous emotions: dread at how many more basements she may have to tumble through before her life resembled anything close to normal.

And an ache of sadness to be leaving this dingy box of a room where she had spent hours learning how to work with clients. Their faces and stories came to her and she let out a sigh, knowing there wasn't anything more she could do for them. Everybody who had walked in that door was now on their own.

In a matter of hours, she had stepped over a line that divided then from now. This morning, her life had been a train inching forward as she struggled to throw herself and her bags on board. Now, neither train nor platform existed, only a void. Her feelings toward Nick swirled between anger and grief.

She stretched out onto the couch as a wave of exhaustion and worry flooded in over her. How was she going to get Trixie and her stuff from Nick? And more importantly, where was she going to live? Could she talk to the graduate program administrators and beg to be let back in for the fall semester?

She'd have to find a survival job. Her time with the newspaper was closed and she'd crawl over glass shards rather than walk into that building again. Too many ghosts. She could go back and live with her mother, but cringed and pushed the thought away. And there was always a job at the Penny Pincher, a karmic twist if ever there was one.

Another slow roll of exhaustion made her arms and legs feel filled with heavy cement. She didn't bother to switch off the humming lights above her, even though they cast everything into a depressing contrast of sharp details and muddy shadows. She closed her eyes and tumbled into a sleep that felt drugged.

* * *

SHE DREAMED SHE WAS floating through her childhood home, around the time after her father walked out on them. The house was as she remembered it, except for a fine layer of dust that covered everything.

As she moved through the house, the furniture stretched and the walls loomed. She went into the kitchen where her mother sat at the kitchen table with her gaze fixed on some point beyond the window. A cup of coffee waited in front of this younger mom who had only a few strands of gray hair. She was unaware of her daughter, even though Julia called her name and shook her arm. Her mother's profile stood out against the kitchen's gloom and her eyes were dull marbles.

By instinct, Julia dropped her hand and backed away. If her mother rotated her head toward Julia, she would see a daughter grown back into a five-year-old. Julia knew those eyes would be flat and black and lifeless. A powdery snow of gray dust floated down and Julia edged away, her footprints dark islands on the kitchen floor among thickening drifts.

Terror clamped around her throat, making breathing

a struggle, and Julia ran down the hall to her childhood bedroom. Opening the door, she felt relieved to find her room was clean and bright with morning light and her collection of stuffed animals were clumped together in front of a pillow on her neatly made bed. Her favorite toy, a black-and-white cat named Moses, lay sprawled on the floor. She picked up the stuffed animal without effort because she had shrunk to the size of a toddler.

A vine snaked out from under the bed, coiled itself lightly around her pudgy wrist, and yanked hard. She slid under the bed and fell through a thick canopy of trees before landing on hard-packed ground. More vines slithered toward her like bark-covered snakes and encircled her wrists and ankles. One vine slipped around her neck and slipped a tendril down her back and wrapped itself around her waist. Its bark scraped against her skin and she screamed for her mother, but it was pointless.

She was utterly alone.

Julia thrashed and fought against the vines, then cast about for something to slice through their rough bindings, which were the width of a man's fingers. A crook of a stream trickled past her, undulating a slow sludge, and it dawned on her that she was in the clearing by the river where fireflies had encircled Walter and her.

But now, rather than a place of beauty, it turned into a mirror-nightmare with the river reduced to a noxious artery and banked by a forest restless with shadows. Behind her, something crashed and grunted through the bramble. As the creature grew closer, the vines tightened their grip until she could only take shallow gasps.

Her lungs burned as though they were on fire and the vine cinched, inch by inch, around her body. Julia's fate was sealed and she waited for whatever beast would explode from the shadows to consume her.

* * *

WITH A YELL SHE AWOKE and jumped from the couch, trembling and looking about wildly. Her heart raced and she moaned, "Oh my God."

She'd never had a nightmare that vivid before, and she lowered herself back to the couch, closed her eyes, and rocked back and forth, praying for the images to retreat.

At a distant sound, Julia cocked her head and listened. A light tapping came from the front of the office. She punched open her cell phone and the screen lit up to read 3:21 a.m. It also showed seven missed calls from Nick and two from Graham, but she hadn't heard any of them because her phone was on mute.

The tapping continued, and grew louder and more insistent. Julia crept down the hallway and peered around the corner, her pulse high and still hammering in her ears from the nightmare. A figure stood on the other side of the glass front door, and when he took a step back the streetlight fell across his face, she recognized Nick. The habit of Nick being her protector and rescuer sent relief through Julia and she hurried to unlock the door.

Nick was the picture of wretchedness and his posture was stiff as if he were standing at alert. "Julia, God. I was worried, especially after you left, and then didn't come home. Are you alone in here?"

Hope flickered in Julia.

We only had a bad patch. We can make this right. Maybe she had been wrong about the whole Calliope thing.

"I'm alone. But you scared me half to death. I was having the worst nightmare and thank goodness you woke me up."

As he backed up for her to swing the door open, he stumbled and the corners of his lips jerked into a smile that held no warmth. The smell of Scotch came off his breath and a surge of fear chased away her fogginess. With a lunge she grabbed the door handle and tried to close it, but Nick knocked back her arm and forced his way into the tiny lobby.

"No, no, no. You say you're alone, but shouldn't I do a bed check, just to make sure?"

"Are you drunk?" Julia knew the truth but needed to buy herself time to think. She had never seen Nick intoxicated like this, and realized with alarm that rather being loose and slurry, his diction had grown more precise and clipped.

He leveled his focus on her as she backed down the hallway. Then he tilted his head up as though considering the question. "Am I drunk?" he mused, then chuckled. "Yes, gloriously so. And for every shot I drank, I toasted you to chase away the memory of your shrew face after you ambushed me at the paper. Maybe I was hoping to blot you from my mind, but instead you just got sharper and sharper. So finally I had to see for myself what you were up to."

Julia reached her office door with Nick a few steps away. She gauged when she could jump and slam the door behind her, but he grabbed her by the waist and pinned her against the doorframe.

"Let's continue the conversation," he said in a voice low and silky, all the while pressing his fingers deeper into the flesh above her hips.

Julia pushed against him, but he was a taller by a head-and-a-half and heavier by fifty pounds. He didn't budge. Her spine pressed against the sharp edge of the doorway frame and pain flared up her back.

"Look. No one's here but me. You're hurting me. Please get off me and go home." Her voice sounded weak and far away to her ears.

To Julia's relief, he retreated a step and lowered his hands. "Okay, I'll leave."

She slid away from him and crossed to the desk where her purse lay against a table lamp with her clutch of keys sticking out from the half-zipped top. There was no sign of her cell phone and she prayed it wasn't buried at the bottom on the purse. She glanced at him. Nick eyed her with calm detachment, betrayed only by a vein running up the middle of his forehead that pulsed a dangerous beat.

"But you're coming with me."

Julia edged closer to her purse. "Sure, just let me lock up. Meet me up by the front door, okay?" Her voice wavered and she swallowed.

As though sensing her fear, Nick gave her a rakish grin and shook his head. "No. I'll be a gentleman and wait right here. I need to walk you to your car. It took me a few minutes of circling around, but I finally found it three blocks away. What was it, Julia? Needed to catch some late-night air before hiding out here?"

Shit. She forgot she had parked on a side road by a chiropractor's office, just in case Nick did drive by the clinic.

Their polite charade evaporated like a splash of water on a white-hot stove burner. Keeping her gaze level with his, Julia slid her feet until she was a few inches within grasp of her purse. Nick watched her with a strange light in his eyes as he stretched his mouth again into that weird parody of a smile. This must be how a mouse feels when it cowers below a swaying snake—hypnotized and frozen, waiting for the strike and the deep, stinging bite of fangs into soft flesh.

He extended his hand in an almost courtly manner. "Shall we go?"

It was as if Julia's tongue was lined with cotton and she

couldn't form enough spit to swallow, much less answer. She shook her head.

"So *no* to coming home with me? But *yes* to allowing your mind to conjure up crazy fantasies about me having affairs with whomever I'm standing next to on a public street? Do I have that right?"

She slid half a step backwards, sliding her hand along the top of the desk, never daring to break his gaze. Her left hand was on the desk's surface and a finger grazed something soft that she prayed was the purse strap. "I saw what I saw, Nick."

"No, you see things that aren't there. I can just as easily say you and Graham were having an affair because anything could have been going on in the photography department."

"Except you know that's not true. You're trying to distract me."

"Why, because it's hard to prove a negative? You believe I'm having an affair with Calliope, so you twist it in your mind until you made it true? Then poof, all our plans out the window. But this?" He swept his ,arm in a half-circle. "This dump of a place is where you'd rather be? You're not making sense. Again."

He paused and crossed his arms, which accented the muscles in his shoulders. "Okay, so if we've established I'm in the clear, then that leaves you. Are you guilty of something?"

He knew how to evoke confusion in her, and his words coiled in her mind. She pushed them aside. "Stop! I've told you my work with the clients means something to me, but you're never interested in listening. I've found out I'm a good therapist. And I've found people who care for each other, and care for me. This is my home and you can't rip it away from me."

Her words rushed out in a flood and to say them out loud filled her with relief. A bead of sweat trickled down the side of her face but she stood up straighter.

A crimson flush crept up Nick's neck as he narrowed his eyes until they glittered. "I refuse to believe this town and whack job are more important to you than me! I can smell a lie and you're not telling me something, Julia. I believe you about Graham, I'll give you that. So what is it? Who is it?" He paused and chewed on the bottom of his lip, a gesture Julia knew all too well—he was running through people as though flipping through mug shots and calculating logical outcomes. His head snapped up. "It's that old guy. The director of this nut case central. At the funeral you talked to everybody but him. Now that I think about it, I'd say you two were avoiding each other."

At the mention of Walter, warmth fanned across her cheeks. "He is my director and he's my friend." But her gaze faltered.

Nick's eyes widened as if he read her mind like a crawl of neon type. "Maybe. Maybe not. But the idea of him has entered your mind. Your *guilty* mind. What's that term therapists banter about? Projecting? So are you projecting your guilty mind onto me? I'm not the sick, cheating one here. You are, Julia. How crazy, exactly, *are* you?"

For a dangerous moment, Julia forgot she was alone in the clinic with Nick, who was more drunk and angry than she'd ever seen him. Her own anger roared forth. "You don't call me crazy! No one does, and I won't accept that from you anymore."

Nick sprang forward, grabbed her, and ground his hips into hers. "Then maybe you'll accept this." He tugged at the waist of her pants.

His erection pushed against her and she breathed in his noxious breath heavy from soured liquor. Pushing against him, she screamed, "No! You're hurting me!"

"You're the crazy one. So crazy you wrote 'Get out now' on your own filthy car window." He yanked at her pants until the top button popped off.

Julia felt as though she was slipping down a dark well, losing consciousness as a way of escape. Nick's breathing grew more labored and a core part of her spirit curled up into a tiny ball of protection as she went limp in his arms. The room was fading away, growing dark and distant. He would claim her body and make her his again.

But a tiny pinpoint of a thought shot through the descending veil, something about her car window. She grasped for the thought, it skittered away, and she willed herself to remember while Nick unbuckled his belt with one hand and lifted up her shirt with the other.

Praying for strength, she focused her dwindling concentration and pushed Nick away. Breath flowed into her lungs as though she came up for air from the ocean's depth. The maddening thought circled and she tried to capture it, and it almost skittered away again. Then Nick's words floated to her as if from a distance.

She gave a cry and planted her hands on his shoulders and pushed him. He went back a few paces with a grunt and they faced each other.

"I never told you what was written on my window. I never said those words to you!"

He paused as surprise and confusion flickered across his face.

As if splashed with cold water, Julia was more awake and present. She lifted her hands to his chest and shoved, which gave her enough room to twist and grab her purse. Its solidness in her hands gave her strength. "You knew the words because you wrote them! You wrote it to scare me. And you wanted to scare me so you'd be the big protector as

I escape Elston with my tail between my legs!"

The truth of her words sent fire through her veins. She thrust her hand into her purse and her fingers touched the cool plastic of her phone. Grasping her phone, she told him, "Go home, Nick. Or go to hell. Either way, leave or I'm calling the cops."

Nick's blue eyes blazed in sharp contrast against his pink-flushed face. He was no longer the least bit attractive to her.

Julia held her breath, could she dial 911 with her shaking hands? The landline phone sat on the other side of the desk and she would have to turn her back on Nick to reach it, an option she didn't dare gamble.

He shook his head as if waking from a trance. With a shuddering breath, he let out a laugh. "Yes, yes, yes!" He pointed at Julia and nodded his head, as though they were in total agreement about something hilarious. "I wrote on your window and, yes, on occasion I've had sex with Calliope. Yes! I admit it. Not that she was any great shakes, but whew! What a relief. Is that what you'd call a cathartic release, Ms. Therapist?"

Even though she didn't give a damn about him anymore, his words were emotional slaps. From deep in her gut, waves of alarms jangled because whomever she had believed Nick to be, this was not the man in front of her now. Her voice shook and her ribs hurt from where he had gripped her. "Go home. It's over. We're over."

His face grew blank and he seemed to relax, as if giving up. "I'm going home, if that's what you want."

She glanced at her phone and pressed the side button to turn it on. Her hand shook and she feared she would not be able to punch in the three numbers to dial 911. "Thank you," she whispered, never taking her eyes off him.

"But..." He looped out his arm and encircled her shoulders. "Not without my bride. Where I go, Julia, you go." With a yank he pulled her towards him and the cell phone flew from her hand and banged against the wall so hard the backing flew off and the battery popped out.

Julia screamed. Fueled by his adrenaline, Nick lifted her with no effort and carried her reeling toward the door. She thrust away from the sour smell of alcohol on his panting breath, which caused him to sway. "Are you insane? Let me down now, and I won't call the police!" she cried, writhing in his arms.

He clamped his arms around her and squeezed tighter, grunting with the effort. "No. We made our plans and we honor our plans. Now we have to go. Tonight. I can't trust you in your state of mind. You'll see, in the morning, this will all be better."

She kicked one leg free as he carried her toward the doorway. Her foot caught the wall where a framed poster hung. It pitched forward off its hook and banged to the floor with the glass shattering into an explosion of shards. Nick jumped and, for a split second, paused.

Julia elbowed him hard in the ribs and he let out a groan. She pushed against the wall and her shoe swiped across the light switch, turning off the light and pitching the room into semi-darkness. Nick scrambled to maintain his hold on her as she arched her back. With a strength she didn't know she possessed, she planted both feet against either side of the door frame and thrust out her legs. A searing hot pain shot up her right thigh and up to her hip as if she had ripped a tendon.

Her efforts propelled them back and they crashed to the floor, with Julia on top. The hallway light shone dimly, and she rolled away from Nick, who lay sprawled on the floor. Her hip screamed in agony as she dug her hands into the thin carpet and inched forward through slivers of glass.

Putting her weight on her left knee, she struggled to stand.

His hand clamped around her ankle and Nick pulled her down. She screeched in agony and fear before wrenching her leg forward and freeing herself, with her foot coming out of her shoe. She crawled like a crab toward the desk where the landline phone sat. The phone cord dangled down the side of the desk like a lifeline. She snatched the cord and the phone fell into a heap in front of her. The blessed dial tone hummed only inches from her face. There was movement to her left and a violent yanking motion as Nick ripped the phone cable from the wall.

Julia wailed in frustration then cried, "Please stop! It's already gone too far." She peered up at him, a monster looming over her, immune to pity.

Nick shambled forward and Julia edged away. He bunched up the front of her shirt into his fist as if to hoist her up and Julia hung onto the side of the desk.

She dropped her head as detachment crept into her body and waited for his next assault. From the corner of her eye she caught a tiny red flickering of a light from the underside of the desk. A memory flooded back of Walter in his rumbled, blue chambray shirt, installing something under her desk from what now seemed a lifetime ago. *The panic button!*

She swung her body forward just as Nick hoisted her from the ground and the blessed red light slid out of her sight. There was only this moment and there would be no other. If she missed it, she would be dead.

Julia slammed her hand down under the desk where she hoped the alarm was installed. Her hand smacked only the cool flat wooden surface and she flared her fingers until she touched something round. She wasn't sure if she hit the button. Was the alarm wired to alert the front desk and Walter's office phone? If so, then both were useless to her now in the empty clinic. But had Walter wired the alarm to send a message to his cell phone? Julia struggled to remember, but couldn't.

Apparently suspicious about what she was doing, Nick crouched down next to her and peered up under the desk at the alarm. "More of your tricks!" he snarled, as he lunged for her. She rolled away toward the corner next to her desk. His face was twisted into a mask of fury, and even if help were on the way, she had acted too late. Nick was beyond being swayed by any cries for reason or mercy she could muster. Both of his hands were now tightened into angry fists. She squeezed into the corner beside the back of the desk, imagining the fine bones in her skull cracking under his blows.

She threw one arm up to protect her head and the other gripped the carpet. Pain bloomed up from her index finger and something soft and feather-like brushed against her thumb. A needle point burrowed deeper into her finger and at last Julia found the missing purple fishing fly that she had lost when it fell off her desk last week, Walter and Luke's last lure.

Nestled between the soft, nylon-threaded body and emu feathers, lay a brass hook, sharp enough with its curbed barb to catch a thrashing trout. She gripped the dumb-bell eyes set at the top of the hook between her thumb and index finger, which were slick with sweat and blood. As Nick swung his hand back to strike her, she shot her hand up and plunged the needlepoint of the hook into the soft flesh of his upper lip.

Nick rocked back on his heels and howled in pain, swatting at his face and forcing the fly to twist into his lip deeper.

Dim streetlight from the hallway beckoned. Julia leapt over Nick and bolted for the light, expecting his arm to snake out again and drag her back down. Her heart pumped out pure fear, but it could not squelch the exquisite pain shooting from her right hip as she reeled away.

Julia hit the front door, lurched out into the fresh air, and hobbled into the parking lot. The night spread out silent around her and she remembered her car was blocks away. Even if she had her keys, she could never make the trek immobilized by pain and wearing only one shoe. From behind her the front door of the clinic gave its metallic squeal. All her efforts had only bought her this last minute of freedom.

Nick's rasping breath and footsteps drew closer and Julia sank to her knees. From the distance a dog barked, and then a second. Closer still, a third dog howled before she recognized what set them off.

Sirens.

Nick's footsteps faltered, then stopped. All the dogs chorused their howls as red-and-blue flashing lights lit up the treetops from the block to her right. A patrol car, with another close behind, roared into the parking lot, their headlights slicing the darkness.

Blinded for a moment, Julia could only make out the silhouettes of two officers running up, one with his hand on his holster. An officer recognized Nick, called him by name, and ordered him to lie down on the ground at once. Julia dared a glance behind her.

Nick had managed to wrestle out the hook from his upper lip, but now shock froze his face as a trickle of blood wound its way down his square jaw. His startled eyes darted between the two officers before he settled on the cop with his hand on his gun. He walked toward him, rearranging his features into a jovial expression. "Hey, Frank! Man, they got you on the third shift? Listen, radio back to headquarters and let them know this isn't—"

"On the ground now!" yelled the officer, as he and his partner advanced.

Nick snapped his head toward Julia and his eyes, blue as sapphires in the halogen lights, poured pure hatred. The officers used that moment to push him to the ground and cuff him from behind. Together they hauled Nick up, and one walked him to the squad car where the officer told him, "You have the right to remain silent. Anything you say can and will be held against you."

The officer Nick had called Frank came up beside Julia and knelt beside her. "Ma'am, what are your injuries?"

She brought trembling hands up to her face and noticed her forearms were coated in blood from crawling through the broken glass. Exhaustion rolled over her, making standing up an impossibility.

A tall figure burst from the glare of the headlights, and Julia screamed and startled back, certain Nick had escaped.

"Julia!"

Walter's voice cut through her terror, and she rose and staggered forward. She made it a few steps, stumbled, and collapsed into Walter's arms.

Pushing back hair from her eyes, he scanned her face. "Are you all right? Did he hurt you? I got the panic alert from your office, so I called the police while I raced here."

Julia tilted up her head and with shaking hands, pulled him towards her and kissed him, not caring who was watching. "I'm okay now. I think I'm finally okay."

Her knees buckled and Walter caught her as the world swirled away from Julia. Her last sensation was of being carried away in his arms and inhaling the sweet scent of wood smoke against his warm skin.

Chapter 48

The sun dipped behind the hills as Julia strode down the town sidewalk. She barely noticed her messenger bag, which was filled with books, as it thudded against her side with each step. She exhaled white puffs of breaths and her cheeks tingled from the cold.

Even though her teeth chattered in the winter wind, she couldn't stop smiling. Not only had she finished the dreaded statistics class she had struggled with over the past semester, she was pretty sure she'd aced the final.

She passed the front window of the Curl Up and Dye Hair Salon, where the woman who cut Julia's hair was trimming a cloaked, wet-headed woman. The stylist waved at Julia, her fingers looped through the scissors' handles. Julia grinned and waved back.

After a few blocks, residential homes interspersed with businesses and Julia veered left onto her final block. A bungalow house came into sight: for decades it had been a home before it was sold and converted into a hardware store, and then, for the past two years, abandoned as it slid into neglect.

Now it was a construction site. The last rays of sunlight reflected off a new silver metal roof with a ladder propped against one side and a curl of blue smoke drifted up from the chimney. Almost overflowing with building debris, a dumpster squatted at an angle near the sidewalk and pairs of sawhorses were lined up side-by-side in the front yard.

A wooden sign lay across one pair of sawhorses with the carved words 'Elston Wellness Center' painted in blue against a white background. A small can of gold gilt paint was set off to the side next to a cleaned artist's paintbrush. Walter's meticulous hand had outlined in gold 'Elston Well' and Julia admired how the embellishment made the letters pop.

Soon after the clinic had closed, Walter and Marlene had pooled their monies and purchased the old house to create a collective private practice. Reluctant at first, because he was going through a divorce, Paulie at last agreed to join in with them, and together they tackled large swaths of the renovations themselves to keep costs down, with the occasional help of contractors.

When she wasn't at the college, Julia tore out rotten boards, sanded, painted, hammered, and stripped off circa 1960s wallpaper until her arms ached. Trust deepened between the four of them as the house evolved from a state of dingy decay into homey, well-scrubbed rooms.

Julia clattered up the front steps and opened the front door, her shadow stretched across the newly polished oak floors. She entered a room to her left that once had been a lawn-and-garden supplies area of the hardware store, and would be her future counseling office. Although it was sparsely furnished, Julia could hardly believe it was hers. In the fireplace, tentative blue flames licked the edges of a stack of logs, more evidence of Walter's handiwork.

Julia cocked her shoulder and let the bag slide onto the desk. She went into the foyer as Marlene came out from the kitchen in splattered jeans and T-shirt, her hair tucked under a red handkerchief. Marlene set down a paint bucket. "How did you do on your finals?"

"Over and done, thank heavens." Julia shook her head. "But graduation in August still seems so far away."

"You'll get there, dear. It'll go by in a snap."

A door across the hall swung open and a line of five men emerged, followed by Paulie talking to the last one, a glum man in his twenties. "You can mail that letter to your soon-to-be ex, but when I asked you guys to express feelings in writing, it was more so you could get them out and share in group. How about shredding or burning this one? No point in stirring things up with her, right?" Paulie pushed his glasses up on his nose and waited for the man to answer as he twisted the limp letter in his hands.

He brightened. "She bought me a crossbow for Christmas a few years back. I didn't even want the darn thing. Why not use this letter here for target practice?"

Paulie clapped him on the back as they walked out the front door. "Perfect!"

Julia said to Marlene in a low voice, "Paulie's divorce support group seems to be going strong."

"Oh, yes," Marlene nodded. "Business always booms during the holidays. Ever since his own divorce experience, he seems to have found a new niche."

A rattle at the front door made Julia think Paulie was returning. A whoosh of cold, fresh air rushed into the hallway as the point of a tree emerged, followed by Walter, pink-cheeked from heaving a Fraser fir tree sideways through the entrance. When he set the tree up on its trunk, the top brushed against the ceiling.

"Christmas tree delivery!" He stepped back to admire the looming tree.

"My, such a beauty. And so big," Marline added, craning her neck to look up.

Walter rocked back on his heels and rubbed the side of his jaw. "Hmm. Didn't seem that tall in the lot."

"They never do," Marlene said with a laugh. "After three months of remodeling while still seeing clients, so what if we have a nine-foot tree in an eight-foot ceiling foyer? Here, let me fill a bucket of warm sugar water for our new addition to sit in and refresh itself."

Marlene's cell phone rang in her jeans pocket and she answered while walking down the hall. "Hi, Mona. What? Can you speak up, I can barely hear you." She disappeared behind the swinging doors of the kitchen.

Julia reached up and stroked the supple, dark green needles tinged in blue. The tree's perfume filled the air and brought a rush of Christmas memories. Winter chill still cloaked the branches. "I think she's perfect."

"She?" Walter pushed his cap back. "What's this thing you have for naming fish and trees 'she'? Well, I guess I better take her outside and trim the base down a bit."

He picked up the tree and Julia hurried to open the door. As he passed, he stopped and smiled at her. She ran her fingers through his thick hair that he was now growing longer. His gaze lingered on Julia before she swung the door wide for him to wrestle the tree back outside.

Quiet settled over the house and Julia closed her eyes and breathed in the calm. A log in the fireplace popped. She opened her eyes and trailed into her office. Flames danced around the logs and filled the room with an amber light while the wind whistled low notes down the chimney. An antique desk she had found at a yard sale sat in the corner, its surface covered in receipts and contractor's estimates.

Walter shared this room with Julia while he oversaw the remodeling, but for the past month he had spent most of his time at his new job as an administrator for the hospital. Marlene and Walter had offered Julia the front office, and she'd protested, saying it was far too nice and should be Marlene's. However, Marlene assured Julia that she preferred the quieter room tucked in the back and away from all the street noise. Especially since Julia had spent the summer working in a windowless junk room at the former clinic. Marlene insisted she'd earned the sunniest room.

Outside the bay window, only a glowing smudge of sunset remained against the luminous lavender sky. A corner streetlight flickered on and gave depth to the shades of purples. Julia eased into the armchair next to the fireplace and allowed the dancing flames to mesmerize her.

Her thoughts still turned to Nick, but they were coming with less frequency and fear. After his arrest, in an attempt to avoid any more publicity than his attack on her had already generated, Nick pleaded no contest to a lesser charge of battery. He was given a one-year probation and ordered to complete an anger management class. Of course, the Dallas paper had gotten wind of his legal woes and the job offer was rescinded.

Julia imagined this was his most crushing loss. She and Nick hadn't spoken since that terrible night six months ago, but she did hear he had taken a job in Virginia. She lacked the curiosity to even Google his name and see whether or not he was still out east, but she hoped he stayed there.

She had found a small rental and moved into the small, upstairs garage apartment with sweeping pecan trees on three sides of the house. Trixie learned how to leap from the open kitchen window to a nearby limb and stalk the network of branches for unsuspecting birds or stretch out in the odd crook of a tree with eyes half-closed. The foliage was so thick outside the windows, it was like living in a treehouse surrounded by dappled shade.

In September, she picked up pecans when they fell around the house and filled sack after sack, baking them into pies and cookies and breads that she gave as gifts. Since the college was nearby, she found herself walking to and from the campus, and eventually extending her walks to the grocery store, coffee house, or friends' houses, like Phoebe from school. The muscles in her legs strengthened and she pushed herself a bit more each day until she could climb stairs without panting. Often an entire week would would go by and she had never started the engine of her car, which she found to be liberating.

One night she was grating carrots for a salad at the kitchen sink while Trixie circled around her ankles. The window was open and a cool evening breeze had ruffled her hair. A wave of contentment flowed into her heart. She knelt down and scooped up the orange tabby and rubbed her chin on the cat's head. Trixie's purrs sent vibrations through Julia's chest.

While she was no longer Rowena's student-therapist, Julia made a point to drop by the animal shelter some Friday afternoons and volunteer in the kitten room. She bottle-fed tiny kittens, many of whose eyes weren't even open. Afterwards she cradled them until they fell asleep with rounded bellies full of formula. Although the kitten room was one of the first jobs Rowena had worked at the shelter when she started as a volunteer, it didn't take long before she was offered a paid position.

On occasion, Julia found her at the front desk answering phones or fielding questions for people looking for a pet. Rowena sailed past Julia, bangs cut at their usual blunt angle and plastered against her forehead framing her squarish head. Sometimes Rowena hauled out trash bags or led out an excited dog dancing on the end of a leash. But always, Rowena kept her eyes resolutely straight ahead.

Once in a while, however, Rowena stuck her head into the kitten room door as Julia sat cross-legged on the floor feeding some tiny scrap of a cat. She pointed to the sink, half-filled with dirty bottles and bowls. "End of shift, make sure everythin' in there's clean enough for you to eat out of yourself."

Julia nodded at Rowena's stern face. "Yes, ma'am."

Rowena then grunted and turned away, but not before

a smile had played at the corners of her mouth.

A log hissed then popped. Julia startled, unaware she had lapsed into a daydream while staring into the fire. The front door opened and closed, and Walter came in, bringing with him a draft of cold air. He knelt before the fire and rubbed warmth back into his red-knuckled hands. "Tree should fit now. I left it on the front porch to enjoy its bucket of sugar water Marlene whipped up."

"Looks like it might fit. Unless she wants to put a star or angel on top," Julia said with a grin.

Walter groaned and cocked his head up at Julia as firelight flickered across the smooth planes of his face. "You women are going to be the death of me yet."

Julia reached out and brushed a lock of hair away from his eyes, then ran her fingertips from his temples to his chin, feeling the light stubble of his beard. Walter took her hand and pressed each fingertip to his lips. As they leaned in to kiss, three brisk raps came from the door.

Marlene stood in the doorway putting on her jacket. "Mona called and invited us to her house for a tamale-making party. From the noise in the background, it sounds like the entire Garcia clan is in attendance. She asked us to bring our card table. Seems they've run out of room in the kitchen and now the assembly line has spread into the living room."

"Oh, man," Walter said. "Last year Mrs. Garcia served a spiced hot chocolate I still dream about. Maybe I can get her to tell me how she makes it." He stood up, his fingers laced through Julia's.

"Don't hold your breath," Marlene said. "I've been asking for the recipe these past five years and she won't budge. In any case, I'm leaving now. And you'll be coming, too, Julia, right?"

Julia laughed. "I've never made tamales before. Isn't it

kind of complicated?"

Marlene waved her hand. "After fifteen minutes you'll be up to your elbows in masa and corn husks and rolling out tamales like a pro. I told Angel I'd drive by and collect him and his guitar, so I'll meet you two there, okay?"

Walter and Julia agreed and watched Marlene leave. "Before we descend into the noise cyclone of the Garcia household," Walter said, "can I hold you a minute?"

"Best offer I've had all day." Julia wrapped her arms around his waist and rested her head against his chest. Through the thickness of his flannel shirt, his heart beat steady as he held her tight. She lifted up her face to his and they kissed, his lips soft against hers. A current hummed between them.

Walter pulled back. "Let's revisit this later tonight, shall we?" He reached into his front jean's pocket and pulled out his car keys.

"Sure, give me a few minutes to collect some things."

He kissed her forehead and left, his footsteps growing fainter as he crunched along the gravel walkway to his truck. Julia knelt before the hearth, took out a fireplace poker, and nestled the logs together. The flames leapt up higher and rolled out waves of warmth. She inhaled the sharp smoke interwoven with a hint of fresh paint from the kitchen.

Her heart filled with gratitude. "Thank you," she whispered to no one, and everyone.

Outside, Walter's truck rumbled to life and Julia grabbed her coat, gazed across the room, and pulled the door closed with a gentle tug.

The truck backed out of the driveway with Julia sitting close to Walter as the headlights swept the room in a wash of white light. A spray of sparks traveled up the chimney and burst out into the crisp night sky. The bright embers danced in the air and blended against a blanket of stars, and for the briefest of moments it was impossible to tell ember from star, before they winked out.

ABOUT THE AUTHOR

Leslie Tourish is a writer and a psychotherapist who lives in a small town in the Texas Hill Country with her husband, daughter, and two terribly spoiled dogs.

www.leslieanntourish.com

ABOUT THE ARTIST

Desarae Lee is a fine artist and illustrator from Salt Lake City, Utah. Her art has appeared in galleries and art shows across the U.S. and she has won numerous

awards for her work including Best of Show, Best Illustrator, and Featured Artist. She is a published author and illustrator and serves as a founding board member at Salt Lake City's Downtown Artist Collective, where she can occasionally be found teaching drawing or printmaking.

www.desaraelee.com

ACKNOWLEDGEMENTS

I am grateful to Cecily Sailer, the editor who guided me through my first draft of the novel. Without her, this book would have stayed an unfinished project.

Thank you to Susie Pruett and Ginny Renfroe, my sharp-eyed writing partners and loving encouragers. Lisa Carlson and SuzAnne Beard, as my beta readers, you rocked the house.

And finally, a profound thank you to Cynthia Stone for her wisdom and humor in getting this book made.